I thought he wasn't coming. I thought he was working in Milan.

He was Naim Ansah.

She opened her eyes and looked up at him looking down at her. He was dressed in a well-tailored business suit and handmade Italian shoes with his hands in his pockets, his silk tie loosened and a smile on his handsome face. "And are you trying to incinerate?" she asked with a little chuckle, showing she amused herself.

He removed a hand from his pocket and smoothed it over his low-cut ebony beard as he nodded. "You're right. It's a party. It's hot as hell. And I want in on the pool," he said, removing his suit jacket to toss it onto the pavement surrounding the pool.

Marisa didn't miss the way his eyes—those intense dark eyes with the most beautiful shape and long lashes—took in her curves in her bikini as she floated. In the years since her cousin Alessandra met and married his brother, Alek, it had been impossible to miss the way his eyes were always on her—probably because she was just as busy eyeing his chocolate good looks from a distance, as well.

The watched watching the watcher.

Naim was delicious looking. Good body. Great face. Gorgeous dark eyes.

In the past, she would have gladly allowed herself a taste of all of his fineness. *I am single and not ready to mingle.*

Niobia Bryant is the award-winning and national bestselling author of more than thirty works of romance and commercial mainstream fiction. Twice she has won the RT Reviewers' Choice Best Book Award for Multicultural Romance. Her books have appeared in *Ebony*, *Essence*, the *New York Post*, *The Star-Ledger*, *The Dallas Morning News* and many other national publications. Her bestselling book was adapted to film.

"I am a writer, born and bred. I can't even fathom what else I would do besides creating stories and telling tales. When it comes to my writing I dabble in many genres, my ideas are unlimited and the ink in my pen is infinite." —Niobia Bryant

Books by Niobia Bryant

Harlequin Kimani Romance

A Billionaire Affair
Tempting the Billionaire
The Billionaire's Baby

Visit the Author Profile page
at Harlequin.com for more titles.

NIOBIA BRYANT
and
LINDSAY EVANS

*The Billionaire's Baby &
The Wrong Fiancé*

HARLEQUIN®KIMANI™ ROMANCE

ISBN-13: 978-1-335-00588-5

The Billionaire's Baby & The Wrong Fiancé

Copyright © 2019 by Harlequin Books S.A.

The publisher acknowledges the copyright holders of the individual works as follows:

The Billionaire's Baby
Copyright © 2019 by Niobia Bryant

The Wrong Fiancé
Copyright © 2019 by Lindsay Evans

Recycling programs for this product may not exist in your area.

Printed in U.S.A.

www.Harlequin.com

CONTENTS

As always, for my mama/guardian angel,
Letha "Bird" Bryant.

THE BILLIONAIRE'S BABY

Niobia Bryant

Dear Reader,

Welcome back to Passion Grove for another story of wealth, power, influence, romance…and excitement. This installment features Naim Ansah and Marisa Martinez—the sexy businessman and the reformed party girl. The baby they created was unexpected, but the passionate chemistry they enjoyed had been stoked for more than a year, and that love promises to last a lifetime.

I hope you enjoy their fiery story set in my beloved Passion Grove, where the small-town atmosphere does not hinder the luxury. I love this place and I hope you all do, too. Growing the series and introducing new characters has been fun…and there is so much more to come.

Best,

N.

Chapter 1

Marisa Martinez had lost count of the laps she swam in the Olympic-size pool, but she was thankful for the coolness of the water against her bikini-clad body and the silence it created. Beneath the crystal clear depths, made all the more brilliant by an intricate pattern of the turquoise glass tile, she could almost forget the party going on around her. Launching off for another lap by pushing her feet against the wall, her toned arms slashed the water before she turned over into a backstroke, taking in air with her head above the water as she alternated her arms in circles and flutter kicked her feet.

She closed her eyes, enjoying the feel of the summer sun on her face as she reached over her head to grip the edge of the pool and float.

"Are you trying to pickle?"

Marisa hid her surprise well. His deep voice and English accent were easily recognizable.

I thought he wasn't coming? I thought he was working in Milan?

He was Naim Ansah.

She opened her eyes and looked up at him looking down at her. He was dressed in a well-tailored business suit and handmade Italian shoes with his hands in his pockets, his silk tie loosened and a smile on his handsome face. "And are you trying to incinerate?" she asked with a little chuckle, showing she amused herself.

He removed a hand from his pocket and smoothed it over his low-cut ebony beard as he nodded. "You're right. It's a party. It's hot as hell. And I want in on the pool," he said, removing his suit jacket to toss onto the pavement surrounding the water.

Marisa didn't miss the way his eyes—those intense, dark eyes with the most beautiful shape and long lashes—took in her body's curves as she floated. In the years since her cousin Alessandra had met and married his brother, Alek, it had been impossible to miss the way his eyes were always on her—probably because she was just as busy eyeing his chocolate good looks from a distance, as well.

The watcher watching the watcher.

Naim was delicious looking. Good body. Great face. Gorgeous dark eyes.

In the past, she would have gladly allowed herself a taste of all of his fineness. But now? *I am single and not ready to mingle.*

Marisa released the edge of the pool and turned to pull herself up and out of the water beside him as he finished undressing.

"Naim, get some swim trunks!" his brother, Alek, yelled over to them from where a small group of family and friends were gathered about the manicured grounds of the Ansah-Dalmount estate enjoying the live band playing and the catered food being served by uniformed staff.

"My boxers are good!" he yelled back as he looked down at her.

"Enjoy the pool," Marisa said, water dripping off her from head to toe.

"We will," Naim said, quickly reaching out with one strong arm to wrap around her waist and pull her into the pool with him as he leaped.

As soon as he released her, Marisa brought her feet to press against his rigid abdomen to push off and swim away from him. She was surprised at the ease with which he caught her, wrapping a hand around her ankle. She kicked away his touch, adjusted her bottom upright and pushed up off the base to break through the water with a splash. He did the same, and she eyed him while she pushed her water-soaked shoulder-length curls back from her face.

Their eyes met.

There was an invisible line between them that neither dared to cross. In the years since they were in each other's company, more time was spent ignoring each other and acting like they were strangers than anything else. But that awareness for each other would not fade, no matter how much they denied the pull.

"Dinner's ready," Alessandra called out, unknowingly breaking their moment.

Marisa and Naim moved away from each other and climbed from the pool. He gathered his clothing and she picked up her discarded towel to wrap low around her waist. She had to force herself not to look in his direction as she strode across the heated stone walkway to the large pergola adorned with strings of white lights above the table large enough to seat twenty.

And every seat was filled.

As she reached for her sheer floor-length coverup and dried her wet hair with a towel, Marisa eyed each one of the people seated at the table as one of the staff turned on the lights as the evening sky began to darken, streaking it with dark blue, lavender and orange colors. They were a large unit brought together by the love of Alessandra Dalmount and Alek Ansah, who were forced to work together as co-CEOs of ADG, a multi-billion-dollar conglomerate, but had willingly fallen in love once they tired of the battle of wits and strong wills. With their union, two families were brought together for family events and vacations.

Marisa took a seat near the end of the table next to Alessandra, the de facto head of the Dalmount family ever since her father's death years ago. She doled out allowances, advice and sometimes strict orders, trying her best to keep a very rambunctious bunch of kin in line while running a business and putting her own small family of Alek and their baby girl, Aliya, first.

God bless, Marisa thought, reaching for one of the many crystal pitchers of citrus punch lining the table, among beautiful floral arrangements and thick, lit candles, to pour herself a glass.

Over the rim of the glass, she eyed the younger brother of her uncle Frances, Victor Dalmount, and his wife, who was nearly half his age, as they shared a secret toast and a laugh together. Thankfully their boisterous twin sons were upstairs in the nursery being watched by a few nannies, along with all the other children in the families.

Aunt Leonora, her mother's lively younger sister, who was dressed in one of her beloved silk caftans in vibrant colors that dimmed in comparison to her personality, enjoyed large sips of her signature Veuve Clicquot as she doled out funny anecdotes and quips, giving her opinion on any and everything. Her personality and age made it all forgivable.

And then there's Momma.

She shifted her eyes to her mother, Brunela Dalmount-Martinez, sitting at the head of the table—a seat most would assume would be for the man of the house. The entire Dalmount clan was well aware that as the eldest Dalmount child, she felt her younger brother Frances had been given *her* birthright to run the family business simply because "he was born with a penis." When she met and fell in love with Mario Martinez, a man of no wealth but lots of affection for Brunela, she married him despite the objections of her brother, Frances, who was the head of the family at that point. Mario's death just a few years after their marriage had been the final blow, and Brunela had turned bitter and resentful as a result.

Marisa looked on as her mother, a tall and regal woman who rarely seemed to smile, watched everything with derision. She seemed to detest the same family money she enjoyed spending so lavishly—particularly on her. It was a bitter pill to swallow, to admit that her mother spoiled her with the family's abundance of wealth, to her detriment.

Marisa had been denied nothing growing up. Designer clothes, lavish lifestyle, missed curfews, surly attitude and eventually an abundance of alcohol and partying. She took her sense of entitlement to the brink and pulled Alessandra down into the abyss with her, nearly destroying her cousin's career as the co-CEO of ADG.

Marisa's partying had eventually spiraled, and she even began experimenting with pills. Alessandra had worried about her safety and come to retrieve her from a house one night where she had been partying to take her home. She, Marisa and everyone else in the house were taken to jail when the police raided the home. The scandal that followed Alessandra when the news hit the press was profound, and the ADG had contemplated asking her to step down from her position.

Thankfully, Alessandra retained her position and offered Marisa a stay in rehab to help defeat what she thought was about to become a serious issue for her cousin. Marisa's choice was rehab or no financial help going forward. Resistant at first, Marisa had resented the order, but with every day of clarity and change, she became thankful that Alessandra had the balls to put her foot down in a way no one else had with her.

At times, when she thought of her past behavior, she felt ashamed. But now, pushing aside thoughts and regrets over her wild past, Marisa eyed Alek's side of the family. His beautiful mother, LuLu, who remained true to her Ghanaian heritage with the gold head wrap she wore like a crown. Marisa smiled when she reached over and closed the case on the iPad her daughter, Samira, had been swiping through, not paying much attention to the summer dinner party around her. Like her brothers, she had inherited the Ansah work ethic and their billions from their father, Kwame—cocreator of the Ansah-Dalmount Group, along with Alessandra's father, Frances.

Alek and Alessandra's chef, Cook, stepped out onto the patio and stood next to Alek's chair. Everyone quieted down. "Good evening," he said. "For starters tonight, you are being served an appetizer sampler of fried crab ball with a spicy aioli sauce, fried oyster topped with a blue cheese slaw and bacon-wrapped seared scallop with a drizzle of garlic sauce. Enjoy." He offered everyone a smile before turning and walking back into the house.

"Thank you," Marisa said as a long and slender plate with the delicacies was set before her.

"It's good to see you, Marisa."

She glanced up at Ngozi Johns-Castillo as she returned to her seat next to Marisa with a glass of sangria filled with sliced peaches, oranges and white grapes. "You, too," she said, shifting her eyes away from the alcohol.

"Does this bother you?" Ngozi whispered in her ear.

Marisa gave her a smile. "No, thank God," she admitted.

Ngozi was Alessandra's personal attorney and good friend who had successfully had them cleared of any drug charges after the raid. It was she who had driven Marisa to the front door of the rehabilitation center for admittance, so she was well aware of her fall from sobriety. "Still working at *La Boulangerie*?" she asked as she cut into her scallop and dipped it into the sauce.

"I am...for now," Marisa added, only hinting at

her plans for her future at the local bakery specializing in French pastries and the best fresh brewed coffee on the planet. "And how's married life?"

Ngozi's dark eyes immediately sought out her husband of the last six months, Chance Castillo—best friend of Alek and self-made billionaire via his invention of two successful productivity apps that had *Forbes* calling him a tech king. "Damn good," she said, her voice soft and her eyes dreamy even as she took a bite of her appetizer.

Chance was sitting across from her and looked up as if he felt her gaze on his. His smile came with ease.

Their love was clear.

Looking away from them, her eyes fell on Naim, Alek's younger and equally handsome brother, as he walked out of the house now dressed in a V-neck T-shirt and cargo shorts. His eyes went straight to her. Her heart swelled and her pulse quickened its pace. He had the kind of dark and intense eyes that drew a woman and locked her in.

They both looked away as if caught.

Everyone enjoyed the rest of the meal of beef sashimi on radishes and sisho leaves followed by seared octopus in a red-wine mole sauce and brandied cherries with whipped vanilla cream on chocolate sorbet. Everything was delicious.

But for Marisa, it signaled to keep a promise to herself to finally talk to Alessandra. For weeks she had been putting it off and effectively stalling her plans for her future. Tonight, she was determined to get it over with.

The worst she can say is no.

Marisa rose from her chair and raked her fingers through her still-damp curls as she walked down the length of the table to reach Alessandra's seat. She bent down beside her. "Hey, can I talk to you for a sec?" she asked.

Alessandra set her wineglass on the table as she looked down at her. "Yeah, sure," she said. "What about? Everything okay?"

"Actually, it's business," she said, amazed that no one else could hear her hard, pounding heart.

Alessandra looked surprised and then cleared her throat as she rose to her feet. "Well, let's go talk business," she said, leading the way around the table and into the mansion via the open French doors.

Marisa licked her lips and wrung her hands as she followed her cousin. At that moment, her nerves made her feel more like a child than a woman the same age as Alessandra. Their lives were so very different. While Marisa was a party girl in recovery working at the local bakery, Alessandra was an educated, married mother who helped run a billion-dollar conglomerate.

"In your office?" Marisa asked, her steps on the tiled floor pausing.

Alessandra turned the knobs of the double doors and pushed them open wide, nodding. "Alek and I have a deal that we only discuss business in here to help keep it separate from home, which is our haven," she said, looking out of place in her strapless bathing suit and sheer palazzo pants as she walked around the two large wooden executive desks that faced each other—one for her and one for Alek.

They were a power couple.

Marisa came inside the large space with its dozens of windows admitting warmth and light as she took one of the three club chairs lined up facing the sides of the desks.

"So, what's up?" Alessandra asked, crossing her legs and leaning back in the chair as she eyed her.

"I hope I've shown you since I finished rehab that I am intent on accomplishing more in life than traveling, wearing the latest designer fashions and being present at every hot event in the city," Marisa began.

"You have and I am proud of you," her cousin said. "We all are."

Knuckle up, Marisa.

"While I've been working at *La Boulangerie* this last six or seven months, Bill has actually been teaching me to be a chocolatier on my off-hours," she said. "And I've been completing an online, part-time professional chocolatier program for the last two months."

Alessandra looked surprised.

"In fact, the chocolate desserts and candies that he has been selling for the last few weeks are my creation," Marisa said.

"Really?" Alessandra asked. "I *love* the toasted almond truffles."

Marisa inclined her head. "Thank you," she said, unable to hide her smile of pride.

Alessandra fell silent but gave her an encouraging smile.

"Bill, the owner of La Boulangerie, is not interested in taking on chocolate making, but he has offered me the opportunity to begin my own small business by subletting me space to sell my chocolate at the bakery," she said. "So, I would like a loan to be able to purchase equipment and supplies...and to be able to move out of my mom's guesthouse and into my own place."

Marisa released a breath.

There, I said it.

"Marisa, you're asking for a loan when you have not accepted your monthly allowance in close to a year—the money you are entitled to by the family trust set up by my father," Alessandra explained.

Marisa looked out the window at the summer sun, searching for the right words to speak life into her truth. "I have been spoiled—ruined—by wealth. No, no. What I mean is I have been ruined by wealth I did not earn," she continued, thinking of every misstep, fall and fumble she'd made. She shifted her eyes to her cousin and locked them on hers with steely determination. "I want a success story that is earned, not easy."

"So how was the chocolate mousse tonight?" Alessandra asked.

Marisa was taken aback by the question, but ready

to respond. "A touch of orange liqueur would have elevated it," she said.

Alessandra chuckled. "Please don't tell Cook that?" she asked.

"I won't."

"Cash or check, cuz, because you've got a deal," Alessandra said, rising to extend her hand to her.

Marisa rose, as well, and shook her hand. "A loan," she stressed.

"A loan," Alessandra agreed.

Naim could not look away from the sight of Marisa Martinez as she followed his sister-in-law, Alessandra, inside the mansion. Just as he hadn't been able to the first time he saw her at Alek and Alessandra's estate on their private vacation island off East Hampton. He vividly recalled the sight of her, young and beautiful, as she went running off the end of the deck in her bright red swim shirt and boy-cut swim shorts to jump into the water without a care. She was so different from the women he knew who wore expensive bathing suits but never dared get in the pool.

Marisa was petite and curvy with a head full of shoulder-length wild ebony curls and doe-like hazel eyes that suited her unmarred medium-brown complexion. Kissable full lips. High cheekbones. So pretty.

He worked out of ADG's Milan office in the marketing division, but he had flown home for any and every family event over the last year and he couldn't take his eyes off of her whenever they were in the same room. When she spoke, her raspy voice intrigued him. When she laughed, he wanted to be in on the joke. But there was never anything between them except distance. They barely spoke or had a conversation. Stolen glances? Plenty. Anything more? Never.

It was clear they avoided each other.

Naim was single with a bevy of beauties he dated, depending on which state or time zone or foreign country he was in at the moment—and all were well aware that he was neither committed nor looking for a relationship. A dalliance with Marisa that didn't end well would hit too close to home and possibly affect other relationships—his with his brother, his with Alessandra, Alek and Alessandra's marriage. He was aware of her past struggles and was definitely not looking for the headache of a relationship with the former party girl. No, he had nothing more to offer the beautiful Marisa Martinez but proof that he could fully deliver on the chemistry simmering between them.

He picked up his frosty glass of imported Star beer from Ghana that his brother kept stocked and sat there with his family, enjoying good food and good music that was a blend of American R & B hits and Ghanaian mainstays.

A good time was just the distraction he needed from his thoughts on Alek's call that morning requesting his presence in his office Monday morning first thing. Right after a business meeting that ran extremely late, he'd taken the company jet to fly back to the States overnight.

His mother, LuLu, reached across the table and grasped his hand with her own. He gave her the same charming smile that had saved him from discipline growing up as a mischievous teen. "I could use some Red-Red," he said, his eyes twinkling at the thought of his favorite Ghanaian dish of the black-eyed peas and smoked fish stewed in red palm oil and tomatoes with fried plantains on the side.

LuLu's devotion was her children, and cooking for them gave her as much joy as they received eating her delicious food. "Dinner at my apartment this Monday, then," she said, giving his hand one pat before releasing it.

Naim frowned. "Not tomorrow?" he asked, more than surprised. "No Sunday dinner?"

"No, Naim, I have plans," LuLu said, picking up her glass of sangria to sip.

"Doing what, Ma?" he asked.

"Things, son," was her reply.

His frown deepened.

"My clothes look good on you, little brother," Alek said as he walked up and gripped his brother's shoulders. "Feel free to keep 'em. Especially the boxers."

"The pants are a little snug around the seat but they'll do," Naim quipped.

"Gross," his younger sister, Samira, said into her glass of sangria.

"Boys," LuLu said, her tone calm but her order clear.

The playful insults ceased.

"Let's dance, nephew," Aunt Leonora said, walking up with a flute of champagne in one hand and grabbing Alek's hand with the other. "My niece is not the only Dalmount with moves."

Alek gave them a playfully frightened look as the older woman pulled him over to the band.

They all chuckled.

LuLu rose. "I am going to kiss the cheeks of my granddaughter," she said, leaving them with a wink.

Naim looked at his sister pick up her tablet. "Make yourself happy with work," he said.

She gave him a long side glance as she opened the cover. "As if you put in any less hours than me," she said. "We both have a lot to prove at ADG, big brother."

"True," he agreed, raising his beer to her in a toast.

Both Naim and Samira had always wanted to follow in their father, Kwame's, footsteps into the family business. Unfortunately, Kwame wanted nothing more than to continue the family tradition and pass the business on to his firstborn son, Alek, the same way his father had passed it on to him. It didn't matter that it was Naim who had the passion and drive for the business, while Alek declined to go into the business after graduating with his MBA to work on charter boats in the hopes of one day being a captain.

Naim took a sip of his beer and eyed his brother dancing with Leonora but skillfully avoiding her getting too close. He harbored no ill will toward his brother being his father's chosen one. He was proud of his older brother and looked up to him. After his father's unexpected death, Naim had been surprised and hurt to find his father had still left the helm of his share of the billion-dollar conglomerate to Alek, but he also knew his brother would soar in the position he had been forced to take by the stipulation of the will to step up to the plate or see the business sold.

Although Naim never revealed it, the fact that his father would rather sell the business than give him his fair shot at co-CEO was deeply troubling—especially since he was very close to his father, unlike the strained relationship he'd had with Alek. It was that feeling of being overlooked that made him so close with Samira. Both held positions at ADG and were as thick as thieves.

"I've been summoned to Alek's office Monday, little sister," Naim said, stroking his low-cut beard. "Any word on the street what that is about?"

She looked up from her tablet. "I didn't know you were flying back from Milan so I am completely out of the loop," she said. "As always."

He chuckled before taking another sip of beer. Nothing but his brother's well-known rule of not discussing business at his home kept Naim from killing his curiosity by questioning his brother. "I'm exhausted," he admitted, pressing his fingers against his eyes before he yawned.

"You going home or staying?" Samira asked.

Naim owned a lavish penthouse apartment in Brooklyn, but any thoughts of it and his bed faded as Alessandra and Marisa came out of the house and walked back into the party. His heart thundered. He didn't think he'd seen anything sexier than Marisa's bikini under her sheer cover-up. Nothing at all.

"You're drooling you want her so bad."

He looked away from her as his sister playfully swiped her thumb against the corner of his mouth. He lightly shoved her hand away.

"Alek would kill you," she stressed.

Naim looked at her.

"*Or* that could make it even more fun," Samira said, looking first at him and then at Marisa. "Sneaky-deaky freaky."

"You're annoying," he said, rising from his seat.

"Especially when I'm right," she called behind him.

And she was.

He wanted Marisa Martinez.

"Shit," he swore when she raised her hands in the air and swayed her hips to the band's music.

Just sexy as hell without even trying.

His body was on high alert and about to expose his desire. Pulling off the V-neck T-shirt, he went running across the yard and jumped into the pool, welcoming the coolness. He lost count of how many laps he did from one edge of the pool to the other before he came up above the surface for air. He did slow backstrokes across the distance before turning and leaving the pool and sitting on the side. The music blended in the air with the conversation and laughter of everyone.

Naim glanced over his shoulder and froze to find Marisa's eyes on him from the dance floor. And he did not miss the way they dipped down to take in his back. He fought the urge to flex and deepen the definition of his muscles. She pursed her lips and let out a little breath, like she was releasing pressure, and her fingertips landed against her chest.

Marisa Martinez wanted him, too.

Uh-oh.

Needing space before the wrong head got him into trouble, Naim rose to his bare feet and crossed the spacious yard to the patio. "I'm gonna catch a nap, Alessandra. Cool?" he asked her when he reached where she sat with her feet in his brother's lap as she sipped sangria.

"I'm sitting here, too, bro," Alek said.

He grabbed one of the rolled beach towels on the teak stand to drag across his body. "Yeah but I'm asking the boss," Naim teased.

Alessandra raised her glass in a toast to that.

Alek shrugged one shoulder. "Carry on, then."

"Enjoy your nap, bro," she said, nudging her foot

against Alek's hand to remind him to continue his massaging of her toes.

Naim avoided looking in Marisa's direction as he walked inside the house and made his way up the rear stairs off the kitchen. He barely heard the noise of the staff cleaning up or the smell of Cook's home-made pizza for late-night snacking once he was off duty. Fatigue defeated him and desire scared him. Sleep would solve both.

There were plenty of bedroom suites to choose from in the three-story, twenty-thousand-square-foot French Tudor, so Naim just opened the first door and entered, pulling off his clinging swim trucks and leaving them on the hardwood floor of the sitting room before dropping down onto the plush sofa before the unlit fireplace cloaked by darkness.

Naim closed his eyes, enjoying the quiet, and soon he was asleep.

Click.

He awakened with a start, raising his head from the arm of the sofa and looking around the darkened room. "What time is it?" he asked aloud, his voice still thick with sleep.

"Midnight."

Naim looked to the door at the sound of the feminine voice as he sat up. A shadowed figure reached to turn on the lights, revealing Marisa leaning against the wall by the door. Her eyes dipped down to take in his nudity, his member dangling between his open thighs. She arched a brow when he reached for a throw pillow to cover his privates.

"This was my room when I lived here," she explained. "I didn't know you were in here."

"My bad, Marisa. I just opened the first bedroom door and crashed," he said, rising to his full height with the pillow still pressed to his groin. "I'll find another bedroom."

Marisa smiled in amusement. "Like that?" she asked, pointing to the pillow.

He shrugged. "It's better than those wet swim trunks," he said, walking across the room toward the door. "Or nothing at all."

"I'm not sure about that," she said, her voice barely above a whisper.

Their eyes locked. A current shimmied over his body. He knew she felt it, as well.

Uh-oh.

Naim felt breathless, and his heart pounded as her eyes dropped down to his chest and she pursed her lips to quickly pant again. It seemed she was relieving some pressure. Like steam built up from desire.

The inches between them intensified the attraction. "Excuse me, Marisa," he said, feeling his resolve weakening with each moment she remained blocking his exit from the room.

She nodded but did not move as she looked up at him again. "You have to stop looking at me like that, Naim," she said.

He liked how his name sounded on her lips. "Like

what?" he asked, feeling his desire for her stir against the pillow.

"Like that. Like you always do," she whispered. "Like you want me."

"I do," Naim admitted, his voice deep and warm.

She gasped and her eyes glazed over as she pursed her lips once more.

His will broke and he wrapped his free arm around her waist to pull her close as he lowered his head to taste her mouth with a grunt of pleasure.

It was Marisa who reached between them to fling away the pillow to press him closer with her hands to his back as they instantly got lost in the passion—and gave not a care for every reason it was supposed to be wrong.

Chapter 2

Two months later

Naim took a sip of coffee as he stood at the floor-to-ceiling windows of his three-thousand-square-foot penthouse condominium on the waterfront of the DUMBO section of Brooklyn, New York, and looked out at the sweeping views of both the skyline of NYC and the Brooklyn, Manhattan and Williamsburg Bridges. DUMBO, which stood for "Down Under the Manhattan Bridge Overpass," was an industrial area ripe with warehouse buildings that had been gentrified and converted to high-end residences and commercial buildings. It was one of the borough's most expensive sections, and where Naim had wanted to carve out his own space in New York, in addition to his chalet in the Swiss Alps. Alek's home base was now Passion Grove, even though he and Alessandra owned residences around the world, including a penthouse in Tribeca. His mother and sister had their own apartments on the Upper East Side. Brooklyn was all his, and he loved it with a particular fondness for the art, culinary delights and reputation as a tech hub.

The clean lines and modern decor with exposed beams and columns of concrete were his style, and he was glad to be back home the last two months. He had chosen the charcoal and ivory decor himself. Although there was more than enough room for staff, he preferred eating at restaurants or at his mother's, and after a lifetime of living with staff, he preferred taking care of himself.

He turned from the view, already dressed for work in a tailored suit and handmade shoes, crossing the terrazzo-tiled floor of the living area and dining room, which opened up into the gourmet kitchen. He set his empty coffee cup on the marble counter-top and pulled a bottle of water from the Sub-Zero refrigerator before grabbing his briefcase from the top of the sleek marble island and heading to the grand foyer to leave the condo via the elevator that opened directly into it.

He ran through his tight schedule of meetings for the day and was anxious to get the workday started. As soon as the elevator doors slid open, he crossed the lobby of the fifteen-story building with long strides, giving the doorman a nod of both greeting and thanks as he held the glass door open for him. His driver already waited behind the wheel of the company's black-on-black GMC Yukon.

"Morning, Mac. It's a great day to do business," Naim said as soon as he was settled on the rear seat of the SUV with his briefcase on the butter-soft leather seat beside him.

The middle-aged man, whose name was actually Victor McIntosh, said with a smile, "Yes, it is. Yes, it is," fulfilling his part of their morning ritual since he was assigned to Naim upon his full-time return to the New York offices of ADG.

Naim busied himself making overseas calls and checking emails during the nearly thirty-minute drive to Midtown Manhattan. While Mac pulled the Yukon to a stop, he looked up at the art deco building that was a testament to its 1940s creation. ADG owned the twenty-five-story building but leased out all but the top four floors, with the co-CEOs occupying the two offices on the top floor with their own private elevators.

"I have meetings all day but I will be going out for lunch, Mac," he said as he opened the door for himself, something he insisted on doing. He found it ridiculous, as a grown man, to sit and wait for another man to do it.

"You got it, Boss."

Naim closed the door and paused to find a clear

flow across the foot traffic on the street. His smile was broad as he strode into the building and across the polished floors of the lobby to the wood-paneled elevators. It had not gotten old that Alek and Alessandra had promoted him to president of the telecommunications division. His time to become CEO would come when his brother chose to step down, but that was so far off that he had been ecstatic when he discovered the promotion was the reason he was summoned back from Milan two months ago. His focus was ensuring the division remained fiscally viable. The drive for success was in his blood.

Naim's grandfather, Ebo Ansah, began a financial services firm in Ghana in the 1950s that grew significantly in the mid-1960s, providing him a good living. His father, Kwame, entered the family business in the late 1970s. Upon Ebo's death in the early 1980s, Kwame took over the running of the business, aggressively taking over smaller banks and insurance and investments firms to catapult himself to wealth. In 1987, he joined forces with his business competitor from England, Frances Dalmount, with the intent to use their combined resources to take on other business ventures. Both Dalmount and Ansah lived in England and New York for a few years before moving to New York permanently to establish the US offices of the Ansah-Dalmount Group and becoming one of the most successful conglomerates in the world, with its business umbrella encompassing financial services, oil, hotels, resorts and casinos, telecommunications and, most recently, shipping.

"Good morning, Mr. Ansah."

He looked over at a svelte brunette with large green eyes giving him a ruby red smile. He didn't recognize her but wasn't surprised she knew him. Lots of women did. His wealth made him the perfect catch to some. "Good morning," he said, his eyes traveling up and down the length of her shapely frame before he glanced away.

Nothing wrong with looking.

But he knew from the look in her eye she would have been pleased with more. With a polite smile, he sped up his steps to the elevator reserved for the top two floors of the building housing the spacious offices of the executive officers of ADG. He stepped on and rode up alone, pleased for the quiet as he prepped himself for his first quarterly meeting of the division heads with the CEOs.

The doors slid open, revealing the modern and sleek design of the reception area. The light beaming through the glass walls of the offices gave it a really open feel. He nodded at the male receptionist as he passed his area to the left and walked along the marbled floors toward his corner office suite. He paused at the doorway to the office of his executive assistant, Judith Leigh. She looked up, her eyes surprised behind her round spectacles.

He tried not to chuckle. Judith was efficient and smart, but he was well aware he made her nervous.

He wasn't sure of the reason, but he tried his best not to do so. With one press of his hand against the panel, the glass door of her office that adjoined his slid open.

"Good morning, Mr. Ansah," the young woman said, rising to her feet. "I have your coffee on your desk and I was just opening the morning mail. Your first meeting is in thirty minutes."

"Thank you," he said, offering her a warm smile. "No phone calls, please."

She nodded several times and bit at her lip as she twisted her hands.

Naim turned and made his way to his office, setting thoughts of her and her nervous behavior aside. The views were spectacular, and he enjoyed the sun bursting through the apron windows, almost blocking the sight of the surrounding skyscrapers and the Hudson River in the distance. Summer was drawing to an end, and soon the frigid cold and snow of winter would rule, demolishing the sunny views.

His steps paused at a small dark brown box sitting on his glass desk.

His heart hammered as he recognized it as Marisa's signature box for the chocolate treats she sold at La Boulangerie bakery in Passion Grove. *Had she been here and left a treat for him?*

Naim felt hopeful that she had. That surprised him.

A steamy vision of him atop her on the couch with

her legs spread wide as she clutched his bare buttocks and begged him for more played out in his head.

Yes, yes, yes, she had cried out in abandon, pushing him to please her. And himself. His gut clenched.

Since that night of wild sex, they had gone right back to how they were before. Barely better than strangers who spoke and kept it moving. When he awakened early the next morning she was gone, and he knew she regretted it.

Most times he could forget that night. Most times. It had been surreal. Very hard to forget.

His manhood stirred as he remembered the feel of her lightly biting his shoulders when she had sat astride him and taken over the ride.

Clearing his throat, Naim neared the desk, seeing the folded stationery beneath the box. He set his briefcase atop his large glass desk and lightly stroked the raised lettering—Décadence de Chocolat—French for "chocolate decadence." He slipped the note from under the box and opened it with his index finger. It was from Alessandra.

"Marisa's newest treat: chocolate scones," he read aloud, pushing aside his regret that the treat was not from Marisa instead.

Attached to the note was a Décadence de Chocolat gift certificate for five hundred dollars. Naim chuckled. A costly gift the billionaire heiress could well afford. He could only imagine the number of scones and gift certificates Alessandra had given out to support her cousin's new business venture.

He removed his billfold from the inner pocket of his blazer and tucked the gift certificate inside before he opened the box and removed one of the two scones.

He felt foolish for reveling in the fact that Marisa's hands had made the chocolate and then baked the scones. He turned with the dessert in his hand to face the floor-to-ceiling windows. Of all the amenities that came with his state-of-the-art office, the view was his favorite. He couldn't count the number of minutes he had stood there looking out at the city and its movement and vibrancy gave him peace of mind as he thought through a business problem, especially once the night reigned and the city was illuminated.

Rocking back on his heels, Naim took a bite of the scone, and within moments he grunted in pleasure. It was delicious. Sweet but not cloying. Tender. Decadent.

She was just as skilled as a chocolatier as she was at making love.

Marisa had gasped and dug her fingers into his shoulders as she arched her back and flung her head back until her curls stroked the middle of her back, all while he had pressed his face between her breasts and gripped her fleshy buttocks.

He closed his eyes at the memory and pinched the bridge of his nose with his free hand.

It was best to move on. Stop thinking about that night. Two months had passed and it was clearly a one-night stand. Nothing more.

And that was how he liked it.

Right?

Bedding her was supposed to kill his lust for her now.

With a shake of his head, Naim tossed the rest of the scone in his mouth, acutely aware that her body tasted way better—and he doubted he would ever forget that.

Marisa smiled as she poured her own special blend of chocolate out onto the marble slab of her work area in the kitchen of La Boulangerie, quickly picking up a spatula to temper the chocolate by working the mix back and forth across the marble, keeping the warm liquid from cooling and turning solid before sufficient fat crystals could form. The fat gave chocolate its shine, smoothness and longer shelf life. There were far easier methods, but she had quickly fallen in love with the traditional tabling method and found it soothing.

Never had she seen anything as beautiful as smooth, warm chocolate.

Well…

She gasped at the memory of Naim's strong arms splayed across the back of the sofa, his chest hard and just as gleaming, as she rode him with her arms stretched high above her head.

"Damn," he'd sworn, looking at her in wonder.

The fleshy bud nestled between her thighs throbbed to life at the memory.

They had mated like they were starved. Not once but twice. Both times equally explosive and fiery.

Marisa closed her eyes as she continued to work the chocolate, allowing herself to dwell in the heated memory of that night…

They'd knelt on the floor, his body behind hers as he pressed kisses from one shoulder to the other. His hands cupped her breasts and teased her hard nipples before easing down her stomach to palm the warm V between her thighs.

She had cried out in pleasure.

"Still at it?"

Marisa glanced up at Bill Landon, the owner of the bakery, a tall man with a blond man-bun who looked more like a sun-kissed California surfer than a man from the East Coast with that distinctive Jersey accent. "Just finishing up a batch of chocolate for the morning," she said.

He leaned against a metal counter and crossed his arms over his chest, covering Bill the Pâtissier embroidered across his apron. "I still can't believe you make your own chocolate from cocoa beans," he said in apparent wonder.

She shrugged one shoulder. "I love my own blend of cream and sugar ratios to chocolate. The perfect sweet spot between milk chocolate and dark," she said, continuing to table the chocolate. It usually took around five minutes.

"I'm proud of you, Marisa," he said.

She had started out as a cashier, wanting her independence from her family, but a love of chocolate and an innocent question to Bill on how it was made led to him teaching her all about chocolate making.

"Thank you for helping guide me to my gift," she said earnestly.

Bill pressed his hands together and nodded.

Marisa gave him a smile before she focused on using a scraper to get the chocolate back into a bowl before pouring it into her specially made silicone molds with her logo. "What's your plans for the night, Bill?" she asked as she began sliding the molds into the fridge.

She already knew it would include a pretty lady. Bill was single and always ready to use his good looks and charming nature to mingle. He was never in short supply of a date.

"Dinner with someone sweeter than your chocolate," he said, removing his apron and walking across the kitchen to his storeroom to toss it into the metal-rimmed hamper.

"That's pretty sweet," Marisa teased, closing the fridge and removing her own apron and hair net.

Bill chuckled. "And I'm looking forward to it," he said. "You?"

"Headed home to soak my feet and watch television before I catch some sleep," she said, using a hot and soapy dishcloth to clean the chocolate from the marble.

"We're starting our night at this fun bar in Edenville called Darby's if you want to join us before we head to her place for dessert," Bill offered as he began closing up his office.

Marisa wrung out the dishcloth and laid it over the side of the empty metal sink to dry. "I've had all the partying my heart could desire, so that's a hard pass, Bill," she said, retrieving her Gucci pocketbook that was a throwback to her days of wearing nothing but the best the family money could buy.

He looked apologetic as they made their way out of the kitchen. "My bad, kiddo," he said, turning off the lights as he followed her out behind the counter of the sizable storefront that was reminiscent of an old-world pastry shop from Europe with its brick walls, wood beams, polished hardwood floors, metal accents, and black bistro tables and chairs.

"No biggie," she said with honesty. "It's my job to remember, not yours."

"Cool."

Before she walked out the bakery, she looked back at her display beneath her sign, Décadence de Chocolat. She smiled, filled with pride that she had started her own small business and was on track to pay back her loan from Alessandra in another few months.

"Have fun, Bill," she said, unlocking her cherry red Bentley coupe—a gift from her mother for her twenty-first birthday. It was the one luxury she clung to. This year her mother offered her a newer version, but she had declined.

That was sacrifice enough. I never said I was perfect.

She drove the ten minutes to the peripheries of Passion Grove, where the original homes making up the small town were more modest. Here the two blocks of two-thousand- to three-thousand-square-foot homes were in abundance, and were considered cottages in comparison to the megamansions built in the last twenty years. She pulled her car onto the drive before the two-car garage, grabbing her bag before entering the English Tudor home she'd rented, using a portion of the money she borrowed from Alessandra to move out of the guesthouse of her mother's estate.

Closing the front door behind her, she kicked off her black sneakers and took a deep inhale, loving the smell of it. "Home sweet home," she said, raising her hands to undo her top knot and free her curls that spoke to her African-American mother and Cuban father she had never gotten the chance to meet.

As she stroked her fingers across her scalp, she closed her eyes, remembering Naim's fingers in her hair as he kissed her that night. Slowly. So slowly.

"Wooo," Marisa said at the recollection.

She could have let him do that for forever and a day…if that night could have led to more. But it didn't. It couldn't. Under the light of day, reality superseded reckless passion, and she had gathered her clothes and what little respect she could muster, leaving him sleeping on the couch.

Forcing the recollection away, she moved about the house turning on lights before climbing the stairs in the center of the house to the second level. She undressed in her bedroom, calmed by the muted tones of the room, before walking into the adjoining bathroom. As she ran a scented bubble bath in the claw-foot tub, she sat on the edge looking around a beautiful space that paled in comparison to the luxury she'd grown up in but satisfied her because it was of her own doing.

No household staff. Fewer amenities. Considerably less space. But it was *hers*.

With a sigh filled with both her pride and fatigue from a hard day's work, she turned and slid into the tub beneath the steamy depths. Tilting her head back against the rim, she looked up at the ceiling, smiling at the changes in her life—for the better. She closed her eyes and rubbed her hands against her arms, enjoying the gentle movement of the water against her body.

It almost felt like the gentle touch of a lover.

Sinking deeper beneath the water until her chin touched the surface, Marisa extended her legs and crossed them at the ankles atop the edge of the tub. She was at peace, and when she closed her eyes she got lost in her steamy imaginings and didn't fight it...

"Miss me?"

Marisa opened her eyes to find Naim standing beside her tub, naked and as glorious as she remembered him from that night. She took him all in. Every delicious, dark inch, including the ten curving away from his body and ready to please. "No," she lied, finally answering him.

He gripped the edge of the tub, his eyes locked on hers, and reached into the water with his free hand to ease between her thighs.

She gasped and arched her back as she opened her legs and allowed him to stroke her intimacy.

His eyes were like a hawk to prey as he reveled in the pleasure displayed on her face as he slipped a finger inside her core. "Now?"

"Yes," she admitted in a harsh little whisper.

He eased in another finger.

Her hips arched up off the bottom of the tub as she bit her bottom lip and nodded eagerly.

He chuckled, low in his throat. "Let's see if we can have a night like we did the last time," he said, stepping over the side of the tub to climb inside with her.

She welcomed him with a moan...

Marisa awakened from her daydream and sat up in the tub, causing the water to overflow onto the floor. "Damn," she swore.

That hadn't been her first fantasy about Naim over the months. Although she played it cool around him as if that night had never happened, secretly she couldn't forget it. He was a skilled lover. Right pacing. Right kissing. Right touches. Slow when needed. Fast and furious when wanted. Just good.

Marisa drew her knees to her chest as she exhaled.

He had been her first lover in over a year. Her

focus had been her sobriety and the change in her lifestyle, but when she walked into her old bedroom and awakened Naim on the sofa, she'd turned on the light to reveal his nudity and found it hard to deny all of his sexiness on display.

Strong chest.

Hard abs.

Muscled thighs.

And one beautiful, glorious tool that was impressive even at rest.

She frowned as a wave of nausea hit her that caused her to cover her mouth with her hand. She took deep, steadying breaths, but the feeling wouldn't pass. She climbed from the tub and took just a few steps before she dropped to her knees in front of the commode a moment before she gagged several times and then vomited.

What the hell?

Marisa frowned at the foul taste and sat back on her haunches, rolling tissue off the roll to wipe her mouth before tossing it into the commode and flushing it before standing. She felt dizzy and reached for the wall, closing her eyes.

Am I sick? What did I have to eat? I don't have time for illness.

Moving over to the sink with slow steps, she rinsed her mouth before looking at her reflection as she ran her fingers through her curls. "Pepto-Bismol," she said, bending down to open the door to the cabinet under the sink.

As she looked through the hair products and makeup, she eyed the unopened box of maxi pads. "Oh," she said, her shoulders drooping as she realized it had been some time since she last used one.

Lots of time.

Months.

"Oh," she said again, this time with a frown.

Marisa rose to her full height and studied her reflection as the pace of her heart began to pick up. She saw the panic slowly flooding her face and felt nauseous all over again. She closed her eyes and pressed a hand to her chest as she felt herself hyperventilating at her missed cycles.

"It's just the stress of the job," she reasoned as she left the bathroom and took the door leading into her walk-in closet. "Stress can throw everything off. Stress is the enemy of a healthy body."

Panting through pursed lips, she quickly pulled on black leggings, a matching fitted tee and sneakers before leaving her room and jogging down the stairs to retrieve her keys and purse. "I have to slow down a little bit, that's all," she said with a little laugh that waned at the end as she left her house and fast-walked to her car.

She drove back to the downtown area in a calm manner. She'd convinced herself that everything was fine. Life would not throw such a wrench in her plans. It was simply stress. "I just need to relax. Maybe get a massage. Sleep more. Drink more alkaline water... eat less of my chocolate. *Something.*"

She parked and walked inside The Gourmet Way, the high-end grocery store designed like a galleria that specialized in gourmet food, making her way to the aisle with the health and beauty products. "Maybe my blood pressure is too high," she said, even though she knew that didn't sound right.

Marisa grabbed the first pregnancy kit she spotted and moved to the lone register that was open. "What time do you close?" she asked the teenage cashier with freckles and oversize spectacles.

"Nine o'clock," he said, scanning the box and then dropping it into a small black paper shopping bag. Marisa paid him and accepted her change and the bag. "The restroom, please," she requested, unable to bear a drive home before she took the test and knew the results.

He pointed a long slender arm toward the rear of the store. She headed that way, eventually seeing the sign and entering the gender-neutral restroom. Locking the door, she tried to steady her trembling fingers as she opened the box and used the kit.

"Five minutes," she said, setting the timer on her phone before she closed the lid and sat on the commode as she eyed the test sitting on the edge of the sink.

What if...

Marisa started to cover her face with her hands but then remembered she had yet to wash her hands. She stood and moved over to the sink to do so, avoiding looking at the test.

Can't be. Won't be. Better not be.

Marisa closed her eyes. "It's just stress. It's just stress. It's just stress," she whispered.

"Thank you for shopping with us today at The Gourmet Way. Currently we are offering our daily Butcher's Closeout Special on the finest USDA grade cuts of meats. Please be sure to stop by our meat department and see the selections being offered."

Another wave of nausea hit her as the voice on the intercom stopped talking. The thought of vomiting over a public commode ironically made her want to vomit.

Ding.

Marisa froze and she eyed her reflection, knowing once she looked at the test that the results could change her life forever. With her breath coming in pants, she looked down—and then swore.

It's a baby. It's a baby. It's a baby.

Chapter 3

Two weeks later

There were just seven more weeks of summer, and Naim was trying to enjoy every bit of his favorite season when he wasn't tied to work. He parked his onyx McLaren 600LT in front of the stables of the Passion Grove Equestrian. Dressed in all black, from his polo shirt to his breeches and riding boots, he made his way across the graveled yard to the sixteen-stall barn. One of the trainers led his chocolate Arabian stallion out of his stall toward him.

Once he learned of the hundred-acre horse boarding facility in Passion Grove, Naim had set about purchasing himself a prize stallion, wanting to get back to his childhood pastime of horseback riding. It had been something he shared with his father and now missed. Living in Brooklyn didn't provide a place to properly house a horse, but Passion Grove did, and he could easily visit his brother and sister-in-law, kiss the chubby cheek of his niece and get a ride in on his horse on the weekends.

The facility provided premium horse boarding, scenic surroundings, plenty of paddocks, large stall barns, an indoor/outdoor arena, vet and farrier. He gladly paid the sizable fee to have his new stallion well taken care of.

Naim patted his neck and stroked the bridge of his nose. "Hello, boy, how are you?" he asked.

The stallion lifted his nose to nudge his hand, causing him to chuckle.

"You haven't changed his name yet, Mr. Ansah."

Naim looked over the back of the horse at the tall and willowy redhead, Greenly Briton. She was the stunning owner of Passion Grove Equestrian. "Lucky Duck doesn't fit him," he said, giving her a charming smile.

Her emerald green eyes dipped down to take in his mouth before she curved her own. "Well, what does suit him?"

Deciding to amuse himself with a little harmless flirtation, Naim stepped back from the steed, taking in his strong build and deep brown coat that gleamed.

Like chocolate.

"Decadence," he said, thinking of both Marisa and her delicious chocolate treats.

"That is perfection, Mr. Ansah," Greenly said, coming around the front of the horse to stand before him. "Or can I call you Naim?"

He took in the fitted V-neck tee she wore with black breeches and riding boots. He was impressed, but not interested. "Either is fine, Ms. Briton," he said politely, turning to grab the horn and lift his foot into the stirrup to climb onto the saddle.

She crossed her arms over her ample chest. "You sit well in that saddle, Naim," she said. "I bet you really know how to ride."

Naim lightly held the reins as he chuckled and looked down at her. "Yes, the hell I do," he assured her with one last leisurely up-and-down perusal of the woman before he galloped away.

He enjoyed the feel of riding the horse, especially when he entered one of the paddocks and really picked up the pace, using the reins, his heel and his stern voice to control the strong beast. His ride became his focus, and for the next ten minutes, nothing else mattered but him and Decadence.

"Good boy," Naim said, patting the stallion's neck as he slowed the stallion down to a trot and then a walk to cool down his muscles.

He walked him over to the trail for new scenery, enjoying the beautiful landscape as he followed the well-worn path that circled the property. Back where they began, he easily dismounted and loosened the girth before putting the reins over his head and walking Decadence back to his corner stall of the barn.

One of the biggest parts of horseback riding, Naim, is the moments of selflessness when you take care of the horse after the ride just as well as he took care of you during it.

Naim smiled at the memory of his father and him sharing that time together on their estate in London. So many hours of enjoyment, life lessons, laughter and selflessness in caring for the horses.

Filling the trough for him from the spigot, he busied himself checking if the animal was overheated, sweating or breathing heavy before removing the tack and storing it away. As he groomed him with a sweat scraper, a currycomb and then a stiff brush, he was happy Greenly never interrupted them. He wasn't sure she wouldn't press him for a lay in the hay—while Decadence watched.

It was late afternoon by the time he was done and Decadence was cleaned, dried, fed and in his stall.

"See you soon, Decadence," Naim said, allowing himself one last stroke of the bridge of his nose before turning away.

He was sweaty and felt the exertion in his bones, but he had enjoyed his day. At his car, he paused at the folded note tucked under the windshield wiper. Looking around first, he reached for it, not at all surprised by Greenly's name and phone number scrawled there with a crimson kiss pressed beside it. As he climbed inside the vehicle, he tossed the note onto the passenger seat and soon was driving down the graveled drive and onto the sedate Passion Grove streets.

Naim slowed down and made the right turn onto Dalmount Lane, a mile-long paved street leading to the sprawling twenty-five-acre estate of Alek and Alessandra. The property had once belonged to Alessandra's parents, Frances and Olivia. In Passion Grove, all streets were named after flowers, so Frances had commissioned a one-of-a-kind hybrid rose in honor of Olivia that he named the Dalmount, which made it eligible to be the name of the private street. Her mother passed when Alessandra was young, and then upon Frances's passing, the estate became her own.

Naim reached the twelve-foot-tall wrought iron gate with Dalmount-Ansah in an intricate bronzed scroll in the center. He pulled up to the security panel and lowered his window to enter the guest pass code. The security guard on duty in the office stationed above the six-car garage opened the gate and Naim accelerated forward down the tree-lined paved road.

At the sight of Marisa's red Bentley parked on the circular drive before the house, his gut clenched and he accepted that he felt excitement at seeing her again. He barely noticed Roje, Alessandra's chauffeur, kneeling by the tires of Alessandra's black 1954 Jaguar MK kVII sedan. Climbing from his low-slung sports car, Naim removed his aviator shades. "Hello,

Roje," he said to the tall and burly dark-skinned man of sixty with a bright white goatee.

"Mr. Ansah," Roje said, his voice strong but polite.

With a nod, Naim walked over to the front door, his heart pounding in anticipation at the thought of seeing Marisa again.

He entered the house, stepping into the foyer and then pausing at the crowd of people in a circle looking down at the polished floors. His brows dipped as he eyed his brother bouncing his daughter, Aliya, his mother looking concerned and several uniformed staff members standing around. All were looking down at the floor.

"What happened?" someone asked.

"She fainted."

"Who fainted?" Naim asked, walking up to stand behind his brother.

Aliya reached over her father's shoulder to press her chubby palm to his cheek, her eyes bright at the sight of him. He grabbed her hand and pressed a kiss to her sticky palm in welcome as he looked over his brother's shoulder.

"Marisa," Alek said, just as Naim spotted her body sprawled on the floor with her head in Alessandra's lap.

Alarmed filled him. Scared him to death actually. But he fought not to break through the bodies to drop to his knees down beside her.

Alessandra lightly tapped her cheek. "Marisa. Marisa. Wake up," she said.

Wake up, Marisa. Wake. Up.

She stirred.

Relief flooded him. The grip on his gut and heart faded.

"My head hurts," Marisa whispered, wincing as she tried to sit up.

"Get her a pain pill and glass of water," LuLu said to one of the servants.

Marisa shook her head. "No," she moaned.

Alessandra looked up. "Get it," she said, her voice firm.

Aliya reached to come to him, and Naim took her from her father's arms, pressing kisses to her cheek as he fought hard to pretend to be nothing more than a bystander. "You happy to see Uncle Naim?" he asked her.

She nodded and giggled before burying her face against his chest.

The housekeeper returned with the glass of water and two pills atop a folded paper cloth. LuLu and Alek moved aside to allow her to pass them and hand the pills to Alessandra. "Come on, Marisa, this will help your headache," she said, trying not to press the pills to her lips.

"No, no. I can't," she moaned, her eyes half-closed. "The baby. Not good for the baby."

Alessandra's eyes widened.

Alek went stiff. "Huh?" he asked, almost on the level of Scooby-Doo.

"Definitely no pain pills, then," LuLu said, covering her mouth with her hand as she eyed Alessandra and Alek with a questioning stare.

The staff disappeared.

Baby? What baby? Whose baby?

He remembered the heated moment they climaxed together…sans condom. Caught up in the moment. Lost in the passion. Not caring about the consequences.

Naim felt like he might just join her on the floor.

Marisa looked up, and her eyes fell on Naim standing in the small crowd looking down at her on the floor—where she had just revealed her pregnancy. She shifted her eyes away from his as Alessandra and Alek helped her to her feet. She was not ready to deal with Naim. Not yet. She was still trying to accept her march to motherhood herself.

She accepted the glass of water and busied herself drinking it down as the flood of questions drowned her.

"You're pregnant?"

"Who is the father?"

"Does your mother know?"

"How far along?"

"Who's the father?"

"How do you feel?"

"Have you been to the doctor?"

"Do you need to go to the doctor now?"

Marisa held up both her hands. "Whoa. Whoa. My head is spinning from all the questions," she said, stiffening her back as she eased past them all. "Yes, I am going to call my OB/GYN and make sure everything is fine. And no, I haven't told my mom so I would appreciate if you all gave me a chance to do so, but in the meanwhile, I'm good and I really am not up for the round of fifty questions. So if y'all will excuse me, I came to drop off a loan payment and I did that. So I'm out."

She crossed the foyer and left the mansion, nearly running into Roje, who brought his large hands up to grab her elbows and steady her. "Sorry," she said to the man who was always so quiet around them.

"Marisa. Wait," Alessandra called behind her.

Roje gave her a smile before he turned and walked toward the side entrance leading into the kitchen that the servants normally used.

Marisa turned as Alessandra reached her. She expected a reprimand or more questions, and was surprised when her cousin pulled her into a comforting embrace.

"Congratulations," she said.

Marisa felt her defense fade as she let her forehead rest on her shoulder. "I just didn't want any more mistakes. I wanted to do something right... and I can't believe I messed up again," she admitted, her voice soft as she revealed the truth of her feelings and concerns. "I am not ready to be a mother."

Alessandra leaned back enough to look down at her. "There was a time when, if someone told me you would own your own business built off your own sweat and that you wanted to work for your own money, I would have laughed, but look at you proving me wrong every day," she said. "And I bet that you can prove yourself wrong in this."

Marisa closed her eyes and tilted her head back as tears rose. "Thanks," she said, pausing when she dropped her head and looked past her cousin to see Naim standing in the open doorway looking at them. "I gotta go."

She rushed to cross the courtyard and climbed behind the wheel of her Bentley, looking in her rearview mirror at Naim still standing there watching her drive away. At the end of Dalmount Lane, she pulled to a stop and pressed a hand to her still-flat belly. No pain. The throb in her head was gone. She still called her OB/GYN in Manhattan, explained what happened and answered questions that reassured her. She already had an appointment scheduled for that Monday. With a promise to eat something, not stand on her feet for long periods of time and not move too quickly, she ended the call.

Marisa returned to the bakery, forcing herself to eat two delicious croissants before returning to selling her treats. Still, her thoughts were on the look on Naim's face at the news of her pregnancy. She couldn't escape it, and it scared her.

"You okay?"

Marisa looked up at Bill and his cashier, Lynette, who were looking at her oddly. She forced a smile and nodded, before focusing on the line of people waiting to buy chocolate. "Good evening. Which Décadence de Chocolat would you like to enjoy?" she asked a twentysomething mother with twins in a double stroller.

"A dozen turtles, please," the woman said.

"A dozen? You're really treating yourself," Marisa said as she used plastic tongs to place each milk chocolate, caramel and pecan treat into one of her signature boxes with a matching chocolate bow on the lid.

"They'll last me a week," she said, taking the box and handing Marisa a black Amex card.

"Good luck with that," Marisa teased, ringing the transaction up on her iPad before presenting it to her customer to sign.

With her worries uppermost in her mind, the last few hours of the workday seemed to drag by. Marisa was thankful when she finally got into her car and made her way home. Her gratitude faded at the sight of Naim's sports car parked in front of her rental house. Her first instinct was to speed past and keep driving.

Where?

Her hands tightly gripped the steering wheel as she slowed down the car and drove onto her driveway. Her heart was pounding so crazily she was afraid she would faint again. As she watched Naim climb from his car in her rearview mirror, she forced herself to take deep, calming breaths before she did the same. "It's not yours," she said as soon as he reached her standing by her car.

"I don't believe you," Naim said, his deep brown eyes searching hers as he looked down at her. "And if you are carrying my child I have every right to know, Marisa. I have every right to be a father. Don't take that from me because we made a baby during a one-night stand."

Marisa hated that his closeness still affected her. Her senses were just as alive as her fears of him knowing the truth. She craved him as much as she hated him being there. "It's not yours, Naim. Forget that night ever happened and move on," she said, turning from him.

"I can't."

Marisa froze and hung her head. *Neither can I.*

"Did you forget?" he asked.

Forget? That night? At that very moment, she was getting lost in the memory...

Marisa reached between them to fling away the pillow to press him closer with her hands to his back as they instantly got lost in the passion. He grabbed the edges of her swim cover-up to pull up over her head. The feel of his hard inches pressed against her belly sent a shot of pleasure coursing over her body as she raised herself up on her toes and then wrapped one leg around him. He cupped her but-

tocks, hoisting her higher against the wall as he broke the kiss and pressed his mouth against her cheek. Her chin. Her neck. The deep valley between her breasts pushed up high by her bikini top.

She shivered as Naim used his teeth to lower it to free her breasts. His breath breezed against her taut brown nipples. At the first feel of his tongue stroking it, she moaned with hunger and pleasure. The first suckle drew a hot gasp as she arched her back and clutched at his head, thinking she might explode from the electricity they created. "Yes!" she cried out, over and over, losing count.

"You like that?" he moaned against the sides of her full breasts, looking up to see the rapture on her face.

She nodded eagerly. "More," she begged in a hot little whisper. "Please."

He obliged with pleasure, smothering his face against her cleavage and rubbing his head back and forth against the sweet-smelling softness before clasping one of her breasts to deeply suck it, drawing a good bit of the brown globe into his mouth as his tongue also stroked her nipple. He grunted in pleasure, his hands deeply massaging her hips and buttocks as she ground against his hardness. "I could suck on these forever," he whispered into the heat they created.

"Then don't forget the other," Marisa teased with a soft smile.

He raised his head just long enough to cover her

*mouth and suckle her lips before lowering it to give
her other breast the same attention. Slowly. Meant
to please.*

*The seat of her bikini dampened against his hard
inches as she gripped his shoulders and wished he
were deep inside her instead of rubbing against her.
The months of ignoring the desire he stoked in her
faded into nothing. Her promise to herself for celi-
bacy was about to be broken. She was ready for him
to deliver on the promise of passion to come.*

*He wrapped one strong arm around her waist as
he walked them backward until he dropped down
on the couch with her straddling him. She rose just
long enough to remove her bikini bottom before reclaiming her seat on his lap. She looked down at his
hardness. Long and thick. His tip was smooth and
tempting, but with a lick of her lips, she fought the
urge to suckle him there. Instead, she clasped the
side of his face and kissed him, drawing the tip of
his tongue into her mouth as he reached behind her
to ease one strong finger inside her core.*

*She arched her hips and cried out into his mouth.
Naim lightly slapped her buttocks.*

WHAP.

*She looked down into his beautiful dazed eyes and
bit her bottom lip.* "Again," *she demanded.*

He obeyed.

WHAP.

*She arched a brow and purred with a soft little
giggle.* "Again," *she whispered into his open mouth,*

so turned on that she thought she might climax be-
fore he even slid inside her.

WHAP.

He gripped her buttocks with his free hand, his
fingers digging into the soft flesh as he licked at
her lips.

"It's been a long time," Marisa professed as she
reached down to stroke his hardness, lightly drag-
ging her thumb across the smooth tip.

His hips arched up off the sofa as he winced in
pleasure. "Then I need to make it worth the wait,"
he said, his breath shaky.

She locked her eyes with his as he circled his fin-
ger inside of her and pressed his thumb against her
throbbing clit. Her wetness made his circular mo-
tions against the warm bud slick and devastatingly
arousing.

She gasped and then exhaled, unable to look away
from his eyes framed by long lashes. "Your eyes are
beautiful," she admitted, dipping her head to suck
his bottom lip.

"You're beautiful, Marisa," *Naim countered.*

She raised up on her knees and pushed the hand
buried between her thighs away to settle the plump
lips of her core around his tip. It was warm. She
moaned at the feel of it.

"It's wet," *he whispered with a shake of his head*
against the sofa where it rested.

"You did it," *she said, arching her back before*

lightly twerking her buttocks and slowly lowering herself down to surround him with the heat.

Naim bit his bottom lip and gripped her buttocks as he flung his head back with a soft swear. "Wait. Don't move. Don't move. Don't," he begged, closing his eyes and tensing his jaw.

"What's wrong?"

"Anticipation is a bitch," he admitted.

"So true."

Naim opened his eyes, looking up at her as she pressed her bosom against his chin and moved her hips to ride his tip. "Nah," he said, wrapping his arm around her waist and turning them over so that she was on her back and he was between her legs. "I need to be on top...for now."

She stroked her hands down his muscled back to his buttocks, spreading her legs as wide as she could. He dug his hands beneath her to lift her buttocks as he stroked inside her, his face buried against her neck. His pace and rhythm were perfection. She eyed him in wonder.

And for the time being, she didn't bother to count how many times they made love. They simply fed on one another. On the sofa. On their knees bent over the sofa. On the floor. Against the wall.

Kisses. Moans. Thrusts.

Passion and pleasure personified.

A sexual wonderland. Every desire sought and met.

And with her once again astride him on the sofa,

they kissed each other deeply, sweat coating their bodies, as she rode him hard and furiously. He had one hand twisted in her hair and the other gripping her buttock to help guide her core down upon him. Her fingers dug into his shoulders. Their tongues were entwined.

"Don't stop. Please. Make me cum," he begged, his voice deep and low.

Marisa felt him stiffen inside and knew his release was near. "We'll cum together," she whispered heatedly into his open mouth, nearly blinded with passion as she felt her own climax building inside of her.

When the first sparks of the explosion lit, she gave in to the passion, releasing a cry as waves upon waves of pleasure burst inside her. His cries blended with hers with his own climax. They clung to one another, riding the waves until they both trembled, kissing each other deeply as they reached the heights together.

She had never felt anything like it before, and doubted she ever would again. And then to learn that they had created a baby in the midst of so much chemistry and passion. She was surprised by how much the thought of that overwhelmed her. Tears welled and she closed her eyes.

"Marisa."

She knew he'd walked closer to her. Her body sensed him. Reacted to him. Her pulse. Heartbeat. Hairs on the back of her neck.

But she couldn't relinquish the control of her mind and body again so easily. Like her family, the Ansahs were billionaires. She believed such wealth and excess did not bode well for her child's upbringing. She was a testament to it. She wanted the normalcy for her baby that she had never received.

He lightly gripped her shoulders and whirled her around to face him.

Marisa felt woozy at the sudden movement and her knees buckled a little. Instinctively she reached out and grabbed his arms to steady herself. "Whoa," she said.

Naim took her keys from her hand and swung her up in his arms with ease. "Are you okay? Why do you keep fainting? Is something wrong with the baby?" he asked as he strolled across the walkway and up the stairs to the front door.

"I'm fine. Put me down, Naim. I can walk," she protested even as she enjoyed the scent of his warm cologne.

He used the lone key on the ring with the fob to unlock the door and carry her inside. "Bedroom or living room?" he asked.

"Neither," she said.

He gripped her body closer to him. "One or the other," he insisted.

She looked up at his profile. It was carved with determination. Resigned to accept his help and loving not being on her feet, Marisa pointed beyond the stairs. "Den," she said, not sure she could resist being in a bedroom with Naim Ansah.

Hell, I want to kiss his jaw right now.

He strode to the right of the stairs, and the space opened up into a family room/kitchen open concept. With his strength, it barely took the effort to cross the room and lay her on the leather sectional sitting before the fireplace.

"Thank you," she said, immediately readjusting from a prone position to a sitting one.

Naim walked over to the kitchen, setting the keys on the wooden island before he began opening cabinets, and retrieved a glass. He filled it with water from the fridge and brought it over to her. "Drink up," he said, sitting down on the sofa beside her.

"I'm *fine*. My doctor says dizziness is normal early in a pregnancy because my blood vessels are expanding to supply blood to the baby," she said.

He looked confused.

"There's more to it but that's the gist of it," Marisa said, taking a sip of water as he turned his attention to the photos and decorative box on the leather ottoman.

"Your dad?" he asked, picking up a photo of a man and a much younger Brunela.

She remained quiet as she took the picture from his hand.

Her pregnancy had her reflecting on memories of her father, wishing he hadn't passed away when she was so young, and thinking of her half-Cuban heritage. She wanted to know more about her culture. She knew nothing to pass on to her child. She couldn't even speak Spanish. All things her father would have taught her. With her thumb, she stroked her father's lean and handsome face.

Naim picked up another photo. "A father is such an important part of a child's life," he said. "Why would you want to deny our baby a father the way death denied you a chance to know yours, Marisa?"

She looked pensive as she released a heavy breath. He was right. She would never overcome her regret of not having her father in her life. And the baby would be part-Ghanaian. Naim and his family were far better suited to pass on their traditions.

"Marisa, is that my baby?" Naim asked.

She looked over at him, her eyes serious as they searched his.

What's to come?

"No," she said. "It's *our* baby."

Naim nodded, his eyes serious. "Our baby," he repeated softly in agreement.

Now what?

Chapter 4

I'm going to be a father.

Naim looked out the window of his corner office as he sat in the chair behind his desk. He was reviewing reports on the acquisition of their own streaming service to rival Netflix and Hulu, but his thoughts were full of Marisa and their baby. He settled his bearded chin in his hand and leaned back in his chair.

"So, Aliya has a cousin on the way."

He flexed his shoulders at the sound of his brother's voice. "Word is out, huh?" he asked, turning in the chair to find his brother strolling across the polished floors toward his desk.

Alek unbuttoned his tailored suit jacket and took one of the clear seats before his desk.

Naim pressed a button on his desk to darken the glass wall separating his office from his assistant's. "Mama told you?" he asked.

"You didn't."

He stiffened at the censure in his brother's tone. "I didn't know I was obligated to. Excuse me for assuming you were only my boss at work, big brother."

"Perhaps your decision making outside of the business gives me a reason to be concerned about those you make in business," Alek countered.

Naim frowned and smirked. "In two months, I have already made tough decisions that led to an increase in revenue of more than 25 percent," he said, his voice hard and unrelenting as he picked up the folders before him and reached across the desk to drop them in front of his brother. "I am currently reviewing streaming services that we can acquire as we liquidate smaller, lesser performing televisions stations. Also, my decision. Two months."

Alek flipped through a folder.

"You were wrong about Alessandra's abilities at ADG. You were wrong when you wouldn't let Samira enter the business because she's a woman, and now you're wrong strolling in here questioning me and my ability to do my job," he said, speaking words he had long held on to. "I thought Alessandra's love had softened you, but then we must have something in common because now I see I was wrong."

Alek tossed the folder back onto the desk, the lines in his face clearly brought on by anger.

"I know Daddy thought you were the end all be all when it comes to running his shares of ADG—"

"Leave him out of this," Alek interjected.

"I wish I could," Naim admitted, rising from his seat and loosening his tie as he stood before his floor-to-ceiling view. "It hurt that he forced you to run this business and completely overlooked me, my experience working here, my education and my willingness."

Alek joined him at the window. "I didn't ask for any of this, Na," he said, reverting to his childhood nickname for his brother.

"I don't blame you for him wanting to continue the tradition, but it would have been nice—especially as close as we were—if Daddy had said to me that I was good enough."

Alek gripped his shoulder. "The plane crash took away his chance to do it, Naim," he said. "Doesn't mean he didn't believe it."

Naim glanced back at the photo of his parent he kept on his desk. "I learned not to wait for anyone to qualify or quantify me. I *know* I'm damn good," he asserted, looking at his brother.

"I had his respect in business, but you had his time, Naim," Alek admitted with one last firm slap to his brother's back. "His expectations for me kept us from being close."

That was true.

"Then don't let your expectations of me do the same to us."

Alek frowned, clearly realizing he was more like their father than he thought. "Marisa, huh?" he said, changing subjects with the finesse of a bull in a china shop.

Naim nodded.

"What's the plan? Are you two in a relationship?"

"No, no, no," Naim rushed to answer, shaking his head. "We're going to coparent."

Alek nodded in understanding, but Naim could tell he was holding back. Opinions. Judgment. Reprimand.

"Listen, a fun night led to more. It's not what we planned, but it is what it is and we're going to make the best of it. It's not like money is an issue. We get along—"

Alek snorted.

Naim gave him a face that he hoped said, *Really, man?*

Alek held up his hands in apology before extending one to him. "Congratulations. Just make sure your child has your last name. He or she will be an Ansah," he said. "And I am thankful that your slipup happened with a Dalmount and not some random chick on the come-up, *but*…to make sure this doesn't happen again…"

Naim looked on as his brother reached into his back pocket and withdrew a sleeve of gold foil condoms that he pressed into his hand before he turned and walked out of the office.

* * *

"Just when I thought you were playing checkers, you make a grand chess move. Bravo, Marisa. Bravo."

Marisa eyed her mother standing on her front porch. She had barely opened the door before she made her proclamation and stepped forward to engulf her into a hug. "Our baby is not a chess move, Momma," she mumbled against her mother's shoulder.

"Of course you will move back in with me," Brunela said, breezing past her daughter in a sheer black silk shirt, wide-leg pants and more than a dozen Chanel necklaces of varying lengths. She set her patent leather tote on the table by the door as she looked around. "There's no way my grandchild can grow up here. I can fit the entire house in my living room and kitchen."

"I'm not moving back in with you, and this house is the same size as the guesthouse I chose to live in on your estate," Marisa said, still standing with the front door open. "I have to get to the bakery."

"The bakery," Brunela said, frowning in distaste. "No. No more of that. You need to be off your feet."

Marisa eyed her mother, a woman of extravagance. Everything was over the top. Her style of dress. Her mannerisms. Her young lovers. Her desire for attention. Her anger over not being the heir to the Dalmount throne.

Her way of showing love.

Marisa couldn't remember a time she asked and

did not receive from her mother. And now, after rehab to avoid a face-first descent into alcoholism and then more than a year of leaving her wild partying lifestyle behind, she knew better. There were times she should have been denied things. No boundaries were set, and she almost fell off the cliff into self-indulgence, immaturity and reckless behavior as a result.

She would no more let her mother ruin her child's life than she would Naim.

Pulling her cross-body bag over her head, she moved her mother's tote to pick up her car keys. "I would think you would be glad I spent my days working instead of drinking and partying," she said, locking her eyes with her mother's.

Brunela looked away. "I just want what's best for you," she said.

"Didn't the past teach us boredom and excess definitely is not it?" she asked, trying to keep the censure from her tone as she held the door open wider.

Brunela saw the move and looked hurt.

"How about I come over for dinner tonight after work?" she offered, along with a soft smile.

Brunela's expression changed and she clasped her hands together. "Oh, good. I will have Chef make your favorite dishes," she said, walking over on her heels to slide her tote over her arm.

And just like that, she's distracted. Thank God.

Marisa followed her mother out of the house. They shared an air kiss before she climbed into the rear of her chauffeur-driven SUV—her mother had never felt the need for a driver's license. Growing up in a house filled with servants had a way of doing that to a person.

Behind the wheel of her Bentley, she pressed a hand to her belly, pleased she had not shared with her mother that she had a doctor's appointment later that afternoon. She smirked at the idea of her mother's over-the-top behavior bundled into a small room. "I just can't deal with it, kiddo," she said.

Bzzzzzz... Bzzzzzz... Bzzzzzz...

She looked down at her phone. "Naim," she read aloud.

Her pulse raced as she answered. "Good morning," she said, still sitting behind the wheel on her driveway.

"Good morning, Marisa."

She loved his English accent. Always had. Always would.

"I know we're not a couple, but I remembered you said you had a doctor's appointment today and I wondered if you would let me go with you. Or take you. Or meet you. Whatever you want."

She smiled at the uncertainty in his voice. Naim was usually so confident and bold; his presence could define the atmosphere of the room he entered. But here he was sounding unsure as he asked her permission. "It's not really necessary—"

"It is for me."

She knew the day would come where Naim's

knowledge of her pregnancy would change everything. "Okay," she said in a rush before she could easily find a dozen or more excuses to keep him from going. "My OB/GYN is in Manhattan, so you can just meet me there at three if you're free."

"I'll get free. This is important."

Her heart skipped a beat. "I'll text you the address."

"Thanks."

"Okay. Bye."

"Bye, Marisa."

She released a long breath before she started her car and slowly reversed down the drive, trying hard not to be impressed by Naim Ansah.

Six weeks later

Marisa and Naim stared at each other across their table at Tuscany Steakhouse in Midtown New York. Neither noticed the neutral decor with dark wood trim and deep brown leather seating of the high-end steakhouse as they continued their stare-off. Not even the clang of cutlery against plates and the chatter of the diners distracted them.

Naim caved first, reaching for his glass of red wine to take a deep sip as he shook his head in exasperation. "Why are you so—"

"Independent?" she offered with a wide smile as she drank from her glass of sparkling water with sliced grapefruit.

"Stubborn," he muttered, reaching for his linen napkin to spread across his lap.

"Our baby is fine. We heard the heartbeat. I'm finally over the dizziness and sickness. My breasts are not as tender—you may not care but I'm *thrilled*. It's a good afternoon. You offered me lunch and I accepted," she said, reaching for a crispy French loaf to spread with butter. "Why ruin it talking about money?"

"May I take your orders?"

Naim let his rebuttal slide as he handed the waitress his menu. "I'll have the bone-in rib eye, medium well, please," he said.

"Same for me, and I'll take a linguini seafood and cheesecake to go," she said, handing the young lady her menu, as well.

Naim eyed Marisa curiously as the waiter left them alone.

"For later," she explained. "This is one of my favorite restaurants, but it's out of my budget right now."

Naim slammed his hand against the table, drawing the eye of the couple at the next table. "That's what I'm talking about. You won't accept your family allowance. You won't allow me to help you financially during the pregnancy. What are you trying to prove?" he asked.

"Well, hello, stranger."

Naim looked up and surprise filled his eyes at the sight of Vena Davenport, a tall and thick caramel beauty currently wearing a deep aubergine sweater dress that looked just a half-inch short of bursting at the seams. He and the cardiothoracic surgeon had enjoyed a fun weekend in the Alps last year but had lost touch. "Vena," he said, rising to press a kiss to her cheek. "It's good to see you."

Marisa cleared her throat.

When he reclaimed his seat, she extended her hand to Vena. "Hello, I'm Marisa and I'm pregnant with his child. It's *so* nice to meet you," she said with a false smile.

Vena's eyes went from Naim back to Marisa as she slid her hand into hers. "Congratulations," she said before walking away.

Naim eyed Marisa as she leaned over to wave at Vena's hasty retreat.

"Jealousy looks good on you, Marisa Martinez," he said with a chuckle.

"Jealousy?" she balked, frowning. "Never."

He eyed her. She was beautiful in a cream wrap dress with her normally curly hair blown straight and her makeup emphasizing her features. Her pregnancy was not yet showing, but she had the glow. Vena looked like a man in comparison. "I was going to introduce you," he said truthfully.

Marisa arched a brow in disbelief.

"So you don't want me but you don't want anyone else to have me," Naim mused, sitting back when the waitress returned with their steaming plates.

"That's not it. I just don't want you patrolling for new lovers while I'm sitting here," she explained, picking up her cutlery.

"Why would you care?" he asked, his attention on her and not his food.

"I'm pregnant, so my sex life is officially over because I don't plan to mate with one man while I'm pregnant with another's child," she said, pointing at him with a piece of meat she pierced with her fork. "You, on the other hand, are free to fidangle—"

"Fidangle?" he asked, amused by her. "What's that?"

She arched a brow. "I could use another F word to be clearer."

"No thanks."

"Good," Marisa said. "As I was saying, you're free to mate like rabbits while I'm on lockdown for forty weeks of pregnancy and six weeks of healing from it. At the very least, you could refrain from lining up your next bedmate in front of me."

He took a sip of wine, letting it float on his tongue to savor the taste before he swallowed. "And that's the only reason, Marisa?" he asked, hating that he was hopeful that her reasoning meant more than that.

Over the last six weeks, he had attended two doctor's visits with her, even flying overnight from Los Angeles so as not to miss one. He felt protective of her, and if he was honest he was pleased beyond measure that another man would not be making love to her for some time. "So that night really meant nothing?" he asked, leaning forward to lock his eyes with hers.

Something in her brown depths danced a bit, revealing an emotion or reaction he couldn't quite place. She set her fork down on the plate next to her succulent steak. "We had great sex. I'll admit it was the best I ever had, but we don't really know each other," she said, tilting her head to the side as she continued to eye him.

"I agree," Naim said, his voice deep and serious.

She squinted her eyes. "To the greatest sex ever or that we don't know each other?" she asked, her curiosity clear.

"Both," he admitted.

She gasped lightly.

He heard it. His gut clenched. They were playing with fire at that moment.

Hell with it. I'm ready for the heat.

"Naim," she said in warning, seeing something in his eyes that was probably similar to what he was seeing flaring up in hers. Desire.

"We could get out of here and see if it's just as good as it was the last time," he suggested.

She pursed her lips and released a short breath.

Her own little pressure valve.

With her eyes locked on his, she raised her hand and motioned with her fingers. The waitress was at their table within moments. "Check, please," she said.

Naim was already reaching inside his suit jacket for his billfold. "ASAP," he urged.

"That was the last time," Marisa said, still waiting for her vitals to return to baseline as they lay in the king-size bed of Alek's former bachelor penthouse apartment.

Their afternoon romp had been good. *Damn good.*

Naim turned on his side, resting his head in his hand as he looked down at her. "I agree," he said. "That could get addictive."

She looked up at him, feeling trapped by his beautiful eyes. Just moments ago, she had stared into the deep brown depths as he stroked them both to an explosive climax. It had felt like free-falling, and yes, that could get addictive. "Do you think Huntsman heard us?" she asked, searching for a distraction from an impulse to kiss him.

Huntsman was Alek's loyal manservant and confidant of over fifteen years. Once his brother wed and moved to Passion Grove, Huntsman remained behind in Manhattan to be of service whenever the family used the residence. Most days he had the large space to himself.

Naim chuckled. "His quarters are on the other side of the penthouse so I doubt it," he said, reaching with his free hand to stroke under her chin.

She shivered and closed her eyes. "What are we doing, Naim?" she whispered as his fingers trailed down her throat.

"Look at me."

She did.

"We're having a baby," he said, reaching under the crisp thousand-count sheet to press his hand to her belly as he smiled down at her warmly.

He really is charming.

Marisa turned and lay her head in the nook created by his bent arm as she took a deep inhale of his cologne.

Lord, he really smells so good.

His hands shifted behind her to massage her back, drawing a deep moan of satisfaction from her.

Get up, Marisa. Leave now.

She pressed her mouth to his neck instead and felt him tremble. "Does pregnancy make you horny?" she asked, feeling the familiar warmth he evoked in the pit of her belly.

"I'm not sure," Naim said, gripping one of her buttocks as he bent his head to bite her shoulder and then kiss a trail to her ear. "But I think it's my duty as the father of our baby to make sure your needs are satisfied."

She raised her arm to lift the sheet, looking down with a hot little grunt as he hardened and lengthened before her eyes.

It's so dark and long and thick.

"It's up to you, Marisa. I'm ready. Just say the word," he whispered against her throat before sucking the spot between his lips.

"Word," she gasped, gripping his shoulder and pulling him atop her.

Four weeks later

"It's a boy!"

Naim double pumped his fist at the doctor's pronouncement as he sat in the corner of the exam room. He watched Marisa smile before looking over at him.

"Go ahead," she urged him as the nurse stepped forward to use wet wipes to clean the ultrasound gel from her slightly rounded brown belly.

"What?" he asked, remaining seated and poised and not doing the victory dance he had promised her he would. "I'm just happy the baby is healthy."

Lies. He was ecstatic to find out they were having a son.

A boy!

"Yeah, right," Marisa drawled.

Dr. Warren laughed. "I will see you both back here in three weeks. Just stop at the desk to make your appointment," she said, giving them a smile before leaving the room with the nurse behind her.

Naim left the room, as well, as Marisa changed from the gown to the bright red lightweight sweater and matching linen wool pants she wore with flats. He strode over to the cute blonde woman behind the desk just before the exit. "Hello, Kylie," he said, reading her nametag.

"Hello. How can I help you?" she asked, her eyes taking him in with appreciation.

Naim removed his leather billfold and pulled out his black Amex. "I wanted to pay the bill for Marisa Martinez and leave my card on file to handle all future payments that need to be made," he said.

"Of course," she said, taking the card and typing on the keyboard of the Mac before her.

He glanced back at the closed door of Marisa's exam room.

"There is a significant balance. Ms. Martinez had made arrangements to make payments," Kylie said.

"Swipe the card for the full amount, Kylie," he said, before giving her a smile to soften his hard tone.

"Right away," she said.

She soon handed him a receipt and a pen.

Naim didn't look at the amount as he signed his name in slashing strokes before handing both back to her. "Thank you," he said, accepting his card and his receipt before leaving the Upper West Side office. They were on the fifteenth floor, and he slid his hands into the pockets of the lightweight wool peacoat he wore as he looked out the windows at the busy New York traffic below. It was October, and the fall winds whipped up stray papers littering the street.

"You didn't have to wait, Naim."

He turned and smiled at Marisa, stepping forward to help her pull on a stylish red lace trench coat. "Is this thick enough?" he asked. "It's chilly out."

She turned as she tied the belt. "I'm going straight to my car," she explained. "I'm fine."

Naim straightened her collar for her. "You look beautiful," he said, loving the bright color against her complexion.

"Thanks," she said, her voice soft as she clutched her large tote and began walking toward the frosted doors of the elevators.

"I thought we might get a late lunch again," he offered as the door opened and they stepped inside alone.

She gave him a side-eye glance before shaking her head. "Let's not. We both know what happened after the last doctor's appointment," she said.

They had made love three times that afternoon before finally parting ways with reluctance.

"Right," he agreed, turning to face forward.

He felt uneasy because he knew he had to tell her about paying her medical bills. He preferred to do it rather than have it catch her off guard and upset her even more. Money was always their point of contention. Other than that, they had found a nice comfortable pace to get along as they prepared for the birth of their child. He called her every night to check on her. At gatherings at Alek and Alessandra's, he gave her space.

The elevator slid to a stop and opened into the underground parking garage.

"Where'd you park?" he asked.

She dug her key fob from her purse and pointed toward the rear corner.

"I really would like to help with the doctor's bill. I don't want you burdened with bills I could easily handle because of your crusade on independence," he said as their footsteps echoed against the concrete.

Marisa stiffened and her lips tightened. "I have it, Naim," she said, tucking her curls behind her ear as she hit the button to automatically start the engine of her Bentley.

"Marisa," he said, reaching to lightly grasp her elbow.

She stopped but eased from his touch as she looked up at him. "What?" she asked.

He licked his lips and pushed aside the urge to kiss away her anger. "Please understand that I feel I am just as responsible for this baby as you are. You have the responsibility of carrying our son and will bear the burden of labor to bring him into this world. The most I can do is show up to doctor's visits. The least I can do is take away the burden of bills."

Marisa looked away from him at some unknown spot.

"The least I *have* done is take away the burden of bills," Naim admitted, clenching his hand into a fist inside the pocket of his coat.

Slowly she turned her head to eye him. "What did you do?" she asked, her voice deceptively soft.

Naim looked up at the fluorescent lighting briefly before locking his eyes on her again. He pulled out the receipt and handed it to her. "Tell me it's okay," he said as she snatched it from him and read it. "Tell me it's okay to help you, Marisa."

She balled the receipt inside her fist before tossing it at his chest. "You can't throw money at everything, Naim."

"At bills?" he balked. "I *damn* sure can."

She swallowed hard. "It's great to be a billionaire Ansah. Isn't it?" she snapped with sarcasm.

Naim looked incredulous. "Just as great being a billionaire Dalmount, right?" he shot back at her.

"I walked away from it," she asserted, poking

her finger against his chest. "Money damn near destroyed me, and I refuse to let the same thing happen to my child."

"*Our* child," he reminded her, his voice cold as he gripped her hand with his own. "Who has every right to his inheritance as an Ansah, even if you refuse to pass on your legacy as a Dalmount."

Fear filled her eyes. It confused him and softened his stance. "Marisa, what is it? Talk to me. I'm trying to understand," he said, holding up his hand. "I'm trying to help."

She blinked and shook her head, taking her hand out of his. "I—I—I gotta go. We'll figure this all out another time," she said, turning and fast walking to her car to climb inside.

"Marisa," he called behind her.

He fought the urge to follow her, not wanting her spooked into an accident.

With a frustrated sigh, he stooped and picked up the balled-up receipt, crushing it further inside his own fist as he watched her taillights as she drove away from him.

Marisa couldn't sleep. Guilt had a way of defeating rest. And she had plenty of that.

She made her way back to her bed after a bathroom break and picked up her phone as she sat down on the edge of the bed in the darkness. It was well after midnight. With a hand pressed to her small belly, she pressed the home button. "Siri, call Naim," she ordered the phone.

"Calling Naim," her phone announced.

The phone rang twice.

"Marisa? Everything okay?"

She closed her eyes and licked her lips. "Naim, I'm sorry for blowing up on you today," she began, rising to leave the room and cross the hall to the bedroom she had designated for the nursery. She leaned in the doorway at the empty space she had to fill. "It's just a lot, you know, and I don't want your way of life to totally eclipse mine because I've chosen not to focus on my family's wealth."

The line was silent for a few moments. She didn't fill it.

"Marisa, I won't lie and say I agree with your disdain for wealth," he began. "But my offer to pay for your medical bills is something I would have done even if I was worth ten thousand and not a billion, Marisa. That offer was about my character, not my money. The money just made it easier."

The moonlight streamed through the window, and she smiled as she envisioned a crib with a baby boy asleep on his back inside it.

I'm going to be a mom.

"We'll split the medical bills fifty-fifty, Pops," she said, accepting that she didn't have to go it alone.

"Pops?" he asked, sounding amused.

She turned and walked back into her bedroom. "I figure that's what our son will call you."

"Let's save that for him because the very last thing I want to be is your father, Marisa Martinez," Naim said, his voice deep and delicious.

Her body warmed in response.

"You sleepy?" he asked.

"Not really," she said, lying back on the pillows. "Your son is playing kickball with my bladder. You?"

"No, I'm in Australia on business," he said. "It's just three in the afternoon here."

She turned on her side, pulling the sheets up around her waist. "You have time to tell me all about it? I really need to get put back to sleep," she quipped.

He chuckled. "Meeting with owners of a TV and movie streaming service that I may acquire for ADG is not boring."

"Eh," she said with a small shrug of one shoulder.

They fell into a comfortable silence.

"How about I stay on the phone with you until you fall asleep," he offered.

"We're in this together," she said, closing her eyes.

"Yup. It's me and you against the world," he said.

Marisa liked the sound of that.

Chapter 5

Seven weeks later

Marisa pressed her hand to her small rounded belly as she felt the baby kick a bit. She smiled and waited to see if he would give her another poke or not. He didn't. "Not like I need a reminder, kid, you're lying on my bladder and I need to pee every hour," she said as she looked around her small walk-in closet.

It was far smaller than her previous closets and was jam-packed with remnants from her extravagant prior lifestyle. She reached for a floral-jacquard fil coupe evening gown with a plunging neckline, fitted waist and A-line skirt that was sheer. She remembered buying the six-thousand-dollar dress and a few more without a blink of the eye. She wore it once to some charity ball she couldn't even remember.

Leaving the closet, she stood before the mirror hanging above her eight-drawer dresser, holding the frock in front of her nude frame. It truly was beautiful, but over the years she had thousands of dresses just as pretty and pricey. Plus jewelry, designer handbags, furs, luxurious shoes—nothing but the best.

The gold Valentino.

The sheer black Zuhair Murad.

A rose-gold metallic Kevan Hall.

Chanel. Gucci. Dior. Louis Vuitton.

Beautiful frocks used to cover up how empty she had felt on the inside.

She walked back into the closet and replaced the dress in its spot, leaving the furs and designer gowns behind to her more casual clothing. It was getting harder to find things that comfortably fit her expanding waistline. She decided on a black velvet tuxedo suit with a sheer black T-shirt beneath it. In her heyday, she would have worn the ensemble sans bra and not given a care as to who her nipples offended. She smirked as she pulled a lace brassiere from her lingerie chest against the wall.

Times have changed.

Leaving the closet, she went into the bathroom and did her makeup and hair, twisting the front and leaving the back hanging in curls. Sprays of her precious Annick Goutal's Eau d'Hadrien perfume scented her with notes of citrus, cypress and ylang-

ylang. She pressed her nose to her wrist and inhaled with a soft moan of pleasure.

She needed the boost.

Once dressed, she left her home and climbed behind the wheel of her car to drive the short distance to Alek and Alessandra's estate. The ebony lampposts on the corners of each street were adorned with cornucopia, and the oversize pots burst with fall flowers and foliage. The sun was bright in the sky, although it did little to beat off the crisp chill in the air.

As she pulled up and parked in front of the megamansion, she looked at the many luxury cars filling the garage and the courtyard. She didn't see Naim's McLaren and glanced at the clock on the dash. Dinner was at six, and it was just a few minutes before that.

Is he coming?

She reached in her beaded clutch for her phone, stroking the screen with her thumb.

Maybe he rode in from the city with someone else.

Marisa pushed the phone back into her clutch and climbed from the car. Last night, like clockwork, since he'd learned the baby could begin hearing at twenty weeks, he had called and sung "Can't Take My Eyes Off You" as she had the phone on speaker. He hadn't mentioned missing Thanksgiving dinner the next day.

Not that he has to fill me in on his whereabouts.

Other than at the doctor's office for appointments, she rarely saw him. But when she did, his smile— that charming, perfect smile—still made her feel light in the chest and weak at the knees. She could use a dose of his charm as she faced the families now.

Please be here, Naim.

Marisa entered the house, not bothering to wait for staff. Most were off for the holiday—even those who lived on the property full-time. The scent of food was heavy in the air as she made her way to the formal dining room. She stiffened her back and took a breath before opening one of the double doors and entering the room. Just as she suspected, everyone was already seated around the custom French Provincial dining room table for twelve.

"Happy Thanksgiving, everyone," she said, her eyes quickly skimming up and down the rows of faces.

Alek and Alessandra were holding down the ends. Aunt Leonora, her mother, Samira, LuLu and baby Aliya were on the left. Then there were Uncle Victor— with a fresh ebony dye job that did nothing to make him look younger than his sixty years—his wife, Elisabetta—who also failed to make him look her age—and their twin boys, Hellion 1 and 2, and a stranger—all bets he belonged to Marisa's mother or Aunt Leonora. Let's just call him Fling, Marisa thought.

And no Naim. No place setting, either.

He's not coming. Cool. I got this.

She gave her aunt and mother kisses to their cheeks before taking the empty seat between her mother and Samira, giving the beautiful young woman a warm smile.

"You look gorgeous, Marisa," Samira said, her English accent elevating the comment.

"Thanks. You, too," she said of her rose-gold sweater dress as she reached for a glass of iced spring water.

"Miguel Santos," the stranger said, reaching across the table to offer her his hand.

He belongs to Momma and favors my dad in his youth. She has a type. "Nice to meet you, Miguel," she said, shaking his hand.

"I thought you weren't coming," Brunela said, clasping Marisa's hand. "I was about to send a car for you."

As per tradition, the family had been gathered since early afternoon, enjoying each other's company and snacking on tasty hors d'oeuvres until dinner.

"It's my first day off in a long time so I rested all day," Marisa explained.

"You need to be resting *every* day in your condition," Brunela said.

And here we go.

"I'll be open for business Monday, Momma," Marisa said matter-of-factly before removing a box from her envelope clutch to reach past her mother and hand to her aunt Leonora.

She winked and set the box by her gold-rimmed dish and decorative charger plate.

Brunela looked from her daughter to her sister. "What is that?"

"Truffles I asked her to bring me," Leonora said,

patting the box. "A bite of one of these with a sip of champagne is a life worth living."

Marisa bit back a smile as her mother rolled her eyes and clenched her teeth as she stiffened her back.

"I can't believe you are encouraging this madness," Brunela said, her lips thinned in annoyance.

"Brunela, please. I'm living my best life and I ain't going back and forth with—"

"Aunt Leonora," Marisa said, cutting off the rest of the song lyric.

The older woman just laughed.

"I'm going to check on dinner," Alessandra said, moving to rise.

LuLu held up her hand to stop her as she rose instead. "I'll go," she said. "I need to check on something, anyway."

Marisa noticed she and Alessandra shared a look. LuLu raised her brows. Alessandra's eyes filled with sudden understanding as she nodded before LuLu left the dining room. Everyone else at the table was talking and enjoying themselves, completely missing the odd moment.

She was intrigued by the exchange but her focus quickly went back to Naim, or his absence. "Excuse me," she said, rising from the table to exit out the side doors leading to a small hall and a powder bathroom.

At the sound of whispered voices, she paused and looked down the length of the hall running behind the wall alongside the large dining room. She couldn't see them. She tensed as she listened to their murmurs.

"Roje, please join us. I want you there."

Roje. Alessandra's driver. Marisa pictured the tall, dark-skinned, bald man with a fit frame.

"As long as we pretend we're not in love, right? Like we're near strangers and not lovers, LuLu?"

Marisa's eyes widened at that reveal.

LuLu and Roje? The widow of a billionaire and a chauffeur? Lovers?

Well, you go, Ms. LuLu, Marisa thought, backing out of the hall and into the dining room to avoid further invasion of their privacy.

"Where's that sexy brother of yours, Alek?" Aunt Leonora asked.

Marisa turned to cross the room, seeing her aunt remove her silver flask and pour some clear alcohol into her lemonade.

"I could use some eye candy, and everyone else at the table is taken," her aunt continued.

The dining room doors opened.

"Good thing I'm here to entertain you, Leo."

Marisa bit back a smile at the sight of Naim striding into the room looking handsome in a dark gray blazer with matching silk shirt and dark denims. The dark skin, beard and those eyes made her heart pump double a few times.

"Happy Thanksgiving, everyone," he said, going around the table to press kisses to the cheeks of all the ladies and slap his brother on the back soundly before he turned and strode toward where Marisa had paused in her path back to the table.

She closed her eyes as he kissed her cheek, as well, and lightly squeezed both elbows in welcome. "I thought you weren't coming," she said.

"And leave you alone to face this crowd?" he asked. "Never."

She smiled as he pressed a warm hand to her belly.

"I flew all the way from Switzerland to make it."

"Switzerland," she said. "Business or pleasure?"

"A little of both," he admitted, locking his eyes on hers as he looked down at her.

Naim was dating. The society pages and gossip blogs made sure to keep the world—and Marisa—updated with his every move.

Dinner with Loren. Charity ball with Heather. Dancing with Sophie. Movie premiere with Onia.

She said nothing as they walked back to the table and he held her chair out for her. Jealousy had spoiled her mood, but she fought hard not to show it.

Naim bent at the waist. "Don't worry, Marisa," he whispered for her ears alone. "They were just dates. Harmless fun to pass the time. Nothing more. I promise you that."

"You don't owe me any explanation," she said, feigning ambivalence.

He unbent his body and moved away from her with a chuckle, revealing his disbelief.

LuLu Ansah was flooded with indecision as she looked up into the eyes of Roje and stroked his smooth cheek with her hand. Her heart swelled with love for him. A love she felt she could never truly claim as she longed to. There were so many tiny battles she would have to overcome to claim him: the acceptance of her children, the legacy of being the widow of a man who had created a dynasty—a man she still grieved and loved—and their difference in station.

A year after her husband's death, she had found a relief from her grief and a spark of passion in bed with Roje. Their lovemaking had helped her to remember that her life, her dreams and her wants did not fade along with the passing of her husband, but she also knew it could only be that one night. Many years later, memories of that night left her unable to deny the imprint he'd left. *They'd* left, together.

That night I left a piece of my heart with you that I will never get back, LuLu.

She fought hard to deny her feelings for him, her desire for him, but in time—with his insistence that they no longer deny their connection—she gave in. Clandestine moments ruled them, each seeming to move heaven and earth to find a few hours to luxuriate in their passion. And then came love.

"I love you, Roje," she whispered to him before pressing a kiss to his mouth.

"And I love you," he said, gripping her hips to pull her closer.

"But it has to be this way," LuLu insisted.

"For now, or forever?"

At her continued silence, Roje stepped back, breaking their hold. "I'll have my dinner in my quarters," he said, his disappointment clear. "Happy Thanksgiving, LuLu."

He turned and she extended her arm, but stopped herself from reaching for him by closing her fist and pressing it to her mouth as she wished things could be much simpler.

Four weeks later

Naim awakened with a yawn, spreading his legs and arms across the crisp sheets as he turned his head and looked out the window of his master suite at the jagged pyramid-shaped Matterhorn of the Swiss Alps. The isolated highland, scattered with snow and ice, was majestic against the blue skies and clouds serving as its backdrop.

Many adventurers and explorers had made the climb on the mountain resting on the Italian-Swiss border, but Naim kept his fascination with it to its views from his chalet. It could be just as deadly as it was beautiful. It was his love of skiing that had led to his purchase of the sixty-four-hundred-square-foot chalet in the Petit Village in the town of Zermatt, known for mountaineering and skiing.

He climbed from the bed and strode, nude, to his en suite to wash his face and brush his teeth before reaching for pajama bottoms and a robe to cover his nakedness. He left his master suite, enjoying the panoramic views and light offered throughout the three-story modern wood structure. The smell of breakfast mingled with that of the pine Christmas decor. He could already hear the family downstairs. *Probably opening presents.*

He paused on the steps at the sight of Marisa in red pajamas and a robe, standing before the twenty-foot Christmas tree in the corner of the spacious living room. Her hair was pulled back in a ponytail and her face was makeup free. *Beautiful.*

Naim's eyes dipped down to her belly. It was clear she was pregnant. Her belly was round and protruding, and her breasts were fuller. Thirty weeks down and ten to go. He had gotten past his fears and concerns of having a child—especially with a woman to whom he was not married—and now he was just ready to hold their son and love him the same way he had been loved by his parents.

"Merry Christmas, everyone," he said, descending the stairs.

Everyone greeted him from their spots in the living and dining rooms.

Marisa looked up at him, and he saw concern in her eyes. "Merry Christmas," she said before giving him a hesitant smile.

Oh, no.

His stomach tensed. Things had been good between them, but she was skittish like an unbroken horse when it came to the baby and extravagances. He was still surprised she had come along with the rest of their families to enjoy the holidays in Switzerland as his guests. If he was honest, her whole "save me from money" bit was tiresome, but he fought hard not to point out the fallacies in her argument.

Yet another reason we could never be together.

He continued down the stairs, eyeing his house-guests for the week. Alek and Alessandra were help-ing Aliya open gifts. Leonora was sipping a mimosa that was clearly more champagne than orange juice. Brunela was in pajamas and a plethora of diamonds as she enjoyed an e-cigarette. The twins were fling-ing wrapping paper over their heads as they tore through their abundance of gifts, while Victor snored in the corner of the sectional and his wife, Elisa-betta, looked on. His sister, Samira, was alternat-ing between watching the kids enjoy their presents and reading the new hardcover novel by her favorite writer, Lance Millner. He was pleased to see her en-joying anything besides work.

There was another sad face in the crowd, and Naim frowned a bit as he eyed his mother, LuLu, as she rose from the sectional to stand at the window looking out at the snowcapped mountains alone. She had been reserved the entire trip, and they weren't scheduled to leave for another three days. From his spot on the stairs, he watched as she stepped outside, still dressed in her nightclothes, and walked to the end of the balcony where she withdrew a phone and made a call. He was curious who she could be call-ing, but left her to her privacy, turning to join the mother of his unborn child.

"How are you?" Naim asked as he came to stand

beside her before the tree, which was well-adorned with gray and brown decorations to match the decor.

"It's too much," she said, looking down at more than two dozen boxes still wrapped and under the tree.

"What?" he asked.

"Now that lazy bones is up, you two can open up my nephew's presents," Alek said, rising and stepping over his daughter clapping her hands at a light-up toy that displayed her name across the ceiling.

Naim eyed her profile, seeing her dismay at the abundance of things purchased for their son who wasn't even born yet. He saw the love and support of their families, who were excited about the baby's arrival, and she saw a future of him being spoiled. "Listen, we'll open them. Select what we want, and what we don't need we can donate to charity," he whispered in her ear.

"No," she stressed, shaking her head.

"Marisa, you're going overboard," he said, finding it hard to swallow his annoyance.

She turned to stare up at him.

"You two okay?" Alek asked, walking up to them.

Naim released a heavy breath.

"Actually, everybody, I'm feeling really tired," Marisa said, moving past the broad bodies of the brothers. "Can I exchange gifts with everyone later?"

"Of course," Alessandra said.

Brunela came over and lightly touched her elbow. "I'll go up with you until you fall asleep," she offered, her face lined with concern.

"Thanks, Momma," Marisa said, accepting her offer as they climbed the stairs to her guest suite on the second floor.

"What's that all about?" Alek asked.

"Nothing," Naim said, looking at the small box on top of the pile of gifts for the baby.

It was an eighteen-carat rose-gold Tiffany charm bracelet he had purchased for Marisa for Christmas—a gift of thanks for carrying their child.

Naim continued to watch Marisa climb the stairs, tilting his head back until she and her mother disappeared into her suite.

"Did you talk to her about the shared custody agreement?" Alek asked, for his ears alone.

Naim shook his head, reaching down for the gift box to slide into the pocket of his robe. "No, not yet," he admitted. "I know it was my attorney's suggestion, but the more we disagree on everything, I'm beginning to feel it's more and more necessary."

Alek gripped his shoulder briefly in a show of support before walking away.

Naim actually appreciated his brother restraining from offering an opinion. This was a decision he had to make, because those papers could very well make their coparenting ideal or tear them apart for good. That had to be his choice and his alone.

Five weeks later

Marisa released a grunt as she stretched her arms above her head and then pressed her hands to her lower back as she released a long stream of breath. "Baby Ansah, you are wearing Mommy out," she said aloud.

"How's Mama Bear?" Bill asked as he entered the kitchen.

Marisa shrugged. "Ready to have my body back," she said, feeling humongous.

Bill paused in loading a tray with freshly baked croissants he'd just pulled from the oven. "Will you still feel that way when you are in the midst of a contraction?" he asked, giving her a smile.

She'd be lying if she said she wasn't nervous about the baby's journey out of her body and how she had to expand to allow for his exit. "I am doing Kegels as we speak to prepare my body," she said, giving him a meaningful stare as she walked over to the island to use tongs to pick up a warm and buttery croissant.

"Kegels, huh?" he asked, wiggling his blond brows. "I'm intrigued."

They shared a laugh.

"So am I."

Marisa's laughter faded as she eyed Naim standing at the entrance to the kitchen. "Hey, Naim. What are you doing here?" she asked, giving him a smile as he eyed Bill and then her.

"I drove in from Manhattan to drive you to the doctor," he said, sliding his hands inside the pockets of his full-length charcoal cashmere coat he wore with a tight-fitting hat to beat off the January northeast winter chill.

"The doctor that's *in* Manhattan," she said slowly.

"That's dedication, dude," Bill said before picking up the tray and walking past Naim and out of the kitchen.

"I could have driven myself like always," Marisa said, checking the time on her iPhone before she removed her apron and washed her hands to free it of chocolate.

"You two look really comfortable."

Marisa paused and looked over her shoulder at him. "We do?" she asked, feigning innocence of his jealousy.

Naim tilted his head to the side as he shrugged one shoulder. "I know I don't have a right to ask, but..."

"But what?" she asked, walking to the office to retrieve her Vuitton tote and the black sable she'd treated herself to two years ago.

"There seems to be something between you," he said, his eyes on her with intensity.

"Friendship and respect," she offered. *"But..."*

Naim looked indignant. "But what?" he balked.

"You're correct that you have no right to question me, with the current parade of women you're enjoying like a pageant," she said.

Naim waved his hand dismissively. "I'm not serious about any of them," he said, reaching to try to close her coat over her belly.

"Why?" she asked, brushing his hands away.

"Why what?" he asked, trying again to close the fur.

Marisa rolled her eyes. "Why aren't you ready to settle down...with anyone?" she added, afraid he would misunderstand her motivation in asking.

Naim turned his lips downward in thought. "I'm

not ready to settle down, and most women who claim to want to settle me down are only after my money," he said.

"Ah. A downside of having a *ridiculous* amount of money, huh," she said, as if proving her entire point on her new contention for wealth.

"I'd rather have than have not," Naim assured her. "And when I'm ready, I'm sure I will find the right woman to love me just for me."

"Yes, you will," Marisa said softly.

Their eyes locked and held.

With a breath that only hinted at her racing pulse, she was the first to look away.

"Is Bill the Baker the reason you won't stop working?" Naim asked.

Marisa spared him a brief glance, wondering if she should bother to explain that her only peace was working with her chocolate at the bakery and that she heavily relied on Bill to discuss things the Dalmounts and Ansahs refused to understand. Admittedly, the man was a blond beauty with a fit frame and a desire for women of color, but she was only interested in his advice and friendship.

"I work because I have bills to pay," she said.

Even with his low-cut beard, she could tell he clenched his jaw. "Bills you don't *have* to pay," he reminded her.

She looked up at him, her eyes imploring him to understand her point of view.

He gave her his warmest smile. "According to the baby app on my phone—"

"The what?" she asked, arching a brow.

"The baby app on my phone," Naim repeated. "You might be feeling clumsy because it's harder to balance your body, and there's something called pregnancy brain—"

Marisa reached up and pressed a finger to his mouth.

"But the long hours on your feet are not good—"

She stuck the finger inside his mouth. His lips closed around it. "Just because I am carrying your child does not entitle you to have complete control over my life," she said. "Understood?"

He shook his head.

She paused in removing her finger.

His gorgeous eyes twinkled as he proceeded to circle her finger with his tongue.

Marisa felt the fleshy bud of her intimacy throb to life, and her nipples ached beyond just them swelling with milk for the baby. She tugged her finger from his mouth and looked away so that he couldn't see the heat of desire in her telltale eyes.

Naim touched his hand to her chin and raised her head. "If you think that I wouldn't absolutely make love to you right now, you are so wrong," he said in those deep dulcet tones of his.

She shivered, and her chin felt warm from his less than innocent touch. "Naim, that's sweet of you to make me feel like I'm not a beached whale, but it's not necessary," she said, leaning back to avoid his touch.

He lightly gripped her face as he bent his knees to match her shorter height. With a tilt and dip of his head, he pressed his mouth to hers. Soft at first. Then deeper. He used his tongue to gently open her mouth and tango with hers.

Marisa literally swooned and reached behind her to grip the island as she locked her knees for stability.

"You okay?" he whispered against her mouth.

She nodded. "Sure," she said, clearing her throat.

"Tell me, which chocolate is sweeter? Your candy or me?" he asked.

"Definitely the candy," she lied, walking past him to leave the kitchen.

Three weeks later

Naim loosened his tie and took a sip of rare Macallan 1988 single malt Scotch, enjoying the taste of the liquor on his tongue before he swallowed as he looked out at the cityscape. The lights reflected against the darkness of the sky and the whiteness of the February snow, creating a captivating view as he stood at the window of his DUMBO apartment. His attempts to focus on completing his reports on the most viable streaming services to purchase and revamp for expansion into the US markets could not hold his attention.

He pulled his phone from the pocket of his slacks and checked it.

No call.

After their appointment at the OB/GYN earlier that day, Naim had expressed his desire to be there when the baby was born and even dared to ask Marisa if he could stay at her house during the last two weeks before her due date. The thought of being there and supporting her from the moment labor began sat right with him. He was surprised—even hopeful—when she asked for time to think about it.

It had been hours since he dropped her off at home, and with each passing minute, he was realizing she was not going to concede.

Turning from the window, Naim took a seat at one of the charcoal suede parsons chairs surrounding the custom-made concrete dining room table as he dialed his mother's number. *"Comment vas-tu, Maman?"* he asked of her well-being in French when she answered.

Like his brother and sister, Naim spoke five languages. Their mother had taught them from a young age to speak them all.

"Excité pour mon petit-fils d'arriver. Et vous?" LuLu said, proclaiming her excitement over the imminent birth of her grandson and then asking him how he was.

"Nervous," he admitted, switching to English as he reached across the table to pick up the folded legal forms. "The baby—my son—will be here in the next week or two, and I don't know how things will be between Marisa and me, but he will be in the world and we have to raise him even while we're not together. Not in the same home. Not on the same page about so many things."

"Parenting is difficult, even for those of us who were in the same home. Everyone makes concessions. Adjusts to different points of view," LuLu said.

"Your father and I clashed many times over you guys. He thought I was too soft, and at times I thought he was too strict, but neither of us denied the love we had for our children."

He tapped the forms outlining a joint custody agreement against the table as his eyes widened in surprise. "I didn't know that," he said. He could rarely remember his parents arguing.

LuLu chuckled. "We handled our business of *any* nature in private, son," she said.

He fell silent.

"Naim, it is normal to have fears about becoming a parent. This is a huge responsibility that you must take seriously," LuLu said, her voice impassioned. "A man is whom his father makes him to be. So figure it out and don't treat it like you do business, Naim. Everything does not have to be war."

In business—when needed—he could be ruthless. He had been on a mission to prove himself.

Bzzzzzz.

He lowered his phone at the vibration against his ear. He had an incoming text message from Marisa. He opened it.

No kisses. No sex. Key under mat.

Naim chuckled, thinking of her reaction to their kiss earlier at the bakery. She wanted him just as bad as he still desired her, but her house, her rules. "Maman, let me call you back," he said. *"Je t'aime."*

"Love you, too," she responded with warmth before ending the call.

Naim rose to walk into his bedroom to retrieve his leather Brunello Cucinelli carry-on he'd packed earlier just in case. It held his casual clothing. Although he planned to work from home while they waited for her labor and delivery, he was having a couple suits delivered to her house in case of an emergency meeting.

Back in the dining room, he gathered his files into his briefcase. He paused, looking down at the legal papers his attorney had drawn up.

So figure it out and don't treat it like you do business, Naim.

His mother's words of advice clung to him as he picked the papers up. With a shake of his head and a pensive look, Naim slid the papers inside his briefcase, as well, before turning to leave his penthouse.

He hoped for the best and dreaded the worst.

Chapter 6

One week later

"At week thirty-nine your baby is as big as a pumpkin."

Marisa eyed Naim from her spot on the couch, lying with her feet in his lap. "I did not need your app to tell me that," she said, pointing to her round and distended belly before looking at him. "You do know Dr. Warren is tired of you and your app, too, right?"

Naim chuckled as he set the iPhone down and began gently rubbing her swollen feet as the lit fireplace crackled before them. "Listen, this might very well be my only child, so I am fully invested in every moment."

Marisa eyed him. "Your only child?" she asked, trying not to let the warmth of his hands distract her.

He locked those eyes on her. "I'm not sure I want kids raised with different mothers in different homes," he said.

"You say that now, until you fall in love and get married," she said, pulling her body to a sitting position.

"Married?" he balked with a frown. "That's not happening anytime soon."

Marisa rubbed her belly as she eyed his profile and let it settle in that she was disappointed in his continued outlook on matrimony. In the last week, they had fallen into a pattern that she found comfortable. He worked from home, using her office, and she busied herself making chocolate treats in the kitchen. In the evenings they fixed dinner together and settled down to watch television or just talked. Or laughed. Or played board games.

Or pretended to ignore the attraction still pulsing between them with the steadfastness of a heartbeat.

Even at that moment as she eyed his profile, she desired him and his presence created a warm glow in her belly that felt good. Something more than just sex. Something she refused to name or claim.

Naim turned his head and caught her eyes on him. He smiled. "We could agree in another five years to have another child," he said, his eyes dropping to her mouth.

She licked her lips. "Together?" she asked before

her breath caught at the thought of him inside her again. "Don't be silly, Naim."

He shrugged. "Yeah, you're right," he agreed.

Her disappointment at that surprised her. She looked away into the fire.

"Are you afraid?" he asked.

"Of labor?" she asked, not allowing herself to look at him again.

"Yes."

"A little, but mostly I'm ready to see our baby and have my body back," Marisa said, easing her feet from his hands and his lap as she sat up with effort.

"And what a body it was," he said, rising to his feet.

"What? This isn't sexy?" she joked.

He paused, looking handsome in a midnight blue sweater and dark denims. "Marisa Martinez, there's not a damn thing you could do to not be sexy to me," he said.

She made the mistake of looking up at him. Seeing his eyes revealed the truth of his words. It was dangerous to her resolve. The last thing she needed was heartache. She had already battled and defeated so much.

"You're just horny," she joked, picking up the television remote from where it had sunk beneath the cushions of the couch.

"That's very true," he admitted with a chuckle as he walked over to the kitchen.

"One week of abstinence has you crazy?" she called over to him.

"One week?" Naim balked, returning with two bottles of water. "I haven't been with anyone since you."

Marisa accepted the bottle of water, touched that he pushed her to stay hydrated as the doctor insisted. "Naim, you don't owe me explanations...or untruths," she said before opening the bottle and taking a deep sip.

"I've never lied to you, Marisa," Naim said, his tone stern. "And I never will."

Their eyes locked again.

"And I think we should promise each other to be truthful as we raise our son," he added. "We are linked for the rest of our lives through him."

"It won't be easy and we will bump heads over things, but I agree truth is always necessary, Naim," she said.

"To truth," Naim said, extending his bottle of water to hers.

"To truth," she echoed, tapping her bottle against his.

He bent to sit down on the floor. "Okay. Truth," he began.

Marisa set the half-finished bottle of water on the floor by her bare feet. "Okay," she agreed, feeling unsure about the road he was going to take them down.

"Do you regret not letting anyone throw you a baby shower?" he asked.

That surprised her. She was sure he was going to ask her to admit she wanted him. "Um, no, I don't, because I kept all the gifts they gave us for Christmas...most of which we used to set up his nursery, remember?" she said.

"Okay, you got a point," he conceded.

"Thank you. Truth," Marisa said, playfully tapping the top of his head. "When were you going to tell me you had nurseries set up in everyone's house—including yours?"

Naim leaned over and ducked as he glanced over at her with a sheepish grin. "Who told you?" he asked.

"Samira," she said, reaching to swat the back of his head.

He ducked again and caught her hand in his.

Her pulse raced.

Damn.

He released her. "I just want him comfortable when we take him to visit," he said.

"Truth."

"Another one?" he asked.

"Yup."

"Fire away."

Marisa tapped the remote against the palm of her other hand. "On a scale of one to ten, how much have you missed your lifestyle this week?" she asked.

Naim chuckled. "It's been interesting," he said.

"Truth," she stressed.

"About a five," he admitted.

Marisa laughed. "Yeah, right," she said. "No servants. Smaller house. No one to announce your name when you enter a room," she said.

"Right, *but* I'm here with you and it's been wonderful getting to know you better and prepare for our son," he said.

"I feel the same way," she admitted, feeling that warmth in her belly that was becoming familiar whenever she was around him.

"Truth?"

"A six," she said.

He chuckled. "Stop reading my mind."

Marisa shrugged one shoulder. "Listen, this isn't easy what I'm doing. Everyone is so focused on what I'm giving up that no one cares about what I'm gaining and that, yes, I miss the servants and sleeping in late and buying whatever whenever I want," she said, unable to keep annoyance from seeping into her tone. "Do you know when I first moved in here I had to hire a cleaning service to teach me how to clean?"

Naim chuckled as he eyed her.

"I didn't know the right end of a mop," she said, slightly smiling at the memory. "But now I do, and I learned how to pay bills, and clean, and cook *a little*, and as a grown woman I am so proud of that. Why isn't anyone else? It wasn't easy. I was a grown woman learning things most people learn as teenagers. It was embarrassing."

Naim leaned his head against her knee. "I never looked at it like that, Marisa," he said.

"I just want to raise a kid who isn't spoiled by excess, you know," she said, stroking his head. "The Ansah children turned out fine. All educated and responsible and driven. But I didn't. I never went to college. I majored in partying. Hard. There's a downside to raising a kid around so much money, and I am that."

"You *were* that," he insisted.

"Right," she softly agreed. "I just hate that everyone acts like I'm overreacting when we all know rich kids who've done numerous stints in rehab or overdosed or run through money or are just horrible, spoiled, rich, entitled people who won't hit a lick at a stick."

He shifted to rest on his knees between her open legs. His eyes were level with hers. "Let's promise not to raise a horrible, spoiled, entitled kid who won't..."

"Hit a lick at a stick," she supplied.

"Hit a lick at a stick," he repeated, offering her his pinkie.

Marisa closed her eyes and laughed a little as she hooked her pinkie with his.

Their eyes locked. A current passed between them. It was undeniable.

"Truth," she said.

His eyes dropped down to her mouth and then back up to her eyes as he nodded.

"I hope he has your eyes," she admitted, her words soft.

"You do?" he asked, seeming surprised.

"Actually, if he is a mini-you I am okay with that," she said.

Naim's smile spread like ice melting under sunshine.

"Oh, God, your ego is ridiculous," she drawled.

"And your compliments are ego boosting."

She rolled her eyes.

"You sure you don't want to make that baby pact and in a few years try for a little girl who looks just like you?" he asked.

Yes.

Marisa patted his cheek and looked away, breaking his spell as the urge to suck his lips faded. *Get out from between my legs. Get out from between my legs. Get out from between my legs.*

Naim checked the time on his Vacheron Constantin watch before climbing to his feet.

Thank God.

"I've got a business call coming out of Australia," he said.

"About the streaming service?" she asked.

Naim had expressed to her his desire to prove his worth in his position to his brother and to himself. She admired his ambition and drive to work, when truly he could just sit back and live quite well off his inheritance. That gave her hope about ensuring he gave that same work ethic to their child.

"Hopefully we close the deal," Naim said, rubbing his strong hands together. "You need anything?"

She shook her head, setting her feet up on the coffee table with a wince as a twinge of pain radiated across her lower belly.

Naim came over and grabbed a woven leather pillow to lift her feet and place it beneath them.

"Thanks," she said, forever touched by his attentiveness.

When he turned to leave the room, Marisa watched him until he was out of her sight. Once the baby was born, he would be moving back to his penthouse in Brooklyn. If she was honest with herself, she would miss him around the house.

Just as much as she missed him in her bed the night before…

Marisa released her full-body pregnancy pillow from between her thighs and sat up on the edge of the bed as her stomach rumbled and her bladder cried for relief. She checked the time on her cell phone— 1:24 a.m. She crossed the room in her sock-covered feet, using only the light from the streetlamp filtering through the window. Once done relieving herself, with her hand rubbing her lower back, she made her way back across the room and out into the hall.

She paused when she noticed the light was on in the room Naim was occupying during his stay. His being up at such a late hour surprised her, and she crossed over to the threshold. Her eyes widened at the sight of him nude and wet as he dried off with a towel. His back was to her, and she released a little pant as she took in the breadth of his strong shoul-

ders and the contours of his back before her eyes dropped to his buttocks and muscled thighs.

She bit her bottom lip at a hot memory of clutching at his butt and wrapping her legs around his thighs as he stroked deep inside her.

He turned, still not noticing her, and her eyes widened at his hard chest, defined abs and the soft bush of dark hair surrounding his lengthy manhood.

Everything on her body that could pulse did, including the fleshy bud nestled beneath the lips of her core. His body was as deep, dark and decadent as her chocolate, and she was hungry for a lick and a nibble.

Naim tossed the towel onto the bed, doing a double take when he spotted Marisa standing there in her floor-length nightgown. He smiled. "Couldn't sleep?" he asked, taking his time reaching for the towel to wrap around his waist.

"Hungry," Marisa said, her cheeks feeling flushed from being caught watching him. She looked down at the hardwood floors and then up at him. "You're up late, too," she said as he came around the bed to lean in the doorway. The scent of his soap was musky and clean and she inhaled it, enjoying how his scent seemed to burst in her chest.

Naim Ansah was a lot of man.

"You may not know it, but there's just enough light to show the silhouette of your body through that nightgown," he said. "And it's sexy as hell."

"Oh, really?" she asked, her voice breathy as she

released hot little exhales. "Your towel isn't doing much to cover you, either."

"Just say the word, Marisa," he said.

She flushed with heat, thinking of the last time he'd said those words to her. This time she denied them the pleasure. "No," she said without much effort. "Complications, remember?"

He nodded.

They had agreed a sexual relationship of any kind would only complicate things between them, and so they agreed to resist...

That resistance got harder with every day...

Naim ended the conference call with a press of the button on the phone. Rising, he stretched his limbs before leaving the office and walking down the hall and past the stairs to the open living area. He smiled at Marisa lightly snoring with her mouth ajar, her hands on her belly and her feet still up on the coffee table.

He leaned against the wall and eyed her, finding the scene hopelessly adorable.

This Marisa, domesticated and swollen with child, with remnants of chocolate on her clothes and her hair up in a tousled bun, was so different from the wild woman he remembered enjoying herself a little too much at ADG's anniversary ball. Far too many glasses of champagne had led to her tempting the telecommunications director with her short sequin dress and long legs to a wild dance. His wife had

not been pleased, and neither had Alessandra. He remembered being both amused and slightly disturbed
at her reckless behavior.

And now she was having his child.

Naim couldn't deny that he was pleased she had
changed for the better, and he felt so protective of
her and the baby. He would go to hell and back on
his knees to make sure no harm came to them. Hell,
living without sex for the last five months had felt
near that…especially lying in bed at night knowing
Marisa was just a dozen feet away from him across
the hall. Looking beautiful, glowing with his child.
Fuller face and breasts and buttocks. Even more gorgeous, if that was at all possible.

Pushing off the wall, he walked over to the sofa and
looked down at her sleeping. Her lashes rested against
the tops of her cheeks and her full mouth was pouted
in her sleep. The urge to press a kiss to her temple and
stroke her hair filled him as it had so many times. But
that was nothing new. The urge to kiss Marisa happened often. At every doctor's appointment. While
they were laughing at some funny meme on social
media. When he rubbed her feet. As she listened to
him intently when they spoke. While they both struggled to make dinner for themselves. While she slept.
Every night when he sang "Can't Take My Eyes Off
You" to her belly and she smiled.

And at the look on her face when they'd finished
the baby's nursery…

"It's perfect," Marisa said as she walked around the room and touched everything with a smile on her face.

Naim was pleased. His first night there, he had mistakenly walked into the room when she gave him directions to the guest room where he would be sleeping. He discovered lots of unopened boxes and packages scattered about the room—mostly their family's Christmas gifts for the baby. The next day, while Marisa was napping, he went back to the room and set about opening everything. The crib his mother gifted them was the hardest challenge, but he tackled it. Handiwork was not his forte, but he got it done.

She looked over her shoulder at him, and his heart tugged to see tears welling in her eyes.

He crossed the room. "What's wrong?" he asked, lightly grabbing her upper arms to turn her body to face him. He cupped the side of her face and stroked the tear that slid down her cheek.

"I forgot all about it," she said, shaking her head at herself. "After you had everything delivered, I closed the door and forgot about it. The thought of it all overwhelmed me and I just pushed it away and forgot."

Naim embraced her, resting his chin atop her head as he rubbed her back instead of pressing a kiss to her temple as he wanted to. "No biggie. It's all done. That's what Pops is here for," he said, hoping to lighten the mood.

He felt her body shake with a laugh before she leaned back and looked up at him. Her eyes were *more cheerful and free of tears as they searched his. She opened her mouth as if to say something but refrained, sparking his curiosity. "Thank you," she finally said.*

Naim nodded, loving the feel of her in his arms with the roundness of her pregnant belly pressing against him. He could stay that way forever. "You're welcome."

The baby kicked, and he felt it against his gut, causing his eyes to widen. "You felt that?" he asked, releasing her to press both hands to her belly.

"If you did, you know I did," she quipped.

"Right," he said, bending down before her to press a kiss to her belly.

Naim was touched when she caressed the back of his head...

And just as it had in that tender moment between them, Naim's heart swelled now with an emotion he was finding harder and harder to deny over the months.

Her eyes fluttered open and she winced with a grunt.

"What's wrong?" he asked.

Marisa looked up at him with discomfort in her eyes. "Pain. I probably need to go up to bed where I can stretch out," she said, setting her feet on the floor.

Naim came around to stand in front of her, extending both his hands. She accepted them and he pulled her to her feet. "When did it start?" he asked, holding her at the waist.

"Just before your conference call," she said, pressing one hand to her lower back and the other under her belly as they walked out of the living space with him right beside her.

"That was two hours ago," Naim said, feeling alarmed. "Do you think they're contractions?"

Marisa shook her head as they reached the stairs and began the climb. "Dr. Warren said first-time mothers usually don't go into labor early," she said.

He frowned. "But?"

Marisa gave him a playful side-eye and shrugged as they reached the middle step of the stairs. "It's probably Braxton-Hicks. Did your *app* explain them?"

"Ha-ha," he said dryly as they reached the top step.

Marisa cried out and squeezed down on his hand as she bent over from the pain.

Naim rubbed her back and watched her with frantic eyes. "You okay? You want me to call Dr. Warren?"

She shook her head as she slowly straightened her frame. When they reached her room, he turned on the ceiling light as she sat down on the side of the bed and kicked off her slippers as she released a breath before lying down on the bed. He pulled the blanket folded across the bottom up over her as she shifted onto her side.

Naim moved to the door to turn the light off.

"Naim," Marisa called out.

"Yeah."

"Don't go."

He smiled a little. "I wasn't," he said, returning to

the opposite side of the bed. He kicked off his shoes and sat with his back propped against the padded leather headboard.

In the darkness, he felt her move, and soon her hand was reaching for his. He clutched it.

As the night progressed, it became clear that her contractions were all too real. Naim was relieved when he called the doctor and was told to bring her into the hospital, since they had a drive ahead of them to reach Manhattan. He fought like hell to maintain his calm, even as his instincts leaned toward alarm.

Outside, holding her bag and the car seat, he looked at their sports cars sitting beside each other in the driveway. He allowed himself a moment to laugh at how ridiculous both were for parents with a small child. Deciding hers didn't sit quite as low as his, he opted for it before rushing back into the house.

She was already swaddled in a sable coat over her sweats with one of his tight-fitting sweater hats pulled down over her curls.

"We both need bigger cars," Naim said once they'd made it back down the stairs and out of the house.

She chuckled. "We damn sure do," she said, sinking down into the passenger seat of her Bentley with effort.

Naim barely felt the frigid cold as he rushed around the car to climb into the driver's seat. He reversed out of the driveway, offering Marisa one hand as he steered with the other. He was relieved when he finally pulled up before the entrance of Lenox Hill Hospital. His mother and sister, dressed in evening wear and furs, stepped outside as soon as he did with the family's driver, Mandridge, and a hospital attendant with a wheelchair.

"Hello, Mandridge," he said to his mother's long-time driver.

"They have valet parking, but your mother thought you might want me to park your car, sir," he said.

Naim nodded. "Yes, thank you, Mandridge," he said as he rushed around the front of the sports car to open the passenger door while the attendant pushed the wheelchair forward.

Marisa eyed them after Naim helped her from the car and into the wheelchair. "Really, ladies, jeans would have been fine," she said before she winced.

"We were at the Met when Naim called," LuLu explained, reaching for her hand as they all made their way into the hospital. "You ready?"

"Even if I'm not, your grandson is," Marisa said before closing her eyes and pursing her lips to breathe through the contraction.

"Alek and the Dalmounts have been called and are on the way," Naim said as the attendant led them through the hospital and to the elevator leading to the labor and delivery ward's private maternity suite—an upgrade he hadn't told Marisa about and hoped she would not deny herself the luxury.

Many hours had passed since the families were left behind in the waiting room of Marisa and Naim's private suite. Everyone was gathered and excited about the baby's arrival. They all wondered about his name, but LuLu was pleased Naim was honoring their Ghanaian tradition just as Alek had by planning to have an "outdooring" ceremony during which the baby was taken outside the home for the first time, given its name and showered with the love and wisdom of family and friends as everyone celebrated.

LuLu glanced over at Brunela and saw the concern of a mother for her child. Rising in her deep aubergine gown, she moved over to sit beside her, taking the woman's hand in hers. "She will be fine and *we* will be grandparents," LuLu said with a reassuring smile.

Brunela topped her hand with her own. "She is my world. Thirty-one years ago, I held her and she looked up at me with those big brown eyes, and I haven't been able to deny her anything since," she said softly. "I need her to be okay."

"She will," LuLu said, looking up as the door opened and Roje entered, carrying two trays of Starbucks coffee.

She took a breath as her heart pounded at the sight of him. Just last night, on his night off, he had driven into the city and spent the night with her, making love to her with an intensity that still made her tremble. It had been so hard to watch him leave early that morning because she knew Samira would be up from her own apartment in the building to share breakfast as they did nearly every morning.

"I thought everyone could use some coffee," he said, his voice deep and warm.

"Thank you, Roje," Alek said, rising to help him give out the cups to everyone.

When Roje stood before her to give her a cup, their hands briefly touched as their eyes locked. All of the love they felt for one another passed between them without a word spoken.

The door opened again and Naim entered, still dressed in his protective gear with a disposable cap balled in his hands. At the look on his face, the excitement in the room vanished and was replaced with concern. Naim moved directly to Brunela, who stood, eyes wide and panicked.

"What is it?" she asked in an emotional whisper.

A tear raced down his cheek. "The baby is fine. It's Marisa. She's in surgery. There were complications. They made me leave the room," he said.

Brunela dropped back down into her seat as if her knees gave out beneath her. Alessandra and Leonora raced to comfort her. Alek crossed the room to grip his brother's shoulder.

LuLu allowed herself a touch of Roje's hand for comfort and strength before she turned and pulled her son into her arms as she patted his back. Over his shoulder, her eyes locked with the man's she loved before he quietly left the room, leaving the family alone, as his station dictated. That tore at her gut.

Naim was rocked to his core.

As strong as he'd been after his father's death and as much as he found himself resilient in the face of adversity, the idea of having to grieve Marisa weakened him like nothing he had ever faced before. He prayed. He paced. His worry was limitless. His fear was stifling. The minutes of the hour that ticked by were like a slow torture.

It was in those moments that he discovered the love he had for Marisa.

The door to the waiting room opened.

Naim and everyone there rose to their feet as Dr. Warren entered, still dressed in her scrubs. She gave them all a smile and their relief was palpable. "Mother and baby are fine. Both should be in their room within the next twenty minutes or so," she said. "We do ask to keep today's visiting to a minimum so that she can get some rest."

In honor of Marisa, Naim pursed his lips and released a huff like he'd seen her do many times before. He nodded and clasped his hands as he came over to Dr. Warren and extended his hand. "Can I see her?" he asked. "Please."

"Yes, you can. I came to get you," she said, turning to the door.

Naim gave his family one last gleeful smile over his shoulder before he followed her out of the room. He barely heard the doctor explaining the details of what had led to Marisa's emergency C-section. As soon as he was let into the recovery area, he moved to her side and bent at the waist to press a kiss to her temple.

"He's beautiful." Marisa sighed as she looked down at her son before looking up at his father. "He looks like you."

Naim smiled and nodded where he sat on the bed beside her in their private room. The family had just taken their leave for the night with promises to return the next day. "You scared me today," he said.

"I did?" she asked softly.

"It made me realize that I want to be more than just the father of your child, Marisa," he admitted, his eyes searching hers.

She glanced away, more than surprised. "You do?" she asked with hesitation, even as her pulse raced and her heart pounded in excitement.

"I do."

Marisa focused on their son, stroking his cheek with her finger, as her mind ran through every reason they shouldn't tempt fate. There were plenty.

"He's worth us giving it a try."

Marisa pressed kisses to the baby's temple as she began to sing "Can't Take My Eyes Off You."

Naim leaned in and chuckled. "He's smiling," he said in wonder.

She looked up at him, seeing the love for their child in his face and accepting the love she had for him in her heart.

Chapter 7

Two months later

Marisa stood on the balcony looking out at the ocean as she soaked in the breeze and the beauty of the sunset in Havana, Cuba. The streaks of burnt orange, yellow and lavender against the deepening blues of the skies were majestic. She felt so connected to the culture and the vibrancy of the country. In it, she found a way to feel closer to the father she didn't remember.

Just as Naim wanted.

For the last week, they had explored and enjoyed the country, taking in the historical landmarks, discovering local haunts, wondering about its art in galleries and museums and enjoying food that spoke to the Spanish, Caribbean and African influences. She was happy she had accepted his urging and made the trip, with baby Kwesi and a nanny hired just for the vacation.

Heritage was important, and Naim understood that. He had the same plans to pour as much of his Ghanaian culture into their son's life as possible. He wanted Marisa to do the same, and encouraged her to learn more of her Cuban roots. The trip was his contribution to her education. That and teaching her Spanish.

She smiled as she gripped the railing of the glass partition as she looked out at the ocean at Naim's thoughtfulness. In the last two months, they'd both had to do some compromising when it came to their relationship and making decisions on the care of their son, but those times when they were in sync were amazing. Fun and loving.

They split their time between her house in Passion Grove and his penthouse in Brooklyn. He was just as attentive to Kwesi's needs as she was, and that allowed her to recover from the ordeal of surgery. So far, all was good.

Still, Marisa wondered how her return to work would affect them. She would need to be in Passion Grove more and they disagreed over the hiring of a full-time nanny. Both his mother and hers offered to care for the baby while she was at work, but that didn't sit well with her, either. She wanted to do it herself. The thought of missing any of his milestones plagued her.

She felt Naim's presence behind her—those telltale hairs on the back of her neck never failed.

"Beautiful, right?"

She turned and watched him walk out onto the balcony in white linen pants that hung low on his hips. He was carrying two drinks, with a cigar between his fingers. "The view is beautiful. I'm going to miss it," she said, taking her virgin *saoco* from him to sip the traditional Cuban cocktail of coconut milk, and fresh lime juice sans the sugarcane rum.

"We can come back whenever you want," he offered before taking a sip of his mojito and then drawing on his cigar.

They'd been to a cigar factory and watched the cigars being rolled by hand before enjoying one in their lounge. He'd purchased the maximum four boxes allowed into America of premium cigars with a large size sixty ring gauge made of high-quality tobacco and aged for eighteen months.

"Thank you for this trip," she said, turning to lean against the glass balcony wall as she looked up at him. "I feel closer to my father."

"Me siento más cerca de mi padre," Naim said, translating her words to Spanish before he tilted his head back and released a thick and steady stream of silver smoke.

"Me siento más cerca de mi padre," she repeated

before smiling. "It's a shame when an African has to teach an Afro-Cuban Spanish."

"I have some other things I want to teach you, too," he said.

She took the fat cigar from his hand and wrapped her lips around the tip to slowly inhale, enjoying the chocolate and nut undertones. His eyes dropped to watch the move. Tilting her head to the side, she pursed her lips and released a stream of perfectly round smoke rings.

His eyes darkened.

She offered him the cigar, and his eyes remained locked on hers as took a deep drag from it. Holding it between two fingers in one hand and her drink in the other, Marisa rested her arms on his shoulder and lifted up on her bare feet. He released the smoke in a stream into her open mouth that she released through her nostrils before they kissed as the smoke faded away amid them. With moans of pleasure, they deepened it, pressing their bodies close together, seeming to blend into each other the way the smoke disseminated into the air.

As the sounds of Cuban music playing on the streets below reached them on the balcony of their rented villa, she swayed her hips and leaned her head back as she gave into the hypnotizing sounds of the batá drums, guitars, cajóns and marimbulas of traditional salsa music. Naim pressed kisses to her neck as he moved his body in rhythm to hers. They moved in sync with one another, in and out of bed. Almost as one.

With a moan of pleasure, she felt his length harden against her belly. She raised her head to look up into his dazed eyes. "How do you say 'I want to make love with you' in Spanish?" she whispered.

"Quiero hacer el amor contigo," Naim said before dipping his head to taste her mouth.

"Quiero...hacer...el amor contigo," she repeated slowly. "Over and over and over again."

Fire seemed to light his eyes.

She released a husky laugh when he set their drinks on the table between padded chaise lounges and outed his premium cigar before coming back to her to scoop her up into his arms.

"If we're skipping dinner, I have to feed you something else," she said against his mouth before hotly licking his bottom lip.

"Something wet?" Naim asked, pressing a kiss to just below her earlobe as he carried her inside their master suite.

"And hot," she added.

"Damn," he swore, crossing the large space to lay her down before he untied his pants and worked them down over his hips and his hanging erection.

She untied and spread out the red satin floor-length robe she had put on after their shower when they got in from sightseeing, exposing her nudity to him. His eyes missed nothing as he lowered himself to his knees between her open legs. She shivered in anticipation as he pressed kisses to her thighs while he jerked her body to the edge of the bed.

He moaned before he kissed her throbbing bud and stroked it with his tongue.

She cried out and arched her back.

He suckled it into his mouth with a sweet one-two motion that was a mix of craziness and pleasure. Heat rose quickly. Her breath was shaky. Heart pounding. Core warming. Desire building.

Blindly she reached to stroke the back of his head as he pleasured her like he was starved. He dipped inside her core before tracing the insides of her plump, shaven lips.

"Naim," she moaned, lost in wild abandon as she wound her hips, bringing her core up against his mouth. Just gone. Without a care. How could anything diminish the heat and vibrancy of Cuba filtering through the open balcony doors along with the sounds of salsa, as her lover feasted on her body and made her feel sexy and wanted?

He brought her to a climax that left her trembling and hot as her heart pounded furiously as she thrust her hips up off the bed and gripped his head until the pleasure was mind-blowing and she fought to back away from it. With a shake of his head and his eyes locked on her face, Naim gripped her thighs with his strong muscled arms. She was unable to move and had to ride the waves even as she felt she would pass out from it. His intensity. The pleasure. Her explosive, long-lasting climax.

When he finally released her, he rose with his hardness curving away from his body, heavy and thick. Finding the strength, she turned over and crawled the short distance on her knees to take him into her mouth. He cried out and thrust his hips forward, tightening his buttocks as his knees buckled.

Payback.

She circled his tip with her tongue slowly before taking his inches into her mouth.

He swore and flung his head back as he twisted his fingers into her hair and gripped the strands tightly.

Loving the feel of his hardness against her tongue and the smell of his soap still clinging to the soft black hairs around his shaft, she moaned as she licked from the base to the tip. Back and forth with a deep suck of the tip with her pursed lips. Over and over. The heat of his pleasure warmed the skin. It hardened like steel. She knew his climax was near. She wanted it, and sucked harder.

Naim stepped back, freeing his erection. "I want to cum inside you," he said, coming around the bed to slap her upturned buttocks as he climbed on behind her and slid his hard heat within her with one hard thrust of his hips.

They cried out in unison.

He cupped a fleshy cheek of her buttocks with one hand as he pressed down on her arched back with the other and stroked away inside her.

Marisa clutched wildly at the bedcovers as she winced from the pressure of his strong loving.

The baby crying out echoed from the monitor on the fireplace across the room.

They both froze.

Marisa looked back over her shoulder at him and then over at the monitor. "The…baby's…awake," she said in between hard pants. "I'll go."

"Okay," Naim said, swallowing hard as he began to back out of her.

"Aww. What's wrong, hungry baby?"

They both froze again at the sound of LuAnn, the nurse Naim had hired for the week-long trip. Even with her stellar credentials and background check being squeaky clean, Marisa had been hesitant to hire a nanny, wanting to be the only one to mother her child. At that moment, however, she was thankful for her.

"You still want to check on him?" Naim asked, the tip of his hardness still resting inside her.

It throbbed.

Marisa dropped her head to the bed, listening in as the baby's tears quieted. She shook her head. "LuAnn is gonna mess around and get hired full-time," she said, glancing back at him.

Naim chuckled before he tilted his head to the side. "Turn over," he ordered.

She did, spreading her legs wide before him.

He pressed her thighs down onto the bed, and with a bite of his bottom lip and a slight shift of his hips, the smooth tip of his erection hit against her quivering bud before he thrust inside her again as he lay his body down upon hers, sinking them into the bed.

She wrapped her legs around his back and held his handsome face as she looked up into his eyes as the room darkened with the full setting of the sun. The music from below still echoed inside their suite as he lowered his head and kissed her with such passion as he circled his hips with a deep thrust.

Slow and steady was just as devastating to her senses as hard and fast.

Marisa sucked on the tip of his tongue as she caressed and gripped his buttocks.

Naim slipped his hands beneath her to cup and lift her buttocks. He swore as he broke their kiss and pressed his face against her neck.

"What is the man singing about now?" she asked as the music became slow and poignant and his voice filled the air with torment.

He lifted up to look down at her. Their faces were just centimeters apart. The vibrant multicolored lights of neighboring restaurants and bars flashed against the brown of their skin. "He's singing about losing the woman he loves and wishing he could win her back," he said, his words softly blowing against her mouth.

Her love for him swelled her heart. She had yet to admit her feelings to him, but had been close to doing so a hundred times before. As she lay, looking up into his eyes, matching his slow strokes with tiny downward moves of her hips, she could swear she saw the same feelings for her in his eyes.

"Marisa," he whispered down to her with a slight shake of his head. "I love you."

I love him. God help me. I love him so much.

"Marisa, Marisa, Marisa," he whispered again.

Their eyes remained locked as they made love to each other, lost in the intensity. Their eyes stayed locked and their panted breaths deepened as they held each other tightly and gave in to their climaxes with heated gasps and pounding heartbeats.

Tears welled, and she let them flow as she gave in to the climax and enjoyed the sweet release. "I love you. I love you so much," she whispered as he kissed away her tears before pressing his mouth down upon hers.

"Welcome back, little brother."

Naim held up a finger to Alek as he strode into his office. "Okay, thanks, Oliver. Excellent. Thanks," he said before ending the call.

"Oliver Minogue?" Alek asked, unbuttoning his tweed blazer before taking a seat in front of his brother's desk.

"Yes. He's flying into the country next week to sign the papers. The deal is done."

Alek leaned forward to extend his hand across the desk. "Good job, Naim," he said. "Daddy would be proud. *I'm* proud."

And that mattered. Naim was smart, confident

and daring in his business moves, but getting the approval and respect of his older brother mattered. "Thank you."

"Life is pretty good for you," Alek said. "Beautiful baby boy. In a relationship. Closing business deals. What's next?"

Naim loosened his tie. "What are you fishing at, Alek?" he asked, rising to walk over to the glass bar in his reception area to pour them two glasses of Scotch on the rocks.

He handed his brother his glass before reclaiming his seat and opening the desktop humidor to remove two corona-shaped cigars. Alek smiled. "I wondered if you were bringing some back," he said, accepting one.

"Four cases," Naim said, quickly cutting the closed end of the cigar with a handheld guillotine before warming the tobacco in the foot of it in the heat off his lighter before lighting it and handing the cutter and lighter to his brother.

Alek grunted as he prepped and lit his cigar, as well.

Naim drew in the smoke, holding it in his mouth long enough to savor the flavor before releasing it in a smooth stream. He thought of how he and Marisa had shared that cigar on the balcony in Havana and smiled.

I love you. I love you so much.

That recollection made him shiver. He loved her, as well, and at times that scared him. Nothing about

Marisa was planned. Not their night of passion, the baby, the relationship or falling in love. Every bit of it had been spontaneous and off the cuff. Completely unexpected.

Alek asked a question that was completely reasonable. *What's next?*

"How did you and Alessandra get over your differences?" Naim asked, taking a sip from his drink.

"Naim, you have a humidor and cigar cutter but no ashtray?" Alek mused.

"Good point, even though the ash won't break for three inches, it's packed so tight," he said, picking up the discarded cup of coffee he'd had earlier to set between them on the desk. "And my question is still on the table."

"Love and compromise, but above all being able to admit when you're wrong," Alek said. "I brought more faults into our relationship than she did, and my love for her—plus her proving to me she was just as good in business as me—wizened me up."

Naim pressed the intercom and looked over past the glass wall separating his office from his assistant, Judith. She visibly jumped in her seat before giving him a jerky wave and knocking over a cup on her desk as she reached for the phone.

"Good grief," he muttered under his breath.

Alek turned to look on as she stood to wipe furiously at the spreading liquid with one hand and attempted to pick up the receiver with the other. The cord was tangled and the entire phone lifted from the desk and banged against her elbow.

Her cry of pain echoed through the phone line.

"What the—" Alek asked, scowling a bit.

Naim eyed him. "She's more adept than she appears," he explained.

Alek looked doubtful.

They both looked on as she dropped the phone and left her office to come and stand in the open doorway of his.

"Hello, Mr. Ansah...and Mr. Ansah," she said, giving them a nervous smile.

Alek waved.

"Judith, could you find an ashtray for me?" Naim asked. "I'm sure there's one around here somewhere."

She nodded eagerly as she pushed her glasses up on her nose. "Or I can order one and have it delivered," she said, wringing her hands.

"Thanks," he said.

Judith turned and bumped into the door as she left.

"I promise you she's only that way around me," Naim. "Maybe she's afraid I'll fire her."

"Or she has a crush on you, doofus," Alek drawled.

It was his turn to look doubtful.

"As many women as you have plundered through," Alek said, "you cannot be that daft."

Naim frowned. "Do I have to let her go? I really don't want a new assistant," he said.

Alek chuckled. "Nah. You don't have real problems until you walk in and she's butt naked on your desk asking for a different kind of *dic*tation," he said with air quotes.

Naim eyed his brother with questions in his eyes.

"Hell, no," he snapped, his face incredulous. "Alessandra is all the woman I need. Trust me."

Naim leaned back in the chair and pondered never being with another woman ever again except Marisa. Visions of her smiling at him, laughing with him, making love to him and growing old with him played in his head. It sat well with him.

That was frightening.

What's next?

Alek rose and tapped the ashes from his cigar. "You really could have gotten me a box," he said before turning to leave.

"It's hidden in your office," Naim called behind him.

Alek stopped. "You cannot be *that* childish," he said.

"I absolutely can. Good luck with that," Naim said, turning on his computer.

Alek chuckled. "I can't believe I started to say I'm telling Mom on you like I'm not a fully grown man."

"That reminds me. I went by Mom's when we got back from Cuba last night, and I ran into Roje leaving the apartment," he said.

"Roje?" Alek asked.

"Yeah, he said he was dropping something off for

Alessandra," Naim said. "It was weird, and Mom looked like she saw a ghost when I got to the door."

Alek looked confused. "Alessandra didn't mention anything to me about sending Roje into the city," he said.

The brothers shared a look. Their eyes filled with the possibility of something going on between their mother and a chauffeur—or any man.

"Nooo," they both said in disbelief, as if the idea of it was nonsensical.

Alek reached for Naim's phone and dialed Alessandra's private line in her office. He placed the call on speaker.

"Go, Naim," she said, sounding distracted.

"Wrong Ansah," Naim said.

"It's me, babe," Alek said. "Quick question."

"Okay."

"Naim saw Roje in Manhattan last night. Did you send him there?" he asked, looking across the desk at his brother.

She paused. It was noticeable.

"You there?" Alek asked.

"Sorry, I had to sign something for Unger," she said. "Um, yes, I did. Why?"

Naim felt relief.

"Naim saw him at our mother's, and he said he was dropping something off for you."

"Oh, yeah, he did me a favor. Listen, fellas, some people have work to do," Alessandra said.

"Me, too. I'm on my way up," Alek said, rising to

his feet as he ended the call and turned to leave the spacious corner office.

Alek left with a shake of his head, leaving Naim deeply frowning at the idea of them being wrong.

"Um, wait," Alek said, returning to the doorway. "I forgot I was co-CEO with the power to transfer you anywhere I—"

"In your closet," Naim supplied.

"*And* checkmate," Alek said with a bow before walking away.

Marisa glanced at the wrought iron clock on the wall of La Boulangerie before looking up at the tall man walking up to her counter. He wore an oversize jacket and a bucket hat worn low over his face, but she recognized him. He lived in the large estate off the lake across from the Dalmount-Ansah estate, and she would always see him, dressed in his normal garb, fishing in the lake early in the mornings. She'd heard the wealthy recluse only ventured off his estate to fish in the lake in the spring and summers or to make rare appearances at stores on Main Street. He spoke to no one and was considered to generally be in a bad mood. Still, he seemed to like her chocolate.

"What can I get for you?" she asked, wishing she could see more of his face beyond the strong chin, mouth and nose.

"You should deliver," he said, his voice deep.

Well, hello to you, too.

"Maybe one day," she said. "Right now, I'm a one-woman operation."

He grunted. "A dozen nut clusters," he said.

She reached for a box and used tongs to line the large clusters of mixed nuts and chocolate. "I have two left and you're my last customer for the day, so I'll add them in," she said, closing the lid on the box and handing them to him as she accepted his cash.

"Keep the change," he said, turning and walking away.

Marisa's eyes widened as she saw Samira enter the bakery, looking down at her phone at the same moment, and knew they were going to collide. She winced when they did. Both moved quickly to keep the things they held from falling.

"I'm sorry," Samira said.

"You should watch where the hell you're going," he said before brushing past her and leaving the bakery with long strides.

Samira walked up to her with a playful scowl. "What a grouch," she said.

Marisa laughed as she turned the sign on her counter from Open to Closed. "Aww, the right woman could put a smile on his face," she said, stacking the empty trays as she gave Bill a playful wink.

He looked just as doubtful.

"Who would even bother trying?" Samira asked.

Bill eyed the dark-skinned beauty and the red flare leg tailored suit she wore. "The right person," he supplied. "Sometimes they're right in front of you."

Marisa shook her head as Samira completely missed Bill's double entendre. "I'm going to clean up and head home," she said, carrying the trays toward the kitchen. "I am ready to press my face in my baby's neck."

"I just stopped by for coffee before heading back into the city," she said, raising a finger to Bill to put in an order. "Kiss his cheek for me. Auntie has to get back to work."

Marisa entered the kitchen and cleaned up her workspace and utensils as quickly as she could. With a wave and smile to Bill, she left via the rear entrance to the parking area in the back and climbed inside her new SUV. It had plenty of room for the baby's car seat and was paid for, thanks to trading in her beloved Bentley.

Naim had also purchased an SUV—a Mercedes-AMG G65.

Even only working half days at La Boulangerie and making a lot of her treats at home while Kwesi slept, Marisa missed her baby and hated being away from him for even five hours. And it was not until she entered her home, kicked off the patent leather flats, dismissed LuAnn and gathered her plump brown baby in her arms that she felt at peace.

She sat on the chaise longue by the window and looked down into his face as he smiled up at her while he kicked his chubby little legs in his teddy-bear-covered onesie. "Am I crazy or are you happy to see Mama?" she asked him. "Is Mama's baby happy to see me?"

Looking just like your Daddy, she thought.

Kwesi blew a spit bubble and Marisa laughed, picking up her iPhone to take photos of him before she texted them to Naim.

Ur twin! #DaddysBoy

Bzzzzzz.

Miss y'all. On my way.

K.

Marisa read to Kwesi and fed him a bottle as they awaited Naim. The time flew by as she pressed kisses to his cheeks and fists.

"Can I get in on that?"

She looked up at Naim leaning against the doorframe. "Always," she said.

He came over to them and squatted by the chaise.

Marisa leaned down to taste his mouth with several kisses before sitting the baby up on her lap. "Say Hey, Pops," she said.

"Hey, man," Naim said, taking his son's little hands in his.

Kwesi smiled and kicked both his feet excitedly again.

"Take him while I grab a shower," she said, handing the baby to him before rising to her feet.

Naim claimed her spot on the chaise.

With one look back at them as Naim sang "Can't Take My Eyes Off You" to their son, she rushed into her room, removing her clothes and lingerie as she did. Naked, she twisted her hair up into a topknot as she entered the bathroom. She paused to check her body in the mirror, pressing a hand to her nearly flat stomach. She wasn't back to her pre-baby-body figure yet, but she was close.

As the steam rose and began to coat the mirror, she stepped inside the shower and closed the frosted glass door, then tilted her head back. The water from the rainfall showerhead felt good against her body.

"Guess what."

She looked through the steam at Naim standing in the doorway holding the baby. "What?" she asked as she pulled on her bath gloves and lathered them with her favorite coconut-scented body wash.

He told her about running into Roje leaving his mother's apartment the night before. Her movement slowly ceased at the censure she heard in his tone at the very idea of his mother being involved with a chauffeur. She frowned as the steam swirled around her and the water pelted her body.

"I'm sure there's an explanation because—"

"Because what?" Marisa asked, thinking of the love her mother had for her father and how it was deemed wrong by the family because he had no wealth of his own.

"Huh?" Naim asked.

She thought of the stolen moment LuLu had shared with Roje on Thanksgiving. "What if she was involved with Roje? What if he made her happy?" she asked.

"Don't be ridiculous, Marisa," he balked.

"Maybe you're the one being ridiculous," she said.

When there was no response, she used the side of her hand to clear away the steam on the glass. He was gone. Possibly done with the conversation.

But she wasn't.

Marisa left the shower, sudsy and wet, and padded out of the bathroom. She had to know if his issue with his mother finding love again would be over any man, or just a man he deemed beneath her. Even with her mother's flaws, and Marisa knew there were plenty, Brunela was able to put aside their enormous wealth for love.

She stopped at the sight of him lying across her bed with the baby on his back next to him.

Naim sat up when he saw her.

"To think you would deny your mother love because of money—or lack of money—is sad, Naim," she said. "And it speaks to something in your character that I don't agree with."

He frowned. "Here the hell we go with this money mess again," he said.

"Yes, here we go because it's still right there be-

tween us. The big elephant in the room that we ignore, but money and the love of it can be destructive,
Naim," she insisted.

He bit down on his bottom lip and closed his eyes
briefly before glaring at her. "You want to have this
argument, Marisa?" he asked, his voice hard.

"I want to have this *discussion*, yes," she insisted.

"Could you get dressed?" he snapped. "I can't
think straight."

Marisa charged back into the bathroom for her
robe, quickly pulling it on and tying it. The ends
flew up into the air behind her as she whirled to re-
join him. "If you are so caught up in classism, how
are you sure I'm not with you for your money?" she
asked, her heart pounding.

Naim looked incredulous. "My money? Hell, you
don't even want your own money. Which doesn't
make a *damn* bit of sense, Marisa."

She froze. "I thought you finally understood me,"
she said, her eyes filled with disbelief.

"No, I just let it go," he said.

"And judged me a fool the whole time. Huh?"
she asked.

Naim looked away from her.

"Truth," she demanded.

He looked down at their son innocently lying
there in the midst of his parents' storm. "I'm tired
of bringing up things concerning money and hearing this spiel of yours," he said.

"Spiel?" she spat, not sure if the heat in her chest was from hurt or anger.

"Yes, just like any time I brought up the trust fund I set up for Kwesi—"

Marisa's eyes pierced him. "You set up a trust fund even though I asked you not to?" she asked, amazed that the heat of anger was replaced with the coldness of rage.

"If you think I am going to deny my son his birthright, you have lost your mind," he said.

"And if you think I'm going to sit by and let you raise a spoiled, entitled child, then you have lost yours," she shot back at him.

Naim jumped to his feet. "You're being ridiculous. That's about parenting, not money," he said. "Make it make sense, Marisa."

His anger revealed that their issues with money ran far deeper than she realized.

"Your billionaire nose is so stuck in the air that you don't even see what's going on around you," she said bitterly, alluding to his being oblivious that his mother indeed loved a chauffeur. "When your decisions and viewpoints are ruled by class and what someone has or does not have, then it's easy to be blind to what's real. That's your world—and it used to be mine—but not anymore and not for *my* child."

"*Your* child?" Naim said, his voice cold enough to freeze the very blood in her veins. "Now he's *your* child?"

Marisa notched her chin high as she walked over

and picked Kwesi up from the bed. "You drew the battle lines, not me," she said, her heart breaking even as she angrily stuck to her resolve. She knew she stood in the remains of their relationship as it crumbled around them.

"Do you want war?" he asked, his eyes locked on hers with an intensity that put pure fear in her heart.

She blinked to keep back the tears that rose like a flood. "I want to raise a child that becomes the best possible person he can be, Naim. That's *all* I want," she said in a whisper before pressing the baby's soft face against her own, realizing she had nothing in her arsenal to use against him if she pushed him too far.

It was humbling to step away from the fight, but for her child, she would do just that.

"And I want you to leave," she added, stiffening her back.

"Marisa—"

"Now," she demanded. "Get out."

His stare was long and hard. She wondered what thoughts and emotions ran through his mind. He said nothing more as he walked up to her to press a kiss to the baby's temple before he left the room.

Kwesi began to stir in her arms and cry as if picking up on their tension. She sank down onto the foot of the bed. "It'll be okay. It's okay. Mama and Daddy will be okay," she comforted him softly, even though she knew those very words were lies.

Chapter 8

Two weeks later

"You lost my number."

Naim turned from where he stood with his brother, Alek, and his brother's best friend, Chance Castillo, to find Greenly Briton standing there looking radiant in a strapless emerald sequin dress with her red hair pulled over one shoulder. He gave her a once-over, not surprised to see the stable owner at the charity fund-raiser for Passion Grove Gives Foundation. Main Street was closed off for the night for an upscale version of a block party complete with food, drink and dance while bands played. "How are you, Greenly?" he asked.

She stepped closer to him, resting one hand atop his as she leaned in. "Wishing I was as well-ridden as Decadence was today," she whispered near his ear.

Naim hung his head and smiled. "You mince no words," he said.

With a lick of her lips, she stepped back. "I have no time for games," she said, reaching in her clutch to pull out a card to hand him. "*Last* invitation."

Naim eyed her as he sipped from his flute of champagne. She was everything Marisa was not, and he considered that that was just what he needed. With a nod, he took the card. She smiled and stroked his chest before turning to saunter away.

"I don't miss those days," Alek said from behind him.

Naim cleared his throat and slid the card in the inside pocket of his tuxedo jacket. "I'm single," he reminded the men as they moved away from the bar.

Chance took a sip of his beer. "Love doesn't fade in two weeks," he said, looking left and then right until he set his sights on his wife, Ngozi, in a brilliant bloodred body-forming dress.

No, it doesn't.

And Naim's hadn't, either, but his anger at Marisa was stronger.

Without consulting him, Marisa had decided that he was only able to visit with their son at Alek and Alessandra's estate on Sundays. In the last two weeks, he had only seen his son twice, and he missed him. To keep him from his son and bar him from her house and life had created a resentment that scorched hotter than the desire they once shared.

"Looks like Marisa has an admirer, as well."

At his brother's words, Naim's head shot up and he looked around like a spooked deer until he spotted the mother of his son dancing with Bill the Man-Bun. Clenching his jaw, he took in the short silver sequin T-shirt-style dress with a biting-lips graphic across the front. He frowned at Bill's hand on her lower back as she tossed her head back and laughed as they danced.

He took a step in their direction.

"Careful," Alek said, placing a restraining hand on the bend of his arm. "She's single, too, remember."

Jealousy stung his gut.

He forced himself to look away from them. "Where's my son while she's lining up a new lover?" he muttered.

Alek and Chance eyed him.

"Don't question her parenting because you're mad at her," Alek said.

"Doesn't she question mine by not allowing me to see my son when I want?" he countered.

"You're both wrong," Chance inserted.

"And the family will not choose sides because both of you won't get it together," Alek said sternly.

"No need for choosing sides when I'm doing what I should have done in the first place," he said.

"And what's that?"

He glanced at Alessandra, who had just walked up and overheard them. "Asking your cousin to sign a formal joint custody and visitation agreement," he said. "My lawyer sent the papers today."

"Oh, Naim," Alessandra sighed.

"Maybe it's for the best, Alessandra," Alek said. "Right now, they're both making a decision based on emotions. Something formal might be best for the baby to establish a pattern."

She looked across the distance at Marisa. "I can't keep this from her," she said.

Naim shrugged. "Then don't. The papers will be served soon and it is what it is," he said, some of his anger dissipating as he looked down at the tip of his polished handmade shoes. "She wants me to jump through hoops and dance to her tune to see my son. That's not fair, and I'm not putting up with it for the next eighteen years of his life."

Alessandra squeezed his hand before moving beyond him to walk over to Marisa and Bill.

The band began to play "Havana" by Camila Cabello and Daddy Yankee.

Marisa hated that she was taken back to their trip. To better times. She had revealed the truth of her heart in Havana.

I love you. I love you so much.

And she still did.

Standing beside Bill, she looked across the distance at Naim to find his eyes on her.

Marisa, I love you.

She shivered.

* * *

As soon as he heard the first strums of the song, his eyes went to her and he felt the happiness they had shared in Havana. The night they both admitted to their love as the Cuban street music from down below serenaded them.

When her eyes sought his, he couldn't find the strength to look away.

His heart pounded wildly, and he wanted nothing more than to cross the divide and pull her into his arms for a sultry dance and an even sexier kiss.

Alessandra stepped in front of her, breaking the hold Naim had on her.

"Hey," she said, glad when the band transitioned into another song.

"Can we talk?" Alessandra asked, giving Bill a polite smile before leveling her eyes on Marisa again.

"I'll give you a moment," he said, nodding his head respectfully before walking away.

"What's wrong?" Marisa asked.

Alessandra reached for both of her hands. "Remember, you're in public," she began.

Marisa tensed.

"The mayor and sheriff are here," Alessandra added.

Marisa arched a brow.

"Naim just told us that he is filing for joint custody of Kwesi," she said.

Marisa leaned to the side to look past her at Naim. Her eyes narrowed to a glare.

Alessandra tightened her grip on her hands. "I think if you two sit down and talk this out—"

Marisa jerked both her hands from Alessandra and breezed past her to walk up to Naim. So many angry retorts flew to the tip of her tongue, but she pressed her mouth closed and just shook her head, feeling hopeless.

Chance, Ngozi and Alek gave them privacy and walked away.

"I had no idea you could be such an asshole," she said, her eyes searching his as she looked up at him.

"I had no idea you would deny me my right to spend time with my son," he volleyed back. "You think I don't miss him, Marisa? You think I don't love him just as much as you?"

"But two weeks ago, you loved me, right?" she asked with a bitter laugh.

"Two weeks ago, I didn't know you and Bill the Man-Bun were playing in the sheets," he shot back.

She reached to slap him but he caught her wrist in his hand with ease.

"Enough," Alessandra snapped, walking up to them.

Marisa looked around to see plenty of eyes locked on them. She walked away with a shake of her head, pausing to squeeze Bill's hand where he stood by looking on. "Thank you for the dance, my friend," she said, barely able to keep back her tears before she ran away on her strappy sequined sandals.

Bill reached for her, but she shook off his touch and avoided the stares of those in attendance as she made her way up the street to her parked SUV. She made the short drive to Alessandra and Alek's estate, where she had left Kwesi with the nanny watching Aliyah. When she entered the nursery, Leila was feeding him a bottle.

"Early night, Ms. Martinez?" she asked.

Marisa nodded as she kicked off her heels. "Yes," she said, walking over to grab a clean blanket and throw it over her shoulder before she took her baby and lay him on her shoulder with her hand securing his back.

"Marisa, your baby was good," Aliyah said, bouncing atop her walking toy unicorn and moving across the room in her pajamas.

Marisa eyed the toddler and her huge afro puffs. "He was?" she asked.

Aliyah nodded eagerly.

"He really is a good baby," Leila said.

"Thank you," Marisa said, smiling down at him.

"Okay, Aliyah, say good night. It's time for bed," she said, picking her up off the white unicorn.

"Bonsoir," Aliya said in French with a wave as they left the nursery.

Marisa sat on the plush round chaise longue, setting the blanket down before she lay Kwesi down upon it on his back. She hitched the hem of her dress up around the tops of her thighs and crossed her legs Indian-style. With a sad smile, she stroked his thick black curls. Naim's hair. Eyes. Smile. Complexion. Face.

Two weeks ago, I didn't know you and Bill the Man-Bun were playing in the sheets.

That stung. As if she could go from loving him to being with someone else within two weeks. Perhaps the old Marisa, but not the woman he knew.

Or I thought he knew, anyway.

Marisa bent down to kiss the bottom of her son's feet.

Joint custody? What's next?

"I'm just trying to do what's right," she whispered, releasing a puff of breath to keep back the tide of sadness she felt.

"So am I, Marisa."

She stiffened at the sound of Naim's voice and took note that her body had not responded to his presence like it normally did. "Bull," she snapped. "Because you are holding my past against me, and that's clear from the shots fired about Bill."

He strolled into the room and stood over them, looking down at Kwesi, whose eyes lit up at the sight of his father. "Can I hold him?"

"You don't have to ask me that, Naim," she said, sounding weary.

"Don't I?" he asked.

She squeezed the bridge of her nose and dropped her head as he bent to scoop the baby into his arms.

"I just feel he's so small. He just had his vaccination. I don't think he should be staying with you or *anyone* overnight. That's all."

Naim bounced Kwesi gently as he stood looking over at her. "Why I am barred from your house?" he asked. "I could stay in the guest room a few nights a week."

She shook her head and unbent her legs to sit on the side of the chaise. "No. I can't have you there. I don't want you there. I don't want to argue or throw shade anymore. I don't want to love you *anymore*. I wish we had never tried because my heart is broken and now I have to figure out how to fix it—and although it's none of your business, I'm not doing that by *playing* in the sheets with Bill."

"I won't lie. That's good to know," Naim admitted.

"Too bad I had to tell you that for you to know it," she shot back, rising to her feet.

He turned to face her, looking down into her eyes. "You're the mother of my child. Although we are different and see the world differently and couldn't make this work, I will always love you, Marisa, and I don't want to get over that."

Inside she melted. "Don't," she begged in a whisper.

"Don't what?" he asked.

"From the very beginning of us…this…there was no respect for rules. No boundaries. Everything was off the cuff, and look where it got us," she said, stepping back from him and the energy between them that she couldn't deny even in anger. "Time for boundaries. Right. That's what those papers you're serving me with are about, right?"

She picked up her heels and stuck them inside Kwesi's baby bag after checking the room to make sure she had all of his things.

With one last kiss to the baby's cheek, Naim handed him to her. "Get home safe," he said, stepping back and sliding his hands into the pockets of his tuxedo pants.

"We will," she said, placing a blanket over the baby before she left the room.

Naim turned from the views of his penthouse to look at the painting lying atop his dining room table. It was an original artwork depicting a carnival scene in Havana with a street band and people dancing beneath colorful lights on a narrow street between colonial buildings with the ocean in the distance. The colorful scene had drawn Marisa's eyes at one of the galleries they'd visited in Cuba. Secretly he'd purchased it for her and had it shipped from Havana.

Ding-dong.

He looked at the front door before walking over to it. The iPad on the wall showed his mother. Visits to his apartment by her were rare. "Hello, Mama," he said as soon as he opened the door. "I see you've heard about the custody matter."

"What happened to not treating it like a business?" she asked, walking past him to turn in the foyer and face him.

And we're off.

Naim closed the door and walked back into his living room. "I tried," he said over his shoulder.

"How? My grandson is barely three months old. You and Marisa ended things just two weeks ago. When did you try?" she asked, her voice unusually sharp. "This is your child, not a business deal, Naim."

"With all due respect, Maman, you don't know everything," he said, massaging his eyes as he sat down on the sofa.

LuLu clucked her tongue in disapproval. "*L'enfant pense qu'il est plus intelligent que le parent maintenant? Eh?*"

The child thinks he's smarter than the parent now?

Naim shook his head and rose to walk over to the copper bar in the corner to pour a shot of Scotch.

"Everything does *not* have to be war, Naim," she asserted again.

"Tell Marisa that," he said, his voice echoing into the glass.

"I plan to do just that."

"Let me handle this. I'm a grown man, Maman."

Naim turned when she fell silent. She was standing by the table looking down at the painting. He walked over to her.

"This is beautiful," she said, touching the frame.

His mother was a lover of art and culture. One

wall of her Upper East Side apartment was covered with art—mainly of Ghanaian descent.

"When we were in Havana, Marisa was drawn to it," he said, eyeing the street band and thinking of the love they had made that night. "She said it represented everything she wanted to remember about Cuba."

LuLu looked over at him. "You purchased it for her?" she said, her tone soft.

Naim shrugged. "You can have it," he said.

"It's not meant for me."

Naim walked over to the window and looked out at the night. "She wouldn't want it. Not from me, anyway," he said, remembering her words from the night before.

I don't want to love you anymore. I wish we had never tried because my heart is broken and now I have to figure out how to fix it...

LuLu came over to stand beside him. "Love is tough but glorious," she said, wrapping her arms around his and resting her head against his arm.

Naim grunted. "Especially when you're not looking for it but it grabs ahold of you, anyway," he said.

"Don't I know it," LuLu drawled.

"Huh?" Naim looked down at her.

"Nothing," she said, patting his hand.

They fell silent.

"I don't think you're wrong for fighting to have equal say about your child," she said. "I just think you should have talked to her before you involved lawyers, son."

"What's done is done," he said. "The papers were served today."

LuLu winced. "Ouch," she said.

"Marisa and I weren't meant to be. I don't understand her crusade against wealth, and she acts like she wants me to rebuke everything my father worked hard to give me. I'm not doing that," he said. "Besides, I wasn't ready to settle down."

"One day you will be ready—that's just life. Be sure when you do that you have no regrets about whom you settle with," she said. "The older I get, the more I realize that love is worth *every* sacrifice."

Marisa woke up with a little grunt of pleasure and a stretch of her limbs against the cool, crisp sheets as she looked out at the sun rising over Hope Island. She had to admit she loved Alessandra and Alek's private island off East Hampton and couldn't think of a better way to spend the weekend.

Even if *I have to share it with Naim.*

She sat up in bed and pulled her knees to her chest, feeling rested. She looked over at the receiver of Kwesi's baby monitor as she reached to make sure it was on and the volume was at the max.

Last night, with reluctance, she had let Naim take the baby for the night.

Truthfully, she felt well rested for the first time in months—perhaps even before she became huge with pregnancy. And while she'd lain in bed listening in on his interactions with their son, she fell asleep to him softly singing "Can't Take My Eyes Off You."

She rolled her eyes heavenward. "Stupid song," she muttered, flinging back the covers and climbing from bed to walk over to the French doors to open them and step onto the balcony. She closed her eyes and enjoyed the slight breeze before sitting on one of the chaise lounges, where she sat in the butter-fly yoga position with her legs bent and the soles of her feet pressed together. She needed all the balance, good chi and relaxation she could get to prepare for the day.

Hell, the whole weekend.

"I will not choke Naim, I will not choke Naim, I will not choke Naim," she repeated.

Humph. He wants three nights a week and alternating weekends with Kwesi. The man is tripping.

Her body tensed.

Knock-knock.

Thinking it was Naim bringing Kwesi, she rushed to rise and raced across the room to open the door. "Oh," she said at seeing Ngozi standing there still dressed in cotton pajamas.

"Well, damn," she said, following her into the brightly lit bedroom. "Hell of a greeting."

"Sorry. I thought you were the asshole bringing my baby back," Marisa said, taking a seat on the powder blue love seat at the foot of the queen-size bed.

Ngozi gave her a chastising look.

"Three days a week and alternating weekends," Marisa said. "*And* he wants a say on everything. Doctors. Schools. Where I live!"

"Yes, I read the documents you stuck in my hand as soon as we arrived last night. I mean literally in the foyer," Ngozi said with a droll expression. "I'm a criminal attorney, but, Marisa, those are the kind of decisions parents make together all the time."

Marisa arched a brow. "When you have a baby, will you consult Chance before you choose a pediatrician?" she said in a snarky tone.

"No," she admitted, coming over to sit on the wide ottoman in front of the love seat.

"Exactly!"

"But for those things he is really concerned about, I will listen to his point of view."

Marisa frowned as she side-eyed her. "Your point?" she said dryly.

Ngozi looked awkward.

"No!" Marisa exclaimed, pointing a finger. "You think I'm wrong."

"I think you're *both* wrong."

Marisa glared at her.

"And I don't think you're being smart about this," Ngozi added. "Think of this as a business deal. Negotiate. Naim would think like that. It's in his DNA. Trust me, Chance is the same way."

"So what are you saying?"

"It's time to accept that you had a baby from a

one-night stand and the daddy wants in," Ngozi said bluntly.

"Brutal," Marisa said with a wince.

"Offer him one overnight a week and a weekend a month," Ngozi said. "And use that time to rest and recuperate. To work on your craft as a chocolatier. To travel. To date. Whatever."

Marisa frowned. "He will win the joint custody if he goes for it. Won't he?"

Ngozi nodded. "Absolutely," she said. "Judges don't automatically favor the mother anymore. It's a different age, and fathers are given just as many rights as the mothers. It has nothing to do with one being better than the other. It's just equality. Plus, your stint in rehab and arrest may even give him more leverage in court. I'm sorry, but it's true."

Damn.

That made her hang her head. "I'd figured that, but it's hard to hear it from one of the top attorneys in the country," she said.

"If you keep it simple I can handle this for you, but if it gets messy and goes to court I would have to recommend a family attorney to ensure you have the best representation. Cool?"

"Cool."

Ngozi squeezed her knee in comfort before rising. "I am going to find my husband to feed him," she said.

"The chef has breakfast ready?" Marisa asked, glad for the change of conversation.

Ngozi opened the door to the bedroom and looked back. "I'm not talking about food," she said.

"Oh," Marisa said in understanding.

"Ooooh," Ngozi moaned in playful anticipation before leaving.

Marisa rose and went back out onto the balcony. She gripped the railings as she looked out at the ocean. It pained her to accept that Naim held the winning cards. Her past ensured she would lose. For too many minutes to count, she stood there and forced herself to cycle through every imaginable emotion before she grabbed the short cotton robe that matched the shorts and tank she wore to bed.

Every step down the hall to Naim's suite was hard, but she made the walk. Knocked on his door. And when he opened it, she smiled.

Naim wore just navy blue sleep pants, and they were far too clinging. "Kwesi's still sleeping. He woke up around two wanting a bottle and to kick his feet," he said.

She forced her eyes up. "I heard. You did well getting him back to sleep," she admitted.

He nodded. "Thanks."

Marisa released a breath. "Um, so I was thinking until he's older we agree to one overnight a week and one weekend a month," she said, her heart pounding.

His face filled with surprise and then wariness. "And child support?"

"My business is doing really well," she said. "We already split the fee for the medical bills and the nanny's pay. We should keep it like that. If it's gifts you want him to have, just purchase them yourself. But I don't want anything from you."

Naim's face became pensive as he eyed her before he ran his hand over his bearded chin. "I never wanted to take Kwesi from you but when I thought you wanted to keep me from seeing him—to not have a say in how he was raised—I was determined to have what is rightfully mine and that is joint custody," he said. "But if you're willing to end this war, then so am I, for our son."

Marisa nodded. "For our son," she agreed.

"Let's go with your terms now and when he's a few months older we can revisit my time with him," he said, extending his hand. "Deal?"

She looked down at it before nodding and sliding her hand in his.

And just like always, her body came alive, betraying her but aligning with her heart. Her love for him still burst inside her heart like fireworks.

Chapter 9

Two weeks later

Marisa paused on the street with the baby's blanket-covered carrier in her hand, looking up at ADG's twenty-five-story art deco building. It was not lost on her the accomplishments of her uncle and Naim's father as men of color creating such a dynasty in the face of every possible adversity. It was something to be proud of, and a testament to hard work and vision. For so long she had let her mother's anger over being overlooked to run the business taint her view of their success. The last year she had put into building her business had changed her outlook for the better.

She entered the building, careful of Kwesi in his

carrier as the automatic door opened. Once they got through security, she rode the private elevator to the top-floor housing Alessandra's and Alek's offices as co-CEOs. Funny how she had been here plenty of times over the years, mostly to get extra spending money from her uncle, but it wasn't until now that she took it all in and was impressed.

Unger, Alessandra's assistant, had already been notified by security and awaited her arrival to usher her into her cousin's three-thousand-square-foot office. It really was magnificent and grand, with floor-to-ceiling windows letting in the sunlight and offering nearly three-hundred-sixty-degree views of Manhattan, with its twenty-foot ceilings and sky-lights.

As Marisa walked across the space, she took in the stylish decor, private spa bath, small kitchen, exercise room, lounge area with a grand fireplace, library and outdoor terrace. "Being CEO has its perks," she said as Alessandra rose, wearing a bright yellow bodycon dress, and came around her desk to take the carrier and fling the blanket away.

Kwesi was sleeping, but Alessandra undid his straps and lifted him from the carrier, anyway, nuzzling her face into his sweet-smelling neck. "Mother-hood has its perks, and this neck is one." She sighed. "Maybe Aliyah needs a little brother or sister."

"Good luck with that," Marisa said.

We could agree in another five years to have another child.

Marisa shook her head as if to clear it, to erase the memory of Naim's words from it. She reached into her wallet and removed a check to slide across the desk with a huge smile. "My loan is now paid in full," she said with a wiggle of her eyebrows.

Alessandra glanced at it as she set the sleeping baby back into his carrier and reclaimed her seat behind the desk. "Congratulations, Marisa," she said. "I am so proud of you. These last two years, you have really turned your life around."

She bowed playfully. "Thank you," she said. "Actually, I need your advice, if you have time."

"Of course." Alessandra nodded for her to go on.

"I think I've been working harder and not smarter," Marisa began. "I've been so focused on selling the candy—and it's doing very well—but I think the real gem is my homemade chocolate recipe."

Alessandra nodded. "I agree. It's *so* smooth, with just the right amount of sweetness without making you reach for a glass of water because it's too cloying."

"I'm thinking of starting out by approaching bakeries and restaurants with an opportunity to have me supply locally made chocolate for them to use in their candy, cookies and other baked goods. If it goes well, maybe one day I can enlarge the business to be a major distributor for candy manufacturers," she said, her excitement and uncertainty clear in her eyes.

"Smarter, not harder," Alessandra said, tapping

an Aurora pen against the blotter on her desk. "I like it, Marisa. I really do."

"I'm just starting to think it through, but I wanted to know if I was wrong to worry about two birds in a bush when I have one in my hand," she said.

"No, come on, our family was built for business. This is in your blood," she said, waving her hand around the spacious office. "Business—big business— is what we do."

Marisa felt excited and light in the chest, pleased to have her cousin's support.

"Now, let me say this," Alessandra began.

Uh-oh.

Marisa released a puff of breath in preparation for a letdown.

"This may one day entail owning and operating your own factory to produce mass quantities, right?"

"I'm sure that's years ahead, but yes, I'm open to growing *Décadence de Chocolat* that large," Marisa asserted, crossing her legs in her seat.

Alessandra looked to her baby cousin in the carrier and then back at his mother. "I won't loan you any money in the future," she said.

"Why? I paid my loan off with interest," she said, knowing her tone mirrored the look of disbelief on her face.

"Because you have an abundance of money that is rightfully yours just waiting to be used to build up your business idea," Alessandra said, rising again and coming around the desk to lean against the edge as she looked down at her. "Your allowance payments these last two years have been held for you. *Waiting* for you."

Marisa groaned in dismay and did a facepalm.

Alessandra removed her hand and held it in hers. "My father worked so hard to create a legacy that would benefit his family—all of us—for many years to come. And even with all of the drama you brought, you were one of his favorites. What better way to honor him and his hard work than to use the money meant for you to grow a business in the same tradition as he did?"

Marisa said nothing, lost in her thoughts.

"You've proven you don't need it, so there's nothing wrong with wanting it," Alessandra added, just as the baby began to stir.

Marisa didn't know whether to be upset or inspired.

"Why are you in the city, anyway?" she asked, rising to once again take Kwesi from his carrier.

"He's going home with Naim tonight, and I agreed to save him the drive to pick him up," she said, still feeling confused as she dug into the bag and pulled out his prepared bottle to hand Alessandra.

"How's it going?" she asked.

"Better. We have a temporary custody agreement filed with the understanding to revisit the matter when he's one," she said, smiling at the way he latched on to the nipple of the bottle.

"How is it between the two of you?"

Marisa shrugged. "We're cordial."

"And miserable."

"And moving on," Marisa insisted with a meaningful stare before she pulled her phone from her tote to text Naim.

We're in A's office.

Headed up.

Marisa set the phone facedown on the desk, hating that she had the urge to check her hair and makeup at Naim's imminent arrival. "Should I bring dessert for the Memorial Day party this weekend?" she asked.

Alessandra looked thoughtful. "No," she said. "But you can provide the chocolate for Cook to make a dessert."

Marisa smiled. "That sounds better," she agreed.

"Chocky-Wocky!"

The ladies both turned to see Samira quickly striding across the room to reach them. "I heard there was some chocolate goodness in the building." She sighed, taking the baby from Alessandra's arms. "How is auntie's Chocky-Wocky?"

Kwesi smiled up at her.

"I can hear you down the hall."

Marisa rose to her feet at the sound of Naim's voice.

"You're leaving?" Alessandra asked.

She nodded. "I just wanted to drop the baby off," she said.

"Marisa," Naim said.

She barely spared him a glance. "Naim," she returned, handing him the baby bag. "I know you have a lot of things for him at your apartment, but this is diapers and milk until you get home. Just in case."

"Thanks."

Their hands briefly touched when he took the bag.

A spark as sharp as static cling emanated. Their eyes met.

I wonder if he remembers today is one year since the night we made Kwesi.

Marisa looked away first.

"Okay, Ansahs—including my beautiful baby— I am out," she said, leaning in to give his plump cheek a kiss.

"What are you doing with your free night this week?" Alessandra asked.

"I have plans," she said, giving Naim a little glance before turning. "Good evening, everyone."

"Marisa," Naim called to her just as she reached the door.

She paused and looked back over her shoulder. "Yes?" she asked calmly, even as her heart seemed to beat at a triple pace.

Naim stood with his hands in the pockets of his suit. So tall and handsome. "Enjoy your night," he said.

"I will," she said before taking her leave.

On the ride back to Passion Grove, Marisa blared the music in a weak attempt to block out thoughts of Naim and memories of that night one year ago today. It had been good. They had clicked. Over and over again.

And made a baby.

She was thankful to walk into her home and kick off the red heels she wore with distressed jeggings and a V-neck white tee. "Get ready for my *plans*," she said aloud as she walked past the stairs and into the open living space to reach the kitchen. "Milkshake and bonbons while I Netflix and chill."

She carried her treats upstairs to her bedroom, with plans of climbing into pajamas and lying in bed while she caught up on her favorite shows. In the open doorway, she turned on the ceiling light and paused with a gasp of surprise. There was a massive bouquet of long-stemmed red roses next to the painting she recognized from the gallery in Havana.

Setting the flute of chocolate milkshake and bonbons on the eight-drawer dresser by the door, she crossed the room to pluck the card from the roses. She recognized Naim's slashing handwriting.

Marisa,
One year ago today we shared a special night.
Although we are not meant to be, I think the
day should be celebrated because we were
blessed that night to make our beautiful son.
N.

"He remembered," she whispered as she felt the weight of the envelope and opened it to find the house key she had given him all those months ago.

A clear sign they were done.

She pulled her cell phone from the back pocket of her jeans and took a picture of the roses and painting to text to Naim.

I thought you forgot.

He replied immediately.

Havana will never be forgotten.

She retrieved her drink and sat down on the edge of her bed as she eyed the painting and remembered a beautiful night in Havana.

One week later

"I thought you were never going to call."

Naim looked across the table at Greenly, admitting to himself that she looked pretty in a royal blue lace sundress. "I was busy with work but worried if I didn't make the time, your invite would be rescinded."

"Very smart," she said with an arch of her brow.

He chuckled.

Greenly had invited him to her estate in Passion Grove for dinner. The dinner prepared by her chef had been delicious, the wine free-flowing and her company delightful, but he had dreaded the entire night. All he could think of was Marisa and how this woman, beautiful as she may be, was not her.

She rose from her seat and came around the table to massage his broad shoulders as she bent down to whisper in his ear. "I found a new signature perfume today. What do you think?"

He took a whiff. It was sweet and sugary like cotton candy. Not fresh and light.

Like coconuts.

His gut clenched. *Marisa, Marisa, Marisa. She was all over.*

"I have it on everywhere," she added as she lightly bit his lobe and ran her hands down his chest toward his lap.

Naim eased out of his seat and her light embrace, wiping his mouth and stroking his beard with his hand.

"What's wrong? You're so rigid and tense," Greenly said. "Only one part of you should be that stiff."

"I can't do this," he said.

"Why? You don't like a little milk on your chocolate?" she asked, stepping closer to him.

"I'm not over my ex," he admitted to her, holding up both hands.

"Then get under me. I'm quite the horse rider myself," she said.

Naim gave her an incredulous look. "Just how many sexual innuendos do you have inside of that head of yours?" he asked.

"Almost as many as the sexual positions—"

"Aw, man, come on, Greenly, don't be a one-trick

pony," he said, and then closed his eyes at the door he'd just opened.

"That's *too* easy," she mused.

He looked at her and smiled. "And you let it pass," he said in approval.

Greenly bowed.

He chuckled.

"Your ex is a lucky girl, Naim Ansah," she said, walking over to pick up her glass of red wine to sip.

"I didn't say she felt the same," he admitted, clearing his throat.

Greenly eyed him over the rim of the glass. "I'm not ready to be married or locked into a relationship, but one day I will be," she said, drumming her glittered gold nails against the wineglass. "Honestly, I would have sexed you all night and moved on to the next adventure. But…when I find the man I want to be with for the rest of my life, there is absolutely nothing that I won't do—within reason, of course—to make it work."

Her words took him back to his mother's advice.

The older I get, the more I realize that love is worth every sacrifice.

"So, no offense," Greenly said, setting her wineglass down to guide him across the dining room and then the foyer to the front door. "If you're not serving up the goods, I need to call one of my handlers to get the job done."

"Enjoy your night," he said as she reached past him to open the front door.

"And you go figure out how to enjoy your life with your girl," she said as he stepped out onto the sprawling front porch of her Victorian-style mansion.

With that said, she closed the front door.

Naim crossed the courtyard to his McLaren, opening the door to slide down into the seat. His hands gripped and ungripped the wheel as he drove over to Marisa's neighborhood and parked down the street from the home she was renting. The lights were on and her vehicle was in the drive. Inside was the woman he loved, and his child.

Inside was where he wanted to be.

Naim climbed from the car and walked up the tree-lined street to cross the front lawn and jog up the stairs. Once he stood before the door, he raised his hand to knock, but it never landed.

I don't want to love you anymore. I wish we had never tried because my heart is broken, and now I have to figure out how to fix it...

He lowered his hand and his head as he released a heavy breath. He ached for his family, but he had no idea if the bad times would outlast the good when they differed so much. He wasn't looking to fight over every penny he wanted to spend on his child.

Naim turned and retreated, making his way back to his vehicle and then speeding across town into the heart of Passion Grove to his brother and Alessandra's home.

Gia, their maid, evidently alerted to his appearance, already had the front door open when he climbed from his car.

"Good evening, Mr. Ansah," she said as he passed her with a nod of greeting.

"Mr. and Mrs. Ansah are in the downstairs family room," she instructed.

"Thanks."

Long strides took him to them. They were lounging on the massive sectional before the television watching an episode of *Peppa Pig*. Comfortable. At ease.

It was a nice scene.

He leaned in the doorway, hesitant to interrupt it.

Aliyah turned suddenly and caught sight of him. Her face lit up and his heart turned to melted butter. "Uncle Naim," she said, forgetting *Peppa Pig* to come running at him full speed.

He caught her and tossed her up in the air to catch her and press kisses to her cheek.

"Were you at Marisa's? How's the baby?" Alessandra asked, using the tablet to mute the volume on the television.

"No, I came to talk to Alek about something," he said, setting his niece down.

"Peppa, Mama," she said, tapping Alessandra's knee.

Alek rose. "Let's go in the office," he said, walking over to him.

They left the room as the sounds of *Peppa Pig* reclaimed the space.

"What's up?" Alek asked.

"I was on a date with Greenly—"

"The redhead?" he asked as they walked into the office.

"Yes."

Alek looked surprised before glancing at his watch. "And now you're *here*? It's so early."

Naim chuckled. "That's the thing. I turned her down," he said, taking one of the seats alongside his and Alessandra's desks that sat facing each other.

"Really?" he said in disbelief.

"I can't think of anyone but Marisa," he said. "I love her. As much as she frustrates me, I miss her."

Alek nodded. "It was like that for me with Alessandra. I started a war with her but I couldn't stop thinking of how much better it would be to just be with her. Have fun with her. Make love to her. Build a life together."

Naim shifted in his seat. "But we broke up because I started a trust fund for Kwesi," he said.

Alek look surprised again.

"Well…after I told her I wouldn't," he added.

Alek's face filled with understanding.

"I'm not supposed to secure the future of my son and give him an opportunity a lot of people in this country who look like us don't have?" Naim exclaimed. "And it would make more sense if she didn't have a trust fund of her own."

"That she hasn't used in two years," Alek reminded him. "It wouldn't be my choice, but I get what she's trying to prove to herself and to her family."

"But it comes down to parenting skills, not money. As if every parent without money is perfect. As if every parent with money raises horrible children. It doesn't correlate," he said with fire and passion as he waved his hand dismissively in the air.

"You ever explained that to her, or just dismissed her belief as foolish without searching for a middle ground?"

Naim clenched his jaw. "No, but—"

Alek eyed him before reaching into the desktop humidor Naim had gifted him to remove two cigars, the guillotine and lighter. He then walked to the large multileveled bar and poured two glasses of bourbon on the rocks. Back at the desk, he set a drink and a cigar before his brother. "You're going to need this," he said, reclaiming his seat and preparing his cigar before passing the tools over to him.

"Why do I feel as if I'm not going to like what you say?" Naim asked.

"Because you're not," Alek assured him.

Naim looked cautious.

"Remember that conversation we had about knowing when you're at fault?" Alek asked, holding the cigar lightly clenched between his teeth.

Naim took several draws on the cigar to make sure the tightly rolled tobacco was evenly lit. "I'm not at fault at all."

"Impossible."

Naim scowled.

"What do you want?"

Naim thought of himself sitting outside Marisa's house and longing to be inside. "My family. I want my family. I want what you have. I want to sit on a sofa and watch my kid watch cartoons and be able to walk in his room whenever I want and kiss his head. And see her wake up in the morning. And be with her every night. And to make more babies. I want all of that with her and Kwesi. They're my family," he stressed, realizing how very real his longings were.

"What's keeping you from being with your family?" Alek asked as he leaned back in his chair and crossed his right ankle over his left knee.

"She—"

"Nah," Alek interjected with a shake of his head.

"Fine. *I* never once even tried to see her point of view. I just figured she would get over it," he admitted.

"And?"

"I thought I wasn't ready to settle down, but now I know I'm not ready to let her go," he admitted. "The thought of her with someone else drives me crazy."

Alek chuckled. "Been there."

"She told me she had plans one night when she was dropping the baby off to me," Naim said. "Man, that night I bundled up my son and drove all the way from Brooklyn to drive by her house to have some relief that she was home alone."

"Oh, you are all the way *gone.*"

"I know," he said.

They chuckled.

"So much so that you would move into that house on the other side of town to be with her?" Alek asked.

"Forever?" Naim asked.

Alek shrugged.

Naim wiped his face with his hands, then set his cigar in the ashtray before resting his elbows on his knees as he looked down at the Persian rug covering the polished wood floors. "Okay, so I *am* a little bit billionaire bougie," he admitted.

Alek laughed.

Naim tried to keep from joining him. He failed.

"You love her?" Alek asked when their laughter finally subsided.

Naim nodded. "I have since before I even knew I did," he admitted, looking his brother in the eye.

"Does she love you?"

He held up his hands. "She said she wanted to figure how to not love me anymore," he said, the pain of hurt and regret tightening his throat.

"Lucky for you, little brother, love doesn't fade that easily," Alek said.

The office door opened and Alessandra strode in.

She eyed her husband and then her brother-in-law. "Sometimes the best advice is a woman's advice, Naim. We can do and think and say everything a man can," she said, reaching into the humidor for a cigar of her own and then skillfully prepping it step by step before she drew in a mouthful of smoke, savored the aroma and then exhaled the silver smoke slowly before turning and leaving the room.

Alek rose and put out his cigar. "You good, Naim? Because my wife smoking that cigar just gave me a lot of ideas," he said with a wiggle of his eyebrows.

"I'm good," he said, nudging his head toward the door that Alessandra had left wide open—figuratively and literally.

With one last squeeze of his shoulder in encouragement, Alek left Naim alone. He sat back in his seat and enjoyed his Cuban cigar as he debated just what he was willing to sacrifice to have Marisa in his life once and for all.

Chapter 10

Marisa carried her cup of coffee from behind the counter of *La Boulangerie* to the table where Bill sat with his sneakered feet up on a nearby chair. The bakery had long since closed, and the kitchen was spotless. They remained behind talking about her dilemma. "Am I crazy, Bill?" she asked as she claimed her own seat.

"I get it, Marisa. I do, but I think the discipline you've shown in your own life for the last two years is proof that you will do right by your kid," he said, tearing off a piece of buttery croissant to chew. "And hell, you've had an example of what you don't want to do, so you know not to repeat the mistakes your mom made."

Marisa sipped from her coffee.

"And you want to know what else?" Bill said, placing his feet on the floor to lean toward her. "You forgive your mother because that is what a lot of your issues with money are about."

"I don't agree with that," she said with a shake of her head.

"You're a parent now, and you are not going to be perfect at it," Bill said, leaning back and kicking his feet up again on the seat. "The last thing you will want is for Kwesi to grow up and hold a grudge against you because of a wrong move or three. Hell, or a hundred. It's life. Parents mess up. There is no such thing as a perfect parent, Marisa."

"I *love* my mother," she stressed, and then winced when she realized it sounded like she was trying to convince herself more than Bill.

"And you should because you didn't turn out bad. So stop living like you are still struggling to find your way. You did it. You're not the screwup anymore. You turned your life around. You're a talented chocolatier with a thriving business, a mother with a *really* cute kid, and you're in love with a great guy."

She looked over at him at the last part.

"Tell me, why are you still punishing yourself?" Bill asked before tossing another piece of croissant into his mouth.

Marisa picked up the rest of his croissant and bit it in half. "I didn't realize that's what I was doing," she admitted around the mouthful—completely against the etiquette training of her youth.

"Since we're on a roll, I have one final observation," he said, rising to carry his trash to the large garbage can by the exit.

"Just go ahead, Mr. Iyanla," she drawled, although she was interested in his viewpoint.

"If *Décadence de Chocolat* becomes the next Hershey's thirty years from now, would you want Kwesi to choose to have nothing to do with it?" Bill asked, opening the door to the bakery.

The very idea of that made her frown as she finished her coffee and tossed away her cup before exiting the building in front of him.

"A legacy is nothing to take lightly," Bill said, turning off the lights and locking the door.

One week later

From the rear of the meeting room, Naim looked on as Alek and Alessandra stood at the podium to the thunderous applause of ADG's shareholders at the annual general meeting. His spearheading of the Australian streaming service had been one of the major focal points of their discussion on moving ADG forward. The co-CEOs also informed the shareholders of their increase in revenue, with a projection for more than 10 percent growth in the upcoming quarter. As they shook the hands of the newly elected board members, he beamed with pride, knowing both Frances Dalmount and their father, Kwame Ansah, were proud.

"Congratulations."

He looked back over his shoulder at his sister standing behind him. "Thanks, Samira."

"I'm ready for more responsibility at ADG," she said, wrapping her arm through his. "It's time to prove myself."

"I believe you," Naim said. "You have a project in mind?"

"Not yet," she said. "But I'm sitting on go. Okay?"

He chuckled. "Okay," he agreed.

"How's my nephew?" she asked.

"I'm picking him up for the weekend after work," Naim said, smiling at his sister.

"Then I'm staying with you all weekend so I can love on him," she said.

"Like you did the last time I had him for the whole weekend," he reminded her good-naturedly, because he loved how much his siblings loved their nephew. He felt the same devotion to Aliyah.

"I can't wait to have one of my own," she said with a sigh.

"Mrs. Corporate America?" Naim teased, look-ing on as the crowd of people began to leave the meeting room, which was on the first floor of the ADG building.

Samira gave him a look.

"I know. I know. A woman can have it all," he

said, having heard her dreams for a career and family before.

"Look at Alessandra…and Marisa, for that matter," she said.

He thought of the mother of his child. After speaking with his brother the night after his date with Greenly, he had decided to give himself more time to see if his love would fade. He wanted to be sure because he knew a relationship with Marisa would mean plenty of sacrifices and vowing to be with her—and only her—forever.

He also needed to know Marisa wanted a forever with him, as well, and he wasn't sure about that or if she would ever make concessions for him. That was just as important. The give and the take.

Alessandra and Alek walked up to them.

"Good job," he told them both, extending his hand for a shake.

They both accepted it.

Samira extended her hand, as well, for them to shake. "Dad and Frances would be proud of both of you," she said, her English accent less pronounced than her brothers'.

"How about lunch?" Alek asked, reaching into the front pocket of his suit for his phone. "I can get a table at Butter."

Bzzzzzz. Bzzzzzz. Bzzzzzz.

Naim reached for his own phone and looked down at the screen. It was Marisa. His gut clenched. She rarely called him. "I have to take this," he said, walking away from them to answer. "Hello."

"Naim. Hi. I know you're picking up Kwesi today, and I wondered if I could speak to you about something before you go?" she asked, her voice sounding hesitant.

"Is something wrong?" he asked, his curiosity piqued and his heart still pounding.

"It's nothing about the baby," Marisa rushed to assure him.

"Okay, see you tonight," he said.

"Thanks. Bye."

As he slid the phone back into his pocket, he forced himself not to let hope bloom. Marisa was a wild card. Always had been and always would be.

Marisa smiled as she looked at her mother loving on her grandchild. She was forever amazed that she was willing to put aside concern for her beloved Chanel clothing and perfect makeup for Kwesi. She couldn't care less about a little dribble and throw-up as long as he smiled up at her.

"You surprised me today, bringing him to see me," Brunela said, looking over at her in the flower-filled sunroom of her home in Passion Grove.

"This is Naim's weekend, and I've been working fewer hours at La Boulangerie, so I decided to bring him to see his grandmother before his father picks him up later," Marisa explained, surprised at how nervous she felt about that. "And I wanted to talk to you."

"Oh? What about?" she asked.

Marisa rose from the club chair to come over and sit next to where her mother relaxed with the baby on a chaise lounge. "I never apologized to you for all the gray hairs I caused because you worried about me," she began.

Brunela's eyes filled with surprise. "You don't owe me any apologies—"

She gave her a chastising look.

"All I ever wanted was for you to be *happy*," Brunela stressed, reaching with her free hand to cup her chin. "Especially with your father passing on."

Marisa released a shaky breath. "In hindsight, what I needed was for you to be firm. To say no. To draw a line in the sand, because I took advantage of it. I was a spoiled, entitled brat," she said. "Can you admit that, Momma?"

Brunela looked down at the baby and then back up at her with tears in her eyes, making them appear glassy. "No," she said with a sad smile. "I will not."

Marisa sighed. "I'm grown and I'm in a better place because I've been honest with myself, and people have been honest with me. I need that from you, too," she said. "Parenting never stops, and I'm giving you the chance to help keep my head on straight. I'm not saying we will always agree, but I want to value your opinion. I want to know we're not dealing in platitudes."

Brunela eyed her with clear doubt.

"The only thing you ever objected to was my working. Where's *that* Brunela Dalmount-Martinez?" Marisa asked. "Momma, was I a spoiled brat?"

Brunela squeezed her eyes shut. "Yes," she said in a rushed whisper.

Marisa smiled. "And I'm still alive," she said.

"I should have been tougher on you, Marisa," she admitted. "When you were a baby, you would scream for what seemed like hours on end and your father would come right along after work and pick you up, and all seemed right in your world as long as you were in his arms. And then he died and I didn't know how to give you that same comfort he did. I was lost, and I can admit I went down the wrong path with you."

She reached for her mother's hand and squeezed it. "You did the best you could," she said. "And I forgive you."

Brunela patted her updo. "Beneath this dye, you caused many a gray hair. I forgive you and I'm thankful those rough days are behind us," she said.

They fell into a comfortable silence.

"You do know they say the trouble you gave your parents will come back on you through your child?" Brunela asked.

"Oh, Lord, I hope not," she prayed, covering her face with her hands.

Naim parked his SUV next to hers on the driveway before exiting it and making his way up the steps onto her front porch. Summer was thick in the air, and the heat was just beginning to lower a little as the sun went down, so he was happy to be without his tie and suit jacket.

The door opened before he could knock, and his eyes took in Marisa from head to toe. She looked beautiful and carefree in a red cotton sundress with her hair loose and her feet bare. He wanted to kiss her. "Hey, Marisa," he said instead.

"Hey. Come in."

When he walked past her, the scent of coconuts taunted him. He wanted to hold her.

"Kwesi is in his swing," she said, moving past him to lead him into the living area.

His eyes dropped down to the back and forth motion of her buttocks in the dress. He wanted to make love to her.

Naim turned his attention to his son, bending down before him. "There's Daddy's boy," he said.

Kwesi's eyes lit up and he kicked his feet.

"Naim."

He looked back over his shoulder. Marisa was sitting on the sofa with one knee bent and her foot pressed down into the cushion. Although her dress still covered her, he couldn't help the erotic thoughts the position brought to mind. *Is she messing with me? Does she want this to work? Because she can absolutely get it.*

Rising, Naim sat on the opposite end of the couch. "So, what's up?"

"I have an idea to expand my business by focusing on selling my chocolate," she began before explaining her idea to him as she had to Alessandra.

He listened, but his disappointment was clear. This was about business. Nothing more. "The chocolate is really good," he admitted. "That's your key selling point. That and your unit pricing."

"I know you were the head of marketing before your promotion," she said. "And I wondered if you could help me figure out the best approach to reach out to possible customers for the chocolate."

"I can help you with some ideas," he said.

Marisa smiled. "Thank you. I would *really* appreciate that," she said. "Especially with things the way that they are."

Naim eyed her. He started to say, *Barely better than hostile?* But he refrained. Shaking his head, he wiped his hand over his mouth and beard. "Um, you're going to need to allocate a good sum of money to be effective. Especially with hiring a quality publicist."

"I've decided to use my trust fund money to back my business," Marisa said, almost bashful. "My uncle Frances would want that in honor of his legacy."

And with her smile, her shyness over her own wealth and her willingness to change, he wanted to love her forever.

But what does she want?

"Actually, if you're not in a rush I took some

steaks out to grill and made a salad for dinner," she said, rising to her feet.

He looked up at her. "To talk about your business?" he asked.

"No," she said simply. "It's just time to get along. Right?"

Naim continued to stare up at her. "Okay," he agreed, rising, as well. "I'll grill the meat if you want."

She nodded and walked around the sofa and into the kitchen. "I got New York strips," she told him, reaching for a plate from the fridge.

Naim washed his hands and dried them with a paper towel before taking the plate from her and removing the plastic wrap. "These look good," he said, feeling awkward and out of place in her home.

"I'm starving," she stressed, pulling tongs from the drawer to mix the salad in a large wooden bowl.

"Won't be long."

Naim made his way out the patio doors to her gas grill. Once he turned it on and placed the steaks on the rack, he looked back over his shoulder through the glass door at Marisa moving about the kitchen. She picked up her phone, and moments later the sounds of Latin music filled the air.

She's messing with me. She has got to be messing with me.

He turned back to the grill to flip the meat with a spatula to keep from piercing it with a fork and releasing the juices too soon.

The door opened, and she stepped out onto the patio carrying two plates and the bowl of salad. "I thought we could eat out here," she said, setting everything down on the patio table before going back in the house.

When they were medium-well, he slid a steak onto each plate. She returned with cutlery wrapped in linen napkins, the baby monitor and a glass of sparkling water for herself and Scotch for him. "Kwesi fell asleep in his swing so I laid him down until you're ready to go," she said, handing him his drink.

Her fingers stroked his as he took it, and his gut clenched from such an innocent touch.

I don't ever want to go.

"That was good," Marisa said, taking a sip of her drink as she looked across the table at Naim.

His eyes locked with hers. That all too familiar current passed between them.

"The perfect summer dinner," he said.

"For a perfect summer night," she finished.

He nodded in agreement before taking a sip of his drink.

"This is so awkward," Marisa said, setting the glass down on the table. Some sloshed over the side.

"Yes, it is," he agreed, shifting in his seat.

Come on, Marisa. Get it together.

"If you want, I can go," Naim offered.

She closed her eyes as he stood up and walked past her to reach the patio door.

"I tried, Naim," she said. "I tried not to love you."

He paused.

She opened her eyes and turned in the seat, taking in his strong physique. "Naim," she said.

He turned to her.

Their eyes locked.

"I love you," Marisa admitted, hearing the pounding of her heart in her ears as she spoke to the emotion nearly bursting inside of her.

Naim stepped close to the chair and reached to stroke her cheek with his thumb as he smiled a little.

"Truth," she stated, rising from the chair and pushing it out of her way. It tumbled onto its side.

"Always."

Marisa smelled his warm cologne and inhaled it. "You said you would always love me. Do you?"

"Always," Naim promised, holding her face with his hands. "I never stopped."

Marisa brought her hands up to grip his wrists as she let her head fall back. She pursed her lips and relieved some of the pressure.

With a chuckle from low in his throat, Naim bent to press kisses along her neck. "I have missed you," he moaned.

"I tried not to miss you," she said. "Tried and failed."

"I want you in my life, Marisa. If that means living a more humble lifestyle, then fine. I'll do it—hell, I'll buy this house for us," he confessed.

"You'd do that for me?" she asked, overwhelmed by the gesture.

"I need you," he told her fiercely. "I love the hell out of you."

She shivered as she took his hand and led him inside the house to the sofa. She spun, and the skirt of her dress rose up like a parasol, revealing she wore no panties. She bit her bottom lip as she looked down at the fire lit in his eyes. "I decided today to have you in every way possible," she admitted softly as she eased the straps down her shoulders and undid the side zip so that the dress fell to a red puddle around her feet. "To feed you. To sex you. To love you."

Naim eyed her body as if saving it to memory, missing nothing as he released a shaky breath and reached to pull her forward by her thighs. He pressed a kiss to the cleanly shaved V at the top of her legs before lightly biting the plump flesh between his teeth as he deeply massaged her buttocks.

She felt her eyes glaze over as she tilted her head to the side and watched him adore her body. "Like the first night, huh?" she asked, her voice thick with desire.

"Damn right," Naim said before he used his tongue to split the lips and stroke her bud.

She cried out.

He lifted one of her legs onto his broad shoulder and tilted his head to suckle more of the fleshy bud into his mouth.

"Naim," she gasped, gripping the back of his head with both her hands.

Flickers of his tongue with the speed of wings pushed her to the edge, until she dropped her leg and backed away from the pleasure as she trembled like a leaf in the wind.

Naim undid his belt and unzipped his pants, raising his hips to work them and his boxers down past his knees. He eyed her as he stroked the length of his hardness. "You missed this, too?" he asked.

One step forward and a drop to her knees between his open legs, and his hardness was in her mouth. It was his turn to try to retreat as she focused her attention on the smooth chocolate tip until she felt his thighs tremble and his gut clench as he hit high notes she worried would wake the baby. Only then did she rise and straddle his hips to ease her wet and hot core down onto his hard and long curving length, until she fit him inside her completely with a whimper. She had to adjust to the feel of him. The hardness. The heat.

She ached. Her nipples were hard. Her pulse sped.

"It's been so long," Marisa gasped, raising her arms high above her head as she finally began to rotate her hips with the skill of a belly dancer.

He watched her move as if hypnotized, and it egged her on and pushed her to do more.

"Did you miss *this*?" she asked with a hot lick of her lips.

"Damn," Naim swore, wrapping an arm around

her waist to jerk her body close and suck one taut brown nipple into his mouth as she continued her ride.

"I'm coming," she gasped, closing her eyes and flinging her head back as he sucked wildly at her nipples as explosions went off deep in her core and sent her on a high.

"Don't stop. Don't stop. I'm coming with you," he whispered just a second before he roughly cried out and filled her with seed as he rocked his hips in countermotion to hers, sending his inches deeper inside her.

They rode the addictive waves and white-hot spasms together, their moans echoing in the air around them. Their bodies were coated with fine sheens of sweat. Both had been relentless, until they were spent.

She stayed atop him with her head on the back of the chair above his shoulder as he massaged the small of her back. She could feel his heart beneath her go from pounding and fast to slow and steady as they both regained control of their bodies.

Marisa kissed his neck. "You think we should take things slow?" she asked, hating the fear that returned to her.

Naim shook his head. "I don't want to spend another night under a different roof from you and our son," he insisted. "We've had more than a year of back and forth. What more time do we need?"

"Forever and a day," she said without hesitation or thought. An instinct.

"Are you ready for that?"

"I am," she swore, lifting up to taste his mouth and loving when he deepened the kiss with a moan.

The baby's shrill cry echoed through the monitor.

They broke their kiss with a laugh. "Looks like the reunion will have to wait a little longer," Marisa said, rising to her feet and bending over to retrieve her dress.

Naim slapped her buttocks. "That's fine. We have forever."

"And a day," Marisa added softly.

Epilogue

One month later

Marisa was filled with peace, happiness and an abundance of love as she walked down the rose-petal-covered aisle. From behind her sheer tulle veil, with the glass-enclosed candles lighting her path, she eyed Naim holding Kwesi in his arms. Both were dressed in tailored tuxedos. Her future husband and his little best man. Two of the greatest loves of her life.

The soloist sang a beautiful rendition of John Legend's *All of Me*. Their family and close friends lined the pews. The decor was resplendent and the scent of the floral arrangements heavy in the air.

My wedding day.

Marisa stroked the photo broach of her father pinned to her elaborate Swarovski diamond bouquet. She'd like to think he was there with her in spirit, walking her down the aisle to her happily-ever-after. It's why she hadn't asked anyone to fill his place. And so, with her old photo of her father, her new diamond earrings from Naim, her borrowed diamond bracelet from her mother, her dark blue lace thong that Naim would enjoy removing later and an actual lucky sixpence beneath the sole of her satin Manolo Blahnik heels, Marisa reached the altar as the soloists ended the song and claimed her seat.

As they practiced the night before, he handed her their son while he held the edge of her veil with both hands before lifting it back to reveal her face.

"You look so beautiful," Naim whispered to her.

Marisa's heart swelled with pleasure. "Thank you," she said as he took Kwesi back into his arms. "And you both look handsome."

"I want to kiss you," he admitted.

The minister, Reverend McDonell, leaned toward them. "Not until my say-so," he said, his tone amused.

The attendees laughed.

Naim looked bashful.

Marisa loved him all the more.

He extended his free hand to her and she took it, loving the feel of his warm grasp as they turned to face the minister of the church.

Throughout the entire ceremony, as they exchanged vows and rings before saying "I do," Marisa was overwhelmed by the love she had for Naim and the love she knew he had for her.

What a journey.

Their love was slow to be accepted by them both, but once they decided to wed, they wasted no time planning their nuptials. After a brief honeymoon to Ghana, they would return to the estate they'd purchased together in Passion Grove—large enough but not too sizable to feel like a compound. A compromise.

Love was always worth the sacrifice.

"Now if everyone will come forward and gather around the altar to surround the couple with your love and hope for them to have a blessed union," Reverend McDonell requested, his voice booming and seeming to echo inside the sanctuary. "Place your hands upon them and repeat after me this wedding prayer."

Marisa and Naim lowered their heads as their loved ones touched them lightly on their arms, shoulders and backs. Their words offering to cover, support, guide and lift them both up during their marriage was profound and touching. Emotions swelled inside her and a tear raced down her cheek as the prayer ended and she looked up into the eyes of her husband.

Naim gently swiped the tear away with his thumb. "I love you," he mouthed.

She nodded. "And I love you," she whispered, smiling as Kwesi loudly cooed.

Everyone chuckled.

She took their son in her arms and pressed kisses to his plump cheek.

"Now by the power vested in me I pronounce you husband and wife," Reverend McDonell proclaimed, his voice bursting with joy.

Naim looked to him.

Reverend McDonell gave him a wink. "Kiss your bride," he said.

Naim wrapped his arm around Marisa's waist, pulling her and his son closer to him, as he used his free hand to tilt her chin up. "My wife," he whispered against her mouth just before he kissed her.

Marisa closed her eyes and returned his kisses, thankful for her happily-ever-after.

* * * * *

"I'm glad we could make this happen," she said to Bennett once they were left to the relatively quiet corner of the roof.

"I'm glad you suggested this outing," he said with a smile. "I won't lie, I'm curious as hell why you'd ask me to lunch when you've been dead-set against enduring my company over the last few years."

Not that her reluctance had stopped him from talking to her, she thought.

"Let me at least get some ice water before you start, please," she said as she set her shades on the edge of the table and the slim briefcase at her feet.

"Of course. Forgive my rampant curiosity." The sarcasm sat too well on his beautiful mouth. He took his own dark glasses off and set them beside hers. His obviously designer shades gleamed like platinum next to her plain white-framed ones. Nonetheless, they looked like a pair, a realization that sent an uncomfortable jolt through her system.

Lindsay Evans was born in Jamaica and currently lives in Atlanta, Georgia. She loves good food and romance and would happily travel to the ends of the earth for both. She writes sensual novels and short stories for the romantic in all of us. Find out more at www.lindsayevanswrites.com.

Books by Lindsay Evans

Harlequin Kimani Romance

Pleasure Under the Sun
Sultry Pleasure
Snowy Mountain Nights
Affair of Pleasure
Untamed Love
Bare Pleasures
The Pleasure of His Company
On-Air Passion
Her Perfect Pleasure
The Wrong Fiancé

Visit the Author Profile page
at Harlequin.com for more titles.

IT MUST BE LOVE, OR EVERYTHING

THE WRONG FIANCÉ

Lindsay Evans

To my readers, for everything.

Dear Reader,

The Clarks of Atlanta is one of my favorite families to write about. It's been so much fun writing Devyn Clark and Bennett Randal's story. Devyn's decision-making skills could use some work. She's lost love, money and even trust in herself by putting her faith in the wrong people. Now she's standing at a crossroads, wondering if she should take a chance on Bennett.

I hope you enjoy this story as much as I do. Right now I'm deep into writing the next book in the series— Aisha Clark's novel—and I can't wait for you to read it, too.

Blissful reading and heart-happy days to you now and always.

Lindsay

Chapter 1

Some men just couldn't be trusted.

Devyn lifted the champagne glass to her lips and watched Bennett Randal prowl across the art gallery. In the heat of a Georgia summer, he looked elegant and completely comfortable in a three-piece suit. He smiled at nearly everyone he met, shaking hands and dipping his head low to pay absolute attention to each person he stopped to speak with.

Although she hated to admit it, he was everything she thought a man should be. Confident, kind and unquestionably brilliant. Leilani's Pearls, a company founded by Bennett's parents, was a breakthrough beauty enterprise that had been floundering on the brink of bankruptcy when Bennett pulled himself from his playboy lifestyle long enough to drag it into modern times and send profits soaring. His Ivy League business degree was definitely not being wasted.

Even while saving the family company, Bennett always found time to play, though. He'd been engaged to her good friend Adah for years but cheated on her constantly. Now the engagement was broken. His former fiancée was married to someone else and he was single. And very happily so.

Dev wrinkled her nose. Well, *happily*, was probably a bit of a stretch.

Since word of the broken engagement had filtered through to Atlanta's gossip mill, Bennett had been everywhere. Even more than before. He turned up in the most random places. Devyn had seen him at poetry readings, a wedding, even an exhibition game where her brother had played charity ball with other retired pro basketball players. And every single time Bennett had managed to come over and say something ridiculous to her before drifting off to bother somebody else.

"You should stop staring at him or people will get the wrong idea." Her sister, Aisha, came out of nowhere and leaned into Dev with a sharp grin. The fruity cocktail Aisha sipped on had turned her lips an interesting shade of green.

"He's a pig," Devyn said automatically. Her defense mechanism when she caught herself thinking anything charitable about the Randal heir.

"I think you protest too much, sister dear." Aisha

stuck out her green tongue at Dev, then took another sip of her glorified green slushy. The skirt of the pale pink, tulle mini dress she wore fluttered in the artificial breeze of the AC and the half-dozen tiny gold rings on her fingers flashed in the light.

Dev curled her fingers around her cool champagne glass and rolled her eyes. Aisha acted like a complete airhead sometimes, but she was probably the smartest one in the family. She certainly knew all the Clarks inside and out. If it wasn't for her, their brother, Ahmed, probably wouldn't have his wife by his side right now, certainly wouldn't be honeymooning on a boat someplace, the happiest he'd been in years.

"Don't try to psychoanalyze me, Aisha. You know that—"

"Devyn." A sharp voice cut through the rest of her words. Her boss appeared out of the crowded gallery in a wicked click of high heels. Her rounded face and body were breathtakingly beautiful, but that lovely impression was usually blasted all to hell once she opened her mouth. "Shouldn't you be working the crowd and getting them to buy instead of chatting?" Tangie snapped.

Barely left unsaid was how much Dev owed Tangie and her gallery after Dev's recent screw up.

Her stomach twisted at the reminder that was never far from her mind anyway.

Aisha turned around with a storm in her eyes, all the sweetness and sugar instantly gone from her pretty face. "Listen, bi—" But Devyn squeezed her sister's arm. Hard. "It's okay," she said under her breath to Aisha. Her sister switched the look to Devyn. "She doesn't need to talk to you like that."

But she had every right. Devyn had messed up, and messed up big-time. She'd trusted the wrong person. Something she'd never do again.

"It's okay," she repeated. Maybe if she said it enough times it would be true.

Aisha snapped a glare at Tangie and stalked off.

"Protective, isn't she?" her boss sneered, letting Devyn know she didn't consider it an admirable quality. "Does she know what you did?"

At the look she must have seen on Devyn's face, Tangie's red lips twisted. "I didn't think so." She snapped her fingers. "Now, get to work and earn me back that money you lost." Then she spun away and slunk back into the crowd. Her sneer turned into a smile the moment she turned away from Devyn to welcome someone to the gallery.

"Thank you so much for coming," Tangie cooed to a tall man in a tartan suit. "It's good to have you here."

A fist clenched at Dev's side, but she slowly forced herself to relax her fingers, one after the other. Tangie was right. She had work to do tonight and needed to get back to it. Weeks ago, before she messed up, things had been going really well. But now...

Dev heaved a soft sigh. No point in crying over spilled money. She should be grateful for what she still had—a job, for one. Her freedom, for another.

She straightened her spine and pinned a determined smile to her face.

"Now that's a look I recognize." Bennett Randal appeared at her side, happy enough that she wanted to bite the smile off his face. "Whose world are you getting ready to take over now?"

"Bennett." She acknowledged him with a cool nod. "Always a pleasure."

He had the nerve to laugh, with a flash of white teeth and dimples that would've made a lesser woman weak in the knees. "I love how your whole body tells me this encounter of ours is anything *but* a pleasure." His laughter simmered down to a soft chuckle. "Good thing I don't take these things personally."

"Maybe you should," left her mouth before she could think better of it.

"What would be the fun in that?" He turned his head and seemed to take in the whole gallery with one glance, leaving Dev with his hard-jawed profile, full and wickedly curved mouth, high cheekbones and strong neck.

He wore his suit well, a dark blue pinstripe with a yellow tie. The strip of yellow silk had tiny sailboats on it. The suit fit his broad shoulders and athletic shape well. Unlike most of the men who came through Tangie's gallery and Dev's art circles in general, Bennett's entire persona was the perfect marriage of strength, elegance and seductive sensuality.

A devastatingly beautiful man...

The thought came out of nowhere and Devyn had

to bite the inside of her cheek in self-punishment. A man like that didn't need anyone else to say or even think of how gorgeous he was.

She cleared her throat and threw herself back into their subtle verbal brawl. "And you're all about fun, aren't you?"

"Of course," Bennett said easily. He sipped from his nearly empty glass of champagne and she couldn't help but notice how strong and capable his hands looked around the delicate glass. "What else is there to life if it isn't fun?"

Work. Obligations. Trying to be a better person despite always screwing up.

But Devyn said none of these things.

"There's much more to life, Mr. Playboy. But if you're rich enough, you never have to find out."

"Dear Devyn. There *are* other things to do in life." His brows rose high over his silt-colored eyes. "But enjoying what you've been given is more important than making a martyr out of yourself just because it feels like that's what society—or certain people in it—expects of you."

"Martyr?" She stared at him in shock, something about his words making the bottom drop out of her stomach. "That's definitely not what I'm doing."

He hummed a noncommittal answer, the lightest of smiles curving his sensual mouth. "If you're not happy with what you're doing, then look for something that lets you celebrate this beautiful world you've been dropped into."

Devyn opened her mouth, then closed it. She didn't want to think about this. And she certainly didn't want to be challenged by this—this cheater and silver-spoon-fed heir—about how she should live her life.

But what exactly have you been doing? What are you doing now?

The tiny voice at the back of her head was mocking. Her mind ran with the question, following the trail of all the things she'd done for herself lately that didn't involve trying to make up for what she let happen at Tangie's gallery.

"That's what I thought," Bennett murmured. "You should change that. Live a little. Enjoy a lot. Be that girl you were in college, if that's what you want."

That girl you were in college.

No. That girl was gone forever. She'd lost something precious and hadn't been the same since.

Dev wanted to pinch Bennett for daring to bring that girl up. But they didn't have that kind of relationship. He was just the man who'd been engaged to one of her best friends for years. A man she met in college when they were both young and had nothing to do but live. Now they both had different kinds of lives. Ran in different circles. Had different commitments.

"It's not that easy," she said finally.

"It is if you just let it be." He tossed back the last of his champagne and bared his strong neck and the sliding thickness of his Adam's apple to her gaze as he swallowed. "What's holding you back?"

My mistakes, she thought. A woman named Tangie McBride. And another named Miriam Alexander, a woman Dev thought she was helping.

They paraded behind her half-closed eyelids, one after the other. The last one lingered the longest. Damning her for a trusting and naive fool.

"What's holding me back?" She parroted his question with a bitter twist of her mouth. "Things that someone like you can't even imagine."

The look he gave her was piercing, like he was trying to see behind her eyes, read her mind and find out all the secrets she kept hidden from everyone. Including the people who loved her the most.

"My imagination is more complex than you think," he said with a knowing smile.

Damn him. He was so confident, so absolutely sure about the way he lived his life and his place in the world.

"Obviously you think so," Dev said with a dismissive gesture.

"Since you don't believe me, you should test my imagination out for yourself and see." A single eyebrow dipped up and down, a wicked slash above his twinkling eye. "I promise you won't be disappointed."

Promises, promises. If she had a hundred dollars for every time a man said something like that to her only to turn out to be an actual disappointment, she probably wouldn't be in the position she was in now. Devyn shook her head. Plus, no, she wasn't about to flirt with Bennett Randal who was as shameless now as he had been while engaged to Adah.

"I'll pass," she said, and took a pointed step back from him.

"You don't know what you're missing," he murmured with another grin.

"Somehow, I'll manage to live with that unsolved mystery. I know I'll be one of the few women in this town who doesn't know all the…ins and outs of dealing with a man like you."

"Interesting word choice," was all he said, then turned his attention back to the paintings making up the exhibition Tangie had personally curated and was desperate to sell. "Just as interesting as the work here tonight."

A clumsy segue, but she allowed it.

Tangie had themed the work around expats so the pieces were about other cultures as viewed through American eyes. Some of them were beautiful, or *interesting* as Bennett said, but most of it was just commercial, the right combination of landscapes and faceless, beautiful bodies that would appeal to people styling a home for sale, a bank lobby, or something equally generic. None of it was inspired. The beautiful, evocative work the gallery had had in storage and should have been gracing an exhibition was gone. And it was all Devyn's fault.

She swallowed the thick bitterness of her regret. "I take it you've seen better?" she asked, sliding an assessing gaze at Bennett.

"I have better at my house," he said with another glance around the gallery.

"Do you?" She didn't hide her skepticism.

That was one thing Dev hadn't heard about Bennett Randal. Playboy? Yes. Man-whore? Sometimes. Any kind of art collector? Definitely not. There were few things she'd heard about him that were actually good.

Truth be told, when people started talking about the positive things Bennett had done, she tended to tune them out. She didn't want to hear anything about the man who slept around while engaged to Adah and who conveniently got let off the hook when his fiancée broke off their long engagement.

It didn't matter that Adah had married a much more suitable man a short time afterward. Bennett must have been the bad guy in all this. It just made sense.

"Yes. I have much better work in my actual basement. The pieces are mostly from the period of the Harlem Renaissance, an inheritance from one of the great-grands that somehow fell to me." He shrugged like it was no big deal, but his eyes toyed with her, bright and teasing, like he knew the stroke of art lust that zapped her right in the heart. "They've already been authenticated but I want to have at least one more expert look them over before I decide their fate."

If he wasn't lying—and why would he be?—those pieces would be extraordinary to see. Did he have any original Carl Van Vechten photographs? Paintings from the period of Zora Neale Hurston or Langston Hughes?

Devyn mentally wiped the drool from her mouth. "That actually sounds pretty incredible. I know at least a dozen people, including me, who'd love to take even a peek at something like that."

"You would?" A smile toyed with the compelling lines of his mouth.

"Absolutely…"

Just then, she caught Tangie's eye from across the gallery. The woman looked speculatively between Dev and Bennett before she pointedly narrowed her gaze.

Right. Convince people to buy this watered-down stuff because she owed Tangie, and owed her big.

Damn, would she ever find a way out of this stupid mess?

Dev drew a deep breath, ready to tell Bennett she couldn't stand around with him all night talking about nothing. But he spoke first.

"I see you're already done with my company for now," he said with a charming grin, like her reason for leaving him behind was part of some fun game. "We should do this again sometime soon. Maybe in a more intimate setting?"

Was this man really flirting with her?

"I don't think so, Bennett." She put all the ice possible in her voice. "Have a good night."

Dev turned and walked away. With every step, she felt the hot weight of his gaze on her back. Like he was trying to melt her from the outside in.

Chapter 2

"Thanks. Have a good night." Bennett slipped the young, female valet a twenty-dollar bill and got behind the wheel of his silver Mercedes convertible.

The Bluetooth automatically connected with his phone and started playing a song by The Roots he'd been listening to before he got out of the car. Bennett absently tapped the steering wheel along with the music.

Slowly and very carefully, he pulled away from the front doors of The McBride Gallery, navigating between cars still arriving and the constant stream of people walking between the gallery, the gourmet ice-cream shop next door and the other places in the exclusive part of Buckhead he rarely visited.

Once free of the parking lot, he shot out into the evening Atlanta traffic and raced toward the highway. The car's powerful engine growled and sent a ripple of excitement up his spine. The usually dense Atlanta traffic opened up and the sports car darted across two lanes, zooming past vibrant lights of the city and onto the highway. Bennett laughed out loud from the sheer pleasure of the drive.

It was good to let go after feeling like a leashed tiger while talking to Devyn Clark.

Bennett hadn't been in his right mind when he decided to go to the gallery opening. The week or two since his ex-fiancée's wedding had been spent rushing between his usually empty Midtown Atlanta office at Leilani's Pearls and trying not to pursue a certain woman.

His work at the now-thriving beauty-focused corporation was exhilarating, even fun. With the help of celebrity friends and some deft business maneuvers, he managed to save the company from bankruptcy and was now strengthening its position in the global marketplace. After an entire adulthood spent indulging his various appetites, he found managing the family business surprisingly rewarding.

But a long day and part of the night spent in front of the computer had weakened Bennett's willpower, and he'd looked one more time at the small invitation with The McBride Gallery information, the name of their new exhibition and the time the opening began. Dev's name was nowhere on the invitation, but he knew more than he should about what she was up to these days.

And so, he'd showered, gotten ready, driven to the exhibit, handed his keys over to the valet at the gallery and walked in, all while telling himself he was *only* going out to one of his favorite city spots. His heart immediately thumped heavy and hard between his ribs when he saw her across the room.

Devyn Clark.

She was exquisite. Gorgeous in a way that consistently aroused and frustrated him. Confrontational eyes, luscious cheekbones and a soft mouth he'd thought of kissing a thousand times. Her body wasn't bad either.

If he was being honorable, he would ignore those feelings. But he often wasn't, so he didn't.

That neck of hers was bitable and long, leading to sexy clavicles and breasts that were more than a handful. Small waist and a curvaceous backside often covered in business-perfect slacks drew the gaze of just about everyone Dev passed. She was the sexiest woman he'd ever seen.

Every time Bennett saw her, he wanted her. Not just to warm his sheets, but to warm his life. And now that he wasn't tucked away in a strange "engaged but available" status, he realized he could have her if he wanted. Or at least *try* to have her. But she seemed to hate him.

Maybe that was part of the reason he couldn't stop

thinking about Devyn. Or stop wondering why she was so cool to him.

There had to be something he could do to change her hatred for him to at least a mild dislike. People had ended up in bed together with less between them. And he hoped they'd end up together in other ways, too.

The sudden sound of his ringing phone distracted him from his thoughts. He looked at the car's Bluetooth display and smiled.

"Hi there, Mrs. Diallo."

A soft laugh burst from the car's speakers, replacing the music that had been playing moments before. "You better stop calling me that. You know I decided not to change my name." His ex-fiancée, Adah Palmer-Mitchell, sounded giddy with happiness.

"Why not?" he teased. "Is Adah Palmer-Mitchell Diallo too much of a mouthful for you?"

"Don't be such a man." She snorted. "Kingsley and I talked about it and I let him know my name isn't something I'm ready to give up."

He chuckled because she was so easy to get a rise out of. "You know I don't care about things like that, sweet Adah."

She snorted again. "Don't pretend you aren't Mr. Traditional behind all that 'do what feels good to you' vibe you always give off."

Adah was partly right, of course. If he ever got married, he'd hope his wife would want to take his last name, want to be closely identified with him. But he'd respect her decision, no matter what it was.

"Don't you worry about that," he said, quickly dismissing any ideas of his own potential marriage, whenever that happened. "What are you up to anyway? Shouldn't you be frolicking in the waves with your new husband or something?"

"You know full well that I came back from our honeymoon a couple of days ago," she said, and sounded a little sad about it. "Now it's back to work and reality for me and Kingsley."

Adah had taken off two weeks to escape to some island with her new husband. Bennett had heard that Kingsley Diallo was a workaholic so was pleasantly surprised at the relatively long trip they'd done together. Diallo was the CEO of one the biggest privately held cosmetic and beauty companies on this side of the world, and Adah had her own business in Atlanta. Some sort of specialized, early childhood learning facility. It was a business she was restructuring, splitting the early childhood education from specialized tutoring services, leaving the original location for her partner to run while she opened a second one in Miami. She and her husband both worked hard.

"That's the thing about reality, it's always there waiting for you," Bennett murmured. A sign up ahead announced his exit so he downshifted and changed lanes, still whipping between slow-moving cars.

"Tell me about it..." Adah sounded like she was

rolling her eyes. "Before getting back into it, though, I wanted to check in with my Bennett to see what he's up to."

In all the years they'd been engaged, they'd been close, but Bennett had never been "her" anything. Once he made it clear he wasn't going to stand in the way of her love affair with the Diallo CEO, though, they'd become even closer. Adah was a sweet, loving woman and he was happy she found the passion she'd been craving all the years they'd known each other.

"*Your* Bennett is doing just fine, thank you," he said. "I'm actually heading back home now."

"Another sexy, rooftop party with half-naked women?" He could hear the smile in Adah's voice.

"Not quite." He wasn't ready to tell her about Devyn and his fixation on her. At least not yet. The two women were friends and he wasn't quite sure what Adah's response would be if he let on that he was interested in getting the prickly but sexy as hell woman into his bed. "It was something small and low-key. Nothing to raise my blood pressure too high."

"Okay, old man." Adah giggled.

He was only a couple of years older than her but that didn't stop Bennett from being a little sensitive about his age. None of them were getting younger. "I'll old man your little behind…"

"Hey, that's Kingsley's job now," she said, surprising a bark of laughter out of him. His mild and sweet little Adah. How she'd changed, and for the better, too. She was happier, more relaxed, more herself. He didn't realize how much their engagement had stifled her. Not just her actions, but her personality, too. Breaking the engagement their parents had arranged for them in college was the best thing they'd ever done for each other.

"Yes, it is his job now, isn't it?" Bennett mused with a smile. He shifted gears and guided the sleek silver car off the highway.

Adah sighed, just like a woman fresh from her honeymoon. "It absolutely is."

"The two of you looked like you belong together," he said softly, feeling something tug inside his chest. "And you seemed like you were finally content." At the wedding, Adah had been radiant, and her smile was the happiest and freest he'd ever seen it.

"Do you sound envious?" she asked him with surprise in her voice.

Damn, did he?

"It must be because I'm tired," he said.

Thankfully, she didn't press him. They talked about other things for the rest of his drive, then disconnected their call once he pulled into his driveway. As the garage door gently rattled closed behind the car, he found himself thinking about Devyn again, about the way she looked in her gun-metal gray dress, her head held high, and her eyes holding secrets he couldn't even begin to guess at.

Whether it came from dislike or desire, the spark that had always been between them flared to brilliant life whenever they were in the same room, and she was still trying to freeze it into submission. But Bennett could see that she was as helpless to stop it as he was. His skin tingled with electricity whenever she was near. The pupils of her expressive eyes always went wide enough to gobble him up.

No, he wasn't done with Devyn Clark. And he had the feeling she wasn't done with him either. Not by a long shot.

Chapter 3

"I don't know how you can stand to work with that bitch," Aisha snarled, showing off her pretty, white teeth.

She tossed her bright blue handbag onto the floor of Dev's Audi before heavily dropping down into the seat and slamming the door shut.

"Sometimes I don't know either." Dev started the car and waited for her sister to buckle her seat belt. It was well past one in the morning, and she was more than a little tired.

Past her sister's shoulder, Tangie's voluptuous shape moved behind the frosted glass of the gallery's front door, as the gallery owner locked up. Despite the fact that the party had finished at eleven, the last potential buyer only left the gallery an hour before. To Dev's relief, they actually bought something before they walked out, snacking on the last two mini cheesecakes from the dessert bar.

Tangie had asked Dev to stay late. Her boss wanted a rundown of how the day had gone, meaning a tally of how much they'd sold versus their expectations, and the whole time she'd looked at Aisha as if willing her sister to disappear. But Aisha lingered, seemingly ignoring Tangie's pointed comments about her needing to be on her way. And now, they were finally leaving. Dev eased the car out onto the main street.

"You want to get your own gallery, don't you?" Aisha barreled on before Dev could answer. "You should do that and leave that crotchety loon in the dust. You can do this much better than her. She was so pathetically desperate in there. I swear people only bought any of that stuff just to shut her up."

Dev couldn't help but smile at her sister's loyalty, even if what she said wasn't quite true. Tangie had charisma and plenty of charm, necessities for a good salesperson. She just didn't waste any of it on Dev.

"I do want to have my own gallery, Aisha, but it's not that easy." Dev needed a stronger reputation in the art world; she needed money.

"How isn't it? There's plenty of money if you want to rent or buy your own space, set up all the business paperwork and hire some staff."

Dev slid Aisha a look as she guided the car through

the nearly empty streets. "You know that our brother's money isn't actually ours, right?"

Their brother, Ahmed, was a retired pro-basketball player. Pretty much everyone in Atlanta had heard of him. He wisely invested his money, including setting up trusts for both of his siblings, their mother and their cousin Sam. But Dev had worked all her life and didn't feel right touching the money. Besides, Ahmed had done enough when he bought a huge plot of land in one of the best, and also most secluded parts of Atlanta. There, he'd built four houses, one for himself, their mother and each of his sisters.

It wasn't something any of them had asked for; he'd simply done it. With that gift of a house, Dev's biggest expense had immediately disappeared. It didn't hurt that the home Ahmed built for her came with every conceivable thing she'd wanted in a home— granite countertops, a pool and plenty of space for her to grow her flowers.

Ahmed would lend her the money she wanted in a heartbeat, but her pride wouldn't allow it. He'd made that money for himself, not to bail out irresponsible siblings—and an older one at that—who ought to have made wiser choices. She needed money for more than just opening up the gallery she'd dreamed of having since she was a teenager.

Lord, did she need the money.

This was her own mess to clean up, though. She'd made it herself, and she'd do the work of taking care of it. Plus, she didn't want her family to know just how much of a screwup she was.

What a laugh they'd all have if they knew that their capable and responsible older sister was anything but.

"Whatever, Devyn," Aisha muttered, staring out the window at the passing city. "You know Ahmed wouldn't mind lending or outright giving you the money."

"But I would mind."

"Whatever, woman." Aisha made a dismissive motion with a beringed hand.

Younger than Dev by five years, Aisha hadn't known a time when they didn't have money. The Clark children were raised firmly middle class by their college professor parents. Their father had passed eight years ago from a heart attack and, although heartbroken beyond repair, their mother had taken over the role of both parents easily and with grace. The children hadn't wanted for anything, really. But once Ahmed started making real money playing basketball and lavishing it on his family, nothing was out of reach. Not for Aisha.

Private university in Europe? Of course.

A just-released, limited edition sports car? Why not?

Aisha hadn't learned to be conservative with Ahmed's money, at least not the money he freely threw into their bank accounts on a regular basis. Dev had used hers to pay off some foolishly acquired debt and to help out friends, who then disappeared as soon as their financial obligations did. She even spent a couple of stupid years trying to keep up with her much-richer friends.

She knew better now, but was all the poorer for it.

Sometimes it was easy to think that "mistake" was her middle name instead of Michelle.

Dev's Audi pulled up to the secured gate that marked the beginning of their six-acre compound and put in the security code. When the thick metal gates slowly swung open, she eased the car in. Although the small guardhouse was empty, she knew the cameras inside it and on top of the gate were tracking her car as it slowly cruised down the curving road. Her phone rang.

When she answered it, her cousin's low voice filled the car. "Dev."

"Everything is cool, Sam. Aisha and I are on our way back from the gallery and about to turn in for the night."

"Hey, Sammy!" Aisha called out from the passenger seat, waving at the car's console as if Sam could see her.

Sam grunted a greeting back at her. "Glad you guys are back home safe," he rumbled a moment later in his deep voice that sounded like he'd just woken up when the security system alerted him about their approaching car. "Sleep well."

"Thanks, Sam. You, too."

Sam, while not their only cousin, was the one closest to them. Recently returned by honorable discharge from the Army, he was dealing with his PTSD by playing bodyguard for Ahmed. But Ahmed was off in Paris on his honeymoon and didn't require Sam's services at the moment. The men were close, but even Sam could see the line had to be drawn at following Ahmed while he was with his new wife in the most romantic city in the world. Dev just hoped nothing would happen to the couple while they were off traipsing through the land of cheese and wine. Neither man would be able to forgive themselves if it did.

Aisha settled back in her seat. "Sam needs a life, don't you think?"

Dev shrugged. "He'll get one when he's ready."

A few minutes later, the car pulled up to the tree-lined drive of Aisha's yellow house. A pair of golden, feline eyes stared out at them from the upstairs window before disappearing.

Dev hugged her sister good-night. "Thanks again for staying with me at the gallery until closing time."

"No problem," Aisha said after giving Dev a loud, smacking kiss on the cheek. Smiling, Dev playfully pushed her away. "You saved me some Uber cash with this fab door-to-door service." She grabbed her purse and shoes before opening the car door. "Get some rest. I hope you sort out what's been bugging you lately."

"What do you mean?" Dev frowned. Was she allowing her worry to show?

Aisha only rolled her eyes. "Whatever, sister dear. You're not as much of a blank wall as you think. I'll see you later." She slipped out of the car, then firmly closed the door behind her.

Dev waited until Aisha opened her front door and the skinny black cat she laughingly called her life partner wound between her bare legs to peek out into the night. The cat's tail waved, then Aisha did the same. Dev pulled out of the drive and headed for her own house. The path was well lit and the ride short, but it gave her more than enough time to run the evening back through her mind. Tangie's constant bullying. Her own inability to do more than snark back at the woman. Bennett Randal's appearance.

Ugh. What a night.

She pulled the car into the garage, grabbed her purse and made her way into the house without turning on any lights. Maybe a bit of ice cream before bed? The idea tempted her as she passed through the kitchen, long enough to make her pause in front of the fridge. Just as her hand moved toward the freezer door to open it, her cell phone rang.

Saved by the bell.

Then she saw who was calling. Tangie. Okay, definitely not saved then.

"Hello?"

"I just found out some interesting news," Tangie said. The gloating in her voice immediately put Dev on guard.

"Did you?" Dev mentally sighed and walked away from the fridge, heading through the house and upstairs to her second-floor bedroom.

"I certainly did." Then Tangie paused like she was waiting for Dev to ask another question. When Dev didn't respond, Tangie made a noise of irritation. "I want you to come in tomorrow."

Dev frowned. They'd already agreed that was going to be her day off. "Why? What's going on?"

"I just figured out a way you can redeem yourself with the gallery—and me."

What, indentured servitude? Dev thought, but waited impatiently for the rest.

"But I'd rather tell you in person," Tangie continued.

Dev cursed under her breath. "What time?"

"Around ten or so, nothing too early."

How generous, she thought with a twist of her mouth. She waited for Tangie to share the "interesting news" she'd opened the call with, but when the woman didn't offer anything else, Dev knew she'd get it the next day and not before.

"All right. I'll be there."

She disconnected the call after getting the barest acknowledgment from Tangie. In her bedroom, she put her phone to charge and, despite her exhaustion, took a cool shower to wash away any remnants of the day from her skin. Too bad, it wasn't that easy to wash it from her mind.

With both Tangie and Bennett Randal on her mind, it took her hours to fall asleep.

Morning sunlight found Dev groggy and irritable. But after a quick shower, nearly an entire pot of Jamaican Blue Mountain coffee, and the daily call with her mother and sister, she felt ready to face whatever Tangie had to throw at her.

Her key to the back door of the gallery easily turned in the lock. "Good morning, Tangie," she called out, closing and locking the door behind her.

It wasn't quite ten o'clock yet, but she wanted to get this thing, whatever it was, over and done with so she could carry on with her day off. Some of Monet's *Water Lilies* were visiting the Lowe Museum and she wanted to take the afternoon to sit with them.

Despite her museum plans, she wore her favorite power outfit, a beige pants suit with blood-red pumps and a red bow at the neck of the white blouse underneath. The gallery, scheduled to open for business at eleven, was still quiet, and she followed the sound of a single voice, Tangie on the phone, to the office next to her own.

Tangie had a folder open on her desk and seemed to be arranging an appointment with a potential buyer for one of the pieces currently on display. Dev took the chair in front of Tangie's desk and crossed her legs, waiting patiently for the conversation to finish.

As her boss talked way more than she needed to, Dev's eyes wandered to the piece on the wall behind Tangie, a mediocre image of a catamaran at sea. Sunlight glimmered on the water rendered in beautiful shades of blue while the boat sailed, majestic and purposeful, toward a strip of land barely visible on the horizon.

The image made her think of Bennett and the solo boat trip around the world that he took a few years ago. She didn't remember how she'd found out about it, from Adah maybe. Another one of Bennett's wild ideas that was supposed to save him from boredom. Inexplicably, worry had dug its claws into her when she found out.

What if he fell overboard and got eaten by sharks? Ran out of fuel?

Storms were unpredictable, especially at sea. One could sneak up on him, toss the boat around like a toy, then drag it down to the bottom of the rough sea never to be seen again. Those thoughts had driven Dev crazy for the entire time he was gone.

Adah, on the other hand, had been very much un-bothered by her fiancé's adventure.

"That's just Bennett," she'd said, laughing. "He'll come back with stories about the mermaids he se-duced on his way there."

Sure enough, Bennett had been just fine. He came home the conquering hero with stories only he could tell. His journey may have even broken some sort of record. But Dev hated that she'd worried about him so much. How could Adah stand to see a man she loved do such dangerous things and not pull her hair out every time?

"Did you hear what I said?"

Dev twitched at the sound of Tangie's raised voice. The other woman was off the phone and had apparently said something she didn't catch.

"No, actually. I didn't." Dev refocused on her boss. "Can you repeat that, please?"

A huff of frustration left Tangie's beige painted lips, and her eyes sharpened with a hint of malice. "I *said*, I know about Bennett Randal's Harlem Renaissance art collection. Someone heard him talking about it last night."

Damn these people... Dev wanted to shake her head but just barely stopped herself. The eavesdropper might be Tangie for all she knew.

She nodded. "He mentioned the collection to me in passing, yes."

"I'm not surprised." Tangie's eyes glittered with a familiar desire. She was on the hunt for art she just had to have. "Which is why I think you should be the one to convince him to sell the collection through the gallery."

Tangie's words stunned Dev into complete stillness. "Through *this* gallery?"

"Of course. Where else?" Tangie snapped. "It's obvious you have a personal connection to him. I suspected something was going on between the two of you, but I wasn't a hundred percent sure until I saw you two together last night. You looked very *cozy*." She made "cozy" sound like they'd been caught screwing in the middle of the gallery among the canapés. "Use whatever you have to get his collection to my gallery. Otherwise I can't guarantee how long your little mess-up will stay hidden."

Blackmail. That's what this was. The thought reverberated through her mind along with her shock. She'd known her boss was upset with her, and that she had work to do to mend that relationship. She'd not figured on Tangie actually using her screwup to get something out of her. Especially something like this.

"You've got to be joking."

It still nagged at Dev that Tangie had never reported to the cops or the insurance company that so much art had "disappeared" from the gallery weeks ago. Tangie had told her she was "protecting" Dev, keeping her bungling from the press and the authorities, but sometimes Dev wondered if that were entirely true. She didn't have time to solve that puzzle, though, with everything else she had to worry about.

"—and you know that means I can't guarantee you have any sort of future here or in the art world," Tangie continued like Dev hadn't said a word.

Dev's thoughts stuttered. Wait. What was Tangie implying here? She clenched her jaw and forced the useless questions to a halt. "I know I made a big mistake but that's no reason for you to make threats." Maybe it would be better if this were taken to the authorities, she thought. Just get it all out in the open and over with.

The other woman drew herself to her full height of five feet nothing, like she was trying to loom over Dev's much-taller frame. "To say you made a mistake is putting it lightly and you damn well know it."

Yes, Dev knew it all too well. She'd trusted someone who'd betrayed her, and artwork went missing as a result. Tangie had made it clear that Dev could be implicated in the loss as an accomplice. Dev also knew the power Tangie wielded in the art world. The thought of what the other woman could do to her budding career in Atlanta and nearly everywhere else in the United States sent a shiver up her spine. She didn't back down, though.

"Ask me to do something else," she said. "Bennett and I may know each other, but that doesn't mean I'll have sex with him to get you what you want."

"Let me be clear so you won't misunderstand me." Tangie braced her palms against the top of the desk and leaned into Dev's space. "I don't care what it takes. I'm not interested in your sex life, or even if you have one. But this is not a request. Get this done and you're free and clear. No more debt to me. Don't do it, and you're finished. No more career."

The threat throbbed between them loud and clear.

Dev bit the inside of her cheek so hard it bled. Her hands clenched and released in her lap.

All the while, Tangie loomed over her, unmoving. Finally, Dev swallowed her anger. All the bad decisions she'd made had led her to this moment. Unfaithful college boyfriends. The man she almost married but wised up about a few weeks before the wedding that would have ruined both their lives. It was no wonder she was in this predicament. She had a history of bad choices.

She had no other option now.

"I'll do this," she said. "But after Bennett signs on

the dotted line with you, you and I are done working together. You'll make me do penance for this for the rest of my life if I let you."

Tangie sat back down in her chair, an ugly look of triumph on her face. "That doesn't seem unreasonable to me. Spending the rest of your life making up for your—"

"Just stop," Dev hissed. She'd had enough. "Stop right now. All you have to do is tell me we'll be even after this. There's no use getting personal." Or more vindictive.

Tangie's hazel eyes were unforgiving. "Yes, we'll be close enough to even after that," she said. "Just get Bennett Randal's collection here."

Bennett Randal.

After all these years she'd spent avoiding the man, now she was being forced to actually seek him out. To ask him for something. And to confront that looming thing between them that she'd never wanted to.

Dev kept her back straight, her face calm, but she felt like she was in a daze. Everything around her was hazy, covered in a fog. All the colors muted, the sound in her world turned all the way down.

She was really going to have to do this.

God knows she didn't want to, but she had no choice. She was the one who'd made the mistake that cost Tangie and her gallery over a million dollars. For the thousandth time, Dev realized what a complete mess she'd made of things. She had to clean it all up, but she didn't at all like the tools she had to use to do it.

Last night, Bennett's cocksure attitude and over-whelming masculinity had almost undone her. She couldn't forgive him his past with Adah, but she couldn't quite get over the powerful effect he had on her either.

For years, she'd kept herself away from him, sure she was doing the right thing. And now she was sup-posed to put herself in the position of asking him for something, maybe even begging. If he was the careless bastard she'd always thought him to be, he'd just refuse her out of hand and put them both out of their misery.

But what if he didn't? What if he wanted her to get on her knees and beg?

Her body shuddered like a plucked harp string.

It wasn't until she was at her car in the gallery's parking lot, standing in the heat of the summer sun, that she realized how cold she was. And that she was literally trembling too hard to properly hold her car keys in her hands.

When the keys dropped from her nerveless fin-gers for the third time, she just stood staring down at them. Her vision swam, the images in front of her eyes floating and surreal.

The pavement under her feet. Her keys. The scarlet exclamation points of her shoes. All of these things seemed like they were wandering away, just like the future she'd once envisioned for herself, drifting, in-tangible, and more out of sight.

Chapter 4

As much as he wanted it to be, Bennett's obsession with Dev wasn't enough of a reason to neglect his job. So, like a responsible future CEO, he spent a couple of good presunrise hours dealing with a tricky patent issue for Leilani's Pearls before opening his front door at nine o'clock on the dot for the art appraiser he'd hired. The man was there to verify the authenticity of the art collection he'd inherited from his grandmother and maybe give him some guidance on what to do with the work.

The appraiser and art authenticator, Alan DuValle, stood at his front door in a dark suit and tie despite the heat of the early morning Atlanta sun. Gray-haired, balding and with a nearly skeletal figure, he looked just like the photos Bennett's security contacts had sent him. Behind him stood someone else, a woman Bennett hadn't invited. Inwardly he frowned but kept his expression neutral.

"Mr. DuValle." Bennett greeted the man with a firm handshake. In return, Alan DuValle, honest to God, bowed over their linked hands.

"Mr. Randal," he said in a surprisingly deep voice for someone with such a skinny frame. He gestured to the woman behind him. "This is my colleague, Melanie Winchester. Apologies for not mentioning her sooner but her company was a last-minute addition. She's the grant writer for Next Generation for the Arts, a local nonprofit geared toward promoting art appreciation and art creation among lower income children." A small wrinkle appeared on his otherwise-smooth forehead. "I hope it's not a problem that she's here."

"I'm just here to observe, Mr. Randal," the woman hurriedly said. She was pretty but unassuming in her wire-rimmed glasses and thick hair pulled back from her face in a businesslike bun.

Bennett gave her a nod of acknowledgment along with a smile so he wouldn't seem rude.

Her presence *was* an inconvenience, but one that Bennett would deal with. He'd already vetted DuValle with ID and security checks and would've done the same with this woman if he'd known she was coming.

"This is not ideal, but please come in." Bennett waved the pair in while taking out his phone. "Your ID, please, Ms. Winchester."

With the pair standing side by side in his hallway, he took a photo of both the woman and her driver's license, immediately sending them to the security firm he worked with.

Crooks of all kinds littered the world, and Bennett didn't have the time or patience to be taken for a ride by any of them. Not when he could be doing more interesting things. Seconds later, his phone beeped. A message from his contact at the firm that the information was received and being processed.

"Come this way, please." Bennett invited them farther into the house.

The house itself wasn't very big. About three thousand square feet of peace and quiet with a backyard just inches from the park. Bennett had a couple clean the three-story house from top to bottom every two weeks and a chef who made him enough meals for his needs when he was in town.

Speaking of which… Bennett stopped. "Would either of you like a drink or—" With a trickle of amusement, Bennett noticed that DuValle was already sweating although Ms. Winchester looked cool as a glass of lemonade in her teal linen dress and heels. "—a kerchief to mop your forehead?"

"No, thank you, sir," DuValle said. "I'd rather see the work as soon as you're ready, then talk with you about my findings afterward with that drink."

Ms. Winchester seemed like she had another opinion but only inclined her head toward the older man. "Whatever Mr. DuValle thinks."

"Sounds good," Bennett said. "Follow me."

He guided the pair through the well-lit upper levels of the house then down the stairs to the cooler and shadowed lower floor where he kept his wine and artwork and other things he didn't want to be destroyed by sunlight.

It didn't take long to reach the set of open rooms Bennett had set up as an impromptu gallery space when he'd unexpectedly received the series of photographs, paintings and first edition books. He'd hired the nearby university's curation department students to uncover and display the pieces in a way that was also accessible. They'd given the pieces the white-glove treatment, been respectful and, most of all, thorough.

"Here we are." Bennett opened up the last door leading into the cool set of rooms. "You'll find white gloves over there on that desk, along with notebooks, pens and anything else you might need."

"Oh!" Mr. DuValle seemed surprised again. "That's very thoughtful of you."

"Yes, it is, Mr. Randal," Ms. Winchester chimed in. She was already looking around her with a critical eye and seemed to be far more interested in the artwork than the conversation they were all having.

"I'm just being practical," Bennett said. "No point in having you search high and low for things I can easily provide." Having strangers poking through his stuff, no matter how thoroughly they'd been vetted, just didn't sit well with him.

"In that case, thank you very much." DuValle bowed again.

"No worries. You can start wherever you like. Give

me a call when you're finished and we can have that discussion over lemonade or whatever's your poison."

"That sounds perfect." With his colleague next to him, the slender man practically glided across the room to get at the small wicker basket containing the white gloves. He looked very anxious to begin, and Bennett was anxious to let him. The collection was an important one, and remarkably well curated before it had even gotten to him. It would be nice to see it displayed in a place where people could appreciate and benefit from it.

Bennett gave him a quick nod and headed for the stairs when his cell phone rang. He fished it from his pants pocket. After a brief and stunned glance at the screen, he brought it to his ear.

"This is a pleasant surprise."

"What, don't I get a 'hello' at least?" Dev's voice sounded forced through the phone, as if she was trying to sound carefree but failed miserably.

"You can have whatever you like from me, Ms. Clark," he said smoothly back. His previous comment was true, though. It was a surprise to hear from her. If they didn't have Adah plus a few other friends in common, he'd wonder how she'd even gotten hold of his phone number. She'd never called him before.

"I bet you say that to all the women who call you up," she said.

"Not all, just the special ones." Bennett kept walking and left Alan DuValle and Melanie Winchester to their work.

With the unexpected appearance of Ms. Winchester, Bennett was even more satisfied with his decision to install and turn on a high-tech security monitoring system, especially for the lower floor. He was a laid-back guy and enjoyed socializing with a lot of people, but that didn't mean he was naive. His trust was hard to come by.

Walking up the stairs, Bennett turned his complete attention to the woman on the line. "So what can I do for you, Ms. Clark?"

After an odd pause, Dev spoke. "I'd actually... like to take you to lunch."

Bennett paused in midstep. "Come again?"

An unexpected snicker burst through the phone, then a soft breath that sounded like relief. "May I have the honor of your presence for lunch sometime soon, Mr. Randal?"

Okay. So since he wasn't actually hearing things there was only one answer. "Of course." Another breath came at him through the phone. Was she actually nervous? "But only under one condition," he said, fisting a hand around the smooth mahogany railing of the stairs.

"Of course, you would have a condition." Her voice changed, becoming tinged with a hint of acid. "What is it?"

"I get to pick the place."

"If it's your house then—"

"No, no. Nothing like that." True, he'd love nothing better than to have her in the place he called home, filling his space with her particular spark and snap, but not on the first date. "Just a restaurant in town I think you'd like. Or at least I hope you'd enjoy it enough to invite me out to lunch again."

He could feel her relief through the phone. What exactly was this lunch invitation about? From the way Dev acted, it felt like more than just lunch.

"In that case, sure," she said without a single hint of meekness in her voice. "Just let me know when and where."

"Perfect. For your future information, that's exactly what I like to hear from the women in my life." Before she could tell him exactly where to stick that comment, he continued. "I'll send you a text with the place. The date and time are completely up to you. For you, I'm completely flexible." He had a couple of upcoming appointments but nothing he couldn't shift around.

"Hmm." She hummed at him through the phone, sounding thoughtful even a little playful. "That's what men always say until it comes time to bend."

"In that case, I look forward to that moment."

"Me, too," she said softly. "Me, too."

"I'll see you very soon then, Dev."

After the call ended, Bennett grinned and fist-pumped the air.

All right now.

Feeling more energized than he had in days, he jogged all the way up the stairs while the faint sounds of conversation from the pair in the basement floated up behind him.

Chapter 5

Walking just behind the uniformed restaurant host leading the way, Dev stepped off the elevator and out to the rooftop of Aerie Atlanta, one of the newest eateries in Midtown Atlanta. The sounds of late afternoon diners' conversation greeted her and she took off her sunglasses, surprised by the canopy overhead that both protected patrons and invited in the brilliant sunshine.

Dev scanned the mostly full rooftop, searching for Bennett. Like he was the steel to her magnet, it didn't take her long to find him.

"Your party is right here." The host in front of her waved unnecessarily to Bennett, who sat at a corner table near the roof's edge, with his shades on.

He looked like a big cat basking in the sun. Instead of another one of his beautiful suits, he wore a thin button-up shirt in some shade of blue that gorgeously set off the deep oak of his skin.

With a hand clenched around the handle of her narrow briefcase, Dev headed across the restaurant to Bennett's table. As she walked between the widely spaced tables, she felt the eyes of the other patrons on her. Curious. Interrogating. It made her glad she'd taken the time to dress well. Or at least appropriately. Her ice-blue vintage Dior with its giant pockets and tucked waist probably wouldn't win her any awards for originality, but it fit in perfectly with the ladies-who-lunch and high-powered execs vibe the crowd was currently giving off.

As she got closer to Bennett's table, he stood up and treated her to the view of his narrow hips and muscled thighs in perfectly fitted designer jeans. The brown leather belt around his waist matched the shade of his watchband perfectly, and probably his shoes, too.

Vain, beautiful man.

To give herself a few seconds of relief, Dev looked away from Bennett to check out her surroundings.

Unlike the main part of the restaurant downstairs, the roof wasn't crowded. Two o'clock in the afternoon found her at the tail end of the lunch rush, but the tail was long indeed. The patrons there seemed in no big hurry to leave. The rooftop, though, was half-deserted and it made her suspect Bennett had waved some sort of magic wand to make the crowd disappear. It was nice.

When Bennett had told her the name of the restaurant where he wanted to meet, she'd been surprised. Of course she'd heard of it. It was one her brother Ahmed had taken his new wife to before they'd gotten married. Ahmed and Elle were so romantic together that it was a little scary. Her brother, a man who believed that romance was never alive in the first place, had fallen head over heels for a die-hard romantic, and now the two of them spent all their time trying to outromance the other.

It was kind of funny, actually. And sweet.

All too soon, she arrived at Bennett's side. She was eager to get this over with, uncomfortable with being forced into this position by her boss, feeling as though she were deceiving both herself and Bennett. She might think he was a player to stay away from, but that didn't mean she liked leading him on as she tried to get his collection for the gallery to handle.

"Thank you," she murmured to the host who didn't move fast enough to pull out her chair before Bennett did. But the man didn't look unhappy that someone else had done his job for him.

"Very good, sir," he said to Bennett like he was approving their marriage.

Bennett sent a subtle wink her way and she had to work hard not to laugh. His brand of charm should really be outlawed. No wonder he had no shortage of bedmates when he'd been cheating on Adah. The thought made her swallow hard and look away from his too-handsome face.

After telling her all about the specials and getting her drink order to convey to the waiter, the host quickly disappeared.

"I'm glad we could make this happen," she said to Bennett once they were left to the relatively quiet corner of the roof.

"I'm glad you suggested this outing," he said with a smile. "I won't lie. I'm curious as hell why you'd ask me to lunch when you've been dead set against enduring my company over the last few years."

Not that her reluctance had stopped him from talking to her, she thought.

"Let me at least get some iced water before you start, please," she said as she set her shades on the edge of the table and the slim briefcase at her feet.

"Of course, forgive my rampant curiosity." The sarcasm sat too well on his beautiful mouth. He took his own dark glasses off and set them beside hers. His obviously designer shades gleamed like platinum next to her plain, white-framed ones. Nonetheless, they looked like a pair, a realization that sent an uncomfortable jolt through her system.

She looked over the menu and plied Bennett with small talk until their waiter arrived. He brought with him an iced tea along with two fresh glasses of cold water. Once he took their food orders and disappeared again, Dev grabbed the iced tea like it would save her life. Her throat felt abnormally dry and she drank and drank until the glass was half-empty.

All the while, Bennett watched her with an amused gaze.

"So..." His eyebrows wiggled playfully.

After taking another fortifying gulp of iced tea, Dev sat back in the chair. She licked her bottom lip to get rid of a lingering drop of tea there. Her tongue nearly stopped in midmovement when she caught Bennett's eyes on her mouth. He didn't look embarrassed at all to be caught leering, and she didn't bother calling him on it.

Directly was the only way to approach this. "Your art collection," she said. "Do you mind telling me more about it?"

"Ah, you only want me for my fantastic art, not my fantastic company." He teased her with a brief smile so she must have imagined the flash of disappointment she saw on his face.

Not knowing what to say that wouldn't get her into trouble, Dev shrugged. Hidden under the table, she curled her hand into a loose fist, digging her fingers into her palms. "It's an impressive collection," she finally settled on saying. "Obviously, I haven't seen it yet but just from the little you mentioned the other night, it sounds intriguing. Certainly fresh and new compared to what's already out there."

"It certainly is that." Bennett nodded absently after a brief look past her shoulder. "Even though I don't know much about art, the collection has inspired me in new and unexpected ways, and apparently still continues to do so. Its scope is interesting and I've been wondering these last few days since getting it appraised again exactly what to do with it."

"Do with it?" Was he already thinking of selling it himself or through another gallery? "What do you mean?"

Another smile flashed across his face, this one more secretive. And unfairly sexy. "Nothing you need to worry about right now." He drank deeply from his nearly empty glass of water, the ice rattling gently. Like it was a summoning bell, a waiter appeared from nowhere and refilled Bennett's glass of water and Dev's iced tea before disappearing once more. "Tell me, why are so interested in my collection?" he asked.

"You have to know why," she said, unable to keep the annoyance from her voice, although she was more frustrated with herself for not being up front with Bennett sooner about what she needed. Tangie's directive angered her, and it showed in her tone. "I work for a gallery, for God's sake. I'm sure by now just about everybody, including my boss, has told you how much they'd love to get their hands on it." She might as well have added, "And getting it is the only way I'll get out from under my boss's control."

"I don't like to make assumptions," he said curtly, and shrugged, which just emphasized the broadness of his shoulders. His mood shifted, and he stared at her with an intense focus. "From what you said to me a while ago, I had the impression you were interested in opening your own art gallery," he said, now soft and sincere.

A slow, scalding blush rushed up Dev's throat and into her face. When had she ever told him that?

Her mind flashed through every encounter they'd had—or at least the ones she remembered. But she couldn't recall ever telling Bennett about wanting a gallery of her own, or even having any really personal conversations with him at all. Her desire to have her own space with specially curated art of all types was an intensely private aspiration.

Suddenly, she felt like he'd stripped her naked for the world to see.

Aside from her family, she hadn't mentioned to anyone else that she wanted to open an art gallery. From the beginning, Tangie had just assumed that Dev was happy where she was and only wanted to move to a more prestigious gallery once their partnership was through. Mentally squirming under Bennett's relentless gaze, she tried to keep still in her chair.

"It's an idea I've had," she said, toying with her newly refilled glass of tea and praying he'd leave it at that.

But of course, he didn't.

"In college, that was all you could talk about. At the time, I thought it was remarkable that you already knew what you wanted to do with your life."

College? That was a million years ago. Why

would he even assume anything she told him then would be relevant now?

But of course, it was. Back then, she was a double art and art history major and she'd gushed about the pieces she liked to anybody who'd listen. Dev never thought in a million years that Bennett had been one of those listeners.

"Things usually change over the course of ten plus years." Still internally squirming with embarrassment, Dev toyed with the fork sitting next to her clean and empty plate. In all those years, she'd managed to accomplish exactly nothing.

"Have things changed that much?" Bennett leaned closer. "Have you?"

No, they hadn't. She hadn't either. The things she wanted then were still the things she wanted now.

Dev swallowed the thick and bitter lump in her throat. She felt like a scratched record. Or at least one that couldn't move on from a mournful song about wanting something she could never have.

The waiter's arrival with their food saved her from answering. Like he was unveiling the rarest of treasures, the waiter presented each plate with a proud, straight-backed elegance. The menu was an interesting take on Southern meets Northern Italy. Both she and Bennett had chosen to dispense with any appetizers and just get on with the main meal. In a deep plate, the creamy risotto with mushrooms and mozzarella smelled amazing. Around the edges of the plate were golden brown pieces of fried chicken. A leg and a breast just like Dev requested.

Bennett's massive shrimp and grits calzone had been slit open on top in the shape of a peach, allowing the steam and scent of the pesto-rich sauce of the shrimp to escape. Warm corn bread and breadsticks in a centered basket and a bottle of red wine completed the presentation. Although she hadn't been very hungry when she got to the restaurant, the food made Dev's mouth water.

"Thank you," Bennett said with a pleased nod. "Everything looks good."

"You are very welcome, sir. Madam. May I bring you anything else?" With his eager smile, the waiter looked ready to serve.

After an inquiring look at Dev, who slightly shook her head, Bennett said, "Not for the moment."

"Very well." Then the waiter was gone again.

Dev cleared her throat. "Where were we?"

But Bennett waved his hand in easy dismissal. His attention was completely focused on the food. "We can talk more about what you want from me later. Let's get to one of the main reasons I chose this place." He tucked a napkin in his lap. "Eat."

As much as she wanted to get back to talking about Bennett's collection, Dev had to agree with him now. The scent of their lunch brought out a deep rumble from her stomach, reminding her that she'd had nothing in it all day except coffee and a few cups of water. Instead of going over to her mother's or sister's this morning like she'd planned, she spent an admittedly long time on the phone with them.

That indulgence had meant she hadn't had enough time to do the research needed before talking to Bennett about his collection. Tangie had sent over all the information she had about it, and Dev had searched online—and found—some interesting tidbits about what Bennett could now have hidden away at his house. But she needed more time to get a fuller picture of the scope of his collection and how it all fit together. She had the research in her briefcase along with some information about Tangie's gallery in case he needed to see it before making up his mind about a partnership.

All of that basically meant she had to rely on him to fill in the blanks about the collection. Although, it really shouldn't matter what pieces he had. The important part of the equation was simply that Tangie wanted his art at The McBride Gallery, and Dev had been tasked with getting it.

Dev was very curious to see what he had hidden away, though. The Harlem Renaissance had been one of her favorite periods to study when she was in college. Now, years later, she was still fascinated by the figures from that time, greedily devouring any books, fiction and nonfiction both, whenever a new one came out. But all that had to wait. This amazing lunch wasn't going to eat itself.

Dev spread the napkin on her lap and got to work. The food was everything its scent and sight promised. The chicken was perfectly seasoned, crisp on the outside while tender and juicy on the inside. Maybe they'd even marinated the meat in buttermilk like her grandmother used to do. The risotto was indescribably delicious, just the right texture in her mouth, and the creamy mushroom sauce and fresh cheese burst with so much flavor that she could barely spare a moment to talk to Bennett as they ate. But he kept what little conversation there was centered around their meal, inviting her to taste from his plate while reaching out to sample from hers in the next breath.

When he first reached out with his fork, she raised an eyebrow at him and he paused the utensil above her plate with a questioning look.

"Reciprocity is important to me," he said, still waiting, not touching anything of hers until she nodded in permission. Then, once he'd scooped some risotto dripping with sauce onto the tines of his fork, she pointedly plucked a giant shrimp, plump and pink, from his plate and popped it into her mouth.

Dev moaned in appreciation. It wasn't until she opened her eyes—not even aware that she'd closed them—to see the hungry look on Bennett's face, that she realized just how it sounded. Heat rushed under her cheeks, but she didn't turn away.

He cleared his throat. "Okay then."

After they finished eating and the plates had been cleared away, leaving only their glasses of water, iced tea and wine, they got back to the reason for the lunch itself.

"I've heard a thing or two about the collection from Tangie," Dev said after taking a palate-cleansing sip of her water. "But I'd love to hear more about it from you."

He shrugged. "It's like I told you that night in the gallery. The collection is a bit all over the place although I love that about it. There are photographs by a black photographer working around the same time as Van Vechten, a few paintings, drawings, the first edition of a Langston Hughes novel, plus a letter that I've just confirmed was written by Zora Neale Hurston." He made a broad motion with a large hand. "There are a few other things I'm forgetting, but I'm impressed by everything I've seen in it."

Dev's heart beat a little faster the more he spoke. Each piece he mentioned sounded wonderful. To actually see such things in person, much less have the privilege of handling them if Bennett ever decided to sell them through Tangie's gallery...

She made a soft sound of appreciation. "That's fantastic. Have you thought about what you'll do with it?"

"I have an idea or two."

"But nothing for sure?" she pressed.

"Not yet, no."

Although she should've been more focused on convincing Bennett to seriously consider Tangie's gallery, Dev's thoughts flew back to the pieces themselves.

"Are you certain the photographs aren't by Van Vechten himself?" she asked.

"I'm absolutely positive. The style is very different, more intimate." He curled his fingers as if inviting her closer. "The photographer is there behind the camera, obviously, but it feels like they are part of the scene they're sharing with the viewer, as well—" Bennett broke off with a brisk shake of his head. "You'll have to see it to know exactly what I mean." An eyebrow curved up and a thoughtful expression took over his face. Dev knew what he was going to say before he even opened his mouth, just like she knew what her answer would be. "Do you want to see the collection?" he asked.

The "yes" jumped out of her mouth before she could second-guess herself.

Just that neatly, she fell into his trap. Dev swallowed the sudden lump of nervousness in her throat. Was that what he'd wanted all along? To get her to his house and—

Then she had to silently laugh at her foolishness. She was the one who'd called him up. If not for her, Bennett would be lunching with and trying to seduce some other woman, one far more willing than her. She'd set the trap, and he was the one falling into it. She'd set the trap on behalf of Tangie and her blasted gallery. This was precisely what she'd wanted, to see the collection and to offer a persuasive argument to him for exhibiting and selling it through The Mc-Bride Gallery.

"I'd love to see the collection," she said, rephrasing her earlier acceptance and trying not to sound overeager. "I'm ready whenever you are."

He grinned, an irresistible flash of deep dimples and white teeth. "No time like the present." Bennett raised an arm to signal the waiter and before his hand had even fallen back to his side, the man was approaching their table.

"The check, please," Bennett said.

The waiter produced a leather check holder from the pocket of his neat black apron. Bennett presented his black card without looking at the bill, batting away Dev's attempt to pay.

"Please," he said. "Don't insult me by offering your money. This place is my treat."

Probably used to seeing people argue over the bill, the waiter immediately took a portable credit card machine from another pocket on his apron and ran the card. Minutes later, Dev was walking out of the restaurant at Bennett's side, car keys in hand and the thought of "What the hell am I doing?" ringing through her mind.

That didn't stop her from following him home.

Chapter 6

Bennett's invitation to Dev had been a gamble.

The moment he'd asked her to come home with him, he could've bitten off his own tongue. The last time they spoke, Dev made it crystal clear that she had no interest in coming to his house, or even any interest in him. But then, she'd said yes.

When the word had left her pretty mouth, Bennett's heart galloped like a runaway beast and he had to look away from her as the shocked pleasure rolled through him. She said yes. Then he had to remind himself that she was only coming over to look at the art in his basement.

He laughed at himself. When had he become such a cliché?

They took separate cars from the restaurant. Dev followed him in her little green Audi, never too far back in traffic. Bennett knew because he kept checking his rearview mirror to make sure she was there.

Instead of pulling into the garage, he stopped the Mercedes at the end of his long driveway and got out of the plush leather interior in time to watch Dev's car ease in just behind his. She gracefully climbed out, already looking up at his house. Bennett cast a glance at his custom-built oasis, trying to see it with new eyes.

He'd had it built a few years ago when he finally accepted that he'd be in Atlanta on a more regular basis. It wasn't that he fought against who he was. Never that. He was his parents' only child and the heir to the company they'd built from scratch. He took pride in their hard work and that he'd had enough intelligence to help Leilani's Pearls grow despite the overwhelming challenges it faced in a changing market.

He'd been so much of a kid in his twenties, as he should have been. Imagining a life full-time in the south of France or anywhere but the city where he was born. After accepting that he would one day become Leilani's Pearls' CEO, his vision had changed a little. Business was international, so he'd pictured himself waking up to a French or Tanzanian morning sun ready to do his work via computer, internet, Skype and everything else. Maybe even from a boat sailing across the sea another world away.

But slowly and eventually, he'd come to crave the steadiness of his home city, the hot and spicy appeal of its women—and one woman in particular—along with the comfort of knowing he was close to his parents who, although aging gracefully and well, were still aging.

So Atlanta it was.

"Your house is beautiful." Dev turned from the tall, flowering trees that blocked the view of the house from the road. "I'd pictured you in something a bit more—I don't know, modern—a condo in midtown or something. But this suits you, too."

"Thanks," he said, gesturing for her to walk ahead of him. "You're right. It's not what I would've chosen for myself a few years ago, but now it's perfect."

The house wasn't as large as those of some of his peers. For him, it was more important to have a manageable place that didn't need an army of servants in constant attendance to maintain. His focus had been on the land, lots of open space to walk through when his mind needed movement to function properly. Most of the backyard was dedicated to a tree-lined trail that looked wild but was maintained by a gardener who came once a month. At the back boundary of his yard was a park.

Bennett unlocked the door, turned off the alarm and waved Dev inside. "Welcome." He tucked the keys in the pocket of his slacks. "You can leave your bag or whatever you want right here if you'd like."

"Thanks." After taking out her phone and dropping it into the hip pocket of her elegant dress, Dev put her little briefcase and car keys on one of the floating shelves in the small alcove nearby.

The old-fashioned coatrack in the alcove already held his chef's handbag and the light coat she wore year-round.

Dev fell in step beside him. Light from high windows created a path down the wide hallway that was decorated with framed photos from his life, a professional portrait of him and his family, a photo of the boat he'd taken around the world a few years ago.

The place was masculine, open, well lit, most of the furniture in African mahogany, dark and classic, but with enough light tones that the house didn't seem oppressive.

As they walked farther into the house, the scent of food reached him. Creamy and starchy. Risotto or maybe something else Italian?

"Good afternoon, Caroline." As he approached the hallway leading to the kitchen, he called out to his personal chef. She usually cooked a week's worth of meals so he wouldn't starve to death—or eat out three times a day.

"Good afternoon, Bennett." Her greeting floated back to him. "I'll be out of your hair in less than an hour." She'd been cooking since before he left.

"Take your time," he called back. "We both know you can't rush perfection. And my stomach wouldn't want you to."

Her low laugh followed him and Dev down the

spiral staircase leading to the gallery area two floors below.

"Is that your stay-at-home mistress?" Dev asked him with a raised eyebrow.

He almost laughed. Was that a note of jealousy in her voice? "Any respectable mistress of mine would be in the bedroom when I come home, not the kitchen."

She looked at him like she wasn't sure whether or not he was joking. "So she's just your part-time mistress, then?"

"Some people would simply call her a personal chef."

Dev hummed in reply but he noticed the twitch of a smile.

Soon enough, they were in the wide, open floor plan of the space he'd originally designed as a game room and movie theater. Since the house was nestled into a slight hill, the basement had a set of double doors leading to the walking path that eventually spilled out to the drive. The group of high windows that usually allowed in the full power of the Atlanta sun had been tinted to mute both the brightness and intensity of the natural light.

After Alan DuValle had left, Bennett had made some decisions about the collection and shifted around the space to look more like a gallery, complete with art-safe lights installed to gently illuminate the documents safely tucked away from curious hands behind glass cases. It was a temporary arrangement but one he felt good about.

"Here we are," he said as he stepped off the last stair.

Walking up from behind him, Dev paused to take in the gentle illumination in the space. After a slight pause, she slipped out of her shoes and walked across the wooden floors in her bare feet.

"Oh, Bennett..."

The bottoms of her feet, pale and delicate, immediately captured his attention. It was hard to miss the tiny gold rings that circled both middle toes. And the way she breathed his name... The sound of it went straight to his crotch. He swallowed hard and curled his fingers into the wooden railing. He wanted to kiss her so badly that it was an actual ache.

Bennett yanked his gaze from Dev's feet moving across his wooden floors and tried to pay attention to what she was saying. She approached one of the long series of glass cases running down the center of the large room. Most of the cases were empty and waiting to be filled.

"These photos are incredible."

She'd taken out one of the picture albums he hadn't been able to bring himself to do anything with. It looked like an old-fashioned family album and held nearly three dozen eight-by-ten photos. Within the next couple of weeks, he would have someone sort and display them, but for now, they were in an album spread out on Dev's lap being reverently handled while she sat in a comfortable armchair well out of the sun's reach.

Bennett crossed the room to peer over her shoulder. "Yes, they are."

The black-and-white photographs were both stark and beautiful, truly intimate. Looking at the pictures of a group of uniformed teenage girls and boys sitting together on the grass gave him the feeling of being part of the circle gathered there, as if he was a participant in whatever was happening, not just a voyeur. The entire collection was like that. Rich and inviting. Image after image of people who looked like him and his parents and who were just enjoying their lives. Images he'd never seen in person before.

Until he'd talked to Dev at the gallery opening, he hadn't thought very much about the contents, or even quality of the collection. Yes, the work was interesting, but he'd simply been intent on passing the collection on to an organization or a collector that could appreciate it better. But he'd since gone back to look at the work with new eyes and found a fresh appreciation.

"What you have here is truly fantastic, Bennett..." Dev turned another page.

After a while, he left Dev on her own while he checked his email and responded to a few semiurgent messages. While he worked, she finished looking through the album of photographs, then stood up to wander from corner to corner of the sheltered room. She looked at every book, every piece of art, every photo. All in silence.

Bennett didn't realize she was done until she lightly tapped him on the shoulder.

"I'm heading up," she said softly as if speaking in a sacred place.

Then she walked toward the stairs where she picked up her shoes and slowly made her way back up to the light of the higher floors. Bennett followed, watching the flash of her bare feet, her ankles, the sway of her hips under the blue dress, the straight line of her back.

Bennett could tell by the silence that his chef had finished up and gone home. Without looking, he knew she'd left him a set of instructions for warming up the food, both by text and on a note on the fridge.

"If you're not too tired, I have more to show you," he said, and almost held his breath waiting for her answer.

"Sure," she said after a short pause. "You've been a gentleman so far."

He guided Dev to the third-floor sitting room with a balcony looking out in the direction of the late afternoon sun. The balcony was wide and comfortable, furnished with a weatherproof padded bench, canopy, and a French bistro table and chair set. Sometimes, if it had been a long day and he was feeling too lazy to walk down to his second-floor bedroom, Bennett would fall asleep on the bench and not wake up until well after sunrise. It was a peaceful place.

Dev dropped her shoes just outside the balcony doors and walked out into the sun. It surrounded her like liquid gold, tangling in her thick hair, curving around her slender and narrow shoulders.

God, she was beautiful.

Bennett couldn't remember a time when he didn't think so. From that first glimpse of her outside a bar all those years ago until now. She was the woman he foolishly measured all others against. When his parents suggested the engagement to Adah for the good of both families' businesses, he hadn't made a fuss, only went along with it, figuring that he'd never feel the kind of love that his father felt for his mother, so why not unite with someone he at least enjoyed and was friends with?

After he'd realized how Dev haunted him, though, he'd worked hard to resist pursuing a sexual relationship with her, knowing it would never be more than sex since his forever was promised to Adah.

And now... Now he didn't know where to start.

He took another hungry look at Dev before heading to the living room's minibar. He poured them both drinks, club soda for himself and an iced tea for her, then went out to join her.

"Here you are." He passed her the iced tea, and she gave a momentary look of surprise before accepting, then taking a quick sip. Again, she looked surprised. In the restaurant, he'd paid careful attention. Like a good Southern girl, she liked her tea sweet but it was a light sweetness, a kiss of brown sugar instead of the way most people he knew drank it, practically half sugar, half water.

"Thank you," she murmured, turning her profile to him in the bright sun. Natural gold gilded her long lashes and glistened on the full curve of her mouth.

"Of course." He drank some of his soda, then put the glass on a nearby table. "At the gallery the other day, you got it right the first time—I never had any interest in collecting art."

"Before now?"

"Not even now," he said honestly. "As intriguing as the pieces downstairs are, I'm still not sure I want to keep them. I feel that they deserve someone else who'd appreciate them better. The only difference between then and now is that I realize truly what I have on my hands."

Bennett took a chance and moved closer to her, hoping that his body didn't give him away and tell the powerful truth of just how much he wanted her.

He continued. "The collecting of things has never interested me. What I enjoy about these pieces is the sense of connection it gives me. My grandmother passed them down to me for whatever reason and I'm grateful for that. I'm the only kid my parents have. Since I don't have any brothers and sisters, the work down there gives me the sense of being connected to something and someone else aside from my parents. It's a nice feeling."

The ice in Dev's glass shifted as she drank again and Bennett couldn't help but stare at her luscious mouth.

"I've never thought of that," Dev said thoughtfully.

"I've just always had a strong bond with my siblings and both my parents before my father passed away." Sadness moved gently across the quiet thoughtfulness of her face before drifting away as if it had never shadowed her eyes. "They mean everything to me."

Bennett felt a twinge of envy but allowed it to pass through him as harmless as a rippling wave at eventide.

All his life, it had just been him and his parents. They were all he knew and he was grateful for them, grateful for the closeness they shared. It may only be the three of them but they had enough love between them for an entire tribe.

Despite the many women who'd graced his bed over the years, he'd been looking forward to inviting a special woman into his small family, then expanding it. For a while, though theirs had been a purely business arrangement, he assumed that woman would be Adah. Obviously, he was wrong.

"What about a lover, or a husband?" Bennett asked Dev. "Is there room in that close family of yours for him?"

He noticed the grip of Dev's hand around the glass as she balanced it on the balcony's railing. She turned away from the bright sun but didn't look at him.

"Of course," she said. "Any man I bring into my life has to love my family. It's a must."

She sounded so convinced that Bennett had to tease her just a little. "But what if you fall hard for some guy your family hate. You have hot sex and fantastic talks over wine and art with him, but he's such a douche bag that they can't stand him."

Dev laughed as if that was the most ridiculous thing in the world, tiny lines forming at the corners of her bright eyes. "That would never happen. I have better taste than that."

"Do you? I've never noticed you with any guys long term over the years."

"You haven't noticed me at all." She flashed a look at him. "When would you have time to notice me when you've been so busy getting ready to marry Adah?"

"You'd be surprised," he murmured.

Dev drew in a quick and sharp breath. "That's not…that's not something I want to hear, Bennett."

"Why?"

When he covered her hand with his on the railing her eyes widened, as if she didn't realize he was so close. "That's not fair to Adah," she said.

"She's married to someone else and has a whole new life now." They were close enough now that every word Dev spoke blew air against Bennett's lips, like she was feeding him her words, her voice. But he wanted more. "Devyn, may I…" He breathed against her lips. Then slowly he lowered his mouth to hers, when she made it clear she wanted this, too.

She gasped and pulled his breath directly into her mouth. But she didn't move away. Her lips felt like silk. Delicate. Precious. She trembled against him and sighed. The scent of the iced tea from her mouth brushed over his senses. His hands tightened on her waist.

Bennett pressed his advantage by keeping absolutely still, allowing her to get used to the touch of their mouths, the warmth of their skin-to-skin contact. And to give his own body the chance to calm down. He was already hard, and only from the light touch of her mouth on his.

Their kiss was soft but dry, almost chaste. That didn't stop his pulse from thudding way out of control. His heart pounded, the blood rushed swiftly to both heads. He felt the sunlight on his skin, through his shirt and sinking deep into his flesh. But he didn't know if it was the sun or Dev's touch that made him feel as if he was on fire, rioting flames burning through his heart, his flesh, his thoughts.

Her moan was what did it. That soft sound, then the abrupt movement of her into his arms, like she was tired of waiting for him to finish what he started. Her lips parted and she breathed into him, her tongue flicked the closed seam of his mouth. Bennett bucked at that hot and sensuous touch and lost all his mind and control.

"Dev."

Groaning deep, he pulled her against him and kissed her deeply, searching for her tongue with his, tasting every soft place in her mouth, every wet space. Panting, she swayed against him and inadvertently rubbed her hard nipples against his chest.

His sex throbbed in his pants. His pulse thundered in his ears.

This was it. This was what it was like to finally kiss Devyn Clark.

Powerful. Visceral. Oh so right. It was more powerful than he'd even dreamed, and he'd spent a long time dreaming about this moment and what came after it. Devyn tumbling into his bed and giving in to a desire she never wanted to acknowledge she had for him. But he wasn't dreaming anymore. No. This was much, much better.

Bennett gripped her hips and pulled her tight against the hard ache in his pants. He moved against her, wanting more. For a few delirious seconds she moved against him, too.

Then suddenly, she jerked back. "Oh!" Her shocked eyes were wide-open and staring at him. "No, this is wrong."

"Why?" Bennett groaned the question.

"You know why," she gasped, fingers flying to her parted lips. Her eyes glistened with guilt.

Still powered by his desire, he reached to pull her back to him but she easily slipped from his hold and backed away. The half-empty glass of iced tea rocked and nearly fell over as she abruptly shoved it on the table near his own glass and practically ran from the balcony, barely stopping to pick up her shoes. Caught off guard, Bennett couldn't get his body into motion to follow.

It was only seconds later before he heard her car

start in the driveway. Tires screamed against pavement as she sped away from him and the house. Still breathing hard, Bennett squeezed his eyes shut, but he couldn't shut out that last sight of her face, terrified and shocked, as if she'd just been confronted with her own demons. And had no choice but to try to run away from them.

Chapter 7

Dev clutched the steering wheel of her car with shaking hands and felt like she was going to throw up.

It was a minor miracle she was able to keep the little Audi on the road and straight between the lanes as she desperately rocketed the car toward home.

She'd messed up. She messed up bad.

The second she kissed Bennett back, she knew she was in trouble, but she hadn't been able to stop herself. The firm and incendiary press of his mouth on hers felt like what she'd been waiting for. Like a breath of fresh air. A taste of paradise. A blessing.

The easy bliss of the kiss took her by sharp surprise, leaving her aroused and overheated, but also wishing she was the kind of friend who would never let this kind of thing happen. She also wished so very much that she could sink into the sensation of the kiss with Bennett and take that sweet connection of flesh as far as it could go.

Kissing Bennett had felt just as right as it did wrong.

Adah was her friend. She couldn't do this to her. It broke the girl code. Even though Adah had moved on, Dev shouldn't be making moves of her own on Adah's ex-fiancé. What kind of friend was she for talking crap in the past about Bennett when he'd been blatantly sleeping with other women during his engagement but now she was literally panting to get him into bed? She was the absolute worst.

Instead of telling Bennett logically and calmly that what they had done was wrong and why, she'd run out of his house like the coward she was, as if her tail was on fire. She was still running and didn't know if she should ever stop.

What Tangie wanted from her was impossible. There had to be another way to pay off her debt.

Dev bit her cheek hard as the desperation threatened to shake her apart, sending her mind scattering in a thousand useless directions.

Beg Tangie to forget what she demanded of Dev.

Ask her brother to give her the money to pay off her debt.

Burrow under the covers of her bed and never come out again.

All options that were no options as far as she was concerned. Dev's foot pressed down harder on the gas.

At home, she hurried through the garage and up to her bedroom where she stripped off the clothes she'd deliberately worn to go see Bennett. The vintage designer dress, professional briefcase and casual businesslike hairstyle had all been calculated to make Bennett see her—and by extension, Tangie—as viable professional, business connections. But all she could think of now was the way his hands had pressed against her back through the dress. Fingers flirting with the zipper in a way that made her knees weak and her panties wet.

She had to get the dress off. Now.

And she had to call Adah.

With the dress and heels in a mess on the floor, she pulled on the first thing at hand, cutoff shorts and a tank top, and headed back downstairs, calling Adah as she walked.

She dropped her car keys on the coffee table in her living room and kept walking toward the bay window with its view of her front yard and the rows of bright yellow lilies growing along the winding footpath to the street.

"Hey," she said into the phone when her friend picked up on the other end. "You have a sec to talk?"

The window's padded bench seat had a bunch of art magazines and business cards scattered all over it. She shoved them aside and sat down, her back to the wall and feet stretched out in front of her.

"Sure. What's on your mind, honey?" Adah sounded slightly breathless but happy, and Dev pictured her gorgeous and sun-kissed, starting life in Miami with her superrich new husband.

"Not much," Dev said softly. "Just checking in to see how things are going with you now that the honeymoon is over and you're back to real life." *And how angry would you be at me if you found out I've been making out with your ex-fiancé?*

"Honestly, we may be back in the States but the honeymoon is definitely not over." Adah giggled.

Then Dev heard a low, masculine laugh in the background and had to smile in spite of the guilt twisting in her belly. It was so good to hear Adah so happy and carefree. Years had passed since the girl she knew in college had that old bounce in her step and vivaciousness in her voice.

"Should I hang up and let you get back to it, then?" Dev asked, only half joking. Adah was happy and didn't need any bother right now.

"No, no," her friend said. "It's fine. I'm just getting settled into this huge house down here and Kingsley is allegedly helping me when he *should* be at work." She laughed, then squealed, high and loud. Definite signs of her new husband tickling or poking her.

Dev smiled. "That's definitely my cue to go. I

didn't want anything anyway. Congratulations and keep being happy. I'll call you later on in the week."

Adah quieted. "Are you sure?"

"Absolutely." Dev turned away from her cheerfully blooming walkway that she'd started the week she moved into the house, inspired by Monet's water lilies in Giverny and the thought of beginning fresh.

"Okay, we'll talk soon then. I'll call you in a couple of days." Adah blew her kisses through the phone before hanging up.

Before she had a chance to put it down, the phone chimed in her hand. Tangie's name and number lit up the screen. She cursed. Then clenched her teeth as she answered.

"I got tired of waiting," Tangie burst out before Dev could even say hello. "How did the lunch with Bennett Randal go?"

Dammit. She shouldn't have even told the woman about the planned lunch. "Did he agree to partner with the gallery?"

"No, he didn't make any commitments. I think he's still deciding what to do." She wasn't going to tell Tangie she'd not even made much of a pitch. She'd been distracted by other things.

"Well, help him make up his mind." Sounds of shuffling papers came through the phone, probably Tangie moving around her office, picking up things on her desk and discarding them seconds later, a habit she had when she was thinking. "Tell you what, why don't you invite him to the gallery after hours?

That way, he can see the space as it would be if we had his collection up on the walls and displayed just the way he wants it. That would tempt him for sure. An intimate view of the space, if you will."

Intimate? What exactly was Tangie getting at?

"I don't think that would persuade him to do a damn thing, Tangie. He's not a man who'll allow someone else to make up his mind for him." Or be manipulated.

"But he is a man, so do what you need to do." All sounds on the other end of the call stopped. "I'm sure you won't mind."

Dev's hand tightened around her cell. "What's that supposed to mean?"

A spiteful laugh crackled back through the phone. "You're a smart enough girl. I'm sure you can figure it out."

Very deliberately, Dev lowered the phone from her ear and ended the call, ignoring the continued chirping of Tangie's voice.

Screw her.

But in the end, she was the one who felt screwed when Tangie cc'd her on an emailed invitation for Bennett to visit the gallery once it was closed to the public. With Dev as his guide, of course. It didn't take long for Bennett to respond with a gracious It would be my pleasure.

The last thing Dev needed to think about was "his pleasure," though, or her own.

* * *

The night of Bennett's private tour of the gallery, Dev wore the least seductive thing she owned.

No point giving him—or herself—any wrong ideas. At ten minutes to nine, she smoothed her hands along the thighs of the loose-fitting smock dress with the white, Peter Pan collar. Gray, with elbow-length sleeves and a hem that hit right at the knees, it looked like it came straight out of a catalog from the 1950s. The matching gray heels almost made it feel like a uniform. Overall, the outfit was safe. Boring.

When the front doorbell to the gallery rang less than five minutes later, she knew without checking the cameras that it was Bennett. Of course, he'd be on time, just to torture her. Dev tucked her phone in one of the big, slit pockets and went to open the door.

Wow.

The vision of him through the glass doors of the gallery nearly made her knees buckle.

When she'd dressed like Julie Andrews from *The Sound of Music* she never expected Bennett to wear gray too and look like a hotter version of Captain Von Trapp. He wore another suit. This one in a shade that somehow managed to match her dress exactly. Slim fit to show off his subtly muscled body, the suit looked like it came straight from a European runway.

Bennett was a work of art himself and Dev could easily stare at him all night. She bit the inside of her cheek to stop herself from doing just that.

Life wasn't fair at all.

"Good evening, Bennett." She opened the glass door with a smile that felt as shaky as her knees. "Please, come in."

"Thank you, Devyn." He matched her formality with a teasing smile and mocking bow that brought his head low enough to almost touch her breasts. When he rose, his eyes sparkled with mischief.

She reactivated the locks once he was inside.

"I was surprised to get the email from the woman you work with," he said once the door was locked behind them. "Tangie, I think her name is."

"Yes," she murmured, then stepped closer to him in silent invitation for him to walk with her. "She thought giving you a chance to check out the gallery without the distraction of other people would help you make your decision about working with us."

"There are many things that would help me make up my mind," he said, equally softly. And then added, "Your charming expertise is one of them."

His low voice caressed her all over like sun-warmed silk. The intimacy of it made her shiver. It felt like they were both speaking in quiet voices so as not to wake the sleeping thing between them. The powerful attraction that had swept away Dev's common sense the last time she and Bennett were together.

She clasped her hands behind her back and invited him forward with a tilt of her head. "I'll show you around."

The artwork on the walls was pretty much the same as it was the last time he'd visited. They'd managed to sell a few pieces but the ones put up in place of the sold paintings were nothing to brag about, so she led him straight through the gallery, the bulk of which was open from the street and visible through its thick, UV protected glass walls.

Relatively late in the evening on a weeknight, the trendy area of Atlanta was quiet. A few couples walked past the doors on their way to or from any number of the restaurants in the neighborhood while less than a dozen cars still sat in the street parking parallel to the sidewalk. Even if she and Bennett stayed in the front of the gallery and under the gentle lights that would allow anyone passing by to see, they would still have their privacy.

"I'm happy to see whatever it is you're ready to show me." Bennett mirrored her pose and walked quietly at her side.

Why did everything he said sound like an invitation to sex?

And why did everything in her want to take him up on that invitation?

Dev licked her lips and turned away from his tempting smile. "I'm sure you remember the gallery from your last visit here." She swept her arm wide to indicate the cool space around them, open and curving in a sinuous S to push the visitors through the entire gallery space and past every painting.

Their footsteps tapped sharply against the hardwood floors.

The white walls—crisp, freshly painted and smelling oddly of lavender—showcased the current collection of mostly grand-scale pieces, paintings and sculptures meant to hang in a hotel or bank lobby.

"Yes, I remember everything about my last visit here." Bennett's eyes swept over her before obediently paying attention to the space around them.

She hurried to get her mind back on business. "We can offer great visibility, and our marketing strategy is one of the most effective in the business. We'd engage in cross-promotional efforts with historical organizations and schools to draw attention to your collection's unique aspects, and we'd, of course, arrange for interviews and news articles that highlighted you and your business savvy," she said as they moved through the space. As she pitched the gallery, she couldn't help but feel his gaze boring into her. She tried to shake off the sensation and get back to her task.

"The gallery is very elegant, very functional," he said. They walked side by side toward the rear of the rooms where a floor-to-ceiling painting loomed over them in wavering shades of copper and obsidian. Bennett walked past the impressive mixed-media piece with barely a glance. "It doesn't feel like you, though."

Dev's eyebrow ticked up. What did he mean by that? Before she could think better of it, the question hopped out of her mouth. "I don't strike you as elegant or functional?"

Bennett stopped and turned, his hands hanging loosely at his sides. A platinum ring she hadn't noticed before glinted from the longest finger of his right hand.

"Well, elegant, yes, but functional, no," he said, and Dev inwardly flinched.

She hadn't yet turned on the lights between the main gallery and the offices. That oversight left a long rectangle of shadows between the public space and the private. They stood together in the cool semi-dark, closer than she intended. The scent of his cologne, something subtle and expensive with a hint of mint, teased her nose.

"A woman like you is *not* meant to be used, or utilized in anyway. Not at all. Savored, yes. Enjoyed, absolutely. And although I'd love nothing better than to unwrap your gorgeous body in these sensuous outfits you always wear, *elegant* is not the first word that comes to mind when I think of you. It's too…cold." His breath brushed over her forehead and she shuddered, realizing he'd stepped even closer. "You're the sexiest woman I've ever met, Devyn Clark, and I want to enjoy every part of you until you scratch all the skin off my back."

Oh. My. God.

If Dev had been a weaker woman, she would've stumbled where she stood, damn near fallen to the floor with her high heels kicked up in the air and her body ready for whatever Bennett had in mind. But she found some strength from somewhere.

"I don't think that's appropriate," Dev said despite her suddenly dry throat and soaking wet panties.

"Why?" He crowded her with his body, bringing more of his scent and the seductive bulk of his masculinity.

"Adah…" Barely able to think with him practically pressed up against her, Dev grasped at her friend's name like a lifeline.

"Adah is my friend," he said, low and deep. "The arrangement we had is in the past and she has nothing to do with what's going on here between you and me."

"That's my point," she gasped, backing away from him despite her determination not to be intimidated by his desire, or her own. The darkness slipped over and past her. Once more, they were in the light, but it was on the other side of the barrier between the public gallery space and the private offices. "There can't be anything between us. What happened at your house the other day was a mistake."

"Lie to yourself all you like," he rumbled. "But don't lie to me."

A wall was suddenly pressed cool and hard against Dev's back while Bennett burned like a furnace at her front. His words scored her deeply, the truth delivered in his desire-roughened voice. Bennett's hands settled lightly on her waist and she gasped at just how good that delicate touch felt. Next to her and

Bennett, a giant painting hung on the wall making her feel like they too were on display. But only to those who knew just where to look.

Her body rippled with arousal, the pulse pounding sweetly between her legs, and he'd done nothing but touch her hips. He was driving her crazy.

"I'm not lying to anyone." But she was, she was. Dev couldn't keep her eyes off his lips. The way they shaped each word he spoke. The very sensuality of his mouth. The deep growl of his voice. Oh…

"Then tell me, honestly, what do you want?" Bennett demanded. His thumbs brushed her skin through the dress. Back and forth in a pulse-pounding rhythm.

Dev couldn't think anymore, only feel. She drew in a desperate breath of air. "I want you to kiss me."

Dev didn't realize she'd spoken out loud until Bennett groaned out, "Hell, yeah," and swooped down to press his mouth to hers. Her mind flew away. Her hands slid up his chest as their mouths slid together, hot and intentional. No more teasing this time.

He smelled expensive and tasted like rock candy. She wanted him in her mouth and for the first time, on the other side of the darkness she'd always feared, Dev allowed herself to admit just how much she truly wanted him.

She needed the hard-sweetness of his kiss. His aroused body pressing against hers. The slick sounds of their wet and passionate kisses that filled her ears like the sexiest music. She moved against him, rubbing her hard nipples against his chest, her hungry hips against the throbbing hardness he didn't bother to hide.

So good...

A moan leaked past her lips, and Bennett gripped her harder, his fingers digging into her skin through the not so boring gray dress.

"You're so damn beautiful." He groaned into her mouth. "Every time I see you, I want to kiss you, touch you. I can't believe the things you do to me."

It felt like a lie, like it was something he said to every woman he wanted to sleep with, but in that moment, Dev's natural skepticism took a flying leap and she twined her arms around Bennett's neck, meeting him kiss for kiss, desperate movement for desperate movement. His hand slid under her dress and up her thigh, aiming for that place that throbbed so fiercely for him. The touch of his fingers was like a stroke of fire, and she gasped again into their kiss. Her thighs fell open, begging him to touch her. Right. *There.*

"Oh!" Light fingertips stroked her through the dark lace of her panties. Agitating. Arousing.

Dev moaned, her senses scattering. Those fingers of his touched her harder, stimulating her clitoris and wringing another desperate cry of pleasure from her. Her hand clenched in the soft material of his jacket and through the layers of cloth she could feel the frantic beat of his heart. His teeth nipped her earlobe, his tongue stroked just under her jaw. It was like he knew just the places to touch and drive her mad.

She whimpered and dug her fingers deeper into the back of his neck, into the suit that probably cost more than her car. Her thighs trembled. The heat of pleasure gathered inside her with more force, more intention. Dear God, he was going to make her climax in the place where she worked...

"Come home with me, Devyn. Come home with me and I'll worship you with my hands and mouth all night long." He slid home the seduction of his words with firm and delicious movements of his fingers around her swollen bud. It was temptation Dev couldn't ignore. Desire poured from her like the sweetest honey and pooled between her thighs.

Yes, she wanted that. His hands on her all night. His mouth driving her to the edge of pleasure and beyond.

A chime from the back door's motion alarm jerked Dev from her fog of lust. She gasped once more and pulled back from Bennett. Someone was coming into the gallery from the back employee parking lot. That could only mean one person. She yanked herself away from Bennett with a rough inhale. Her chest heaved from her aborted desire.

"We have to stop!" She braced her palms against his chest, ignoring how wildly his heart beat against her skin through the expensive cloth of his suit.

"Devyn, are you still here?" Tangie's voice sang through the gallery from a few feet away. "I came to help you talk with Mr. Randal about our idea for his collection."

Why now?

By the time Tangie appeared from the back office, Dev had pulled herself together. She stood practically on the other side of the room from Bennett, who was casually examining the massive bronze and black painting he hadn't given a damn about fifteen minutes before.

"Tangie," Dev said with a smile, as if she didn't want to tell the other woman to go straight to hell. "What a surprise to see you here tonight."

Chapter 8

"And what else did you say to her clit-blocking ass?" Aisha chuckled over the phone. "I swear that job you have is the absolute worst."

This was one of her sister's favorite things to say lately but Dev couldn't see how she was wrong. Every day working with Tangie felt worse than the last.

Dev sighed and opened the double doors leading out to her back porch.

At just after eight in the morning, the balmy summer air brushed over her face and shoulders with a calming touch. Sunlight rippled over the sparkling turquoise pool and freshly cut grass. Barefoot and only wearing a thin chemise, she walked down the stone path to sit on the side of the pool and stick her feet in. The water was deliciously warm.

"I just told her I had everything under control and she didn't need to be at the gallery while Bennett and I talked," she finally said to Aisha.

But Tangie hadn't taken her words for reassurance. Instead she'd lingered until Bennett pulled the plug on the visit altogether and excused himself, saying he had an early morning meeting. After he left, Tangie grilled her about the entire evening, asking what he said, if it looked like he would say yes. Endless questions that Dev didn't want to answer even if she could. Bennett had certainly been receptive, but he'd given no indication of what his final decision would be on the collection.

Aisha made a rude noise and Dev could easily imagine the accompanying gesture. "Why do you even work for her anyway?" her sister asked.

Dev sighed and moved her feet back and forth in the water, sending ripples dancing across the pool's surface. "You know why." She'd told Aisha she owed Tangie a lot of money and just left it at that.

"Damn, Dev. Just let me or Ahmed give you the money, already. This is killing me!"

But Dev wouldn't do it. Despite what people thought looking at Aisha and the way she lived her life, she was the more responsible of the two sisters. Her success as an architect was something the entire family was proud of. She'd sneaked money into Dev's bank account before, but Dev had immediately given it back.

"I can't, Aisha. I just can't." It would feel as though she was letting them fix her mistake, instead of just investing in a new business. It would feel like a lie.

The sound of clanging pots came through the phone. Aisha was mad. Or maybe getting ready to put something in the Crock-Pot for dinner later that day. Their mother had already hung up on them a few minutes earlier to get ready for a conference she had downtown.

"You're worse than Ahmed about stuff like this," Aisha muttered. "Where did you get all this stubbornness from?"

As if she had to ask. Dev was her mother's child all the way.

"It's all fine, or it will be once I get Bennett's collection where Tangie wants it," Dev said even though the words left a bitter taste in her mouth.

"Is that what you really want?" The clanging faded away on Aisha's end of the call. "Tangie is a very unpleasant person, and that gallery of hers has some serious bad energy. Why would you want a freakin' fantastic collection of Harlem Renaissance art to end up there?"

"I don't want it to be there, not really. But I don't have a choice. I really don't."

"We always have choices, Devyn. Just know what you're messing around with is sure to come back and bite you in the ass."

"Come on, Aisha…" Dev whined, even though her sister wasn't saying anything she didn't agree with. "I need to do this." Water splashed over her legs as she moved her feet faster in the pool.

"Whatever you say, sister dear."

She was just going to add something else in support of her latest questionable decision when the phone chimed, the sound of another call coming in. Dev looked at the screen.

"Hey, can you hold on for a sec? Bennett's on the other line."

"Bennett? You're ditching me to talk to a guy?"

"Stop it. This won't take more than a couple of minutes." Before her sister could say anything else, she clicked over. "Good morning, Bennett."

"Good morning." His voice rolled over her like a soothing wave. "I hope I'm not interrupting anything."

"I'm talking with my sister on the other line."

"In that case, I'll make this fast." She heard his sharp and deep breath over the line. "I'm making a quick visit to someone who claims to have a piece that would fit well with the Harlem Renaissance collection. I'd like you to come with me."

Her feet stopped moving in the water. Oh my God, yes!

The words hovered just a breath away but she clamped her teeth together so they wouldn't just fly out. With Bennett, it was too easy to get carried away.

But oh my God, the chance to see more work from that time period in person and in private? What a rare opportunity!

Screw it.

"That would actually be really nice," she said, trying not to sound overeager. "Thanks for—" *turning my world upside down* "—including me."

"You're the first person I thought of to share this little adventure with," he said. "I'd love to leave this Friday and stay through the weekend. Can you make the time?"

This Friday? Tangie wouldn't mind her being gone from the gallery as long as it was in pursuit of Bennett's precious collection. As for the weekend, all she had planned was another session in front of the computer searching for a great gallery space to rent or buy when she could finally afford it.

"I can," she said, nodding, already thinking of what to wear for a long weekend in Bennett's company. Obviously the boring gray dress wasn't quite going to do it.

With a splash of the water, Dev dragged her feet from the pool and stood up. Her feet made dark footsteps on the cement as she headed back for the house.

"Where are we headed?" she asked.

"The place is a bit far away so pack an overnight bag with clothes for three or more days."

"So, an oversize weekend bag?" she said, noting he still hadn't answered her question.

"Sure, if you want to put it that way." His low laugh rumbled at her through the phone. "Don't forget a bathing suit and passport."

Passport?

Chapter 9

"Yes, I'll be gone the whole weekend," Bennett said to his father on the phone. "But I told her I'd be back in time for our lunch date." He crossed the cabin of his private jet and sat down at the gently illuminated desk. With a touch of his fingers, his laptop woke up.

"Don't miss that lunch or she'll find a way to blame me somehow." There was gentle laughter in his father's voice.

"I'll avoid that at all costs," Bennett said.

"Good. Now go enjoy yourself, my boy. I know you have some crazy scheme going on. Just don't get yourself hurt."

"No scheme, Pop." Unless he counted this pursuit of Devyn Clark that he was on.

"Somehow I don't believe that." He could practically see his father shaking his gray head. "Be safe, and call your mother to let her know you haven't been eaten by a herd of wild Spanish pigs or something."

"I don't think it's called a herd, Pop."

"Whatever it's called, run if they start chasing you. I hear those things are vicious." His father hung up on him after a gruff but affectionate goodbye.

Still laughing, Bennett tucked the phone away in his pants pocket. Talking to his father had been a welcome distraction. All day, he had worried if he was doing the right thing. If he had made a mistake inviting Dev.

That didn't stop him from checking his phone every five minutes, though. Bennett tugged the cell from his pocket and looked at the screen again. No missed calls. No messages from Devyn saying that she wasn't coming.

That was something, right?

Right.

With a few clicks, he opened the document he'd been working on before his father's call. But after a few minutes, he realized he was looking at the lines of data over and over again and not making any sense of them.

Okay. Enough of this.

Bennett saved the document, closed the laptop and shoved away from the desk. After another look at his watch, then his phone, he started to pace the aisle of the small plane.

He was as nervous as a high schooler on prom night, and he hated it.

Part of him half expected Dev not to show up.

The bait he tossed out to Dev had been—he hoped—irresistible to an art appreciator like her. A trip to a mysterious place to take a look at an equally mysterious piece of art that may or may not belong with the collection she was already half in love with? He'd gambled everything that she'd say yes.

He wanted her with him in on this trip. Hell, he wanted her with him for all the intimate moments in his life that she would allow. But Devyn Clark was a stubborn woman with ideas of what she and Bennett could or couldn't be to each other just because he and Adah had once been engaged and Adah was her friend. Adah treated their long-gone engagement as simply another part of their friendship, just as he did. Dev had other ideas, though. And Bennett needed to change them.

Damn, where was she?

Just as he looked at his watch one last time, the sound of footsteps on the tarmac just outside the open door of the plane reached his ears. Bennett abruptly stopped pacing and settled back at his desk, trying to look calm and unaffected.

Then Dev came into sight.

She walked up the small steps like she'd stepped directly from his dreams. Black flats on her slender feet, a soft-looking pair of gray yoga pants and a thin black blouse long enough to cover her butt. A pale yellow scarf draped gracefully from her throat and her hair, tucked up in a neat French roll, shone in the soft light. She looked almost professional. But she smelled of comfort, flowers and other female things that made him ache to pull her into his lap and kiss the tentative smile from her face.

The relief at seeing her finally there made him light-headed.

Bennett got to his feet and greeted her with a gentle grip on her elbow, taking her purse from her shoulder and putting it on the seat nearby.

"Welcome," he said.

Dev rolled her eyes but it was a look filled with a reluctant type of affection. "You *would* have a private plane."

He shrugged. "Why not?" His business decisions had made the family a lot of money in the last few years, plus he liked nice things. He hoped to spoil Dev with some of these things over the weekend.

The staff woman who'd escorted Dev passed him a clipboard with their flight plan and arrival time. He'd arranged for Dev to be picked up because he'd been afraid she would have asked too many questions and then changed her mind about coming. Once he thanked his employee and nodded his approval, she made her way toward the front of the plane.

From outside the plane, someone closed the door. Okay, they were just about ready.

Dev sat down in the seat across from him. It figured that she'd want to put a desk between them.

"So where are we heading?" she asked. "You never told me."

"Sandin de la Frontera." He smiled, happy he'd been able to keep this a secret. It added to the sense of fun somehow, and intimacy.

"Since I have my passport, I'm assuming that's not in Florida someplace."

"Correct assumption," he said, his smile broadening. "It's in the south of Spain."

Her mouth opened, then closed again. "We're going there for a weekend?"

"Yes. The business with the painting shouldn't take more than that to sort out. Three days at the most."

Dev belted herself in while, around them, the plane made its preparations to leave Atlanta. "Tell me more about what we're doing there, and why you invited me."

Bennett clicked his own seat belt closed. "I enjoy your company and you'd love to take a look at the painting," he said. "Do I need more reason than that?"

"You don't need more but something tells me there *is* more."

Did she want him to confess that he'd been thinking about her nonstop for weeks now? That this trip was the best way he could think of to get her out of her comfort zone and her mind off Tangie and whatever games that woman was playing? He knew, from the moment she'd shown up in the gallery at precisely the wrong moment, that Tangie desperately wanted to seal the deal on getting his collection. It burned him that Tangie was using Dev in this way.

No, that type of honesty wasn't an option right now.

Bennett leaned back in his chair, hands draped over his stomach. "Like I told you over the phone, you're the first one I thought of when the news about this painting came across my radar. A friend of mine based in Spain said this might be a good piece to add to the collection, even if I do eventually get rid of it."

She looked at him, incredulity all over her pretty face. "So you're only going to see this painting on the off chance that you'll buy it and resell it?"

"Of course. In life, nothing is certain." Especially not the plans he'd put together for this weekend.

"Wouldn't it have been cheaper to just Skype with the painting's owner? What if you don't like what you see?"

He shrugged. "Then I'd have gotten a few days out of the office. A win-win as far as I'm concerned."

Not that he spent that much time at the corporate office. It felt a little *too* corporate for him, too confining. His mother loved the new space, the three top floors of a skyscraper with views of Atlanta and parts of Decatur. But he'd rather do his work from a boat, a sunlit balcony, hell, or even his bed. Being confined in any way just wasn't his thing.

"Well, for your sake, I hope the painting blows your mind," she said. But she couldn't hide the excitement shimmering in her eyes.

A similar excitement stirred in Bennett's belly. Not to see the painting that a few people who knew of his collection swore was an early piece by Lois Mailou Jones, but to see the changes that being away from her worries would do for Dev. Already her cheeks glowed with a different warmth, and although the desk lay firmly between them, she leaned ever so slightly toward him, smiling.

The plane settled into its cruising altitude and Bennett smiled back at Dev, enjoying this relaxed version of her beauty.

"Would you like some wine?" he asked Dev as the flight attendant parted the curtain separating the main cabin from the small galley in the front and approached them.

"Sure," she murmured with a shrug. "It'll put me right to sleep and that's just exactly what I need right now."

As promised, just after drinking her single glass of red wine, Dev curled up into the fully reclining seat and slept for most of the trip.

When they arrived at the small airport in Cádiz a little over eight hours later, gently touching down on the smooth tarmac, she shifted under the blanket Bennett had covered her with and opened her eyes. "We're already there?" Her voice was barely above a whisper and her once-neatly pinned hair now tumbled around her shoulders and sleep-soft face. She looked adorable enough to kiss.

He finished up the email he was working on and closed the laptop with a gentle snap. "Yes, Sleeping Beauty. We are." Bennett hid a smile at her owlish blinking and the vulnerable curve of her mouth. "There's a car waiting for us. We'll be staying with a friend a few miles away. Once we get to his house, you can get some proper rest and a shower if you like, or we can just go check out the painting."

Dev sat up. "Let's just go," she murmured with a luxurious stretch that tumbled the blanket from her shoulders and pooled it at her waist. Then her gaze flickered to him and the laptop he'd just closed as well as the papers in a neat stack near his elbow. He saw her make the mental calculations. How long they'd been flying and how long he'd been awake.

"Actually, let's rest for a bit, maybe have some of the famous Spanish cuisine I've heard so much about."

Bennett tucked the pile of papers away in his briefcase. He'd look at them again later tonight before sending the final versions to his assistant. "I'm not sure what famous cuisine you're talking about. I'm afraid my experience of Spanish food comes down to pork. And potatoes."

"Which you apparently don't like all that much," she said with an amused look.

"Which I definitely don't," Bennett agreed. "But

the fish here on the coast is very good. I think you'll enjoy it."

Dev picked up the blanket in her lap and began neatly folding it.

"Don't worry about the blanket," Bennett said. "The flight attendant will take care of it." He checked his phone to confirm that the driver was already waiting for them with the car. He was. Good.

"But it'll be one less thing she has to worry about." Dev finished folding the blanket and grabbed her purse. She stood up. "Let me go freshen up before all of Spain gets a look at my crushed face and crazy hair."

"They should be so lucky," he said, feeling lucky himself that she had allowed herself to be that vulnerable in his presence.

But she only rolled her eyes playfully and with a smile, before disappearing into the bathroom. By the time she reappeared, Bennett had his briefcase in hand. "Ready?"

"Of course." In the bathroom, she'd done something to her face that made her look well rested. Her thick hair was neatly pinned up once again. Dev slipped her purse over her shoulder and walked with him to the now-open door of the plane. It didn't take them long to get through immigration, then they were in the black Peugeot being driven by an attentive chauffeur down a quiet highway toward their destination.

Nearly an hour later, Bennett climbed from the

car and reached down to help Dev out, as well. She slipped her hand in his and stood, looking around them, wide-eyed, at the villa where they would stay for the next few days. The sun danced over her as she turned, as graceful as a ballerina doing a pirouette on a grand stage. In the brightness of the sun, he realized the long shirt she wore was see-through and she had on a formfitting tank top underneath it.

"This place is beautiful," she said with an appreciative sigh.

Bennett managed to stop gawking at her long enough to reply. "I wish I could take credit for it, but the house belongs to a friend who made a very good investment some years back." He squeezed her fingers, then she blushed and gently tugged her hand from his. Bennett swallowed his disappointment and ignored the sensation of loss her withdrawal from him left behind.

The house was massive, wide and rectangular. It was built in the Moorish style with a series of enclosed courtyards, soaring ceilings and curved archways, and it gleamed large and pale on the edge of a cliff with a direct, private path to the sea. Alonzo had gotten it for a steal years ago, then spontaneously relocated to Spain after losing most of his family in a car accident.

"You've never thought of buying some palace like this just so you could play by the sea a few days out of the year?" She teased him with a look from the corner of her eyes.

"I love making money, but I don't like wasting it," he said. "I enjoy being here but it's much more fun to let Alonzo treat me like a prince for a few days than deal with the upkeep of a monster like this."

"Hmm." A smile curved her bright lips. Approval maybe?

Just then a set of joyous footsteps tapped across the tile toward them. Bennett and Dev both turned in time to see a tall man dressed in sand-colored linen pants and a matching short-sleeved shirt jogging down the steps toward them.

"Bennett, my friend!" Alonzo Rice, his friend from college and member of the happily idle rich, drew Bennett in for a quick hug that he gladly returned. "Glad to see you here at a reasonable hour. I thought for sure you'd take the scenic, restaurant route and not get here until after dark."

A soft laugh came from Dev. On the ride over, they'd talked about the artwork on the buildings they passed on the way through the town. Incredible murals on the sides of white buildings Dev had wanted to stop the car and take a closer look at. They'd only made a single quick stop for her to take photos on her iPhone even though Bennett had been tempted to pull over at one of his favorite local tavernas for a drink and some seafood tapas.

"It was a challenge, but I made it." He waved Dev closer. "Mostly because of this woman right here. She is a little tired after the long trip and I didn't want to keep her out of a bed for too much longer."

"Uh-huh." Dev held out a hand for Alonzo to take but he gallantly brought it close to his lips instead. "Devyn Clark," she introduced herself with a smile. "A pleasure to meet you and see your gorgeous house. I can't wait to fall asleep in it."

Alonzo laughed. "Good to have you both here. Nice to finally meet someone interesting in Bennett's life." He looked between them and chuckled again like he knew a secret they didn't. "Come in and get comfortable."

He tucked Dev's arm in the crook of his and lured her away from Bennett with his charm. If Bennett didn't know Alonzo meant nothing by it, he'd have felt something close to jealousy. So instead of complaining, he grabbed Dev's rolling suitcase along with his duffel bag and followed them into the house, waving off the servant who was trying to take the luggage from him.

"I prepared a couple of rooms for you both with some coffee, tea and a light breakfast waiting if you feel like eating," Alonzo said. "If you don't feel like food, just leave the trays right where they are."

He took them through the large house, their footsteps ringing against the pale tile as they passed antique tapestries and paintings hanging from lushly painted walls and under soaring, decorated ceilings. Everywhere they looked, something glimmered gold or royal blue.

Uniformed household staff flitted, ghostlike, between rooms as they passed. Not for the first time,

Bennett wondered why Alonzo needed an army of people for the house when it was just him and, when he was lucky, his girlfriend, who insisted on living in town.

"Here you are." Alonzo came to a large door and pushed it all the way open. "This is the common salon." He then pointed to two doors on opposite sides of the room. "Those are your bedrooms and they each have a bathroom. If you need anything, just tap that bell by the salon door and someone will get you whatever you need."

Bennett wanted to protest that he didn't need anything, that he could jump immediately into the reason they were in Spain, but the grittiness behind his eyelids told another story. He was more tired than he thought. A yawn cracked his jaw.

Alonzo's skeptical smirk let Bennett know his friend thought they'd do anything but sleep once they had the suite to themselves. "Get some *rest*, my friend. I have a few things to take care of in town. I should be back in a couple of hours, but if you wake up before I return, I'm sure you can keep yourselves occupied." Then he winked at them in the most obvious way.

Bennett didn't have the energy to tell Alonzo he had the wrong idea. He dropped the duffel bag on the floor near the ornate-looking sofa. It wasn't until Alonzo and Dev both looked at him with various expressions of amusement that he realized just how loud a sound the bag had made falling to the floor.

"On that note…" Dev said with a soft laugh. "I think we'd both take you up on the offer of rest."

"Of course. *Rest* for as long as you like." Alonzo exchanged the European double cheek kiss with Dev and a shoulder slap with Bennett before quickly leaving them alone.

"You're dead on your feet, superman. Go get some sleep." With another low laugh, Dev grabbed her bag from where Bennett had abandoned it and headed for one of the closed doors. "I'll see you in about an hour or so," she called over her shoulder before slipping into the bedroom and closing the door behind her.

Chapter 10

Despite the six plus hours of shut-eye she'd had on the plane, Dev fell immediately asleep once she got into bed. The sheets were sinfully soft and the bed had just the right amount of firmness to cradle her right into dreamland.

Dreams came to her. Unfocused images of Bennett's smile, his eyes, intriguing glimpses of his hard and muscled chest between the edges of his unbuttoned shirt. They were back in the gallery that night not too long ago and this time there was no Tangie coming in to interrupt them.

The dream sharpened.

Bennett's gray suit jacket lay in a designer heap on the floor. He leaned back against the pale wall with his hands loose at his sides, lashes low over passion-darkened eyes. His chest, muscled and firm, moved gently up and down with each breath. His defined abs rippled when she lightly touched them. Beneath the zipper of his pants, his desire for her bulged hard and insistent.

He was stunning.

All of Bennett was a work of art she craved to have for her very own.

Softly, he said her name and the sound of it on his tongue was an invitation to the filthiest sex, the most complete fulfillment, the giving in to her most powerful craving.

Dev's mouth watered, and she wept with surrender.

In the dreams, she touched him and he allowed her to do whatever she wanted, pushing the crisp white cloth of his shirt off to bare his chest completely. In a haze of desire, she thumbed his dark nipples and moaned in appreciation at his encouraging sounds of pleasure. Slowly, she moved lower and kissed his hard abs, licked between each firm and distinct ridge of gorgeous flesh. Her knees hit the floor. Her fingers, deft and unhesitating, flipped open the button of his slacks. Tugged down the zipper and reached into his tight boxer briefs…

Sunlight arched across Dev's face and forced her eyes open.

"Oh no…" The denial of reality burst from her.

She blinked up at the ceiling, disoriented, as she slowly woke up.

Spain. The ride in Bennett's private plane. A place called Sandin de la Frontera.

Her legs shifted against the sheets and the damp between them made her lick her lips and sigh softly. Even the very breath moving past her parted lips stimulated the delicate flesh and swept fine tendrils of sensation through her. Fiercely, she clung to the last remnants of her dream.

Bennett.

In the art gallery.

Her name on his lips.

She on her knees and ready to sate her desire for him.

"God, I'm such an idiot…" Dev groaned.

But saying it out loud didn't make her want him any less.

This isn't going to turn out well, so you might as well just end it all now. Her sister's voice ringing out with irritating clarity from the back of her mind made her groan again and cover her face with her hands.

"But I don't want to end it," she muttered out loud.

You're being selfish. You're being a crap friend. Aisha might as well have been sitting next to her on the bed, her voice was so loud.

Aisha's proxy voice wasn't telling Dev anything she didn't already know.

She stared up at the ceiling of the unfamiliar bedroom and willed her body to calm itself and give her space to think. With both windows open, a breeze tinged with the salt of ocean air floated through the room. All around her was silence. The desire for Bennett aside, her body felt absolutely content, her mind at ease and empty of everything but the luxuriousness of the sheets she lay in and the anticipation of seeing the painting Bennett was in Spain to buy.

All things considered, she felt like a queen in a fairy tale.

Grown-up. Catered to. Wooed.

This gorgeous man had flown her in his private jet across an entire ocean and had his very sweet friend put her up in his palatial home by the ocean. The weather in the small town was perfect. And, most importantly, she didn't have to think about Tangie and her ridiculous demands for an entire weekend. For the first time in a long while, she felt weightless. Almost free.

She sighed. God, it was going to be hard letting go of this freedom once she got back to Atlanta. To think it had barely been a few hours since she landed in the country. Laughing at herself to stop from crying, she buried her face into the soft pillow that now smelled faintly of the rose-scented leave-in conditioner from her hair.

Queen, my butt. It was time to let that fantasy go. Dev sighed and rolled over in the bed, the soft sheets whispering across her body like a promise for all the things she wanted but was afraid to ask for.

A faint knock sounded at her closed door.

Dev fumbled for her cell phone to check for the time.

Oh damn. Nearly two hours had passed since she shut herself away in the room for a "nap."

"Who is it?" she called out.

"The man busting into your dreams to drag you back to reality," Bennett's voice said clearly through the door. "Alonzo isn't back yet but we have a date with a certain painting."

She sat up, excitement fluttering in her chest. "Already?"

"Why? You're not ready to go see it?" Laughter threaded like gold through his deep voice.

But she was already shoving the sheets aside and getting ready to jump out of bed. "Give me five minutes!"

Four minutes later, she pulled the door open, purse over her shoulder, teeth brushed, and she'd changed into a thin pair of jeans, a white blouse tucked in at the waist and red high heels. An outfit much more suited to the sweltering Spanish weather.

"I'm ready." She flashed Bennett a smile as she stepped into the room.

He stood by the tall window with his cell phone in hand, in an outfit that nearly matched hers—jeans, a white T-shirt, soft-looking Italian shoes on his feet. His back pocket bulged from the shape of his wallet and he looked much better than before. At least it didn't seem like he was about to fall over where he stood.

"Get enough sleep?" she teased.

"I'd have rather had the kind of *rest* Alonzo was talking about, but at least I feel less like road kill and more ready to take on the road and everybody on it."

"Bold words," she said, fighting back a blush at the way he said *rest* and the images it brought to mind. Specifically, the ones from her dream.

"But these bold words of mine are all true." He tucked his phone into his hip pocket and gestured to the main door of their suite. "Shall we?"

Turned out that Alonzo had gotten "tied up" in town and wouldn't be back until much later. At least according to one of the maids who'd shyly given Bennett the information before dashing off. But he left them a car and word that he'd be back in time for dinner that night. Which, according to the Spanish meal schedule, probably wouldn't be until eleven.

"I'm sure we can occupy ourselves until then," Bennett said with a faint smile as he started the big, boxy Mercedes and struck out for the open road.

Sandin de la Frontera was a quiet town. The winding road that led downhill from the house was edged on both sides with rolling fields of nothing. The scenery was pretty but not at all like the acres of olive groves Dev had imagined when Bennett mentioned they'd be heading to Spain. A tall, ancient-looking tower rose high above the village of white-painted houses, its thick stone face and open windows surprisingly well maintained. The ocean was the defining feature of the landscape, glittering and blue on a day clear enough that Dev could see a wide land mass on the other side.

"What's that?" she pointed beyond the windshield.

"Morocco, I think."

"So, Africa?"

Bennett's dimples flashed when he grinned at her, looking briefly away from the road. "Yes, Africa."

"Wow. That's kind of amazing. I've never been so close to the continent before." She slid the window all the way down and stretched her neck out as far as it could go. The bit of land she could see remained just as obscure as before.

"You want to head over there for a visit?"

Dev tucked her head back into the car and smoothed down her flyaway hair after putting up the window. Without asking, she knew without a doubt that Bennett would arrange for them to make it to some part of Africa before they left. All she had to do was say the word. But they weren't here on this trip for her.

"One day I'd love to," she said, unable to keep the wistfulness from her voice. She'd done a lot of things since having access to some of her brother's money but, to her regret, traveling hadn't been one of them.

"But not this week?" Bennett pressed.

She nibbled on her lip and considered the temptation. It would be *so* easy just to give in and ask for that. But she already felt like she was asking—well, begging—too much of Bennett where his art collection was concerned. She didn't want to use him in that way.

"No, not this week," Dev said. "We have a few other important things to take care of first."

Bennett took his eyes off the road again to spare her another quick, dimpled smile. "Well, it's not off the table if you change your mind about making a quick trip over."

"I'll keep that in mind."

They continued down the winding road, sometimes making small talk, other times surrounded by comfortable silence and the calming sound of the car's tires skimming over smooth pavement. Dev allowed her thoughts to wander back to her long-ago dreams of traveling and seeing the different types of art created in other parts of the world.

"We're here." Bennett's low voice brought her back to the present.

The car was stopped in front of a normal-sized house, which was to say it looked nothing like Alonzo's palace. Also, unlike at Alonzo's house, there was no immediate rush of welcome, no one bounding down the stairs to offer them a comfortable bed and questions about a pleasant journey.

"Are they expecting us?" Dev asked.

"They should be. I talked with the owner's husband on the phone before driving out here."

Dev peered outside the car at the surprisingly lush driveway they'd driven up, grass on both sides, green as spring in Atlanta. White marble steps led up to a wide porch elegant with tall Grecian columns and a pair of gray cats sleeping in the shade. Bennett took out his phone and dialed.

"I'm going to look around," Dev said, and climbed out of the car. Bennett acknowledged her words with a nod while putting the phone to his ear.

Despite all the marble and Greek columns, the place didn't feel intimidating at all. Just homey. Maybe it was because of the cats.

From the driveway and to the left, a paved stone path led away from the front of the house and past a vibrant, blooming garden. Roses of just about every color glistened under the bright Spanish sun. The earth around them was dark and rich like the flowers had just been tended to. The faint scent of natural fertilizer mingled with the smell of the roses and other flowers Dev couldn't begin to name.

The path led farther back than she realized and, after a quick look behind her, she discovered she'd lost sight of Bennett and their car in the drive. An iron privacy fence suddenly loomed over her, but after a quick glance Dev noticed that its gate was merely pulled closed and not locked. After only a moment's hesitation, she opened the gate and kept following the path into an obviously private backyard.

More flowers. A pool. The sound of people laughing and splashing around in the water. A radio played what she assumed was Spanish pop music, lively and fun. Very faintly, the musical tones of a ringing telephone rose and fell between the sound of music, laughter and conversation.

There were three people in the pool, all of them talking and laughing at once. A telephone rang again. On a tray near the pool sat an empty bottle of wine on its side plus another that seemed full enough to be worth keeping upright. Three glasses with sparkling golden liquid in them were scattered around the edge of the pool. The image was one of light-hearted pleasure, an enjoyment of what life had to offer in this moment.

The telephone rang again but nobody in the pool seemed inclined to answer it.

"Good afternoon!" she called out. Then, remembering where she was, pulled out her rusty high school Spanish. *"Buenas tardes."*

The trio, two men and one woman, continued to play. The men were bare chested while the woman splashed in the water in a bright floral bikini. They bounced a large plastic ball between them, laughing for the sheer joy of it. Or maybe they were all just buzzed from the wine.

"You're terrible at this game, Mari!" one of the men said in thickly accented English.

"Oh, but I'm great at other things, including teaching you English," she called back and clumsily sent the ball bouncing out of the pool and to the grass a few feet away. The woman laughed. "Not my turn to get it!" And slapped the rump of one of the men. With a good-natured laugh, the man climbed out of the pool to retrieve the ball. Luckily, it rolled toward the gate and near Dev's feet.

"Hey," she said when the nearly naked man, dripping with water and rippling with muscles, his crotch barely covered in a Speedo, bent down to get the ball.

He stared at her with curiosity, standing up slowly with the ball in hand. "Are you coming to join our party?"

"No, not quite." She responded with a smile of her own to his offering of bright white teeth. He was gorgeous enough to be a model, or perhaps a retired one since he was at least in his fifties. "I'm here with a friend to see a painting from someone who lives here."

"Painting…?" He looked puzzled, but before she could answer with some clarity, he made a low noise. "Oh yes…" Ball held between both hands, he made a beckoning gesture to her with his seal-sleek head. "Come. Mari said a man was on his way to look at something in her salon but I didn't think you'd be the one."

Dev waved behind her. "He's in the driveway trying to do the polite thing and call."

"Politeness is not on today's menu!" he said, laughing. With the ball tucked under one arm, the man jogged back toward the pool. "Mari!" he called out. "I think you forgot something."

"Oh, one second," Dev said, although with all the yelling he was doing the man probably didn't hear her.

She walked back quickly through the gate and yelled Bennett's name, telling him to come round the back. Dev didn't wait for him to appear, just strode briskly back toward the pool where the man was already swimming again, continuing with his enjoyment of the sun-drenched day. The woman, Mari, treaded water at the deep end and watched Dev come closer.

"Good afternoon," Dev greeted both Mari and the second man. "I hope Bennett and I aren't disturbing you."

Solid footsteps sounded behind her and moments later, Bennett appeared at her side. His warmth settled close, and in this festive atmosphere it was hard to ignore the rightness of it, even though the sweltering heat should've made the contact unbearable.

Dev briefly met his eyes and he raised his eyebrow at her, the smallest of smiles playing around his sensuous mouth.

"Mr. Randal! It is you, right?" Mari thrust her hand out of the pool up at Bennett.

For a moment, Dev thought the woman was going to pull him into the pool with her and her friends. But she only shook his hand as if they were meeting across a boardroom table.

"Just give me a second," Mari said a moment later. "I completely ignored my phone. Forgive me." With a quick look over her shoulder, she tossed the ball toward one of her men, but it bounced off a bare chest and rolled toward the opposite end of the pool.

"I'll be right back. Don't lose the game without me, Evan."

"I'll do my best." The man dived after the ball.

At her side, she noticed Bennett give the pool a wistful glance, then he met Dev's eyes again. She nodded back. The water did look tempting in the day's heat.

Mari climbed out of the pool, shamelessly fit in the bright, hibiscus-patterned bikini that showed off her gorgeous, well-seasoned curves. Like the man Dev met at the gate, she must have been in her fifties, too, but she wore her age well. Grabbing a robe and towel from one of the poolside chairs, she quickly dried her hair and threw on the robe. The wet towel landed back on the chair with a sound like a slap.

"Come this way," she said.

She led them into the house that, despite its regal appearance on the outside, felt very "lived in." At least three pairs of shoes lay crooked on a shoe rack by the door, clothes hung over various chairs they passed, and not a single maid lurked nearby. They ended their procession in a softly lit room, an office or library with built-in floor-to-ceiling bookshelves on two of the three walls. The wall without shelves had been painted a deep gold and held a few framed black-and-white photographs and a single painting.

"This is it."

Dev drew in a slow breath.

The painting Mari showed them was nothing like the pieces in Bennett's collection, and it certainly hadn't been done by Lois Mailou Jones. Dev could tell that at first sight.

Peering at it closely, she figured it had obviously been created much later than the 1920s or 30s. The subject was a landscape near the water's edge, maybe Central Park, with dogs and green space and well-dressed, brown-skinned people enjoying themselves on blankets scattered on the grass. They wore the fashions of the 1920s, but that was about it. More than anything, the painting seemed like a reproduction of Seurat's *A Sunday Afternoon on the Island of La Grande Jatte*.

Dev inspected the brush work, the style, the date and artist's name printed in tiny script in the bottom corner of the canvas. She released a small sigh of disappointment. It wouldn't fit at all with what Bennett already had.

"What do you think?" Bennett's breath brushed against her ear as he came closer than she realized.

"It's a beautiful piece—" From the corner of her eye she saw Mari's pleased nod. "But it might not be what you're looking for."

She was surprised when he didn't look all that shocked. As much as she'd been looking forward to seeing the painting, she realized then what a disappointment it must be for him to come all this way for what was essentially nothing. He nodded his head, accepting her opinion.

"This is one of our favorites." One of the men—not Evan—from the pool drifted in, clothed now in white drawstring pants and a matching shirt that billowed around his body. "Mari and I picked it up for a steal years ago in New York."

He introduced himself as Giles, Mari's husband.

"Well, at least you weren't cheated," Bennett said with a quick smile. "The painting is pretty good as far as I can tell, but Devyn is my expert, so..." He shrugged.

The smile fell off Giles's face. "Are you sure? Did you look closely enough?"

Mari squeezed her husband's arm but spoke to Bennett and Dev both. "I'd hoped you'd pay us a small fortune for it, but oh well." She laughed a little to indicate there were no hard feelings. "We still enjoy having it here."

"But you wanted to sell it," Giles argued, his voice going deep and protective.

"It's okay, *cariño*." Mari smiled and Giles relaxed. "I wanted to sell the painting when one of our contacts told us how much it might be worth. I am just as happy to keep it."

Mari turned back to Bennett and Dev. "Sorry you came here for less than what you expected, Mr. Randal," Mari said with true apology in her voice.

"It's not a wasted trip, Mari. I love any chance to travel and, of course meeting wonderful people like you." He bowed over her hand, a gesture Dev thought was charming. "You and your pool have actually inspired me," Bennett continued. "All this sun, sand

and water is ripe for enjoying and that's exactly what I plan on doing."

Dev mentally agreed. The water party here had her yearning for her own bit of fun. A swim in Alonzo's pool, then maybe a late dinner before getting back on the plane tomorrow would be perfect.

"Oh good!" Mari clapped her hands. "A man after my own heart. What is the saying—seize the day? I'm glad you were able to get something out of this trip then."

"Thank you for your time," Bennett said warmly.

"We'll see our way out," Dev added, already tugging at Bennett's arm and leading them toward the door. She felt like doing precisely what Mari had mentioned: seizing the day.

When they were back in the car, they looked at each other.

"Well, that was interesting," Bennett said with a soft laugh.

"Yes, that's definitely the word for it." Dev buckled her seat belt and drooped in the seat. "Sorry the trip didn't give you what you wanted."

He gave her an odd look. "It hasn't been that much of a disappointment."

"What do you mean?"

With a growl of the impressive engine, Bennett started the car. "You heard me in there. There's sun and a beautiful day we can still take advantage of. Come on—maybe we can't run off to Morocco like you want, but we can take a closer look at it from the beach."

Dev's smile felt like it was about to split her face in half. "You don't have to tell me that twice."

Bennett took to the road they'd come in on, winding close to the town and the white, terraced houses built into the hills. He drove slowly down the winding cliff road, allowing Dev a longer look at the mist-shrouded land mass across the water.

In its mystery, it was beautiful.

The car eventually turned down an unfamiliar road, winding again, before appearing below Alonzo's impressive hilltop palace. A dirt road led them to what seemed to Dev like a deserted beach. Thigh-sized branches, crookedly placed, marked off the place where the makeshift parking lot ended and the beach began. Their car was the only one there, and even though it was hard to tell from the rocks that loomed on the smooth sand as big as SUVs, it looked like they were the only humans there, as well.

"Is this beach private?" Dev asked.

Even though, less than fifteen minutes before, they drove past a beach with quite a few people dotting the golden sand, here it felt like they were completely alone. Waves rushed up to the shore like a whispered invitation to enjoy everything they could of the hot and beautiful day.

Bennett turned off the car. "*Very* private."

His answer seemed like a dangerous one.

The car door opened and Dev looked over to see

Bennett taking off his shoes and socks before rolling up the cuffs of his jeans to his knees. She didn't want to find the way he curled his toes into the sand charming, but she did. The act was so unexpectedly boyish, so genuine.

"You coming?" He tossed her a challenging look as he swung the car door shut.

"Just try to stop me." She wasted no time kicking off her shoes. The sand was warm under her feet and between her toes, warm and wonderful.

"That's something I would never try to do." Then he took off for the water's edge.

Despite what she'd seen from the shore, Dev somehow expected the ocean to be wilder up close, foamy and lashing the sand with a tempestuous fury she didn't understand. But the blue water rippled like silk under the bright sun.

"This place is beautiful," she said as she fell in step with Bennett on the sand. The waves tumbled up languidly toward their feet but never close enough to touch. "I can imagine renting a house here and hanging out for a few months just thinking about life."

Bennett glanced at her. "Only for a few months? Not for good?"

And be so far from her family forever? No way she could imagine that. "No. I'm not Alonzo or anyone else who could just pick up and leave their home country. I love Atlanta too much to leave for good. Even with all the crazy things about the city, it's too much in my blood for me to just say goodbye forever." Then she thought about the nature of life. "If I had a choice, of course."

A low hum of sound left Bennett's throat. "I used to think the opposite. I couldn't wait to leave Georgia and start a more interesting life someplace else."

"And now…?"

"And now, there's nowhere else in the world I'd rather be," he said.

"I'm sure it helps that you've already seen most of the world." Dev stared across the water to the other world opposite them.

"I *have* seen a lot, true," Bennett agreed. He kicked his feet in the wet sand as they stood side by side. "But there's even more that I haven't seen. That fact doesn't make me want to be in Atlanta any less." He tilted his head back and caught the sun with his smile. "The peach is it for me. I'm not going anywhere."

Was that really true? Men like Bennett always had something better to do and somewhere more interesting to see. Yes, he loved Atlanta now, but what about in a few years?

"I'm sure Atlanta is happy to have captured one of her native sons," was all she said. "My mother says a lot of folks are moving out west to California or even up to New York."

"Those places are all right, too, but I know what's for me." He looked at her with heavy significance in his eyes and, after meeting that intense dark gaze for too long, she tore her eyes from his and looked back across the water to Morocco instead.

Its dark and seductive landmass captured her attention just like Bennett often did. The urge to explore it and surrender to its mysteries tugged fiercely at her. Her doubts had a stronger grip, though.

"I wish I were as certain as you," she said, and couldn't keep the longing and regret from her voice.

"Certainty sometimes just happens." Bennett once again captured her with his piercing eyes. "You can't wait for it. You either leap with it, or you risk never having it."

That sounded like the words of a wealthy man who already had it all. Not someone like her, struggling to correct mistakes and wanting success so badly that she could almost taste it.

Dev shook her head, both in dismissal and denial.

This trip wasn't about her. It wasn't about helping her to drag her mind out of the low, circular pit where it had been spinning for the last few weeks. It was about the painting. She was still surprised at how easily Bennett had released the idea of having the painting once he realized it wasn't what he desired.

She wanted to allow herself to do the same thing. To let go.

Of Tangie.

Of her mistakes.

Of wanting Bennett the way she had no right to.

"You're absolutely right," she said with a forced smile.

Morocco's shadowy coastline beckoned to her like something from a dream. The ocean's water looked crystalline and cool, the perfect antidote to the late afternoon heat and the unwelcome thoughts of Tangie that had suddenly surfaced. She closed her eyes and let the spirit of contentment she'd felt at Mari's house wash away memories of Tangie. She wouldn't allow worries to cloud this wonderful day. She was in Spain, the sun shone brilliantly on the inviting water, and she was lucky enough to have a handsome man at her side. And not just any handsome man either.

Suddenly, Dev yanked her blouse over her head and threw it behind her away from the water. Bennett gaped and she laughed out loud, tickled to have caught him off guard. Her jeans went next. Then, with only her bra and panties on, she ran into the low waves.

"Oh my God!" she shrieked.

The water was colder than she thought it would be, splashing up her legs, thighs and her belly. But she kept going, running and laughing, splashing with her arms thrown wide like she was embracing the wide darkness of Morocco from where she stood. Then she dived into the water.

She swam away from the shore and kept going until her feet no longer touched the ground. It felt so free, so liberating. Laughter burst out of her like bubbles of spontaneous and unexpected happiness.

God, she wished she could feel like this all the time.

Smiling, she turned to face the shore. Bennett stood where she had left him, watching her with a look of surprise still on his face.

"Are you coming?" she called out. She made a show of splashing in the water and enjoying its refreshing caress on her skin.

For a moment, he seemed to consider. Then, with a slow grin, he gave back her answer from earlier.

"Just try to stop me."

Without a single ounce of shame, he pulled off his clothes—underwear included—and slowly walked into the water toward her.

Chapter 11

"Just try to stop me!" Bennett shouted toward Dev right before he plunged, naked, into the ocean.

Damn! The water was cold.

It shriveled up bits of his anatomy he wasn't ready for Dev to see diminished but he was committed to this swim like nothing else right now. He'd invited her to Spain. Pretty much confessed how badly he wanted her. Told her she was one of the reasons he was staying in Atlanta.

After that, the next move was hers.

Well, with this spontaneous, near-naked dive into frigid foreign waters, it looked like she just made it.

At the thought of finally having what he'd wanted for years, the blood rushed through his veins, heady and hot. Not even the cold Atlantic Ocean managed to cool him down.

Twenty or so feet away from him, Dev treaded water, her bare shoulders sparkling with droplets and sunlight. She looked like a mermaid from those old stories, ready to seduce an unwary man into the sea and beneath the waves to a quick but euphoric death.

Whatever death she promised him, Bennett wanted it. He wanted it all.

He swam deeper into the water.

Across the space that separated them, Dev's eyes seem to glow, reflecting the light of the waves. They challenged him.

Danger, they said.

Come closer, they beckoned.

As Bennett moved toward her, those eyes of hers widened and she licked her lips, her gaze skimming down his body from his face to everything she could see above the waterline, and maybe even below. The water was clear enough for it.

When he reached her, any words he could have said to her completely escaped him. All he had was the heavy breath in his lungs, the wild blaze of desire in his body, the thick heat of his sex aching to take her.

"Hey," she said. The breath of sound whispered past her moist lips. An invitation.

He swam close enough for their bodies to touch. Then she kissed him first.

A brush of her lips, salty and wet from the sea, the kiss cool, then immediately turning hot. The desire roiled in Bennett's gut, snaking lower to grab his sex in a heated vise. Her fingers gripped his shoulders and her legs brushed his. Though the water was cool, he wasn't aware of it anymore. All he felt was the heat of the sun, the blaze of desire, the weight of her eyes on him. But as much as he wanted it to be, that wasn't enough.

They had kissed before. Intense kisses that had felt like a prelude to sex. After each of them, though, she had pulled away with regret in her eyes. He didn't want that to happen again.

Bennett moved back. With a mewling cry deep in her throat, she chased his lips with her own, trying to intensify their kisses.

"Devyn…" He groaned under another hot press of her mouth, the salty stroke of her tongue seasoned by the flavor of the sea. "Do you want this?"

She groaned again. "Yes, yes." Her hands tightened their grip on his shoulders, fingernails sinking deep enough for him to gasp at the pain, and pleasure. "Kiss me, Bennett. Touch me."

A hand slid lower on his chest, moving through the water to stroke his nipples, one after the other. His breath bucked. His sex surged toward her in the water. Although a voice told him to ask her again, his body was more than satisfied with this answer.

Bennett crushed her lips under his and took what she so eagerly offered.

If someone were to ask Bennett what happened between him and Dev in the time between when she said yes to him and the moment they ended up on the deserted beach, tangled together on top of their clothes, he couldn't tell them. In the instant she said yes, the door to every possibility opened up to him and he was right there where he wanted to be. With her. On top of her. With her smooth and wet body beneath his, slippery and panting with desire, her thighs around his hips while he kissed her as if she was trying to breathe for them both.

She tasted salty and wet and in need and he doubted he tasted any differently as the monster of desire that woke up urgently inside of him couldn't get enough of her lips, her body, her mouth. The sun burned into his back. Her nails raked his shoulders, her soft and panting cries drove him insane. He would have taken the moment to its explosive conclusion, if not for his concerns for her comfort and safety.

"We should stop," he groaned out.

She looked up at him, confusion in her eyes. "Why?"

"Having sex on the beach may sound really hot in theory, but the reality of it isn't something you're likely to appreciate." He licked his lips and congratulated himself on putting together such relatively coherent sentences when all he wanted to do was pounce on her again.

"What?" Her thick lashed eyes blinked at him, blinded by desire.

God, he just wanted to devour her. Everything about her was so beautiful to him. So incredible.

"Getting sand in sexy places isn't my idea of a good time," he said slowly even as his hips pressed down into hers in the sand. "And once you experience it, it won't be yours either." He shot a glance up into the hills. "And no matter how private this place is, some sneak could grab a photo that would give you grief. I don't want anyone to hurt you."

She licked her lips and unhooked her trembling thighs from around his hips. "Then let's get someplace where we can finish this."

Yes, please.

It was a relief that she still wanted to do this. He half expected her to pull back and say it was all a mistake. She had done it often enough, and he was this close to accepting that she just didn't want him the way he wanted her. But he wanted her to be fully comfortable with this. With other women, he might not have cared as much and would have let events overtake them. Not with Dev. Dev was special.

"Let's go back to the house," he said, although his body wanted to substitute "house" for "car" and give in to the recklessness he hadn't felt since high school and make love to her in the back seat of the big Mercedes. But Alonzo probably wouldn't appreciate it.

Dev licked her gaze over his body to his sex that still throbbed and ached for her. "Yes. Hurry."

They fumbled back into their clothes and made it through a tension-filled car ride back to Alonzo's house. When Bennett pulled into the circular driveway, he bit off a groan of disappointment. Alonzo was back home.

His friend would want to hang out. Do lunch or dinner or whatever. Bennett didn't have it in him to wait through a long meal with Alonzo with Dev sitting tempting and finally willing across from him at the table. Dev's face mirrored his reluctance.

"Okay, let's just get this over with," she said. "We can't be bad houseguests. Leaving him eating by himself just to…" She dipped her head and slid her gaze toward the still-closed front door of the house. A faint smile played around her mouth.

The things he could do to that mouth of hers right now…

"You're right," Bennett forced himself to say. "Let's go and be social."

They got out of the car together, brushing sand from their clothes while Bennett took particular care not to touch Dev. Every touch between them now felt like throwing sparks on a river of gasoline.

Together, but with necessary inches separating them, Bennett and Dev made their way from the driveway and into Alonzo's grandiose house. They made it as far as the main hallway before their host appeared out of nowhere.

Alonzo, dressed in a suit of pale blue linen, looked like he was on his way to Easter service. At a queen's palace. For some reason, he laughed when he saw them.

"I don't have to guess what you two have been

up to," he said with a chuckle. "But I suppose it was only a matter of time, hmm?"

"Don't worry about what we've been up to," Bennett said although only extreme willpower kept his face blank. He didn't want Dev to feel ashamed about what they'd been doing. "We figured we'd come back to the house and join you for an early dinner if you're around."

Alonzo let loose another round of laughter. "I'm around but I'm not hungry. And I bet neither are you. At least not for food." He winked at them both. The gold watch at his wrist flashed briefly as he glanced at it. "Go upstairs and get it out of your system for the rest of the afternoon before you both explode. I have a date in town myself in just a few."

Bennett would've liked to tell the other man to go someplace else with his foolishness but he felt so bright with his lust, so full to nearly bursting with it right there in Alonzo's hallway, that it was useless to deny anything. As it was, he couldn't even look at Dev. His flesh vibrated with her just being near. If he threw so much as one glance in her direction, every lustful thought he was having about her would only become more obvious.

"Fine." He cleared his throat. "Use us as an excuse to go out and party again. We'll be fine."

"I know you will. See you crazy kids later on." Then with a wave, Alonzo was gone.

Bennett didn't want to feel so obvious, but it was

a lost cause at that point. "Shall we?" He waved a hand toward the suite they shared.

"Sure." Dev bit her lip and looked briefly his way, a glance that was both shy and sensual at the same time. Then she walked ahead of him toward their rooms.

Bennett's heartbeat settled heavily between his legs. If they started now, he wouldn't be able to last very long.

At the entrance to their suite, he paused. "I have sand and seawater all over me. I'm going to take a quick shower before I join you, okay?"

He went toward his part of the suite in what he had a feeling was a mad dash instead of a masculine and confident stroll.

"Okay. I think I'll do the same." Dev's low voice reached him just as he opened the door to his bedroom.

While he got himself ready, Bennett left his door ajar, just in case she had it in mind to come to him instead of the other way around.

Once he was showered, scrubbed and in better control of his too-excited body, he threw on his sleep pants, which, fortunately, had pockets. Into those he slipped some condoms from his toiletry bag and headed for her room.

Her door was closed. But that didn't mean anything. Certainly not that she'd changed her mind.

Right?

Bennett knocked.

"Come."

Believe me, I want to.

The response rolled through his mind just as he opened the door. Then everything inside him stopped.

Thoughts. Logic. Breath.

The vision spread out on gold sheets utterly paralyzed him.

Dev lay on the bed, her beautiful skin barely covered by the tangerine-colored bra that cupped her ripe breasts just so and offered them up like the most delicious fruit. The tiny thong panties curved a sensuous line just beneath her flat belly and barely covered her sex. As he watched, Dev shifted in the bed, her smile sensuous and welcoming.

"Once I remember you saying any mistress worth your time would be in bed waiting for you when you got home." She flicked her fingers in the air, the smile on her soft lips becoming playful. "Yes, I know, this isn't home and you were hardly gone to toil the day away in front of your board of directors. But…"

Bennett licked his suddenly dry lips. "Is that what you are? My mistress? I didn't think you were into that sort of thing." He didn't know how he was able to speak so calmly with the steel pike in his pants and his rational mind completely gone from the building.

"A different country, different rules." She shrugged and the ripples of flesh in the neckline of her bra nearly brought him to his knees. "If you want me to be your mistress, here I am."

Damn. What happened in the few minutes he'd been in the shower? Then he shook away the thought. That wasn't a question for a moment like this.

He swallowed thickly and the small action rolled all the way through him. His body throbbed with savage desire. He didn't want her to be his mistress. He wanted her to be much more than that. But if that was what she was willing to give him now, he'd take it. Striding toward the bed, he struggled to maintain a steady pace, to control the surge of energy pulsing through him. A growl of desire rose in his throat. The want thickened his sex and he could barely walk without hurting himself. But each step took him to her and so he would gladly endure any discomfort.

"I don't want you to be my mistress," he rumbled. "I just want you. All of you."

"Then come take me," Dev said softly.

He retrieved the condoms and threw them on the nightstand, then pulled down his sleep pants, hissing when the weight of his sex caught at the loose waistband before bouncing back, heavy and already leaking, against his belly. He dropped the pants on the floor and, naked and ready for anything she wanted, climbed on the bed to claim Dev.

Chapter 12

Dev's desire for Bennett had dried up every drop of sense from her mind.

The few coherent thoughts she had looped around only one thing: Bennett.

Having him. Allowing him to have her. Then dealing with the consequences later.

In this country and city where no one knew her, she could finally have what she'd wanted for so very long.

No excuses. No shame. No more lying to herself.

The day itself had seduced her first. The excitement about the painting, the eagerness to see it, the strange visit to the home where the hosts were living and loving so openly and happily. Even the disappointment over the painting had been colored by some joy. It hadn't been what they'd been looking for, but it was still a vibrant picture, filled with sensual colors, and a reminder that life's beauty was out there, waiting to be plucked, just like the roses in the garden. After that, the spontaneous swim had provided a bright and exciting overture to her passion for Bennett.

While he went to his own room to shower—an excuse she felt that was meant to give them both enough space to reconsider what they were doing, she'd thought—with embarrassing envy—of how happy Adah was with her new husband. She desperately wanted just a little taste of that. So she'd showered and changed into sexy lingerie her sister had stuffed into her luggage when she wasn't looking.

Then she waited for Bennett on the bed.

When he finally came in, masculine and beautiful with his chest bare and the desire equally naked in his eyes, need winged through her belly with the exhilaration of a thousand butterflies set free from their cocoon. And Dev welcomed it.

"If you want me to be your mistress, here I am." She offered him what she thought he wanted.

But then he demanded so much more. "I don't want you to be my mistress," he rumbled. "I just want you. All of you."

"Then come take me."

Dev opened her arms, her thighs, her heart. All for Bennett. She gasped as their mouths fell together, her lips electrified and her tongue eager to tangle with his. His lightly muscled body was heavy on top of her and she loved it.

"More!" she gasped into his mouth.

Bennett's fingers latched onto her hair and held her head still while he made sensual love to her mouth. Her entire body tingled and she moved desperately against the firm body pressing her down into the bed. She found the muscular globes of his butt and pulled him deeper between her thighs. Dev's body wept for more of him.

"I need you…" A moan of pure desire arched from her throat and, in answer, Bennett pushed her thighs wide and pressed his hips between them, nudging the thick ridge of his desire against her. A powerful pulse of sensation made her cry out his name.

"That's it, baby," he groaned.

Already, the heat of an impending orgasm was pooling low in Dev's belly.

"Oh!" The rush of their physical connection took all of her breath away. And her body only wanted to replace that breath, that air, with more of him. Each stroke of his tongue in her mouth tugged sensations from her breasts, between her legs, deep in her heart.

He pulled away, and the light in his eyes nearly burned her to ashes. The tide of her orgasm retreated.

"At last," he gasped, his hard chest heaving, hands roaming over her skin with tender care. "Devyn…"

His every touch sent sparks of electricity shooting through her. It was exhilarating, like being caught in a storm. Her heart raced, her pulse thudded like frantic drumbeats. Under his hands, Dev teetered on the brink of destruction. But she also felt perfectly safe.

Bennett kissed her deeply, his mouth tender and ravenous over hers while his fingers tugged at the sensitive nipples and roamed between her thighs. It felt like he couldn't get enough of kissing her, just like she couldn't get enough of kissing him. Their breaths merged, their panting and desperate moans wove through the room.

Dev fumbled between them for the source of his desire but, after all too brief a touch, he jerked back. "If I touch you like you want, this is going to be over way before it starts," he panted into her mouth.

"But I want to feel you."

His fingers slipped over nipples, one after the other. "Don't worry, baby, you will."

Then he was kissing her again, his tongue a slow and leisurely stroke, exploring and claiming every inch of her mouth. Just as his fingers moved between her thighs, pushing through her wetness and plucking her desire higher and higher.

"Bennett..." She gasped his name as the tension and heat gathered inside her again.

Her skin was on fire. Her breath was out of control. Dev moaned his name again and again, jerking against the sheets, her hips moving uncontrollably now, her thighs wide-open and her sex a steadily dripping fountain of want.

"Bennett!" His name screamed past her lips as the orgasm exploded inside her.

The heavy weight of his body dropped down onto her, holding her in the sheets as she shuddered through her pleasure. Tears ran from the corners of her eyes and slid down into her hair. Uncontrolled breath rushed from her parted lips.

It seemed to take a beautiful forever to drift back down to earth.

When she opened her eyes, still panting from the most intense orgasm she'd ever had in her entire life, Bennett was kneeling between her thighs, a condom on his hard and ready flesh. Dev's eyes flicked down to that intimate part of him, then back to his face. Immediately, her body wanted him again. Shivering from the force of her desire, she ran her hands up his sweat-covered arms, up to his neck and over his cheekbones.

He sucked one of her fingers into his mouth. "Ready, baby?"

"Yes…" She'd waited this long for this man. She only wanted more.

Bennett put a hand on her hip, the other on his sex, guiding its thick length into her.

"Yes!" she whispered, then gasped, the breath jolted from her throat by the hard stroke of him inside her.

His name burst out of her again. Her legs wrapped around his hips and she pulled him deep.

"Make love to me, Bennett." Dev raked her nails

down his back and clung to him, wanting him even deeper. Wanting more. "Let me feel you! Oh!" She cried out when he stroked a particular sweet spot. "Please, just let me feel."

She felt like she was babbling, lost to the ecstatic plunge and retreat of his sex inside her.

"This feels like—ah! a dream—so good, Dev. I can't believe—ah!" Bennett sank deep between her thighs again and again, rocking the big bed under them.

"Just give me this." Dev whimpered and moaned and met him movement for movement. "If this is all I get from you—oh… I'll take it."

Their senseless words overlapped each other. Heat rolled through Dev's body. Bennett's thick sex filled her up almost to the point of pain while the rhythm of their lovemaking went from slow to fast then slow again. His powerful back and hips moving with relentless force, Bennett drew out their pleasure, filling her up, then withdrawing to the very hilt before abruptly slamming into her again. He shifted the angles of his thrusts until he found that one that made her scream. Then he hit that spot again and again, a man on a mission.

Dev's fingers slid over his damp back.

"Oh!" Dev bit his shoulder, screaming her pleasure into his sweaty skin, her legs locked tightly around his back, her sex gripping him hard.

Then she shattered, her whole world in pieces under his passionate and relentless assault.

"Devyn! I—I—" A shout of pleasure erupted from him and he quaked on top of her, inside her as his release claimed him.

Their breathless sounds filled the air for long moments. Then with a deep groan, he pulled out from her body and rolled over on his back. Dev's body clutched at the sudden emptiness, still quaking with delicate ripples of pleasure. She didn't watch him deal with the condom but she knew it was gone when he pulled her close and on top of him despite the dampness covering both their bodies.

Her mind floated in the aftermath of her satisfaction.

"Dev…" Bennett groaned her name into her hair. His lips pressed into her forehead, her cheeks, her throat. He said her name again but that was all.

She knew exactly how he felt. All the words she could have said had flown away; all she had now were the sensations their coupling had left her with. The only word that came to mind for her was simply *more*. She wanted more than an afternoon in the south of Spain. More than a stolen weekend away from Atlanta with him.

Frightened by the unexpected and completely unwelcome thoughts, Dev rolled away from the furnace of Bennett's body and buried her face in the only pillow miraculously still left on the bed.

"That was…" Again, words failed her.

"Agreed." Bennett didn't look any steadier on his feet—well, on his back—than she did. His chest heaved with each breath and his entire beautiful body was covered in sweat. Dev barely stopped herself from touching him again.

"That was even better than in my fantasies," Bennett panted. He dropped a heavy hand low on his belly, fingers tangling in the thatch of hair just above his now-sleeping sex.

"Fantasies?" Dev lifted her head from the pillow to stare at him in surprise.

Well, Bennett was a man, so he'd probably had sexual fantasies about every woman he ever came in contact with who wasn't related to him. Still, he had fantasies about *her*?

He flicked her a glance, one tinged with a hint of *what can I say?* "Since we met, I've had my fair share about you. You're a beautiful woman and…and I'd have to be dead not to notice how sexy you are."

Although his words stroked her from the outside in, she couldn't help but notice that he didn't reach out across the inches separating them to touch her. Was he just pouring on the compliments because he thought she wanted to hear them?

"You know, I hope you don't think I need you to say these things to me." She rolled over to her stomach and propped herself up on her elbows to better see his face.

"I'd be a terrible judge of character if I thought that. Hopefully I'm better than that at this seduction thing." The corner of his mouth lifted in a half smile.

She found herself smiling back at him. "You're

perfect at this seduction thing. All it took for you to get me into your bed was an invitation to look at your etchings. Quick and efficient." Then she flinched, realizing what she'd hinted at, that she'd only slept with him because he flew her to the other side of the world to look at a possibly expensive painting.

And it wasn't exactly a lie.

Dev opened her mouth to apologize or redirect, but Bennett's eyes wandered deliberately down her body.

She felt every stroke of his eyes along her skin, on her breasts half-hidden from him because of how she lay, sphinxlike, her bottom bare and turned to gold by the sunlight coming through the windows. The long mirror high up on the wall gave her the perfect view of the two of them in bed together. The sight was both ridiculously clichéd and exciting at the same time.

With her lower lip caught between her teeth, Dev watched Bennett sit up. The way he moved, slowly and with the natural light emphasizing every motion, sent the beautiful muscles under his skin rippling in the sexiest ways. Incredibly, the long eel of his sex twitched against his thigh and began to grow. Low in Dev's belly, a spark of lust flickered to new life.

"In that case, Ms. Clark," he murmured. "I have something else to show you…"

A sensuous laugh spilled past Dev's lips as she took in the slow awakening in his lap. "Hmm. Is all that for me?"

"Every last inch," Bennett said as he once again covered her body with his own.

* * *

Greedy for each other, they spent the rest of the weekend in bed, only crawling out for meals and counterproductive showers together. Their host allowed them to enjoy each other and only sent maids with trays of food at appropriate times of the day. By the time they left for the airport to return to Atlanta, Dev was sore but happy, stubbornly pushing aside the gnawing question of "what next?"

That she would deal with once she was on the other side of her Spanish paradise.

Chapter 13

"Have you made a decision about your grandmother's Harlem Renaissance collection?" Bennett's mother asked as the waiter took away the last of their empty plates.

"Yes, I have, actually."

Bennett was with his mother at her favorite restaurant, an old-world establishment where you had to reserve a table months in advance, or know someone who could slip you in at the last minute. On a Wednesday evening, the dining room was relatively quiet, just like she liked it, the low conversation of other diners flowing over them in an elegant hush. Sometimes he wondered where she got her bougie tastes when her parents had been strong, working class people and her grandparents had been law-breakers back in the Prohibition days. Yet Stephanie Randal was as refined and Southern as they came.

Wearing a pale green dress with a glittering crystal and citrine brooch pinned on the breast, she sat at the dinner table like a queen. Her thick silver hair was cut short and straightened, the youthful style the perfect frame for her delicate features and gently lined face.

"You're happy with your decision then?" She delicately sipped the last of her red wine from the long-stemmed glass like it was champagne.

Bennett nodded. "Happy enough."

It was a decision he'd made days ago. Long before the trip to Spain with Dev. Long before their heated kiss at Tangie McBride's gallery. He hadn't told Dev about it yet but planned a dinner date before the end of the week where he would let her know all his decisions about the collection.

"I'm glad." His mother removed the cloth napkin from her lap and neatly folded it before putting it beside her water glass on the table. "Will you tell me or keep it a secret until the last possible moment?"

"You know I love springing a good surprise."

"Yes, you do." Her smile was wry and unamused.

When his parents had asked him to pay more attention to the family company and find a way to keep it from going under, he worked in secret for weeks straight, testing his theories in select markets while they wrung their hands, thinking the company was going to disappear at any second. He only let them in on his plan when he was absolutely certain it would work. His parents had been relieved but Stephanie Randal nearly pinched his ear raw for not saving her and her husband weeks of worry.

A waiter slipped close. "More wine, sir? Madam?"

"Another glass of the Chianti for her and a brandy for me, please." Bennett named his preferred brand and the waiter disappeared after giving them both an energetic nod.

"So what are you willing to tell me for now, at least?"

With a satisfied smile, he explained what he was putting together. Somehow, word about his collection had reached a large part of the art world. Collectors and academics had been bugging him for a while now. They wanted to see the pieces in the flesh, and most were very interested in what he ultimately planned to do with them.

After a few conversations with Dev, he decided to have an exclusive opening, a once in a lifetime chance for a few select people to see the collection in one place before he sent the pieces off to their final destinations.

He'd worked hard on the planned event—or at least his assistant had—and was looking forward to the night.

He wondered what Dev would think of his decision regarding the collection.

"I'd like you to come," he finished by saying.

"You know I wouldn't miss it unless you don't want me there," she said with a shrewd light in her eyes.

A moment later, he realized what that meant.

Dev would be at the opening. He hadn't invited her yet, but he would. Then she and his mother would meet.

He drew in a careful breath at the thought of the two most important women in his life meeting each other. Would that be such a bad thing? After all, he and Dev were on a different playing field with each other now.

Beyond his collection of Harlem Renaissance art, Bennett now knew without a doubt that Dev wanted him. She had proven it again and again in Spain, not just by surrendering to his desires but confessing some of her own.

His back still burned from the rake of her nails. His muscles were still sore from their weekend of marathon sex, not just at Alonzo's place but in the plane on the way back to Atlanta.

If he hadn't been in love with her before now, the way she opened herself up to him in Sandin de la Frontera would have tipped him firmly over the edge. In bed as well as out, she had challenged him, made him laugh, made him ache. Made him want more of her in every way.

As the plane had flown closer to Atlanta, he could see her hesitation in returning. She didn't meet his eyes as firmly as she had when they were miles away from everything familiar. Her touches became tentative. Although she probably needed the space to figure it all out, when he dropped her off at her door, he kissed her deeply, passionately. Stroking her tongue with his and joining their breaths. Her soft groan of deprivation as he'd broken the kiss curled triumph in his belly right alongside the desire to tug her into the house and make love to her against the front door.

But Bennett had given Dev her space and driven away to his own home.

Now it had been two days since he'd seen her.

"Bennett Randal, are you actually listening to me?"

He turned away from his thoughts of Dev to focus on the woman on the other side of the table.

His mother tilted her silver head at him, ignoring the waiter who moved behind her to refill her glass of red wine. Bennett flashed her his most carefree smile. "Of course I am."

"So what are you thinking about so hard that you're ignoring your poor mother?"

His "poor mother" was anything but. Not only was she sharp enough not to be fooled by any of his deflections, she was still the very active co-CEO of the company she and her husband started when they were young. According to his mother, they were just keeping the CEO seat warm for Bennett while he finished sowing his wild oats.

"I'm only thinking about the usual," he said, equivocating, hoping she'd pick any one of his "usual" worries out of the air and run with it.

"Which is exactly what, my only son?"

"Making the company more profitable?" He didn't mean to make it sound like a question but there it was.

"That I think you can do in your sleep," his mother said. "Or at least in your spare time."

She picked up her wine and swirled the deep red liquid under the light. A smile gently chided him.

"What are you hiding from me, Bennett?"

He shook his head and hid his grimace, amazed as usual how she seemed to see through him so effortlessly. His father had no such talent, which was probably why he and his father got along so well. Sometimes secrets made for better relationships.

Bennett cleared his throat and searched for a way to redirect his mother. "Adah just got back from her honeymoon."

Stephanie Randal smiled, a genuine response to the woman they both liked, even if his mother had been thinking of Adah as a daughter-in-law for the handful of years she and Bennett had been engaged. Now, she was getting used to the idea of Adah being just a family friend. A friend to Bennett instead of a fiancée or wife. It was the best thing for everyone concerned.

"Oh!" She paused with her glass of wine near her lips. "Wonderful! Honeymoons are one of the best traditions. Such a perfect way to start a marriage."

He glanced at his mother sideways. "Please don't tell me anything about your honeymoon with Pops."

"Why would I do such a thing?" But her smile told him she was about to do just that. "Anyway, seems like you might be thinking about having a honey of your own." She left a meaningful pause. "Are you?"

A honey? He deliberately steered his mind away from Dev. "Life is much more than romance and business deals you know, Mother?"

"Is it? How boring for you then. I was hoping you'd at least get a little sex with a side of romance." She swirled the wine in the glass before taking a sip. "Obviously, you can have one without the other but romance does make the bed play a little sweeter."

Was he really having this conversation with his mother?

"No comment." He took a long drink of his brandy, wincing only a little from the burn.

"Oh good! There *is* a girl in your life. Someone special, right?" She didn't wait for him to agree or disagree. "That's wonderful. Just the other day I was telling your father that it was time you stopped watching other people connect and form a real romantic relationship of your own."

He carefully placed the brandy glass on the table. "I don't have a problem making connections, Mother."

His mother managed to make a grunt sound lady-like. "I'm not talking about getting women into your bed, Bennett. I think all of Atlanta and the greater part of Europe know you're quite skilled in the catching and claiming of romantic prey."

"Prey? Really?"

"Do you prefer me to say 'hoes,' Bennett dear?" Now she was just laughing at him. "Seriously, I worry for you. I want you to find some contentment. Maybe not exactly what your father and I have but something that makes you happy, at least." She pursed her lips. "And I don't mean with Leilani's Pearls. I've already asked you to be certain you're ready for the responsibility of running the company after we step away. You said yes. Now I want you to be sure about the type of personal future you're moving toward, as well."

It was strange. Nearly everyone Bennett knew usually remarked at some point how happy he was and how they envied that happiness. His mother was the only one who seemed to see past everything. Maybe she didn't know he had simply resigned himself to doing what was right for his family and for the company instead of for himself. Maybe she didn't know he'd fallen hard for Devyn Clark the first time he saw her. But she knew something wasn't quite how he made it all seem.

His usual honesty came to the fore, unadorned by the usual layer of bull. "I'm working at getting what I want, Mother. With the direction of the company, and with my life. I promise. It's just taking a little while to get there."

"As long as you're walking toward it, my love. That's all I ever wanted for you." She grinned around a small mouthful of wine. "Well, that and a couple of babies to keep you out of the henhouse. But that's a conversation for another time."

Thank God.

Bennett reached for his brandy with a low sigh of relief.

Chapter 14

Being with Bennett, in bed and out, had been even more incredible than Dev thought it would be.

More than just the sex—which was mind-blowing—was the ease with which they'd fallen into a rapport with each other. Now that she wasn't holding him at arm's length it was easy to see all the things they had in common, how well they fit together. It was frightening and she was still trying to deal with it.

Less importantly, she was getting sick of Tangie and what the woman was trying to force her to do. Sitting across from her boss's desk, she crossed her legs and bit back a sigh.

"Are you even listening to me?" Tangie's voice reached her from far away.

"Oh, I'm sorry," Dev said, although she obviously wasn't. "Just having a hard time adjusting to being back."

Tangie crossed her arms under her breasts and fixed a disbelieving stare on Dev. "Back? You were barely gone for the weekend. Your jet lag can't be that bad, if you actually have any."

Dev ignored the other woman's rudeness because she pretty much had to.

After she'd returned from Spain, Dev reluctantly told Tangie where she and Bennett had gone in search of the new piece for the collection.

"Lucky girl" had been her boss's only reply along with a knowing glance that made Dev feel a little dirty. Then Tangie said, "Too bad the painting wasn't what Randal expected. It would've been nice to have a special piece that traveled all the way from Europe to end up right back here on American soil where it was first created. And in my gallery, of course."

Dev crossed and recrossed her legs, restless and wanting to be anyplace but there.

Obviously it wasn't really jet lag responsible for her wandering mind. It had been spending the last few hours in Spain—and later on the massive bed on the private jet—being Bennett's lover in every way she'd dreamed. They'd kissed, they'd touched, they'd laughed and been closer and more emotionally connected than Dev had felt with any other lover.

The time with Bennett had been absolutely magical, but she hadn't known exactly how they were expected to be with each other now that they were back in Atlanta. It was like being away from here had opened possibilities for them that hadn't existed before. Now, though, despite the passionate kiss they'd shared at Dev's front door when he dropped her off, Dev didn't quite know where they stood.

"Anyway..." Tangie tapped a manicured fingernail against the surface of her recently cleaned desk. "So while you two were soaking up the Spanish sunshine, did he tell you anything at all about his plans for the art collection?"

"Not a thing." While they'd been tangled together, Dev had avoided any conversation at all about the collection. It was one thing to approach him about selling the work through Tangie's gallery when he was barely even an acquaintance. Now it just felt too wrong to continue, as if she'd be using him.

One thing she hadn't told Tangie was that she was thinking about backing out of the agreement they'd made. Dev's mistake had led her to this untenable position but it was too uncomfortable, too much like whoring, for her to continue. Earlier, Tangie had asked her if she was any closer to getting Bennett to do what they wanted. Dev could only admit that she was closer only to falling in love with Bennett. Every moment she thought of his collection and Tangie's plan to get it, she felt sick.

Her boss made an impatient noise. "Well, use your charm to get him where we need him to be. I didn't plan for this thing with him to be a long game."

In her pocket, Dev felt her phone vibrate with a message. "Excuse me," she said to Tangie, then pulled out the cell. It was a message from Bennett.

I'm having an art premiere of sorts in my glorified basement. Private and invite only. Showing off the collection a bit before settling on where it needs to be permanently. I'd love for you to be there as my guest. Please say you'll come.

He'd attached a professionally done digital flyer with the date and time as well as the address of his home.

"It's Bennett," Dev said when Tangie started to visibly squirm as she read the text. "He's having a little showing of the collection. A private list of invited guests."

Tangie cursed and leaned across the desk to glare at Dev. "He's not trying to sell the collection himself, is he?" A look of worry tightened her mouth.

"I doubt that. He doesn't have the time, or the inclination."

"Good. That's a relief. Well, work harder on getting that collection for us when you go to his little opening. It'll help put this gallery on the map. Not that we aren't already pretty well-known, but we could always do better."

Dev nodded, thinking that *she* could do better too and stop being a pawn of a woman she didn't even respect. Especially if it meant no longer trying to manipulate the man she lo—wanted more than she should.

Knowing what that would mean, she swallowed a hint of nervousness that rose up in her throat, but presented Tangie her calmest look. She put her phone away.

"I have serious doubts that the preview will change anything, but I'll go and let you know what happens."

"I don't suppose you can wrangle me an invitation to this opening...?" Tangie tapped her sharp nails against the desk in an uneven rhythm, looking thoughtful, almost diabolical. "Maybe if I get the chance to talk with him while the work is hanging on the wall, it'll go a long way toward bringing him over to our way of thinking."

Not this again. "I don't think so. If you show up there, it'll only make Bennett more guarded." Not to mention she didn't want Tangie anywhere near Bennett. The woman's presence was enough of a taint in her own life; she didn't want to bring her around Bennett any more than necessary. He was a good man. Dev cleared her throat. "I'll talk to Bennett again, although to be honest, after what he told me in Spain, selling the collection through us seems less likely by the day."

"Why do you say that?"

"Because he knows we want it, so I'm assuming he would have said something by now." She didn't think Bennett would keep her in suspense. "I'm wondering if he wants to let me...us...down easy."

"Don't speculate, just do," Tangie said. "If his 'no' ever seems like it's about to be final, I'll step in."

"That's probably not a good idea," Dev cautioned. "He doesn't like being cornered. When he is, he doesn't do what you'd expect." He would only answer Tangie's challenge with one of his own.

Tangie scoffed. "All men are the same. You just have to find which buttons to push. In the end, their knees all buckle the same."

Then this woman really didn't know Bennett. Did she understand anything at all if this was what she believed about men?

Dev picked up her purse and tucked it under her arm, standing up. "I'll leave you to your speculations. I've got to drop the Wharton deposit off at the bank plus a few other errands that can't wait."

They'd just sold one of the big floor pieces, a predictable sale to a law office with a new branch opening in Buckhead.

Tilting back slightly in her chair, Tangie shook her head. "No, don't worry about that. I'll deal with it after I lock up today."

Dev frowned. For as long as she'd worked with Tangie, her job had been to make sure all the big cash and check deposits got dropped off at the bank before close of business on the day the money came through. What? Did Tangie have so little faith in her she wouldn't even let her handle such a simple task anymore?

"Okay…"

"Don't get that look on your face. I have good reason to take care of these deposits now until you earn back my trust," Tangie said dismissively. "Now, get out of here. I'm sure you have better things to do this afternoon."

That was true enough. She had a few things that needed to be dealt with before she fell into bed tonight. Worrying about what her boss was up to didn't even make it to the bottom of that list.

One of those things included making sure she had a dress nice enough to impress at Bennett's opening. They might be on uncertain ground as to where they stood as lovers or, whatever. But she still wanted to look irresistible when she stepped through his front door.

Speaking of which. "See you later, Tangie. I'll call you if anything comes up."

"Of course," Tangie said, which basically translated to "You better."

Taking the back door, Dev ducked out of the gallery. She grabbed her phone on the way through the parking lot.

"Hey," she said when her sister answered the phone. "Can I get you to do me a favor?"

"Sure, sugar pie," Aisha chirped.

"I have a little problem and I want you to just listen and let me know what you think." When

Dev started her car's engine, the call automatically switched to the Bluetooth.

"That's not a favor! You know I love telling you what I think." Aisha giggled and Dev could practically see her sister toss her too-long hair and settle her mouth closer to the receiver. "Now, tell your little baby sister everything and don't leave out a single detail."

Dev drew a deep breath and spilled it all as she drove home. This was her first time telling anyone what she had done, what she had gotten herself into and how she planned on digging herself out of it. As the words left her mouth in a flood, she felt lighter and lighter. The burden was now shared and she could breathe a little bit easier.

"Are you out of your freakin' mind?" Aisha's shocked voice sounded abruptly closer.

"What?"

"Why would you agree to something like that? If you'd asked me about this weeks ago I'd have told you that giving that crazy woman what she wants is not the way to go. Devyn! I thought you were the smartest one of us." The tease was still in Aisha's voice but Devyn knew she was serious.

"I'm not doing it anymore," Dev said. "I can't keep pushing Bennett toward Tangie's gallery."

"Forget that little fact. You don't feel at all strange sleeping with him while trying to convince him to do something he probably has zero interest in doing?"

"You make it sound like I'm prostituting myself!"

"You said it, not me," Aisha snapped.

Devyn clenched her jaw tight.

She was wrong, and she knew it. Even if Dev hadn't been using their physical attraction to get Bennett to think kindly of her business proposition, he might think that if he learned the full extent of her deal with her boss. It was slimy on so many levels.

The messed-up part of it all was that she *did* want to share her body with Bennett. She *did* want to make love with him and have more adventures on the road together.

His collection, she knew now, would be much better off someplace else. Maybe a school. Maybe on display in an African American history museum. Just about any place other than Tangie's gallery, where her boss would just make money from the work and help to scatter the collection all over the world.

With a low sigh of defeat, Devyn clenched her hands around the steering wheel. "I was thinking of borrowing the money from Ahmed to pay her back."

"That sounds like your last resort," Aisha said, because she knew Devyn didn't *ever* want to do something like that.

"It is. I don't want to, but I can't think of anything else." Asking Ahmed for the money seemed the very definition of desperation. After paying off her student loans, the money she'd been saving to open up her own gallery was nowhere near enough to cancel her debt to Tangie.

"I just don't know, Aisha. I have to think of something. You may not have any ideas of what else I can do, but at least you're a good sounding board."

"Hey! I'm way more than that."

"Well, I wish you were a solution machine, stuff problems in get solutions out."

"I'm thinking," her sister said. "Just give me a second. I may not have any ideas now but that doesn't mean my brain cells won't start activating after another cup of tea. Or another of those yummy muffins Mom brought us from that tiny bakery in Grant Park."

Her sister made an appreciative noise then; the sounds coming through the phone indicated she'd started snacking on something sweet.

Okay. The usefulness of this call was officially over.

"Anyway, thanks for listening, Aisha. I just needed to work this through out loud. It's… It's been a heavy weight to bear on my own."

Her sister's frustrated sigh reached her in the midst of her delicate, chipmunk-like chewing. "I don't know where you got this lone wolf mentality from. You have a family that loves you and cares for you. Share your problems with us. We only want to help you, Devyn."

"I know…"

But sometimes it was hard to keep that in mind. She loved her mother and siblings, but they had their own lives and didn't need to see just how helpless she was sometimes, especially compared to all of them who were so damn efficient and brilliant.

Her brother had converted his talent at tossing balls around into a stellar decades-long career complete with sound business investments. Her sister was a brilliant and prizewinning architect, while their mother, in addition to just being plain amazing at life, was a tenured college professor beloved by all her students.

All Devyn had these days was an impossible debt and feelings for a man she should stay away from.

"Anyway, I have to go," she said. "No rest for the indebted and underpaid." Her thoughts flashed to Bennett's upcoming opening and the massive pressure Tangie was putting on her to get his collection at McBride.

Yes, she had to deal with that, and deal with it soon, before, as Aisha said, it bit her hard in the butt.

After the call with Aisha ended, Dev was pulling into her garage.

Once upon a time, she would've called up some of her single girlfriends and invited them to go drinking at one of the many hot places in Atlanta and forget about her problems for a while. But somehow, over the years, she'd drifted away from most of those girls.

They were all *women* now and most of them had found success of the type Devyn could only dream of. Of the four she used to spend most of her time with, one was now a pediatrician, happily single and dating, at least according to her very active social media. The others had also found professional happiness, although they were either married or in serious relationships. Dev was the only one with nothing to show but her isolation, debt and foolish regrets.

Okay. Enough of that. This pity party was getting out of control.

In the house, she exchanged her high heels for flip-flops, then went to check the mail.

"Oh!" Wow.

Someone had sent her flowers. On the porch sat a large bouquet of yellow and white roses sprinkled with small purple blooms. Whoever had delivered them had tucked them carefully in the shade but also in a place where Dev was sure to see them. A card was perched on the side of the large bouquet. Her heart tripped in her chest as she reached for it.

Have dinner with me this week. Tomorrow?
Just because we're back in the real world,
doesn't mean the magic between us has to end.
Bennett

A warm ball of happiness floated in her chest. She was a fool where this man was concerned. But at least she was consistent.

They hadn't seen each other since they got back from Spain. Only a few quick phone calls and text messages here and there. She was ashamed to say she'd been afraid of finding out what he had in mind for them. If he wanted to continue what they had or pretend it all never happened or something else. But the real shame of it came because she didn't have any idea what *she* wanted.

Bennett said what he and Adah had in the past didn't matter where he and Dev were concerned. But that wasn't true. He was a man. He didn't understand the girl code. *Do not date your friends' exes.* It was law. It was a rule that protected friendships.

She *did* know, though, but that hadn't stopped her from hopping on top of Bennett the first chance she got.

All this plus her conflicted feelings about using him to get to his art collection seemed to create an insurmountable wall between what she wanted and what was possible.

Dev shook her head. Still, she reached for the flowers and drew the thick vase close to her chest, inhaling deeply. They smelled incredible. Sun warmed and filled with intention.

And they made her happy.

Fighting through the conflicting feelings, she took the flowers into the house and put them in the center of her small dining table. Her mother and sister would ask where they came from. Then she'd have to confess. To every single thing.

But maybe it was time to finally come clean to them both.

Chapter 15

Dev never managed to get together for dinner with Bennett before his art opening.

She wanted to, but things kept getting in the way. Between running around doing her usual work for the gallery and trying her hardest to find solutions to her Tangie problem, she'd had to put off seeing Bennett until the evening of his event.

Maybe it was for the best. She still hadn't resolved in her heart whether she was doing the right thing dating a friend's ex, let alone doing the right thing seeing a man she originally only agreed to go away with because of a potential business benefit.

"What about this hot man of yours? Did you tell him about the deal you have with Tangie yet?" Aisha shifted across Dev's bed, her head propped up on a pillow, bare feet hanging off the bed as she watched Dev finish getting dressed. "Or shouldn't I ask questions I already know the answer to?"

Standing in front of the floor-length mirror, Dev barely glanced over her shoulder at her sister. "I'm going to tell him tonight. I've been running around like a headless chicken this whole week without a solution to any of my problems. I need to at least face this situation with Bennett head-on, though."

The only real decision she made this week—except for accepting the humiliation of having to inevitably ask Ahmed for a loan once he got back from his honeymoon—was to tell Bennett why she'd been so insistent about acquiring the collection for Tangie.

Aisha was right; the whole situation sat like a piece of volcanic rock in her stomach. The discomfort of it took over her days and made the simplest things seem like agony as her focus drifted. Her mind just wouldn't let her rest.

With deliberately steadied hands, Dev smoothed the material of her dress over her hips and thighs, then checked her reflection one last time.

Simple. Elegant. Sexy without trying too hard.

At the last minute, she'd gone into the bathroom to switch from her glasses to her contacts, only to find that she'd didn't have any more of the disposable lenses. So, wearing much more eye makeup than she was used to, she put on the dark-rimmed glasses she usually only wore at home.

With a pretty dress and "Oprah at the 2018 Golden Globes" specs on, she felt ready for anything.

The fuchsia sheath dress hugged her body and looked fantastic with her glowing skin. Her yellow stilettos made her look taller than usual and she still had a little tan from the couple of days in Spain, despite spending most of the time under Bennett.

Bennett.

She would tell him tonight. Not the reason she owed Tangie, just the broad strokes. Then she would let him know she was no longer going to press him about the collection. It was his to do whatever he wanted with, obviously, and she wasn't going to try to convince him otherwise.

She was up to all that, right?

Behind her, she heard the click of a cell phone camera. Aisha sat up in the bed, her camera aimed at Dev's backside. She clicked a few more pictures, then put the phone down beside her. "You should get going. You don't want to be late for your confession."

"Shut up."

Aisha stuck out her tongue, then smiled. "Good luck, sister."

"Thanks." Dev checked her dress and makeup one last time. "I think I'll need it."

Less than an hour later, she pulled up to Bennett's house with her stomach full of butterflies. She made it out of the car and followed the trickling line of guests to the back entrance of Bennett's house.

At the door, she showed her invitation to one of the two uniformed men.

"Thank you, Ms. Clark," the long-haired one said to her with a smile, his eyes making a subtle sweep of her curves as he handed her back the invitation.

She stepped inside.

Unlike her first visit to Bennett's house, this was a very different experience, more impersonal as she kept to the route everyone else had to take. Once inside, the air-conditioning brushed a cool breeze over her bare arms, and the presence of so many people, maybe no more than thirty, made Bennett's basement feel like a very different room.

From the way it looked and felt, Dev could have been in any professionally designed Atlanta art gallery. And she could have been any one of the dozens of people invited.

Jazzy music from the 1920s, low but infectious, played from hidden speakers. Voices hummed from the mixed crowd and the room itself had the gentle hush of a museum. Wide pedestals with prettily presented appetizers stood in various areas of the large room like they were part of the art collection themselves. And security was very present. Just from a quick glance, she could see at least four people in dark suits obviously keeping their eyes on the art as well as the people gathered to see it.

Everything was very beautiful. Tasteful.

Bennett had told her to call as she was coming out to the opening so that he could greet her personally. But nerves and everything else she had to do beforehand had stopped her. She was jittery and afraid, knowing what she needed to say to him tonight, how she needed to reveal her deal with Tangie.

Basically, she was a coward.

The gathering was a group of diverse people who seemed as though they had little in common. Some looked like college students with their statement T-shirts and dreadlocks, others like high-powered executives, other still like women on the prowl in their short skirts and glitteringly seductive smiles.

Their only shared trait was that they wanted to see the artwork Bennett had displayed in his home.

And speaking of Bennett... Dev spotted the man himself across the room, in his element and very definitely in charge of the night's event.

He was all casual elegance tonight. Charcoal slacks and matching coat, a pale green T-shirt underneath the jacket. No tie. Just gorgeous. Now she wished she'd moved heaven and earth to meet with him before the party. In that moment, she wanted nothing more than to feel his strong arms wrapped around her, his chest and strong beating heart under her cheek.

A soft breath left her body in a rush. Heat coursed through her, concentrating in her chest. Inevitably, the sensation moved south, rolled down into her lap, that warm and womanly place that he could basically have whenever he wanted.

God, she was such a fool for Bennett Randal.

It wasn't the first time she'd ever had that thought

looking at him, and she knew it wouldn't be the last. Without effort, he easily overwhelmed her senses, leading her to try things she'd never entertained before. His very presence brought promises leaping to her lips that she wished she could keep.

Dev couldn't count the times she'd promised herself to stay away from him.

She'd been able to years ago. But not now.

The first time she saw him was at school. Her first year in college, hopped up on hormones and ready to try anything and everything the adult world could throw her way. It was the weekend, a Friday, when she walked past a town bar with Adah and a couple of their new college girlfriends.

Dev had had her first art appreciation class that day and was stammering out her experience, trying to convey her excitement about the class to Adah and the other girls. They didn't care, but she didn't care that they didn't care.

And then she happened to turn her head at just the right time and saw a boy. Obviously older. Drinking at the bar and laughing with someone next to him. He looked up too and Dev fell into the deep ocean of his eyes from across the space that felt abruptly smaller than before. The laughter dropped from his face and he stared back, his eyes devouring her body before coming back to her face. He started to get up—she would swear it—then one of his friends grabbed his shoulder and said something to him that made him look away, then Dev and Adah kept walking and the moment was lost.

He was lost. To her. Because the next time she saw him, Bennett was being introduced as Adah's fiancé.

The disappointment she felt in that moment was nothing to the agony she experienced each time she saw him with Adah, or just saw him around Atlanta knowing that he could never be hers. So she put up a hard shell for self-protection and convinced herself that she hated him. She took pleasure each time he seemed like the bad guy in some situation she knew nothing about. He became the epitome of bad choices, things lost for a good reason, a bullet dodged.

Now she couldn't ignore her real feelings for him anymore.

She'd had a crush on Bennett when she was a girl in college. And now, thanks to a collection of incredible artwork and a stupidly self-indulgent weekend in Spain, she was deeply and hopelessly in love with him.

Dev's chest ached as the truth settled there.

Yes, she was in love with him.

Yes, she was a fool.

No, she wouldn't change a thing.

Across the room, he stood with supreme confidence. Hands in his pockets, his head nodding once then twice as he listened to the man he shared a conversation with. The dark slacks and jacket were perfect on him. The cloth looked both soft and elegant, perfectly fitted to his tall and narrow-hipped body.

Dev's lips tingled. Her hands heated. The urge to seduce him into a dark corner and allow him to kiss her breathless overwhelmed her. It had been far too long since they touched.

The regret gnawed at her again. What had she been thinking, depriving herself of his touch, of his heated kisses and passion for so long? None of the tasks she'd had to finish over the last few days had been worth the loss of times she could've been in his arms.

A flash of dark green moved across her vision, hiding Bennett from her sight. She automatically tilted her head to see around whoever it was that just stepped in her way, on the verge of moving herself just to keep him in view.

"Is it his art you want, or his body?"

The sound of a familiar voice, a voice she hoped never to hear again except on the other side of a jail cell, jerked her from her contemplation of Bennett.

Miriam Alexander stood in front of her. Tall, elegant, free. The woman who'd pretended to be someone else, an innocent, eager-to-learn intern, when Dev had taken her under her wing at Tangie's, trusting her with easy access to the gallery's inventory of art.

Now Dev faced a different version of the Miriam she'd dealt with before. This one looked more grownup with her straightened hair, a beige skirt suit and wire-rimmed glasses, but she didn't have to wear the ripped jeans, T-shirts and braids in her hair for Dev to recognize her.

All of Dev's attention sharpened to a knifepoint. Her skin flushed cold with fury as every thought of Bennett flew out of her head.

Ready to fight, she stepped closer to the woman, a fist clenched at her side and her cell phone gripped tight in her free hand.

"What the *hell* are you doing here?" she asked the woman who'd stolen half a million dollars' worth of artwork from Tangie and left her to take the fall.

Chapter 16

Bennett's stomach did a little somersault when he saw Dev across the room.

Even though he'd been chatting up everyone he invited to the private showing, he was also keeping half an eye on the door and hoping to spot her when she walked in. An hour in, he was about to give in and call her when she finally showed up.

Hot pink dress. Bright yellow heels. Her hair loose around her face. For a moment, Bennett lost the flow of the conversation he was supposed to be having with one of his mother's old friends. Watching Dev, it felt like his heart was being tightly squeezed in her little fist.

Earlier that week, he'd planned on taking her on a

real date. Something intentional and special where he would also tell her about his plans for the art collection. But something had come up suddenly on Dev's end and she insisted on meeting him at the reception instead. Finally, here she was.

"What you've got here is pretty remarkable, Bennett." Professor Rik Tarkadian, one of the literature scholars from the local university and friend of the family, lightly touched Bennett's arm.

The man, bearded and bespectacled, tucked his hands behind his back, smiling. "I can't wait to see what you'll do with it. I'm sure whatever you do will be quite remarkable."

"Thank you for having such faith in me, Professor. I hope not to disappoint." He was one of the first people to reach out to Bennett wanting to see the collection. And when Bennett had reached back, he'd been relieved to find that the professor was just simply curious about the pieces and how they ended up in Bennett's possession.

Now that his curiosity was satisfied, the professor seemed happy.

"From what your mother tells me and from what I've seen with my own eyes, disappointment is the only thing you can never deliver. The community is very proud of you, young man."

A warmth of satisfaction glowed in Bennett's chest. Although the party had only been going on for an hour or so, everything he'd heard so far had been good. Even the skeptics who'd doubted the authenticity of the paintings, photos and manuscripts, came up to congratulate him or angle for a donation or a cheap sale. What he was most happy about, though, was the excitement of the students he'd invited. Many had never seen work from the Harlem Renaissance in person before. Their energy and enthusiasm crackled through the room of otherwise-sedate art lovers and academics.

His mother, who had promptly been ambushed by a young woman with a new product idea for Leilani's Pearls, had disappeared to talk business. After a quick kiss and greeting for Bennett, of course.

Overall, the night was going well. All he needed for it to feel complete was to talk to the woman he couldn't get off his mind.

After the professor walked away, Bennett looked where he'd last seen Dev. She wasn't there but couldn't have wandered too far.

Ah, there she was. Next to one of the high pedestal snack tables, she stood talking to a woman dressed in beige. Something about the woman was familiar but he only spared her a quick glance. Something was off about Dev. A strange stillness surrounded her and her back looked unnaturally stiff.

Yes, something was definitely wrong. Dev's face was completely calm and erased of all emotion. She was mad as hell. Curious and trying not to be worried, Bennett slipped through the crowd to get a better look at who she was talking to.

Wasn't that…? He moved in closer.

It seemed like the rage rode Dev so hard that she didn't notice him, only the woman in front of her. Strangely, the woman was smiling. Her teeth looked very white and very sharp. Although she wore a plain beige suit, something obviously designed to blend in, along with wire-rimmed glasses and low-heeled shoes, there was something about the woman's predatory expression that seemed completely out of place.

Just like she'd seemed out of place when she'd come to his house that morning with Alan DuValle to appraise the collection. Although they hadn't found anything outwardly suspicious about the woman calling herself Melanie Winchester, his security guys had decided to keep an eye on her and advised Bennett to do the same. They said her ID was too perfect. And when DuValle had received an invitation to this event, DuValle's boss had asked for an invitation for Melanie Winchester to come to the showing, as well. Bennett had given one, but he never forgot what his guys told him.

After a dismissive look at Dev, Melanie Winchester said something that Bennett didn't hear and walked away. Dev followed closely behind her, only allowing a foot or two of space between them. Together, they slipped from the main exhibition space, past a sign marked Private hanging from a black velvet rope. The hallway and rooms beyond the rope were darkened and, as promised, very private. Silently, Bennett followed.

Chapter 17

"What am I doing here? Probably the same thing you are," the woman who Dev knew as Miriam Alexander had said with a particularly predatory smile when Dev confronted her. "Working on getting Randal to loosen his grip on those beautiful pieces so they can fall into my hands."

Fear for Bennett had gripped Dev's stomach in a vise.

"You *will* leave him alone and leave him out of this." She'd hissed the words before she realized just exactly what Miriam said.

She was setting up Bennett to be the next gullible idiot who fell for her lies and trusted her just enough to get away with whatever she wanted to steal.

"There's no use getting upset, Devyn." Miriam had flicked her eyes from side to side, seeming to look at the whole room without once turning her head. While the space wasn't overcrowded, people moved constantly past and around them. "Why don't we have this discussion someplace a little more private?" Her chin jerked toward a darkened and empty passageway leading out of the otherwise-well-lit gallery space.

Without waiting for Dev's agreement, she turned and headed toward the hall, her stride sure and unhurried, apparently confident that Dev would trail after her. Dev gritted her teeth. Miriam walked like she belonged in the building and at the party, like she knew where she was going and anybody would be foolish to try to stop her.

Dammit. Dev knew it was a bad idea, but she still followed Miriam. Anger flashed through her like a dangerous and all-consuming fire, and every step she took was an exercise in not choking the woman to death.

She'd stolen from Tangie and then left Dev to take the blame for it all. Now she wanted to steal from Bennett, too. Hell no.

In the deep shadows of the hallway, Miriam turned to her. That smug smile that Dev remembered all too well from her last glimpse of Miriam dirtied her pretty face now.

"I know you don't want your rich stud to see us talking, so here we are in the dark." Miriam put her hands on her hips, still smirking. "Although he'd be very interested in this conversation we're having."

But Dev wasn't ready to hear anything from the woman except for one thing.

"Where are the paintings you stole?" she snapped.

"Gone, of course." Miriam waved a hand indicating the air above them. "That's the point of *stealing*." She said it like Dev was stupid in the extreme. "Do you think I've had them in my garage for the last six weeks just waiting for you to confront me and snatch them all from my thieving hands?"

Dev didn't dignify that crap with a response. "I want those paintings back!"

"We all want a lot of things…"

The smirk grew and Dev wanted nothing more than to slap it off Miriam's face.

"Basically, you're never going to see that amateurish batch of scribblings again. I already got my money for them and they're someplace out in the world being someone else's problem, or pleasure."

Dev's jaw locked tight from her anger. Her stomach plunged with disappointment.

Although she tried to control the emotions on her face, Dev knew she must have looked stunned. Miriam was far from the shy recent college graduate she'd pretended to be when she came to Tangie's gallery looking for an unpaid internship. That was how she'd gotten to Dev with the soft voice and slightly lost manner paired with surprising competence while working at the gallery. That version of Miriam—or whatever her real name was—had disappeared, leaving a cunning and cruel woman in her place.

But the past was over. Dev had been gullible and she had been taken; now she only needed to push forward and fix the things she'd broken with her stupid naïveté.

"I'm gonna go ahead and assume you're trying to get Randal's collection for Tangie, or maybe for yourself…" Whatever she saw in Dev's face sparked her crack of laughter. "Christ. Are you sure you're not the one who just fell off the turnip truck rumbling out of a small college town? You never even thought of getting those paintings for yourself, did you?" Miriam couldn't seem to stop laughing.

Dev stepped threateningly toward the other woman. "Enough of this crap."

Miriam didn't look the least bit worried. In her simple but expensive beige suit, she stood under the faint trails of light with Dev like they were only talking about what flavor of coffee they liked. Her laughter faded into soft chuckles.

"Okay, because we have a history I'm going to do you a solid and tell you a version of the truth." Miriam lifted her hand with one finger out. "First of all, you're not going to get a damn thing from Bennett Randal. He's already decided what to do with the collection, which is donate it to some backwater nonprofit." She put out two fingers. "Second, Tangie will never see any of this work inside her gallery. And neither will you." An attitude of malice and triumph radiated from Miriam. "As a representative from Next Generation for the Arts, I have about ten times more of a chance of getting my hands on the work than you do even if you do wise up and realize what you can get out of this man."

As a representative for…? No, that had to be fake. Miriam only represented herself. Not any university like she'd claimed months ago, and certainly no nonprofit. The only cause she raised money for was herself. If she got her hands on any of Bennett's pieces, she'd try to get it for free, then turn around and sell it for an obscene profit.

Then she'd leave this nonprofit, if it really existed, in hot water for being associated with her.

The two things Miriam told Dev rang in her head like loud signal bells.

Bennett had already made up his mind about what to do with his collection, and he never told her. He just let her believe she had a chance at swinging his decision her way. She was being as naive about her chance of getting some part of the collection for Tangie as the schoolgirl Miriam had pretended to be months before.

But Dev latched onto what frightened her the most.

"Like I told you before, leave Bennett Randal alone. He's not as much of a fool as I was all those months ago when you showed up in your little schoolgirl's outfit."

"He's a big boy," Miriam said with a roll of her

eyes. "I'm sure he can handle anything that little old me can dish out. And if he folds like a cheap tent the way you did, then the whole world will know just what type of guy is about to take over his parents' company."

A growl rolled up Dev's chest. She felt all animal in that moment, protective of Bennett in a way she'd only felt before about family. "I said, let him the hell alone or I'll tell everybody who will listen just who and what you are. A cheating con artist."

"What are you going to tell them?" Miriam's almost-playful manner disappeared. She stepped toward Dev, hands on her hips. "You know if you say anything about the art in Tangie's gallery that went missing, I'll say you were in on it. That's what Tangie thinks, too. You're in a corner. You don't know a damn thing. You don't even know my real name."

"I'm sure it won't take too long to find that out, *Melanie*." It was Bennett's voice.

Dev spun around. She'd been so focused on her confrontation with Miriam that she hadn't noticed him walk up behind the other woman. Dev felt her face grow scorching hot.

Had he heard her defending him like some lovestruck teenager in a high school melodrama? Her mind tripped back to the other thing, equally important, that she'd let slide in Miriam's threat to hurt him and his reputation.

"Is what she said true?" she asked. "Did you already decide what to do with the collection?"

After another hard glance at Miriam, he nodded to her once. An expression like remorse crossed his face. "Yes. I decided a while ago—"

"But why didn't you tell me?" Then a truth occurred to her, that he was just stringing her along to keep their strange little sexual affair going. God, that thought hurt. Dev pressed a hand to her belly. "I thought what we have going on was separate from the situation with the art collection. Did you just string me along so you could keep sleeping with me?" And here she'd been worried about doing that to him. He'd been the one with the secret.

A soft snort of laughter came from Miriam, who Dev almost forgot was there.

"This is rich!" the con woman said with a malicious gleam in her eyes. "You screw him to get his art and he played you. Poor Devyn Clark. Gullible until the end, huh?" Miriam sneered, then, after a swift and frightened glance at Bennett's thunderous face, slipped past them both.

Bennett motioned with a hand and a security guard Dev hadn't noticed before appeared from one of the dark corners to follow Miriam.

Oh God! Embarrassment rushed through Dev. Somebody else had overheard her pathetic questions to Bennett plus all the things Miriam said to her.

Please, let the earth open up and swallow her now…

Her hand tightened around her phone and she

turned to follow Miriam and her security guard pursuer out of the dark hallway.

"Dev, please wait."

She wanted to run out of there as fast as she could, but her feet had other ideas. Bennett's voice froze them where they stood. "Wait for what?" she asked, slowly dying inside. "For you to humiliate me some more? No thanks, Bennett. Even I'm not that self-flagellating."

"This isn't about punishing yourself, Dev. I just want to make sure you know what's going on."

She swallowed the humiliation and forced herself to keep standing there under his intent regard. "Okay, I'm listening. Let me know how much I've misunderstood what's going on." She crossed her arms across her chest and waited.

He bit out a curse and ran a hand over his face. "It's true that I already made my decision about where the collection is going—"

"Before Spain?" She just had to know.

Although Bennett didn't move, Dev got the impression of sudden nervousness from him. His wide-braced legs seemed less of a stance of confrontation or power and more one of protection. In his pockets, she noticed his hands tightening into fists. "Yes," he said slowly. "Before Spain."

A cry almost broke past her tight throat.

Can you blame him, though? A voice at the back of her head spoke. *You've been chasing him just for his collection. That was the only reason you allowed yourself to go along with him to Spain and every other thing he suggested that led up to you being in his bed. If he used the collection to get you into bed, then you used him, too.*

But Dev didn't want to listen to that too-logical voice. It burned with too much truth. Truth she wasn't willing to face in that moment.

Just then, Bennett's phone rang. But he ignored it. "Dev..." He paused and the corners of his eyes tightened. "I may not have gone about this the right way, but I promise what I did was for the right reasons. I want us to be more than cuddle buddies or whatever they call it these days."

"No!" She nearly screamed the word, then forced herself to lower her voice so people wouldn't come running. "I should've followed my instincts and stayed away from you. This is...this is so messed up." Adah was her friend. That was the most important part of it all that she'd allowed herself to forget. Everything else was secondary. "I can't... I can't even think about that right now."

Even with her concerns about Adah, it was the humiliation of being manipulated that burned deep and hot. It wasn't something she could push away, even though she desperately wanted to.

Aisha had warned her. Hell, even her own conscience had told her this wasn't the way to go. But here she was.

The phone in Bennett's pocket rang again.

He stepped closer while the device chimed. "Give me a chance to make this right, Dev."

She shook her head and stepped back. "There's nothing to make right. This whole thing was wrong from the beginning and I knew that." At the end of the day, she had been selfish and dumb as a box of rocks.

The phone stopped ringing and immediately started again.

"You should answer that." She jerked her head toward his phone.

Bennett cursed and yanked it out of his pocket. "Yes?" His steely eyes remained on her face. "Keep her here and call the police. And don't let her out of your sight."

The person on the other end of the phone said something else and Bennett turned away, frowning. He snapped a question to whoever he was talking to, but Dev didn't stay to listen to their conversation. The anger and embarrassment and pain were too much. In a clatter of sharp stilettos, she escaped the dark hallway, running away from the enclosed place as if all her dreams had been lit on fire and the flames were chasing at her very heels.

Chapter 18

Waking up was a challenge Dev wasn't quite up to.

Her alarm blared, insistent and loud, and she reached from under the covers to fumble for her phone and turn it off. But it was a Saturday morning and it wasn't her alarm.

"It's crazy early," she muttered to whoever was calling. "What's so important it can't wait until a decent time of the day?"

"Have you seen social media this morning?" Aisha grumbled at her. Her sister sounded a little faraway. Oh, Aisha must have her on speaker.

"Why would I look at Twitter?" Dev muttered. She pushed away the thin covers wrapped around her like tentacles and sprawled on her back.

Aisha was the one nearly obsessed with Twitter and the rest of them. With their brother being a celebrity and a once-available Hotlanta bachelor, she kept tabs on his mentions all over social media. Because she had the luxury to not care, Dev didn't.

"Your name is all over the internet, Dev! All the art blogs and gossip rags are talking crap about you."

"What?" She shoved her hair out of her face and sat up. "Why would they talk about me? What would they even say?"

Dev subscribed to a few art blogs but that was about it. That and her contacts in the industry were all she needed to keep in touch with things going on in the art world. The gossip rags didn't interest her. Even if they were based on the internet.

"Are you joking?" Aisha sounded like she was about to come through the phone and throttle her. "Not only are you Ahmed's sister, you've also been seen all over the place with one of the most eligible bachelors on the East Coast!"

Bennett. It figures.

"Okay, so what are they saying?"

Her sister fell silent. Then: "You should probably see it for yourself."

Dev huffed and struggled past the sheets twisting around her legs to get out of the bed. She swayed for a moment, light-headed.

Oh right. I didn't eat anything yesterday.

"No, ma'am. You're not going to call me to tell me there's news I should know about, then refuse to tell me exactly what that news is." In the bathroom, she scowled at her reflection before grabbing her toothbrush to scrub the overnight scum from her mouth. "What's going on, Aisha?"

Her sister drew a loud breath. Kitchen sounds from her end came through the phone. She was probably about to make coffee. "I'm sending you some links now, but basically you're screwed."

"How?" She asked the question around her toothbrush and the foamy toothpaste working its magic on her bad breath. Her sister was notoriously excitable and Dev often prided herself on her own calm nature. Chances were that whatever Aisha was up in arms about would blow over with no real consequences after a couple of days.

"Well, first, apparently, by Bennett Randal and very well, too, if the pics are anything to go by."

"What?" The toothbrush almost dropped out of Dev's mouth.

She hurriedly pulled the toothbrush from her mouth and tossed it in the sink. A quick gush of water rinsed out her mouth. Dev put her sister on speaker and began clicking through the links and images Aisha just sent. What the…?

Incredibly, there were pictures of her and Bennett from Spain. Getting out of the car at Alonzo's place and walking much too close. In one shot, he had his hand on the small of her back. And it would have almost been nothing if not for the look on her face, sensual and warm.

Then the most damning one. A shot of the two of them on Lorenzo's beach, kissing. They both wore their bathing suits but from the passion obviously sizzling from the photo alone they might as well have been naked. Bennett had been right about the possibility of paparazzi sneaking photos.

Oh my God...

Dev bit the inside of her cheek as she walked back into her bedroom and sank into one of the chairs there. That wasn't too bad. So what if she was photographed kissing Bennett? Nobody cared about her reputation, and as for Bennett, she was just another in a series of women he'd been linked to sexually. The only person who this could really affect was—

"And most of the articles are actually talking about the paintings that were stolen from Tangie's gallery under your watch. They're calling you Butter Fingers."

Miriam's theft? How did they know? Tangie never let it slip... Dev quickly scanned one of the so-called articles.

Aisha made a scornful sound. "Most of these rags are talking about a secret source but I'm sure we can both guess who that is."

No. Tangie would never do something like this. She had been adamant that nobody find out about the stolen artwork. She told Dev again and again that her reputation as a trusted gallery would be ruined.

Then who?

"Miriam," Dev growled.

"That chick who stole the art in the first place, right?" Aisha sounded livid on her behalf.

Dev cursed softly as her stomach lurched. She was going to be sick.

"What are you going to do?" her sister asked.

She didn't know. Not yet. She did know she wanted to call Adah, to apologize for not letting her know, for having her find out on social media that Dev was with her ex.

She jumped when her phone flashed, letting her know another call was trying to come through. Tangie. On a damn Saturday morning.

Another curse jumped from her lips.

"Tangie is calling. I have to go." She really didn't want to talk with her boss but preferred to face this monster of a problem head-on instead of putting it off.

"Screw her," Aisha spat. "She doesn't want anything more than to gloat over what's going on."

"But I don't know that for sure. Let me see what she wants and I'll call you back."

Her sister was reluctant but muttered "okay" before hanging up.

"Good morning, Tangie," Dev greeted as soon as she clicked over.

"You're fired."

Dev took the phone away from her ear and blinked down at it. "Excuse me?"

"I'm looking at Twitter right now. All your dirty laundry and mine is out there. I just got calls from two artists who're backing out of a deal to show at my gallery because of the mess with you and Miriam."

"Because she stole from us?"

"From me. Yes." Tangie sounded cold as ice. Coldly livid. "I've told you over and over again, Dev, but you refused to listen. Reputation is everything in this town, and in the world. It helps to get you the life you want, and it can also take away the kind of life you have. I can't afford to have you dragging me down anymore. Don't bother coming in to get your stuff. I'm having a messenger drop it by your place this afternoon. You're lucky I'm not pursuing legal action against you for bringing that thief onboard." And with that, her ex-boss hung up the phone on her.

As she looked down at her phone, a notification came through. A message from her sister with another link attached.

It was another gossip website. The headline of the article just about stopped Dev's heart.

DEVYN CLARK SCOOPS UP LEFTOVER FIANCÉ OF COSMETIC EMPIRE HEIRESS AND NEW DIALLO BRIDE.

The featured photo was another one of Dev and Bennett, this one from before their affair. She, Adah and Bennett standing side by side at some fundraiser. Bennett had his arm around Adah, but his smile, an intimate curving of his lips, was directed at Dev. The photo looked damning, like she'd been sleeping with Bennett before he and Adah ended their engagement.

This can't be happening. Feeling truly sick, Dev clutched her stomach. *Adah can't see this.* Not before Dev had a chance to explain. With shaking fingers, she rushed to call her friend.

"Hey, Adah." She pressed her lips together to stop herself from immediately rushing out with an apology as soon as Adah picked up the phone.

"Devyn. How are you?" her friend chirped happily at her. "I have you on my list to call for a lunch invite when I'm back in Atlanta next week."

Dev winced. With the drama Miriam was stirring up, she'd never get that invitation now.

She swallowed the thick ball of guilt in her throat. "It'll be good to see you, Ade. Everything happened so quickly after your guy decided to come up here after you."

Her friend laughed. She sounded so damn happy. "Yeah, I know. Isn't Kingsley just crazy?" She giggled. "Not to mention I didn't even think moving down to Miami would be an option. Not with my business being in Atlanta."

"What, you thought that man would've been okay with you living part-time here *and* Miami?" Adah's rueful chuckle dredged up an answering smile from Dev.

Each word she spoke to her friend felt like a delaying tactic, unnecessary and painful. Dev had to bite the bullet and just tell Adah what was going on.

Dev nibbled on the inside of her cheek. "Um, listen. Before we talk about a time for our get-together next week, I have to tell you something."

"Sure. What's that?"

Adah sounded so innocent, so unaware of the ball Dev was about to drop on her that Dev almost chickened out. She knew Adah was happy, but she also knew that Adah had at one time thought Bennett was the one for her. To have him move on, and move on to Dev, would surely sting, even a little. Maybe a lot. But she clenched her jaw.

The information was out there, waiting to ambush Adah. Dev couldn't let her friend find out from reading it online or in some other cold-blooded way. She had to hear it from her.

Fear clenched her stomach tight. "I…I don't want you to find out about this from anyone but me." She licked her dry lips. "Bennett—Bennett and I slept together. Not when you were engaged to him, but…" The tears of regret and fear rushed down her face before she could even finish speaking. "Even though I did it with my eyes wide-open, I…I didn't mean to betray you."

"Oh. Is that all? I thought it was something serious."

"What?" Dev blinked stupidly into space.

"You didn't betray me, Dev."

"But I slept with your man!"

"First of all, I hope it was more than once because I hear Bennett's fantastic in bed."

What?

"Secondly, Bennett and I are like brother and sister. We've never had sex. We may have been engaged but it was something our parents set up years ago for the businesses. I love him like the brother I never had."

Surprise rocked through Dev. *Like brother and sister?*

"Are you...are you sure you're not upset?"

"Of course I'm not." Adah paused. "Didn't Bennett tell you how things are between us?"

Didn't he? Dev suddenly recalled the times that Bennett had talked about his relationship with Adah, describing it as deep and lasting but also not what she thought it was. The most he'd ever said about the intimate details of their engagement was that they were friends and Adah wouldn't be bothered if he became involved with Dev.

Dev hadn't believed him, though. He was a man. He lived by a different code. According to a few of the men she knew, and mostly in passing, it was nothing for them to relinquish a past lover to a friend. Which was why Dev sometimes thought men and women were a different species altogether.

"He said something like that but..." Dev's voice drifted away.

"But you never trusted him," Adah finished.

When her friend put it that way, it made Dev feel

unworthy of him. Small. Especially now that she realized what Bennett had really been doing. He'd been protecting Adah. If he'd provided more detail about their relationship, it might have made Adah appear shallow, as if she'd only committed to him for business reasons. He'd done the gentlemanly thing by not divulging details of the relationship he'd had with his ex.

"But I understand where you're coming from, Dev. I do. A lot of men just say what they need to to get us into bed. It's hard to completely trust."

And Adah knew the kind of men lurking in Dev's past. The ones who'd betrayed her. The man she almost married.

"Honey." Adah's voice came softly at her through the phone. "Are you crying?"

Heat glowed under Dev's face and fed the steady drip of tears from her eyes. The tears clogged her throat and all she could do was make a pained, animal sound.

"Dev. Devyn. Please. Don't cry." Now Adah sounded like she was crying, too. "I promise you, there's no betrayal. Bennett is his own man and if you love him, the way is clear for you."

Dev's tears stopped with the suddenness of a hiccup.

Love him?

Chapter 19

"Do you know my friend is tearing herself apart over you?" On Bennett's balcony, Adah turned away from her view of the long stretch of rolling hills and trees beyond the backyard.

The early morning sun highlighted her casual elegance in pale jeans and a cropped white T-shirt, glinting on the thin gold chains falling in a cascade at her throat. With a low sigh, she sat down cross-legged on the cushions Bennett brought out for her from the upstairs living room and leaned back against the railing. Her knee nudged the tray containing her breakfast—a glass of spinach and pineapple juice, a toasted croissant with slices of Havarti cheese and a glistening giant tomato.

"Is that what she told you?" Bennett asked. He lay back, bare chested, on the balcony's twin-size padded bench with his arms crossed under his head. Gritty from being up all night, his eyes squinted behind dark glasses. The sleep shorts he still wore stuck to his thighs as the burning sun heated his skin.

"Pretty much," Adah said. A smile played around her mouth as she brought the juice to her lips. "She called me, very apologetic. I think she was more worried about the consequences of what you two have going on than the situation with that thief."

That thief.

Bennett was still a little shocked about what had gone down with Melanie Winchester aka Miriam Alexander. She'd stolen more than those paintings from Tangie and Dev all those weeks ago. She'd also stolen Dev's confidence in herself, made her forget she had people she could be honest with and who could help her.

He'd been up all night dealing with Melanie Winchester and the things she revealed in that shadowed hallway with Dev. His lover had obviously been ashamed of being taken advantage of. While the two women had spoken, her beautiful face had twisted into lines of embarrassment and regret. The anger at him having already chosen what to do with the collection had come later. And even then, it seemed a reaction to personal betrayal more than anything else.

And he had betrayed her.

He wasn't that far gone that he didn't realize what

he'd done. It didn't matter the reason. Dev was hurt. *He* had hurt her.

"I don't want her to be in pain," he said to Adah. "I didn't want to confuse her or make her think she was doing something wrong by being with me. I tried to tell her things were cool with you and me." But he hadn't revealed to Dev he'd decided not to give the collection to Tangie's gallery. He hadn't realized how much of Dev's self-image was tied up in that choice.

"You're a man," Adah said with a quirk of her lips. She got up and, in the kitchenette of the little sitting room, poured coffee into two mugs. One she put on her own tray and the other she gave to Bennett when she came back to the balcony. "She probably didn't trust anything coming out of your mouth unless you said it in bed."

No way was Bennett going to discuss with Adah any part of his sex life. Not even a little bit. He thanked her for the coffee. Instead of risking first-degree burns all over his bare chest, he sat up to drink it.

"So what did you tell her?" He eagerly guzzled his coffee, needing every ounce of caffeine to keep awake and stay coherent.

"I did what I could to reassure my friend that my other friend wasn't doing anything wrong. But the end results all depend on you." Adah sat down, biting into the red tomato. Its juices immediately squirted everywhere. Because it was Adah, none of it ended up on her white shirt. "Hmm. This tomato is crazy good. I bet it's from that organic garden Caroline has in her backyard." She licked tomato juice from her fingers with a grin of pure happiness. "Did I ever tell you what a great decision it was for you to hire Caroline as your chef?"

"Every time you eat something of hers," he said dryly.

Adah nibbled on the edge of the ravaged tomato before putting the whole thing in her mouth. "She's incredible," she muttered around the big mouthful. "You're a very lucky man to have her."

Bennett glanced down into his coffee mug and considered a refill. "It's not like she's my wife, Adah."

"I know. There's already someone else you want to fill that position."

His stomach clenched, threatening to bring up the coffee he'd sucked down so quickly. "We're definitely not talking about this."

"What do you mean? That's the only reason I'm even here." She finished up the last of her coffee and stood up, not seeming bothered by Bennett's resulting silence.

Adah brushed off the pristine bottom of her jeans and ambled to the balcony to look down. Stretching her arms up toward the bright sun, she loosened a yawn.

She was tired. Bennett winced, feeling guilty that she'd rushed up to Atlanta on her husband's private plane because of him, leaving Kingsley Diallo and her life in Miami behind just to tend to his wounds. Although, to be fair, he'd done that and more for her in the many years they'd been friends.

"You're exhausted," he said, stating the obvious.

With an impatient motion, she turned away from the view. "I'll sleep when I get back home tonight. For now, I want to make sure you're good."

"I'll survive," he said, the best that he could do. He wanted to run to Dev and pour his entire soul out in front of her so she could understand why he messed up the way he did. Bennett just wasn't sure it would do any good. He'd tried last night and she'd just walked away.

"That's not what I want for you," Adah said. "You're the second-best guy in the world—" she chuckled at that "—and you deserve to be happy."

Bennett nearly rolled his eyes at her unexpectedly maternal role. "Just because you're married doesn't mean you can start mothering me, Mrs. Diallo."

A smile flashed across her face at the mention of her husband's name. "I'm not mothering you. I'm just concerned about my friend."

"Your concern is duly noted."

"Screw that." With a few steps she was looming over him, the sun haloing her figure and keeping her face in shadow. "Bennett Randal. Do you know what you want?"

He frowned up at her silhouette. "Of course, I do."

Adah's hands landed on her hips. "Well?" She

sounded exasperated, and amused. Like he was her child not doing what he was supposed to.

A thought floated up from the deepest part of him. It was time to be honest. It was time to end the bull, especially since she could see through him so clearly. "Devyn," he said, and her name rolled over his tongue like honey. "I want Devyn."

"Then go get her," Adah said very softly. "It won't be as easy as everything else in your life, but you've never backed away from a challenge before."

Chapter 20

The water lilies were immense, and beautiful.

Sitting on one of the long wooden benches in the middle of the mostly silent museum, Dev felt small, diminished. People walked through the exhibit, staring up at the large canvases, many lost in thought, some taking selfies with the famous series of paintings on temporary loan to the Lowe Museum.

She breathed slowly in and out, feeling lonely and isolated. Feeling lost.

She'd been fired from her job at Tangie's gallery. Whatever reputation she had in the art community was in shambles. And any moment now, her brother would come back from his honeymoon to see what an incredible mess she'd made of her life.

The only positive thing she had going for her so far was that Adah wasn't pissed at her for stealing her ex-fiancé.

That morning, she hadn't been able to bear the daily call with her mother and sister, and dodged the worst of it by pretending to get another call as soon as Aisha had swung the conversation over to Dev's failures. It was only partly a lie to disconnect. She'd missed a call from Bennett while on the phone, but he hadn't left a message. Just as he hadn't left one yesterday when he'd called and she'd not picked up. She didn't call him back. What was there to say? She'd been less than honest with him about her desire to get close to him, and he'd withheld important information from her about his decision concerning his artwork. If she'd known he wasn't interested in using Tangie's gallery, would she even have gone with him to Spain?

That question left her with a dark emptiness. To have missed that magical trip, their lovemaking… She wished she could just go back in time and start over.

With no job to go to, she'd taken refuge at the museum, heading for escape, and hoping for a plan to appear out of thin air.

Two hours later, she was still at the museum, her escape, such as it was, was well underway, but otherwise her brain had pretty much shut down.

She had no job. Tangie still expected her to pay

for the artwork Miriam took or she'd implicate her in their theft. And Bennett had lied to her.

Bennett. God… At the thought of him, her heart ached.

After she'd gotten off the phone with Adah, she didn't know what to do with herself. The realization her friend had led her to—that she was in love with Bennett Randal despite all caution and despite all the supposedly good sense her mother had gifted her with—rocked her world like the biggest earthquake of all time. Even her bones shook.

It had been over twenty-four hours and she still felt like a rag doll, tossed onto the rocky shores of a realization she hadn't been ready for.

You love him. Adah's words echoed in her mind as if her friend was standing right there, whispering them to her over and over.

"As nice looking as these flowers are, I still can't understand why people are so obsessed with them."

She nearly jumped out of her skin at the sound of Bennett's low voice.

The woman at the opposite end of the long bench flashed him an annoyed look. Then passed that same look to Dev.

"They're peaceful," Dev replied. She folded her arms across her lap. "When there's chaos everywhere else, the lilies remind me that order returns eventually." When order would return to this particular phase of her life, she had no idea. But the lilies were a much-needed placid cove while she waited for the waters to calm.

Although she loved the entire *Water Lilies* series, this one was her favorite. In the painting, the water was an almost too-sharp shade of blue. The rippling currents carried along the green of the lily pads and the unexpected flashes of yellow from the open cup of the flowers. Hints of the robin's egg sky flickered in the water. Because it rarely left the museum in London where it was on permanent exhibition, this was the first time she was seeing the painting in person.

It calmed her. Or at least it had until Bennett showed up.

Dev pressed her lips together and looked away from the large canvas looming over her. "What are you doing here, Bennett?"

"Coming to find you. I hope that much is obvious." In brown leather ankle boots, tobacco-colored chinos and a button-up shirt with the sleeves rolled up to show off his powerful forearms, he was a distracting sight. "They arrested Miriam," he said before she could snark back at him for his rudeness. "And they recovered most of the paintings she stole from Tangie's gallery."

The hostility wafted out of her like smoke from a snuffed candle.

"What?" Even though she was sitting, it felt like she rocked back on her feet, her foundations abruptly shifting once more in his presence.

"Yep." Bennett sat next to her and gave her a version of his familiar grin, but it quickly disappeared. "She was actually telling the truth. In a way. The paintings were mostly at some sort of holding warehouse that the feds had been watching for a while. Some international art theft sting. They're wrapping up their investigation any day now so Tangie should have her art back soon enough. And it's clear she didn't have inside help at the gallery."

"I...I... That's—wow! I don't even know what to say." Was it all really over?

"You don't have to say anything, really. I wanted to give you the news so you're aware you don't have to pay Tangie back for anything or fear repercussions."

A blush scorched her cheeks at the reminder of how utterly ensnared by the other woman she had been. How damn helpless.

"I should pay her back for just being stupid," Dev muttered.

"Don't say that. You're anything but stupid. You're one of the smartest women I know." His hand landed on her arm, large and warm. "You're a good person, Dev. There's nothing wrong with wanting to believe the good in people around you."

Dev drew in a hissing breath. The single touch from him, like always, took away her ability to properly draw air. She cleared her throat and pointedly slid away so he had to move his hand. His face flashed a moment of hurt before his expression closed off.

"What about you?" she asked. "Was I just being

naive when I took what was going on between us at face value?"

A beat of silence turned into agonizing seconds, then minutes.

Finally, he dipped his head. "I *did* take advantage, I'm sorry." For the first time since they'd known each other, he looked uncomfortable. "I've wanted you for years."

Dev jolted against the bench, the hard wood biting into her thighs through her thin slacks.

"I've never told anyone. I never even told you when we were in Spain basically making some of my most intense fantasies come true." The corner of his mouth curved up but it wasn't with amusement. "Before that night at Tangie's gallery, until I told you about the art collection, you weren't interested in anything I had to say."

The breath caught in Dev's throat and she licked her painfully dry lips. The nerves twisted in her belly.

Bennett wasn't saying anything but the truth.

Despite what she'd felt for him for years, it wasn't until Tangie basically ordered her to "do whatever it takes" to get Bennett to let the gallery handle his collection that she'd approached him. On the face of it, Dev had gone about it reluctantly but the permission it gave her to be in Bennett's personal space, to enjoy him the way she'd wanted to for years, made her insides sing like a choir on Sunday morning.

But he didn't know that.

At the time, she *didn't* want to know.

And now, it was all one big mess.

Dev swallowed her shame.

"At any rate…" Bennett shifted at her side, still ignoring the woman who glared at them for daring to speak in the hushed gallery of the museum. "You don't have to give Tangie any money and you can go on to do whatever you want without worrying about her debt or any of this hanging over you. That's what I came here to tell you."

"That's all?"

He shifted again, looking like there was more as he stared at the space between them, the space she'd created when she'd slid away from his touch. But finally, he simply stood. "I think that's all that matters to you." Bennett toyed with the phone in his pocket. "Enjoy your time in the museum," he said.

Then he nodded briefly to the woman still staring him down and walked out of the gallery, his boots clicking softly against the wooden floor.

Don't go. Bennett, stay! Please stay so we can finally talk. Dev wanted to shout all these things but the words stayed locked behind her clenched teeth.

For a long while, she stared at the doorway he walked through until it wavered and became blurry. She looked down at her hands clenched tightly in her lap. Hot tears splashed over her fingers and the words she'd swallowed back threatened to choke her.

Like a fool in love with another fool, she was crying.

Chapter 21

With each step he took away from Dev, Bennett felt like he was leaving something important behind.

But he didn't turn around, he didn't look back. Whatever had been driving him to pull Dev into his life was still there, but she didn't want him. At a certain point, a man had to realize that what he wanted didn't matter if the person his desires were firmly fixed on didn't feel the same way. He'd done everything to show Dev his heart, and after seeing it all, she still pulled away. He didn't want it to be over, but even he had to admit defeat.

It hurt.

To give himself time to consider what he'd say to Dev when he found her, he'd parked far away from the museum, in the residential area down the hill from Peachtree. He headed there now.

No. A drink. A drink was what he needed to numb him for a little while. Then he'd give his friend in Tanzania a call. Ismael had been inviting him to check out Dar es Salaam for a while now. No time like the present. Wi-Fi worked just fine there. He could still get his work done for Leilani's Pearls while escaping his relentless thoughts of Dev.

Hands in his pockets, he waited at the red light to cross the busy avenue.

Looking up at the high-rise across the street, he saw a glowing sign advertising one of his favorite brands of beer. This bar would work just as well. Day drinking wasn't usually his thing, but why not? The light changed in his favor and he crossed.

Car horns honked behind him and he thought he heard his name, but when he looked back, all he saw were a couple of tall trucks trudging their way through the intersection and a harried mother pulling her two kids along in the crosswalk. At the building, he grabbed the heavy chrome handle of the glass door and pulled it open.

When he got to the wide bar with the gleaming counter and top-shelf drinks, a sadness tugged at him when he saw he wasn't the only one there. The television at the side of the bar was on CNN but muted and closed-captioned. The other day drinkers were scattered around the bar as far from each other as possible. He climbed on a bar stool and felt the entire heaviness of his body settle onto the black leather.

The bartender came over, cleaning a glass. "What can I get for you?"

"A glass of pineapple juice."

The bartender's expression was confused. "Just juice?"

"Yeah, just juice." He didn't know why he changed his mind but he'd never been much for superficial escapes. When he ran, he took his whole body with him, not just his mind. "But keep my tab open for now. I might change my mind later."

"Of course." The bartender drifted away with a nod.

"May I join you?" a low woman's voice asked from just behind his shoulder.

He turned to tell her he'd rather be alone just as his mind caught on to what was going on. Bennett adjusted the air in his throat. "Are you sure you want to be here?"

"I'm sure."

"Then, please." He gestured to the seat closest to him.

Dev sat. A dark purse she'd been carrying under her arm, elegant and sleek, slid on the bar next to Bennett's elbow. Strangely, she looked different in the low light of the bar. In the museum she'd seemed vulnerable and aching; now there was a strength about her he hadn't seen in a few days.

"I'll have what he's having," she said when the bartender made his way over.

"It's just juice." Bennett motioned to the glass near his hand.

"Even better."

Silence settled around them while the bartender got Dev's drink and slid it in front of her. Dev's purse vibrated but she didn't open it to look inside. She took a sip of her juice. The tip of her tongue appeared at the corner of her mouth to lick away a lingering trace of moisture.

"I don't want to play games," she said softly into the silence.

"Good. I don't want to play games either." The heaviness in the room pressed down on him and he forced out a joke. "Unless it's the kind of games we played in Spain." He smiled faintly.

Dev pressed the back of a hand to her upper lip where a fine sheen of sweat was beginning to form. "What we did in Spain...that wasn't a game to me."

Against his will, Bennett's hand fisted on top of the bar. But he said nothing. The ball was firmly in Dev's court. "I want that," she continued. "I want that with you for as long as I can have it. It was about the collection at first—getting close to you. But then... it wasn't. It was about what *I* wanted."

"You want me?" Bennett asked, because sometimes he could be relentless.

Dev's purse vibrated again. "Yes."

He toyed with the cool highball glass of pineapple juice but didn't drink from it. The things on his mind were much more important. "How do you want me, Devyn?"

"Any way I can have you. In every way if you'd let me." She bit the corner of her lip and glanced up at him through her long lashes. There was an emotional nakedness there that drew him.

At this point, her purse was vibrating constantly, but she still ignored it. "I'd like us to start over with nothing between us but the feelings we have for each other."

The tension Bennett didn't realize was all across his shoulders and his belly gradually loosened. He gave another smile, this one much more relaxed. "What exactly are your feelings for me?"

"Oh God... Are you going to make me say them?"

"I think so. Sometimes a guy likes to hear these things."

Dev gulped down her juice like it was tequila. "I've been in love with you since I saw you in that bar a million years ago. I thought it would go away. I hoped really hard for it to disappear but the feelings have only gotten worse, not better." She flicked him an annoyed gaze. "Happy now?"

He was grinning. "Not quite." He leaned close, catching the aroma of the pineapple juice on her breath and the hint of the expensive scent of her lipstick, an old-fashioned blend he knew for a fact his company made. "Kiss me. Then I'll be happy."

"God, you're such an ass," she grumbled, but leaned in with her full lips gently smiling.

Her mouth was soft under his, a dizzying relief after the past few days of worry and fear and everything else he didn't want to acknowledge. With the heaviness in his chest finally floating away, Bennett tightly gripped the woman he loved.

"Thank you for coming back to me," he whispered in her ear.

Her fingernails sank into the back of his neck and he felt the delicate shudder that ran through her body and vibrated into his. "I've always been yours," Dev whispered back.

Another series of vibrations from her purse had her pulling away, frowning, but she kept her hand locked with his. He squeezed her fingers.

"Maybe you should answer that. Whoever it is seems pretty persistent. It could be important." He brushed a hand along her cheek. "It could be your family."

"You think so? I already let them know I'd be at the museum and that I was fine." But with worry in her soulful eyes, she reached for the phone in her purse.

"Yes, it's my sister," she said, already hitting the callback button. "Hey, Aisha! What's wrong?"

Her body tense against his, she listened for a few seconds. "What?" Her eyes flickered to Bennett and stayed there. "No," she said, her voice low. "I didn't realize that. No, I…I'll be sure to tell him." A pause, then Dev blushed and looked away. "Yes, he's right here. God! Stop it. I'll talk to you later!" Then she ended the call.

"Everything's all right, I assume?"

"You know very well everything's fine." She stared at him in accusation. "That was Aisha. She said you made an announcement about the Harlem Renaissance collection early this morning. Half the collection is being donated to the HBCUs here in the city and…and the other half is mine."

"Ah, yes. That." He tightened his hold on her fingers knowing what she was going to say. "And yes, I'm sure."

Dev leaned into him. "But you said it yourself, Bennett. I don't need to give anything to Tangie. She recovered the paintings that were stolen, and whatever she didn't get back, the insurance more than covered."

That damn Tangie. He should have her thrown in jail for extortion. "I think the insurance covered it in the first place," he said. "She probably didn't want to report it so her rates wouldn't go up, and she was running a game on you, but that's a discussion for another time."

He'd always been cautious where Tangie McBride was concerned, but when he found out she was pressuring his woman to replace something that was lost through no real fault of her own, his apathy turned quickly to dislike. He wanted to ruin the woman.

"But Bennett, I can't take the paintings." Dev

leaned into him, her eyes dark and sincere. "I don't need them."

She really had no idea he would do anything for her.

"You don't need them, but I want you to have them," he said. "They're the first pieces for you to show and sell in your new art gallery."

Her eyes went wide. "My—my—my new what?"

"That's what you've always wanted, and because it's in my power to make it happen, it's what I want to give to you. Please don't give any of it back. It would hurt my feelings." He gave her a puppy dog look, complete with blinking.

She giggled and rolled her eyes. "But seriously, Bennett…"

"Make your dreams come true, Devyn. You've already made mine come true by simply being in my life. Please. Allow me to do this for you, for the woman I love."

The look of shock on her face was adorable. Gently, Bennett tapped her jaw to click her mouth shut before she could start catching flies. "I love you." He gave her that precious word once again. "Now go and do what you love."

Tears glittered in her eyes but they didn't fall. She moved even closer to him, her mouth trembling with emotion.

"That means I should be doing you right now then." Her words startled a laugh from Bennett.

"I'm definitely not going to complain about that," he said, tugging her close for a soft kiss.

"Good, then let's get out of here." She grinned at him despite the tears still making diamonds of her eyes.

"Yes, let's." Bennett tossed a twenty-dollar bill on the bar and curved a hand around her waist.

They left the bar together and stepped out into the warmth of the summer sun.

* * * * *

**Soulful and sensual romance featuring
multicultural characters.**

Look for brand-new Kimani stories
in special 2-in-1 volumes starting March 2019.

Available July 2, 2019

Love in New York & Cherish My Heart
by Shirley Hailstock and Janice Sims

Sweet Love & Because of You
by Sheryl Lister and Elle Wright

What the Heart Wants & Sealed with a Kiss
by Donna Hill and Nikki Night

Southern Seduction & Pleasure in His Arms
by Carolyn Hector and Pamela Yaye

Get 4 FREE REWARDS!

We'll send you 2 FREE Books plus 2 FREE Mystery Gifts.

Harlequin® Desire books feature heroes who have it all: wealth, status, incredible good looks... everything but the right woman.

FREE
Value Over
$20

YES! Please send me 2 FREE Harlequin® Desire novels and my 2 FREE gifts (gifts are worth about $10 retail). After receiving them, if I don't wish to receive any more books, I can return the shipping statement marked "cancel." If I don't cancel, I will receive 6 brand-new novels every month and be billed just $4.55 per book in the U.S. or $5.24 per book in Canada. That's a savings of at least 13% off the cover price! It's quite a bargain! Shipping and handling is just 50¢ per book in the U.S. and 75¢ per book in Canada.* I understand that accepting the 2 free books and gifts places me under no obligation to buy anything. I can always return a shipment and cancel at any time. The free books and gifts are mine to keep no matter what I decide.

225/326 HDN GMYU

Name (please print)

Address   Apt. #

City   State/Province   Zip/Postal Code

Mail to the Reader Service:
IN U.S.A.: P.O. Box 1341, Buffalo, NY 14240-8531
IN CANADA: P.O. Box 603, Fort Erie, Ontario L2A 5X3

Want to try 2 free books from another series! Call 1-800-873-8635 or visit www.ReaderService.com.

---

*Terms and prices subject to change without notice. Prices do not include sales taxes, which will be charged (if applicable) based on your state or country of residence. Canadian residents will be charged applicable taxes. Offer not valid in Quebec. This offer is limited to one order per household. Books received may not be as shown. Not valid for current subscribers to Harlequin Desire books. All orders subject to approval. Credit or debit balances in a customer's account(s) may be offset by any other outstanding balance owed by or to the customer. Please allow 4 to 6 weeks for delivery. Offer available while quantities last.

Your Privacy—The Reader Service is committed to protecting your privacy. Our Privacy Policy is available online at www.ReaderService.com or upon request from the Reader Service. We make a portion of our mailing list available to reputable third parties that offer products we believe may interest you. If you prefer that we not exchange your name with third parties, or if you wish to clarify or modify your communication preferences, please visit us at www.ReaderService.com/consumerschoice or write to us at Reader Service Preference Service, P.O. Box 9062, Buffalo, NY 14240-9062. Include your complete name and address.

HD19R2

SPECIAL EXCERPT FROM

*Completely captivated by his new employee, André Thorn
is about to break his "never mix business with pleasure"
rule. But amateur photographer Susan Dewhurst is
concealing her true identity. Although she's falling for the
House of Thorn scion, she can't reveal the secret that could
jeopardize far more than her job at the flagship New York
store. Amid André's growing suspicions and an imminent
media scandal, does love stand a chance?*

Read on for a sneak peek at
Love in New York,
*the next exciting installment in the
House of Thorn series by Shirley Hailstock!*

As she turned to find her way through the crowd, she came up short
against the white-shirted chest of another man.

"Excuse me," she said, looking up. André Thorn stood in front of
her.

"Well," he said. "This time there isn't a waiter carrying a tray of
champagne."

"I apologized for that," she said, anger coming to her aid. She was
already angry with Fred and had been expecting this sword to drop
all day. Unprepared to have it fall when she thought she was safe,
her sarcasm was stronger than she'd expected it to be. "Please excuse
me."

She moved to go around him, but he stepped sideways, blocking
her escape.

"Let me buy you a drink?"

Susan's sanity came back to her. This was the president of the
company for which she worked. Susan forgot that she could leave and

get another job. She knew what it was to be an employee and to be the owner of a business.

"I think I've had enough to drink," she said. "I'm ready to go home."

"So you're going to escape my presence the way you did at the wedding?"

Her head came up to stare at him. Instead of seeing a reprimand in his eyes, she was greeted with a smile.

A devastating smile.

It churned her insides, not the way Fred had, but with need and the fact that it had been a long time since she'd met a man with as much sexual magnetism as André Thorn. No wonder he fit the bill as a playboy.

"I guess I am," Susan finally said. From the corner of her eye, she saw Fred sliding out of the booth. He should know who André Thorn was, but if he planned to put his arm around her in front of another man, he would be making a mistake. "Excuse me," she said and hurried away.

Susan stood in front of the bathroom mirrors. She freshened makeup that didn't need to be, stalling for time. Why had she reacted to André Thorn that way? Embarrassment, she rationalized. She'd run into him at her friend Ryder's wedding. Judging from where he'd sat in the church, he must know Ryder's bride, Melanie. He would. Frowning at her reflection, she chided herself for the unbidden thought. It was a total accident that she'd slipped and tipped the waiter's tray filled with champagne glasses. André had reached for her, and the comedy of flying glasses and fumbling hands and feet would have made her laugh if it happened in a movie. But it had happened to her—to them. And there was nothing funny about it.

Too embarrassed to do anything but apologize and leave, Susan had rushed away to try to remove the splashes that had hit her dress and shoes. She hadn't returned.

She'd never expected to see the man again, so their eyes connecting across the orientation room had been a total surprise, but the recognition was instant. And now she had to return to the bar where he was. Snapping her purse closed, she went back to her group.

Don't miss Love in New York
by Shirley Hailstock, available July 2019
wherever Harlequin® Kimani Romance™
books and ebooks are sold.

Love Harlequin romance?

DISCOVER.

Be the first to find out about promotions, news and exclusive content!

Facebook.com/HarlequinBooks

Twitter.com/HarlequinBooks

Instagram.com/HarlequinBooks

Pinterest.com/HarlequinBooks

ReaderService.com

EXPLORE.

Sign up for the Harlequin e-newsletter and download a free book from any series at **TryHarlequin.com.**

CONNECT.

Join our Harlequin community to share your thoughts and connect with other romance readers!
Facebook.com/groups/HarlequinConnection